WHEN BLOOD LIES

WHEN
BLOOD
LIES

A Sebastian St. Cyr Mystery

C. S. HARRIS

BERKLEY
New York

BERKLEY
An imprint of Penguin Random House LLC
penguinrandomhouse.com

Copyright © 2022 by The Two Talers, LLC
Penguin Random House supports copyright. Copyright fuels creativity, encourages
diverse voices, promotes free speech, and creates a vibrant culture. Thank you for
buying an authorized edition of this book and for complying with copyright laws
by not reproducing, scanning, or distributing any part of it in any form without
permission. You are supporting writers and allowing Penguin Random House
to continue to publish books for every reader.

BERKLEY and the BERKLEY & B colophon are registered trademarks of
Penguin Random House LLC.

Library of Congress Cataloging-in-Publication Data
Names: Harris, C. S., author.
Title: When blood lies : a Sebastian St. Cyr mystery / C.S. Harris.
Description: New York : Berkley, [2022] |
Series: A Sebastian St. Cyr mystery
Identifiers: LCCN 2021032938 (print) | LCCN 2021032939 (ebook) |
ISBN 9780593102695 (hardcover) | ISBN 9780593102701 (ebook)
Subjects: GSAFD: Mystery fiction.
Classification: LCC PS3566.R5877 W4716 2022 (print) |
LCC PS3566.R5877 (ebook) | DDC 813/.54--dc23
LC record available at https://lccn.loc.gov/2021032938
LC ebook record available at https://lccn.loc.gov/2021032939

Printed in the United States of America
1   3   5   7   9   10   8   6   4   2

For October,

May 2017 to May 2021

It will have blood, they say; blood will have blood.

MACBETH, ACT 3, SCENE 4

A Note on English Titles

As the acknowledged son and heir of the Earl of Hendon, Sebastian St. Cyr carries the courtesy title of Viscount Devlin. Although it seems counterintuitive to most Americans, his wife would typically be known as "Hero Devlin" rather than "Hero St. Cyr" (compare with the famous Almack's patroness Sally Jersey, wife of George Villiers, Fifth Earl of Jersey). As a third son who came into his title only after the death of his brothers, Sebastian tends to think of himself as "Sebastian," although his friends, father, and even Hero most often call him "Devlin."

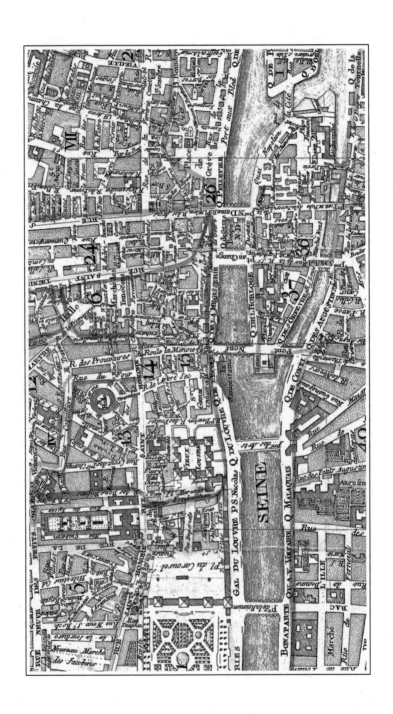

WHEN BLOOD LIES

Chapter 1

Paris, France
Thursday, 2 March 1815

*O*ne more day, *he thought; one more day, perhaps two, and then . . .*

And then what?

Sebastian St. Cyr, Viscount Devlin, walked the dark, misty banks of the Seine. He was a tall man in his early thirties, lean and dark haired, with the carriage of the cavalry captain he'd once been. For two weeks now he'd been renting a narrow house on the Place Dauphine in Paris, near the tip of the Île de la Cité. He was here on a personal quest, awaiting the return to the city of his mother, who had abandoned her family more than twenty years before.

Waiting to ask for answers he wasn't sure he was ready to hear.

The night air felt cold against his face, and he thrust his hands deeper into the pockets of his caped greatcoat, his gaze on the row of fog-shrouded *lanternes* that ran along the quai des Tuileries before him. The great ancient city of Paris stretched out around him in a sea of winking candles and the dull yellow glow of countless oil lamps. He

could hear the river slapping against the stones of the embankment beside him and the creak of an oar somewhere in the night, but much was
hidden by the mist.

Ironic, he thought, how a man could strive for years to achieve a
goal and then, once it was almost within his grasp, find himself shaken
by misgivings and doubts and something else. Something he suspected
was fear.

He turned away from the dark, silent waters of the river and climbed
the steps to what had been called the Place Louis XV before it was renamed the Place de la Révolution. It was here that the guillotine had done
some of its deadliest work, whacking off well over a thousand heads in a
matter of months. The blood had run so thick and noisome that in the
heat of summer the people who lived nearby complained of the smell.
Not about the roaring crowds or the haunting pall of death that even today seemed to hang over the enormous open space, but about the smell.

Pausing at the top of the steps, he stared across the vast lantern-lit
intersection, still surrounded by the stone facades of its once-grand prerevolutionary buildings. Even at this hour the place was crowded, the air
ringing with the clatter of iron-rimmed wheels on damp paving stones,
the clip-clop of horses' hooves, the shouts of frustrated drivers mingling
with the cries of street vendors selling everything from sweet-smelling
pastries to pungent medical potions. The guillotine was no longer here,
of course. At the end of the Reign of Terror, they'd rechristened the
space the Place de la Concorde—the place of harmony and peace. But
with the fall of Napoléon and the return of the Bourbon dynasty, the
sign plaques had been changed back to "Place Louis XV." He'd heard
there was talk of renaming it once more, this time to Place Louis XVI in
honor of the king who'd lost his head here.

So much for harmony and reconciliation.

It was a drift of thought that brought him back, inevitably, to his
mother. She had lived in this city off and on for over ten years—the estranged wife of an English earl turned mistress to one of Napoléon's

most trusted generals. Why? It was one of the many questions he wanted to ask her.

Why, why, why?

The church bells of the city—those that hadn't been melted down to forge cannons—began to chime the hour, and he turned his steps back toward the Pont Neuf. It wasn't a stylish place to stay, the Île de la Cité. The British aristocrats who'd flocked to Paris since the restoration of the Bourbons tended to take houses in the Marais district or the newer neighborhoods such as the Faubourgs Saint-Germain and Saint-Honoré. But it was on this elongated ancient island in the middle of the Seine that Paris had begun, and it called to his wife, Hero, for reasons she couldn't quite define but he thought he understood.

He could feel the cold wind picking up as he stepped out onto the historic bridge that cut across the western tip of the island. It was still called the Pont Neuf, the New Bridge, even though it dated back to the sixteenth century and there were now much newer bridges over the river. Built of a deep golden stone with rows of semicircular bastions, it consisted of two separate spans: a longer series of seven arches leading from the Right Bank to the island, and another five arches that joined the island to the Left Bank. In the center, where the bridge touched the Île de la Cité, stood a large square platform that had once featured a bronze equestrian statue of Henri IV but now held only an empty pedestal.

Earlier in the evening he'd noticed a painfully thin *fille publique* soliciting customers beside the old statue base. But the ragged young prostitute was gone now, the platform deserted, and he paused there to look out over the ill-kept stretch of sand, grass, and overgrown plane trees that formed the end of the island. The gusting wind shifted the mist to show, here and there, a patch of black water, a weedy gravel path, the bare skeletal outlines of branches just beginning to come into leaf. Something caught his attention, a quick glimpse of what looked like an outflung arm and delicately curled, still fingers that were there and then gone, lost in the swirling fog.

His fists clenched on the stone parapet before him as he sucked in a
quick breath of cold air heavily tinged with woodsmoke and damp earth
and the smell of the river. His imagination?

No, there it was again.

He bolted down the flight of old stone steps that led to the water's
edge. A tall, slim woman lay motionless on her side in the grass near the
northern span's heavy stone abutment. This was no wretched prostitute.
Her exquisitely cut pelisse was of a rich sapphire blue wool accented
with dark velvet at the cuffs and collar; her blood-soaked hat was of the
same velvet, trimmed with a jaunty plume; the gloves on her motionless
hands were of the finest leather. Her face was turned away from him, her
cheek pale in the dim light and smeared with more blood.

Then she moaned, her head shifting, her eyes opening briefly to
look up into his. She sucked in a jagged breath. "Sebastian," she whispered, her eyes widening before sliding closed again.

Recognition slammed into him. He fell to his knees beside her, his
hands trembling as he reached out to her, his aching gaze drifting over
the familiar planes of her face—the straight patrician nose, the high
cheekbones, the strong jaw. Features subtly changed by the passage of
years but still recognizable, still so beloved.

It was his mother, Sophia, the errant Countess of Hendon.

Chapter 2

In Sebastian's happiest memories, his mother was always laughing.

A beautiful woman with golden hair, sparkling blue-green eyes, and a brilliant smile, Sophia Hendon—Sophie to her friends and loved ones—had charmed everyone who knew her . . . everyone except her own husband, Alistair St. Cyr, the Fifth Earl of Hendon.

Even as a young child, Sebastian had been painfully aware of the tensions between his mother and the man he'd believed to be his father. As he grew, the brittle silences became longer, the inevitable scenes uglier. Those were the memories he tried to forget: Sophie's tearful pleadings; the Earl's angry voice echoing along the ancient paneled corridors of Hendon Hall; the clatter of galloping hooves as Hendon drove off to London while Sophie wept someplace alone and out of sight.

Four children had been born to that troubled marriage: first a girl, Amanda, followed by three healthy sons. But then the eldest son, Richard, drowned in a rocky Cornish cove. And four years later, in the blistering heat of a brutally hot summer when their mother had defied the Earl and taken them to Brighton, the second son, Cecil, died of fever.

The marriage ruptured. Sebastian could remember his eleven-year-old self sitting on the floor in a corner of his room, his legs drawn up to his chest, his arms wrapped around his head as he tried not to listen to the furious accusations and threats the grieving parents hurled at each other. But afterward, he wished he had listened. For just a few days later his mother sailed away with friends for what was supposed to be a pleasant day's outing.

She'd kissed him that morning, the day she sailed away, and laughed when he ducked her embrace in that way of all eleven-year-old boys. But the pain in her eyes had been there for him to see, even if he hadn't understood it.

Lost at sea, they'd said.

He'd refused to believe it. Every day of what was left of that miserable hot summer he'd spent standing on the cliffs outside of Brighton, his nostrils filled with the smell of brine and sun-blasted rocks, his eyes painfully dry as he stared out to sea, watching for her, waiting for her to come sailing back. Steadfastly, he continued to insist that she must be alive, refused to believe he'd never see her again. But eventually acceptance had come.

He didn't discover it was all a lie for another twenty years.

Chapter 3

A single branch of candles lit the small old-fashioned room, the golden light flickering over the pale face of the woman who lay motionless in the bed, her eyes closed.

Hero Devlin sat beside her, a bowl of water on a nearby chest, a bloodstained cloth in her hand, her gaze on the even features of her husband's infamous mother. Until today, Hero had never met—had never even seen—this woman. This woman who had caused her son the kind of damage that was difficult to forgive.

Hero had seen portraits of the Countess in her youth. She'd been so beautiful, her smile wide and infectious, her eyes thickly lashed and sultry. She was still beautiful even in her sixties, with classical bone structure, smooth skin, and an aura of gentle vulnerability that might or might not be deceptive. But Hero was having a hard time tamping down the anger she'd long nourished toward the notorious Countess, for she knew only too well what the discovery of his mother's betrayal had done to Devlin. How does any man recover from the knowledge that his mother played her husband false, then staged her own death to run off with her latest lover, never to return?

Since learning the truth, Devlin had been quietly searching for her across Europe. As long as the war between France and Britain raged, it hadn't been easy. But the coming of peace brought reports that the Countess lived here, in Paris, although she traveled frequently—sometimes to Vienna, sometimes to other destinations that proved surprisingly difficult to uncover. In the end they'd decided simply to join the horde of British aristocrats flocking to Paris and wait there for her to return. She had been expected back sometime in the coming week, but not today. Not yet.

"I don't understand what she's doing here," said Hero, leaning forward to gently wipe away a trickle of blood that rolled down the side of Sophia's temple. She kept her voice low, although she was afraid Sophie Hendon was beyond hearing anything. "She wasn't supposed to be in Paris."

Devlin stood with his back pressed against the nearest wall, his gaze on the pale woman in the bed, his face a mask of control that carefully hid every emotion, every thought, every betraying trace of pain. A streak of his mother's blood showed on one lean cheek; more of her blood stained his waistcoat and the cuffs of his shirt. Uncertain of the extent of her injuries and afraid to move her himself, he'd found a couple of street porters with a board to carry her up the stairs and across the bridge to the house on the Place Dauphine. They'd sent for a physician, but the man hadn't arrived yet and Hero was afraid there wasn't much he'd be able to do anyway.

"I don't know," said Devlin, his voice carrying a strange inflection that Hero had never heard in their nearly three years of marriage. Then he swung his head away to stare at the blackness beyond the window, his nostrils flaring as he sucked in a deep breath. *"Where is that damned doctor?"*

Hero set aside the bloodstained cloth and reached to take one of the Countess's limp hands in her own. It was a strong hand, aged and fine boned but not delicate. Beneath her fingertips Hero could feel the woman's pulse, erratic and faint. So faint. She lifted her gaze to study again that pale still face, tracing there the ways Sophie was like her son and the ways in which they differed. "Do you think she fell from the bridge?"

Sebastian shook his head. "How do you fall from a bridge with a high stone parapet?"

"Was thrown, then. If she fell from that height, there could be other injuries. Internal injuries we can't see . . ."

Hero's voice trailed off, for the wounds they could see on the Countess's head were bad enough. Her breathing was becoming as erratic as her pulse. *Please,* thought Hero, her throat so tight it hurt. *Please don't die. He's fought so hard to find you. Please, please, please . . .*

But the pulse beneath Hero's fingers grew ever fainter, then skipped, skipped, and was no more. The Countess's shallow, ragged breath stilled.

Hero leaned forward. *Breathe!* she was silently screaming, her fist tightening around that limp hand. *Please breathe!*

Then she heard Devlin say, his voice sounding as if it came from a long way off, "She's gone."

Chapter 4

*T*he physician arrived some ten minutes later.

They were still seated beside the Countess's deathbed when a house-maid brought word of Dr. Pelletan's arrival. A small fire crackled on the hearth, but the bedroom was in heavy shadow, and for one long moment, Sebastian could only stare at the servant. He felt numb inside, so numb he wondered if he'd ever feel anything again. A part of him knew that somewhere beneath the numbness must, surely, lie pain and grief.

Surely?

He felt Hero's hand touch his arm, heard her say to him quietly, "Would you like me to go down to thank him and tell him he's no longer needed?"

"No." Sebastian pushed to his feet. He had the strangest sensation, as if he were moving through someone else's life, or as if he were outside of himself, watching his own actions with a wooden sense of detachment. "No. I'll see him."

He found Philippe-Jean Pelletan standing near the window at the front of the house's small salon, his gaze on the darkly shifting, wind-tossed trees beyond. The physician was a slim man of just above average height, his thick dark hair mingled with gray, his long, thin face dominated by a prominent jaw, his dark eyes deeply set. Although Sebastian knew the man must be somewhere in his sixties, he looked and seemed younger, his movements quick and energetic.

"*Monsieur le vicomte*," said the doctor, turning from the window with a bow, "I came as soon as I could. Is the patient—"

"She's dead."

Pelletan was silent for a moment, his gaze on Sebastian's face in a way that made Sebastian wonder what the physician saw there. He had met the Frenchman the week before in a courtesy call, for Pelletan's daughter now lived in London and was known to Sebastian. But that had been a social occasion, whereas this was a professional visit and therefore quite different.

"It's a pity. You know this woman?" said Pelletan.

Sebastian walked over to where a decanter and collection of crystal glasses stood on a tray. "May I offer you a drink?"

"Thank you, but no."

Sebastian splashed a hefty measure of brandy into a glass. "I hope you don't object if I have one?"

Pelletan shook his head.

Sebastian replaced the stopper in the decanter with studied care. "For some years now she has called herself *Dama* Cappello. But her real name is the Countess of Hendon." He paused, then looked over at the French doctor. "She is—was—my mother."

Pelletan pursed his lips, his brows lowering in a way that suggested *Dama* Cappello was not unknown to him, at least by reputation. "Please accept my sincere condolences on your loss, *monsieur.*"

"Thank you." The brandy glass cradled in one hand, Sebastian went to stand at the window, his gaze on the small triangular-shaped Renaissance-era square below. For one shuddering moment, the physical ache of his grief was almost unbearable, so that he had to force himself to go on. "The circumstances surrounding her death are . . . confused. I would like to ask you to examine the body, perhaps give us some idea as to the cause and circumstances of her death. She was found lying in the grass beneath Pont Neuf in a way that suggests she might have fallen from above. There are significant head wounds, but I don't know if they are the result of the fall or if she was perhaps struck before being thrown from the bridge."

Pelletan stared at him. "You're asking me to perform an autopsy? Here? Now?"

"Not an autopsy precisely. More along the lines of a preliminary examination and analysis." He hesitated and, when the doctor still looked reluctant, added, "If you would be so kind?"

In France a man could be both a physician and a surgeon, for the professions were not separated here the way they were in England by centuries of custom and prejudice. Thus Dr. Pelletan was both a long-time professor at the Faculté de Médecine de Paris and chief surgeon at the ancient hospital known as the Hôtel-Dieu, positions he'd held for the past twenty years. And it occurred to Sebastian as he watched Pelletan consider his request that the man was both a respected professional and a consummate survivor, for he'd somehow managed to maintain his places despite the Restoration, despite having served as consultant-surgeon to the Emperor Napoléon, despite having once performed the autopsy on the body of the ten-year-old uncrowned boy king, Louis XVII.

Pelletan thoughtfully swiped one long, fine-boned hand down over his mouth and chin, his palm rasping against the blue shadow of his day's growth of beard. "Very well. Perhaps you could send Lady Devlin's abigail to assist if there is a need to remove her ladyship's clothing?"

Sebastian sucked in a deep breath. "Yes, of course."

It was more than an hour before Pelletan came back down the stairs from the guest bedroom, his features grim. He was in his shirtsleeves and waistcoat, for he'd stripped off his coat, and he apologized to Hero for forgetting and moved quickly to draw it on again as he entered the salon.

"There's no doubt she fell from a great height," he said, adjusting the collar of his coat. "Presumably, as you suggest, from the bridge near which she was found. Her right femur and right humerus are broken, along with several ribs and perhaps several vertebrae. I presume there is also considerable internal damage, although without a more invasive examination there's no way to know for certain."

Sebastian held himself quite still. "And the blows to her head?"

"The injury to her right temple is, I believe, a result of the fall. It's difficult to be certain about the more severe blow to the back of the head. But the knife wound in her back was obviously not caused by the fall."

"She was stabbed?" How could he have missed that?

"She was, yes. By a stiletto, most likely. It's a small but deep wound that bled very little, at least on the outside. I suspect the internal damage was considerably more severe."

"She was stabbed only the once?" said Hero.

Pelletan glanced toward her. Another man in his position might have resented being questioned by a woman. But Pelletan's own daughter had studied to become a physician in Italy, and he answered without hesitation. "Just the once, yes, my lady."

"Would a more invasive examination provide any additional insights?" asked Sebastian.

"Probably not." Pelletan paused, his gaze on the cuffs of his shirt, which Sebastian now noticed were stained with blood. "But I did notice one other thing. . . ."

"Yes?" prompted Sebastian when the physician's voice trailed off.

"There are bruises on her arms that were not caused by the fall."

"Show me," said Sebastian.

She looked so small lying in the center of the heavy old-fashioned bed, the white coverlet drawn up over her chest, her bare arms resting outside the covers and straight down at her sides. A delicate gold chain with a single pearl pendant lay around her neck; in her earlobes were simple pearl drops. Her eyes were closed, her features composed, almost at peace. With the help of Hero's abigail, Pelletan had removed and set aside her clothing and washed the worst of the blood from her face and head. In the dim light cast by the flickering candles, she might have been sleeping.

Might have been.

"If you look at the bruising here, on her forearm," said Pelletan, going to lift one arm gently and turn the delicate inner flesh to the light, "and there, on the other"—he paused to nod to where her right arm still rested at her side—"you can see quite clearly the marks left by a man's fingers digging into the flesh. The bruises are not old; they were made essentially at the same time as her other injuries, within an hour or so of death. Going by these marks, I'd say it's highly probable someone stabbed her in the back, either before or after possibly striking her on the back of the head. He then left these bruises while lifting her up to throw her over the bridge's parapet."

Sebastian stood with his arms crossed at his chest, his breath backing up tight and painful in his throat. The dark purple oval-shaped bruises showed quite clearly against Sophie's pale skin, and he felt a rush of rage so hot and powerful that he was shaking with it.

Pelletan laid her arm down and said quietly, "Have you notified the police?"

Sebastian cleared his throat and somehow managed to say, "Yes. But we haven't heard from them yet."

Pelletan nodded as if he found this unsurprising. "How much do you know about Sophia Cappello?"

Sebastian felt himself stiffen. "Why do you ask?"

"She was . . ." The Frenchman hesitated as if searching for a delicate way to phrase it, then settled on "quite close to General McClellan, one of Napoléon's marshals."

"So I've been told," said Sebastian.

Alexandre McClellan was something of a legend. The descendant of a proud old Scottish Jacobite family that had taken refuge in France after the disaster of 'forty-five, he'd long been considered one of Napoléon's most brilliant generals.

"Like most of the former Emperor's marshals, McClellan has now sworn allegiance to the Bourbons," Pelletan was saying. "I believe he's in Vienna, working with Talleyrand to secure the best possible terms for France from the Congress."

Sebastian studied the French doctor's solemn profile. "What exactly are you suggesting?"

Pelletan snapped his bag closed and turned to face him. "I'm saying there may be more to this death than a simple robbery somehow gone terribly wrong. It's not easy to unite a country again after so many years of trauma and bloodshed. In the past quarter century, France has seen half a dozen different governments come and go—absolute monarchy, constitutional monarchy, republic, directorate, consulate, empire. Now here we are once again, back to monarchy. In the past eleven months, we've torn down the tricolor and raised the white Bourbon flag, chipped the Emperor's bees and eagles off our buildings, renamed squares and bridges, and replaced the prints of Napoléon in our shopwindows with those of Louis XVIII. Such external changes are easy. But beneath it all, resentments and hatreds linger. Fester. And unfortunately, certain powerful people are far more interested in retribution than in reconciliation."

There was no need for him to mention any names. The newly restored King Louis XVIII might be genuinely interested in compromise, but he was lazy and weak. The real power in the family lay with the King's younger brother and heir presumptive to the throne, Charles, the comte d'Artois, and with their niece, Marie-Thérèse, the only surviving child of Louis XVI and Marie Antoinette. Both were filled with bitterness and wrath and an unquenchable thirst for revenge.

"What does any of this have to do with my mother's death?" asked Sebastian.

"I don't know that it does. But . . . I would advise you to be careful, my lord. Be careful what questions you ask and be very careful whom you trust." He reached for the hat he'd set on a nearby bureau. "There. I've probably said more than I should have. Good luck to you, *monsieur*. You're going to need it."

Chapter 5

*M*arie-Thérèse, Duchesse d'Angoulême—niece of the newly restored Bourbon King, Louis XVIII; wife of his nephew and presumed eventual heir; and daughter of the martyred King Louis XVI and Marie Antoinette—sat on an elevated thronelike chair at one end of a salon in the southern pavilion of the Tuileries Palace. It was a long, narrow room, aggressively opulent and dripping with gilded carvings, tall pier mirrors, red velvet hangings, and massive Rococo paintings of heroic Classical scenes. A string quartet played Vivaldi out of sight behind a screen. The sweet melody was virtually the only sound beyond the discreet rustling of silken skirts and a quickly stifled cough.

As was her habit, the King's niece worked her needle in and out of the canvas in her lap with quick, aggressive strokes. Her longtime *huissier du cabinet* and *premier valet de chambre*—a lanky, dark-haired, monkish man with a hawklike face and the eyes of a fanatic, named Xavier de Teulet—stood just behind her chair and slightly to one side, staring woodenly into space. Two long rows of expensively dressed, stony-faced ladies stood on each side of the red carpet that led to Madame Royale; but there was no conversation. This was the protocol for Marie-Thérèse's receptions: The ladies lined up strictly according to rank and endured the honor of their attendance in rigid boredom while the Duchess attacked her needlework and ignored them.

As was typical of her, the thirty-six-year-old Madame Royale wore a somber black dress with a severe high neckline and Renaissance-like ruff. Only occasionally would she acquiesce to the entreaties of her uncle the King that she "please try to look a little less ghoulish" and wear colors. Marie-Thérèse was in a perpetual state of mourning for her murdered family and she wanted everyone, especially the people of France, to know it. She also wanted them to know that she held them responsible for her loss and endless suffering, and that she would never, ever forgive the ways in which they had individually and collectively let her down. As a result, most of the residents of the country who had once pitied her had learned after less than a year to heartily despise her.

"We expected you nearly an hour ago," she said imperiously to the man now approaching her along the carpet edged by those two rows of rigid ladies.

His name was Charles, Lord Jarvis, and he was a distant cousin to the poor old mad British King George III and his son the Prince Regent. But that simple description was deceptive. A ruthless, eerily omniscient man with an enviable network of spies, informants, and assassins, Jarvis was generally acknowledged as the real power behind the Hanovers' wobbly throne. It was the reason Marie-Thérèse had called him here today.

"My apologies, *madame*," said Jarvis, bowing low.

He was a large man, well over six feet tall, big-boned, and tending toward flesh now in late middle age. In his youth he had been an attractive man; he was still handsome, with an aquiline nose, a deceptively winning smile, and gray eyes that blazed with a rare and piercing intelligence.

"You know why we wished to see you?"

"Not exactly, *madame*."

The Duchess lifted her voice and said, "Leave us," to the two rows of

ladies in attendance. She waited while the air filled with the swish of silk
gowns, the quick patter of slippered feet, the breathy little sighs of what
Jarvis suspected was profound relief. Then she said, "We understand
there are disturbing rumors on the streets of Paris—rumors that the
Beast, Napoléon, may attempt to escape from the isle of Elba and return
to France."

Jarvis threw a quick glance at the Chevalier de Teulet, but the Duchess's *huissier du cabinet* did not meet his gaze. Such speculation had been
common for months, and Jarvis found himself wondering why someone
had chosen to tell Madame Royale about it now.

"It remains a possibility, *madame*," said Jarvis with another bow.

She stabbed her needle down through her canvas with enough force
to make a loud popping sound. "He should have been executed. If he'd
been shot—or, better yet, hanged—we would not have this worry now."

It was on the tip of Jarvis's tongue to suggest that executing a mon-
arch whose coronation had been blessed by the Pope might not be a
wise practice for royals to encourage, but he swallowed the temptation.
Anything that reminded Marie-Thérèse of her own parents' executions
twenty-some years before was liable to set her off into a bout of hysteri-
cal weeping and prostrate collapse that could last anywhere from hours
to days.

He was aware of the Duchess's brittle blue eyes upon him. She was
not a particularly intelligent woman, and she was far from wise. But the
blood of murderous generations of Bourbons, Hapsburgs, and Medicis
flowed through her veins; one underestimated her at their peril.

"You have heard nothing from London regarding Buonaparte?" Her
lips curled into a sneer as she gave the Corsican's name its original Italian
pronunciation.

"Only that he resents the French King's failure to pay the annual two
million francs as agreed to in the Treaty of Fontainebleau."

"Does he find himself in straitened circumstances?" The sneer turned
into something like a smile. "What a pity."

"Men in straitened circumstances can become desperate. Perhaps desperate enough to make a push to recover their lost thrones."

"He can try." Her needle flashed in and out with a vengeance. "It would give us the opportunity to hang him, as he should have been hanged last year."

He thought she might press him for more details of Napoléon's sequestration on Elba and of the guard the British had set upon him. Instead she surprised him by saying, "I hear your daughter, Lady Devlin, is in Paris."

"She is, yes," said Jarvis, wondering where she was going with this.

"She must come to one of our receptions."

Somehow, Jarvis managed to suppress a smile at the thought of Hero meekly taking her place in those hierarchically correct rows of silent, bored ladies. "I have no doubt she would be honored."

The needle flashed in and out, in and out. "And what do you hear from the Congress of Vienna?"

"Only that they are close to agreement."

"That would be welcome news. Except that there are those who suggest Napoléon may be waiting until the Congress breaks up before attempting his return—the idea being that the Allies would find it more difficult to unite in opposition to him once the Congress is no longer in session."

Once again Jarvis found himself wondering who had told her this and why. The truth was, any knowledgeable person advising the exiled Emperor would probably tell Napoléon to make his move soon. Dissatisfaction with the Bourbon restoration in France was growing steadily and might easily erupt in a revolt that could end by putting the more popular Orléans branch of the French royal family on the throne. But Jarvis had no intention of explaining that to the wife of the man who expected to someday, after the deaths of his childless uncle and father, be king.

"The Allies will oppose any attempt by Napoléon to return to

France," he said instead, "whether the Congress of Vienna is still sitting or not."

For a moment, her needle stilled. She met his gaze, and he knew by the flair of triumph in her hard eyes that this was why she had called him here, what she was hoping to hear. "Good." She nodded his dismissal. "You may go now."

Jarvis found his own aide, a fair-haired, green-eyed former army major named Ashur Kemp, awaiting him in the salon's antechamber. Kemp was typical of the men Jarvis employed: tall, strong, intelligent, loyal, and lethal.

"Someone is filling the Duchess's head with fears of Napoléon's possible escape from Elba. I want to know who it is."

Major Kemp's eyes gleamed with the anticipation of a bird of prey setting out on a hunt. "Yes, sir."

Chapter 6

*A*fter Pelletan's departure, Sebastian went to stand in the doorway to the nursery at the top of the tall, narrow house, one hand curled around the frame at his side. His heart was heavy with a suffocating weight, his gaze on the two little boys who slept together in a low bed. There were two beds in the room, but the boys frequently chose to fall asleep like this, holding each other, for one of the boys had already suffered far too much loss in his young life.

Only the younger child, two-year-old Simon, was Sebastian's own son. The slightly older boy, Patrick, was the son of a mysterious tavern owner who'd looked enough like Sebastian to be his brother—and died because of it.

Sebastian was aware of Hero coming to stand next to him, her hand a caress at his side. At nearly six feet, she was almost as tall as he, and he rested his head against hers and felt his breath ease out in a painful sigh.

"It hurts," said Hero softly, her gaze, like his, on the sleeping children. "Knowing that she'll never see Simon. And that he'll never have the opportunity to get to know her."

Sebastian nodded, the ache in his chest so intense that for a moment he didn't trust his voice. He'd discovered that all the questions he'd burned to ask his mother, even his own desperation to see her again, were eclipsed by *this*—this realization that his infant son would never know the beautiful, brilliant, complex, wayward woman who was his grandmother.

The sound of the front door's knocker echoed up the elegantly curving staircase from below. Hero turned, her gaze meeting his. "The authorities?"

"Hopefully."

The "authorities" turned out to be a small, officious *commissaire de police* named Monsieur Bernard Balssa. Somewhere in his middle years, he was short and vaguely pudgy, with lank flaxen hair, a pronounced overbite, and an air of suspicion Sebastian suspected was habitual.

For an Englishman accustomed to London's archaic and woefully inadequate system of law enforcement, Paris's police apparatus was impressive, vaguely intimidating, and highly confusing. The city was divided into districts, each with its own *commissaire de police*, an official Sebastian gathered was roughly equivalent to an English magistrate, although not really. But the city also boasted twenty-four *officiers de paix*, who were scattered around the various *arrondissements* and seemed to operate separately from the *commissaires* in ways Sebastian didn't understand. Then there were the *gendarmes*, an almost quasi-military force, and police agents, and something else, something called the *Sûreté nationale*, a peculiar organization run by an infamous ex-criminal named Eugène-François Vidocq. With such a formidable law enforcement presence, one would expect Paris to be virtually crime free.

It was not.

Shown into the salon where Sebastian now stood beside the hearth with Hero seated nearby, the *commissaire* looked Sebastian up and down and said in French, "You are in truth the *vicomte* Devlin? The son of the

English Earl of Hendon? He who is the British Chancellor of the Exchequer?"

Sebastian answered him easily in the same language, for despite the long war, Hendon had raised all of his children to be fluent in French. "I am, yes." It was only partially true, of course, but Sebastian had no intention of providing this little man with the details of his genealogy.

Monsieur Balssa bowed to Hero, then cast an appraising glance around the small old-fashioned salon. "And you stay *here*? In the Place Dauphine?"

"I am a student of history," said Hero in a voice that would have quelled most men but seemed to have little effect on the *commissaire*. "And the Place Dauphine is literally in the middle of everything historic."

"So it is." Monsieur Balssa sniffed and turned to Sebastian again. "This woman you say you discovered near the Pont Neuf—you are certain she is indeed Sophia Cappello?"

"Yes." Sophie's true identity would undoubtedly be revealed in the investigation of her death, but Sebastian found himself unwilling to disclose it now to this deliberately abrasive man. "Dr. Pelletan has confirmed her identity."

A pinched expression flitted across the *commissaire*'s pasty features. "Dr. Pelletan examined her?"

"He did, yes. At my request."

"And he agreed that she had fallen from the bridge?"

"Actually, it appears that she was thrown from the bridge after being stabbed in the back."

"The knife was still in the body?"

"No. But there is a deep wound, most likely from a stiletto."

"Was she robbed?"

It occurred to Sebastian that he had seen no sign of Sophia's reticule. But then, he had been too concerned with getting her medical help to even think of looking for it. He said, "Possibly, although neither her earrings nor a necklace were taken."

"So she could have jumped and impaled herself on something as she fell."

Sebastian struggled to keep the rage provoked by the man's words out of his voice. "She did not jump."

Monsieur Balssa sniffed again. "You were acquainted with *Dama* Cappello?"

"In the past, yes."

"Interesting." Balssa turned toward the door. "I will view the body now."

Reluctant to have this nasty functionary anywhere near Sophie, Sebastian lit a chamber stick and led the *commissaire* up the stairs to the small guest bedroom. In just the short time that had elapsed since he'd left her, Sophie seemed to have shrunk in on herself, her body looking increasingly pale and insubstantial, like a frail husk abandoned by the vital force that had once inhabited it.

The *commissaire* went to stand at the bedside. He stared at her in silence for a moment, then jerked off one glove and reached out to touch the back of his hand to her cheek. "Mmm. She is definitely dead." He shifted his attention to the wounds on her head, leaning forward to study them more closely. "Pelletan thinks this is what killed her?"

"That, plus the knife wound and various internal injuries."

"Hmm." Balssa straightened and turned toward the door.

"There will be an inquest, I assume?" said Sebastian.

The *commissaire* started down the old, gently curving staircase. "Given the signs of violent death, interment may not take place until after an officer of the police, assisted by a doctor in physic or surgery, has drawn up a statement on the condition of the body and the circumstances relative thereto." His voice had taken on a singsong quality that suggested he was simply quoting the relevant section of the *Code Civil*. "As well, no interment may take place without an official Act of Death, which shall contain the deceased's Christian names, surname, name of consort if any, and the names of any and all close relations still living."

That might be awkward, thought Sebastian as he followed the *commissaire* down the stairs. The French were famous for their voluminous official paperwork.

"If you'd like, we can send a couple of men to fetch the corpse," Balssa was saying. "Transfer it to the city morgue."

Sebastian had heard of Paris's famous morgue, where unclaimed bodies were displayed naked for public viewing before being sent to the city's medical schools for dissection. "That's quite all right," he said, his voice tight as he followed the *commissaire* down the next flight of stairs. "We will be taking care of the funeral. We are . . . close to the family."

"As you wish. An official will attend sometime tomorrow with the doctor."

"Where do you intend to begin your investigation?"

"There will be no investigation," said Balssa as they reached the ground floor.

"What?"

The *commissaire* settled his hat on his head as he crossed the small entrance hall to the front door. "It will doubtless be decided that the woman either jumped or leaned so far over the bridge's parapet that she fell. Believe me, there is enough unrest in this city without setting tongues to wagging with a needless investigation into the death of a notorious noblewoman."

A notorious noblewoman. Sebastian felt a renewed flare of hot emotion somewhere between fury and fear. "I understand there is an office here called the *Sûreté nationale* that—"

Balssa made a rude noise. "Vidocq? That *galérien*? Bah."

Sebastian studied the officious *commissaire*'s narrow, ferretlike face. A *galérien* was a gallerian, or galley slave. He'd heard rumors that the head of the *Sûreté* had several times escaped from the galleys, although he hadn't believed it. Aloud, he said, "But the *Sûreté* does investigate murders, yes?"

Balssa reached to open the front door himself. "Believe me, *monsieur*, even Vidocq is smart enough to stay away from this. Good evening to you and to the *vicomtesse*." He touched a hand to his hat and left.

It had begun to rain, a soft patter of drops that splattered on the worn cobbles of the old triangular-shaped square and filled the air with the smell of dust. Sebastian was still standing at the open door when Hero came up beside him, her gaze on the *commissaire* striding away toward the stone bridge at the end of the island.

"What an unpleasant little man," she said.

The rain was increasing now. Sebastian watched Monsieur Balssa disappear around the corner to the bridge, then said, "They're not even going to investigate her death."

Hero turned to meet his gaze. "Then we'll do it ourselves."

Chapter 7

$\mathcal{S}$ebastian left soon afterward for the northern outskirts of the city.

Rather than disturb his young groom by calling for his own carriage, he took a *fiacre*, the Parisian version of a London hackney. It was past midnight by now, the city's narrow, aged streets dark and quiet in the rain, but he knew he would be unable to sleep until he'd attempted to answer at least some of the questions whirling in his head.

The woman who'd called herself Sophia Cappello lived in an impressive *hôtel particulier* in the rue du Champs du Repos, not far from the ruined church of Notre-Dame-de-Lorette. This was an area where the teeming streets of the city gave way to open countryside, where the detached houses were fronted by high-walled forecourts and boasted extensive gardens that stretched out around them. Sebastian had come here several times since his arrival in Paris to speak to the aged Frenchwoman who served Sophie as something between a companion and a chatelaine. She had answered his questions courteously and yet evasively, claiming she did not know where Sophie was and willing only to say that her return was expected in early March. Yet she had known both Sophie's true identity and her relationship to Sebastian. And when he'd asked why Sophie called herself *Dama* Cappello, the Frenchwoman had simply looked at him with troubled eyes and said, "That is a question I think her ladyship should answer herself."

He became aware of the *fiacre* drawing up before the *maison*'s heavy wrought iron gates, jerking him from the depths of his thoughts. "Wait for me," he told the driver, thrusting open the carriage door.

"As long as you pay," said the man in a provincial accent so heavy it took Sebastian a moment to decipher it.

He hopped down, his gaze on the house before him. "I'll pay."

The rain had stopped, leaving the air heavy with moisture and the lime trees along the lane dripping. Built of golden sandstone with tall, evenly spaced windows, the *maison* dated to the reign of Louis XIV. It was small but exquisite, of two stories plus the extensive attics tucked into its mansard-style gray slate roof. He was expecting to need to rouse the ex-soldier who served as gatekeeper, but the man must have been watching for his mistress's return, for he appeared immediately, limping badly on a peg leg. The left sleeve of his coat hung empty at his side.

"*Dama* Cappello is not here," he said, his lantern swinging wildly as he hurried forward with his awkward gait. He was thin to the point of being cadaverous, his eyes sunken and ringed by dark circles, his skin a sickly white.

"I know. I'm here to see Madame Dion."

The gatekeeper lifted his lamp to shine the light on Sebastian's face and peer at him intently. "Ah, 'tis you, *monsieur*." He unlocked the small pedestrian gate to swing it inward. "She is up, waiting for *Dama* Cappello."

"When did her ladyship return to Paris?" asked Sebastian, his gaze drifting over the *maison*'s classical facade. Only a few of the downstairs windows showed any light; the rest were in darkness.

"Just today, *monsieur*."

Conscious of a painful tumult of emotions he had no desire to face, let alone untangle, Sebastian crossed the entry court, the gravel crunching beneath his boots. He could hear a lamb bleating somewhere in the distance, hear the rattle of harness behind him as the *fiacre's* horse shook its head. Then the front door opened and golden light spilled out across the wet stretch of flagging.

"*Monsieur?*" said the older woman who stood there, a fine paisley shawl clutched around her shoulders with one hand, a flickering candle in the other, her face drawn and tight with worry. "What is it? What has happened?"

He paused before her, finding himself at a loss for words. Madame Geneviève Dion was somewhere in her late sixties or her seventies, silver haired and delicately boned but still fiercely upright. He knew little about her, only that she had been with Sophie for some years. Her patrician accent and manner suggested that she was from that legion of gentlewomen impoverished by the Revolution and the endless wars it had spawned, but she had never told him her story.

He was aware of her glancing beyond him to the *fiacre* that waited in the lane. Her worried gaze returned to him. "Where is she?"

Sebastian looked into the woman's dark, haunted eyes and saw the fear there—a fear that turned into dawning certainty as he said, "I'm sorry, but . . ."

"*Mon Dieu,*" she whispered when he couldn't quite bring himself to say it. The candle dipped dangerously as she swayed, and he put out a hand to steady her. "She's dead, isn't she? Sophie is dead."

"She arrived home this afternoon," said Madame Dion, her gaze on the fire that crackled on the hearth before them. They sat in the salon just to the left of the entrance, a small, intimate room painted a soft pastel peach with carved garlands of roses and entwined foliage picked out in white on the paneled walls. "She said the roads were good, so they made better time than she'd expected." The Frenchwoman paused, then pushed on. "I told her you were here in Paris—that you'd said you'd been trying to trace her for years."

"What did she say?" Sebastian asked quietly.

The chatelaine twisted the handkerchief she held around her fingers. "She didn't say anything at first, just walked out of the house to stand in her garden, by the rose arbor. I left her alone for a time, then went to her. She didn't look at me, just stared off across the distant fields and said, 'I should have known he would come once the war was over.' Then she turned to me and said, 'This is going to be hard, Geneviève. So hard.'"

Her voice cracked, and it was some moments before the woman could go on. "I told her . . . I told her she was tired from the journey, that she should rest and wait until morning before going to see you. But she said, 'No. I need to do this now before my courage fails me.' And she called for her town carriage and left."

"What time was this?"

"When she left? Perhaps an hour or so before sunset. I don't recall precisely."

So around six o'clock, thought Sebastian. "And she said she was going to the Place Dauphine?"

"Yes. I told her you'd taken a house there."

"Do you know if she was planning to go someplace else first?"

"She didn't say. But she sent the carriage back right away."

"She did? From where?"

The Frenchwoman looked troubled. "I don't know. You would need to ask Noël, the coachman. I've been sitting here all this time thinking she was with you."

Sebastian was half out of his chair, intending to go to the stables and wring answers from the coachman, when the clock on the mantel began to strike the hour.

Two o'clock.

He sank back into his seat and forced himself to swallow his frustration. For the past four years, he had dedicated himself to finding justice for the victims of murder; he understood the need to approach an investigation with patience and reason. But how do you exercise patience when the victim is your own mother?

He watched the aged chatelaine bring up one hand to cover her eyes, her throat working as she swallowed. He said, "When I spoke to you before, you told me you didn't know where Sophie was. Do you still say that?"

She let her hand fall back to her lap. "In truth, *monsieur*, I do not know where she went. She said it was best that way, and I didn't press her."

"But you have some idea?"

She was silent for a moment as if considering her answer. "I gather from one or two things her abigail, Francine, let slip that they'd come up from the south of France. But were they there all the time they were gone? I don't know."

Sebastian studied the woman's tightly held features. "Why would she say it was best that you not know?"

The Frenchwoman glanced at him, then looked away again. "These are unsettled times for France," she said simply.

It was an answer that raised a host of troubling possibilities. He wanted to ask her more, to press for the answers he suspected she knew yet was reluctant to give. But he was aware of the fatigue dragging at her aged features, of the shock and bone-deep grief that had left her shattered. He pushed to his feet and said instead, "It's late and I know you're tired; I'll come back in the morning to talk to the staff and perhaps look around the house, if I may."

Madame Dion rose with him. "But of course, *monsieur*. The house is yours now, after all."

Sebastian turned from the door to stare at her. He had assumed the house belonged to Sophie's famous lover, the marshal now negotiating for France in Vienna. "You know this for certain?"

"*Mais oui.* She asked me to witness her will."

Sebastian studied the older woman's heavily lined face and sad eyes. "Who do you think killed her?"

She looked away, her eyes swimming with unshed tears, her lips quivering before she set her jaw hard. "I have no idea. How could I?"

But he was coming to know her better now, was more able to discern truth from evasion. And he was fairly certain she was lying.

Chapter 8

*T*he rising sun was little more than a rosy pink glow on the horizon when Sebastian stood at the water's edge near the massive, bastionlike stone abutment of the Pont Neuf's northern span. The air was heavy and wet smelling from the previous night's rain, the budding limbs of the chestnut and plane trees at the tip of the island shifting in the cold wind, the stone facades of the aged buildings edging the quai du Louvre on the far side of the gray river still wreathed in mist.

Last night, before leaving for the rue du Champs du Repos, he had searched the pavement and roadway of the Pont Neuf, looking for any trace of what he suspected had occurred there. But if Sophie had dropped her reticule on the bridge, some desperately poor soul must have come along soon after to pick it up and carry it off. And the heavy rain had washed away any blood the attack might have left.

And so he was here now, at first light, searching the winter-browned grass and straggly shrubbery near the base of the bridge for—what? Her reticule obviously, but also anything else that might help him understand what had happened to her and why.

He was aware of the increasing rattle of cart and wagon wheels, the clip-clop of horses' hooves on the bridge above as Paris came awake around him. And he knew a whisper of something he recognized as fear: the fear that no matter how he tried, this murderer, *his mother's murderer*, might be the one to slip away from him.

A soft step behind him brought his head around and he saw Hero walking toward him through the wet grass. She was wearing a hunter green pelisse with a black collar and a shallow-brimmed hat tied beneath her chin with green ribbons that fluttered in the wind.

"I couldn't sleep," he said as she came up to him.

"I know." She stared off across the wind-ruffled waters of the Seine to the walls of the Louvre, now glowing golden with the rising sun. She was silent for a moment, then said, "I still can't believe this happened."

"Neither can I."

She brought her gaze back to his face, her own features troubled. But all she said was "Have you found anything at all?"

"Not yet."

"I'll help you look."

They began at the water's edge and walked back toward the central jutting platform that supported the vanished statue's pedestal. When the platform was first built in the early seventeenth century, the Île de la Cité had ended there, at the bridge. But in the last two hundred years the natural sandbar-building action of the river and the island had extended the land downstream. Sebastian had heard that before the Revolution, a local nobleman had amused himself by turning the stretch of wasteland into a garden. But in the years since then, most of the plantings had been lost, ravaged by vandals and occasional floods and the foot traffic to and from the bath and laundry barges that often tied up there.

"I sent a message to Hendon telling him that something has happened and asking him to come right away," Sebastian said as they turned to walk back toward the river's northern channel. As Chancellor of the Exchequer and a member of the Prince Regent's cabinet, the Earl had been in Paris these last three weeks taking part in important discussions with the newly restored Bourbon King and his powerful brother and niece.

Hero kept her gaze on the ground at their feet. "You didn't tell him why?"

"No. I think he'd want to hear it in person."

She nodded, her face still turned half away from him. "Do you think Hendon knew Sophie was living in Paris?"

Sebastian glanced up at the white sky; the sun was now well up but hidden by the high, thick clouds. "If he did, he never said anything about it to me. But then, we didn't tell him exactly why we're here, either, did we?"

She shook her head. "No."

The discovery that Hendon had hidden the truth about Sophie's sham death had seriously strained the relationship between Sebastian and the man still known to the world as his father . . . that truth and all the other truths hidden by a cascade of lies. But the worst of the tension between the two men was now in the past, and they were slowly sliding back into the prickly camaraderie that had been theirs before.

Sebastian and Hero were crossing a muddy stretch near the platform when they came upon a small round mirror with a pretty *chinois* enameled back. "Think this could have been hers?" said Hero, bending to pick it up.

He shook his head. "I've no idea. Anyone could have dropped it."

Hero turned it over to study the fine work on the back. "It can't have been here long."

"True."

They spread out after that, moving farther and farther away from the bridge. Eventually they were so far out that Sebastian was about to call it quits when Hero said, "Here."

He turned to see her crouching down at the edge of a tangle of winter-bared shrubs. She said, "I can't reach it, but there's something in there."

By hunkering down beside her, Sebastian could just see it: an embroidered dark blue velvet reticule that lay tangled in the middle of the stand of half-dead bushes. Its strings had come undone, spilling its contents around it.

Swearing softly, he stood up to push his way into the thorny thicket and retrieve both the reticule and the scattering of items that had fallen from it: a tortoiseshell comb, an embroidered silk handkerchief, and a coin purse that clinked when he picked it up. The reticule was beautifully embroidered with a peacock worked in vivid blue, green, and gold silk threads; both the reticule and the handkerchief were still damp from last night's rain. For a moment he simply held the reticule in his hands, the skin of his face suddenly feeling oddly tight. He could smell the pungent scent of the woodsmoke drifting across the water and the heavy, fecund odor of the damp earth. It was a moment before he realized Hero was saying something.

"Madame Dion should be able to tell us for certain if it's Sophie's," she said, watching him.

"It's hers," he said. "She always loved peacocks."

He was working his way back toward her when he felt a branch snag one of his pockets. "Here," he said, reaching out to pass the reticule to Hero so that he could use both hands to free his coat.

Her lips parted in surprise as the coins clinked and she felt the reticule's weight. Whoever killed Sophie had obviously not been motivated by theft. "Where was she when you found her last night?"

"Over there." He nodded toward the abutment some fifteen feet away.

Hero's gaze met his. "So how did her reticule end up all the way over here?"

He gave up trying to free his coat and came out of the shrubbery with a loud ripping sound. "The only thing that makes sense is that who-ever killed her deliberately threw it—threw it hard. Either before or af-ter he dropped her body over the side of the bridge." He watched Hero tie and then untie the reticule's strings, and said, "What?" as her brows knit in thought in that way she had.

"I suppose it's possible that the strings came untied as it fell, or maybe when it snagged on the branches of the shrubs. But the mirror we found closer to the bridge suggests it was open when it was thrown. And that means . . ."

She paused, her gaze meeting his.

He finished the thought for her. "It means that whoever killed her probably opened her reticule looking for something. And whatever it was, it obviously wasn't money."

Chapter 9

*A*listair James St. Cyr, the Fifth Earl of Hendon, stood with his hat in his hands, his face ashen as he stared down at his dead wife.

He was a big man, barrel-chested, with a large head and slablike face framed by white hair that had once been thick but was now beginning to thin. His most distinctive feature was his intensely blue eyes, a characteristic of his family so unique and consistent that they were known as "St. Cyr eyes."

Sebastian's eyes were a startling feral yellow.

He stood on the far side of the bed from the man he'd grown up calling Father—the man he still called Father, although Sebastian knew now that he was not, in truth, Hendon's son. He wasn't sure what he had expected from the Earl—a brusque nod in confirmation of his estranged wife's death, perhaps, or even a controlled hint of residual rage. What he hadn't expected was this—this profound grief tinged by what he realized was guilt.

"She's still beautiful," said Hendon, his voice husky. "So beautiful."

Sebastian nodded, not trusting his own voice.

More minutes passed. Then Hendon said quietly, "Did she suffer much, do you think?"

"I honestly don't know. The pain from all those shattered bones must have been beyond horrific. But I don't know for how long she was conscious." It was a thought that haunted him: How long had she lain there in the dark, alone and afraid and in pain?

How long?

Hendon said, "I blame myself, you know." He must have seen the surprise in Sebastian's face because he said, "Oh, not back then, not when she ran away. Then I was all puffed up in my righteousness, blaming her for everything from Cecil's death to her endless infidelities to—" He broke off, but Sebastian knew what he'd been about to say: *To leaving me with an heir not of my own loins.*

Hendon reached out one shaky, blunt-fingered hand that hovered over her head. "We never should have married. She was the wrong wife for me, and I was the wrong husband for her. She was so beautiful, so vivacious and accomplished, and that's all I saw. I wanted a gracious, well-bred countess, a devoted mother for my children, and I didn't give a thought to what *she* wanted—to what she needed. I thought she should be content with the roles society expected of a noblewoman. And it infuriated me that she was not."

Sebastian drew a deep, painful breath and kept silent.

"She was brilliant, you know," said Hendon. "Far more brilliant than I. Brilliant and restless and frustrated—so frustrated with what society and I demanded of her. We quarreled constantly, and in time . . . I think she came to hate me. Hate me for what I was doing to her. And so she punished me in the only way she could."

He brought his hand down gently on her head, stroking her blood-stained hair, then raised his gaze to Sebastian's face. "You knew she was living here, in Paris?"

"Yes. Did you?"

Hendon nodded. "But I'd heard she was traveling. I was relieved. I . . . I hoped you'd be gone before she returned."

Sebastian knew a spurt of anger that came close to rage and forced himself to swallow hard. How long had Hendon known? All those years Sebastian had been searching for her, and Hendon had kept silent.

But then, of course he had. He'd kept silent about everything.

"She was traveling," said Sebastian. "She arrived back in Paris only late yesterday afternoon."

Hendon let his hand fall back to his side, and Sebastian noticed it then curled into a fist. "You've no idea who did this to her?"

"Not yet. But I will."

Hendon nodded and turned away abruptly. "Have you told Amanda?"

"No. I thought it would be better coming from you." There was little love lost between Sebastian and his elder sister, and there never had been. "She's still here in Paris, isn't she?"

"She is. She won't be happy, having it come out—that her mother has been living in France for years under an assumed name, I mean."

"Perhaps it won't come out."

"It will come out," said Hendon, descending the winding stairs. "These things always do."

Sebastian hesitated an instant, then followed him downstairs. "Did you know about General McClellan?"

He saw Hendon's back tense. Then the Earl said, "I knew."

"What else do you know?"

Hendon drew up on the landing and turned to face him. "Very little. And I say that in all honesty. I was kept apprised of where she was living, but I had no desire to know more than that. Why would I?"

Why indeed, thought Sebastian.

Hendon cast a disparaging glance around the old-fashioned stair-well. Like all the houses fronting the Place Dauphine, this one had been built over two hundred years before, in the days of Henri IV, and even then it hadn't been particularly grand. "I don't understand why you choose to live here, of all places."

Sebastian found himself smiling. "You sound like Amanda."

"Huh," grunted the Earl, descending the last flights of stairs. "I was hoping to see my grandson again."

Simon wasn't really Hendon's grandson, of course, but that didn't stop the Earl from considering the boy his. Hendon's obvious, intense love for the little boy was one of the things that had helped reconcile the breach between the two men.

Sebastian said, "Hero's taken the boys to watch the street performers by Notre Dame."

"Best to get the children out of the house, I suppose." The Earl paused while the footman moved to open the front door. "You'll be handling the funeral arrangements?"

"Yes—well, Hero will be."

She'd quietly taken responsibility for dealing with both the government officials and the *pompes funèbres*, something for which Sebastian was profoundly grateful.

Hendon nodded. "Let me know."

"We will."

Hendon stepped out into the cobbled roadway, then frowned at the sight of a footman in Angoulême livery trotting toward them.

"*Monsieur le vicomte?*" said the tall young footman, drawing up before him with a bow.

"Yes," said Sebastian.

"A message from the *Duchesse*, my lord."

Sebastian took the missive in some surprise and broke the seal.

"What is it?" asked Hendon, watching him.

Sebastian ran his gaze down over the flowing script. "It's from Madame Royale's *huissier du cabinet*. He writes that the Duchess wishes to see me immediately."

"What the devil for?"

"I've no idea." Sebastian handed a coin to the footman and said, "Thank you. Tell *madame* I'll attend her sometime this afternoon."

"She won't like that," said Hendon, watching the footman trot off. "She's not accustomed to being kept waiting."

Sebastian shrugged. He and the French King's niece had met before, in England; their interaction had not been cordial. "She can wait. There are things I need to do first."

Chapter 10

The *officier de paix* promised by the *commissaire de police* had arrived at the house in the Place Dauphine earlier that morning carrying a worn, ink-stained leather satchel bulging with papers and bringing with him a stoop-shouldered, elderly doctor in an old-fashioned frock coat who smelled strongly of snuff.

The officer was younger than Hero was expecting, with slicked-back black hair, a pointed nose, and an officious, condescending manner. He looked annoyed when told Devlin was out and gave a pained sigh. "Very well, *madame*. You may conduct us to view the victim."

"Of course," said Hero crisply, and showed the two men up the stairs to the room where Sophie lay.

"Hmm," said the doctor, his lips pursing as he leaned over that silent pale form. "You say she was found beneath the Pont Neuf?"

Hero stood in the doorway, her hands clasped behind her back. "That is correct."

Reaching out, he cradled Sophie's chin in one snuff-stained hand and tried to turn her battered head, only to find the neck locked with rigor mortis. He frowned, his eyes narrowing as he peered at the wounds that were visible. Then he straightened and turned away. "Yes, it's quite obvious she died from a fall."

"But she's also been stabbed in the back," said Hero.

The doctor *tsk*ed and patted her arm as if she were a child. "I don't think so, my dear. Simply another injury caused by the fall."

"If I may, *madame?*" said the *officier de paix*, setting up his inkwell on the small table beneath the window and pulling an official-looking paper from his satchel: the Act of Death, required for burial.

"Of course," she said.

He peered at the nib of his pen, decided it would suffice, then dipped the pen in his ink and said, "Name of victim, please?"

"Sophia," said Hero. She hesitated a moment, then said, "Cappello. Sophia Cappello."

The officer nodded, the scratching of the pen filling the silence in the room. "Name of consort?"

This time Hero didn't even hesitate. "None."

She thought he might ask her how she knew this, but he didn't. He simply nodded again and said, "Any offspring?"

"No. No offspring."

After that, Hero spent what was left of the morning with the two little boys and their nurse, Claire Bisette, at the parvis de Notre Dame, the bustling open square before the city's ancient crumbling cathedral. The day was sullen and blustery, but the space was historically the center of Paris and crowded despite the weather with everything from street musicians and acrobats to shoe repairmen and street vendors hawking pastries and steaming hot cider.

At one point the boys paused, hand in hand, to stare wide-eyed at a puppet show set up near the base of one of Notre Dame's towers. "Why cain't we never un'erstand what any of dese peoples is sayin'?" asked Patrick, turning to Hero.

"Because they're speaking a different language," she said, hunkering down beside him. "We're from England, so we speak English. But this country is France, and they speak a language called French."

It had been three months since Patrick had come to live with them. There were times—such as this—when he seemed happy and at peace, lost in the moment. But there were other times when she'd catch a sad, faraway look in his eyes and know he was thinking about his mother and father. Yet he never asked about them, and that troubled Hero more than anything.

Patrick glanced up at his nurse, a speculative expression coming over the features that were so much like Simon's and Sebastian's that the resemblance could still catch Hero's breath. "Claire is French."

"*Mais oui*," said Claire with a laugh, then switched back to English. "And I'll teach you to speak French, too, if you like, *mon enfant*."

"As soon as he learns to speak English without sounding like a Bishopsgate barmaid," said Hero in low-voiced, rapid French as she pushed to her feet, and heard Claire choke back another soft huff of laughter.

Hero was still smiling when she felt a strange chill pass over her.

Turning, she scanned the boisterous crowd that packed the noisy square, her gaze shifting from the mutilated whitewashed facade of the once-grand cathedral to the hospital known as the Hôtel-Dieu and the collection of decrepit old medieval shops and houses that hemmed in the small space.

"What is it?" asked Claire.

"I don't know. I have the strangest feeling. It's almost as if . . ." She paused, trying to identify the sensation, and finally understood what it was. "As if I can feel someone watching me."

Claire glanced around the square, her eyes narrowing. "Pickpockets sizing us up as targets, perhaps?"

"Perhaps," said Hero. But she doubted it. It wasn't greed she felt, but a lethal purposefulness that bled the joy from what had been until then a pleasant outing filled with the laughter of children.

They left soon after. Hero insisted on walking with Claire and the boys back to the Place Dauphine. Then she went in search of an undertaker.

Known officially as *pompes funèbres*, French undertakers were more commonly called *croquemorts*, which translated literally into "dead-biters." According to Claire, there were three theories as to how this rather macabre nomenclature had come about. The most popular explanation contended that in the Middle Ages, undertakers were required to bite the big toe of a corpse to make certain the person was dead. No reaction? Then the body was safe to bury.

But there were others who dismissed that tale as mere legend, insisting the term dated to the plague years, when undertakers used meat hooks to drag infected bodies to mass graves. A meat hook was *un croc de boucher*, and since *croc* sounded rather like *croque*, the practitioners of the professions came to be known as *croquemorts*.

"I'm not sure that's much better than the toe-biting explanation," Hero said.

"Perhaps," agreed Claire. "But there are some who claim both are inventions, since an old meaning of the verb *croquer* was 'to steal or make disappear.'"

"As in the Grim Reaper?"

"Yes, like that."

Whatever the real explanation, there was no denying that, compared to the English, the French had a much more pragmatic, down-to-earth attitude toward everything from sex to death.

Although Hero had to admit she still found it hard to get used to the French word for the dead—*les défunts*. The defuncts.

It was when she was leaving the establishment of the Pompes Funèbres Berges on the quai de l'Horloge that she felt it again: She was being watched.

She looked around quickly, her glance raking the crush of horses, carts, wagons, and carriages that filled the narrow street running along the river. She studied the men and women around her—an emaciated one-armed ex-soldier begging at the foot of the Pont au Change, a ragged flower girl, an aged broom seller, a humpbacked poodle clipper with his box. She saw no one she recognized from the parvis de Notre Dame, but she was now more convinced than ever that someone was watching her.

The question was, *Why?*

Chapter 11

Charles, Lord Jarvis, was in the eastern arcade of the Palais-Royal, his gaze on an exquisite little porcelain clock displayed in the glazed window of a jeweler, when Major Ashur Kemp walked up to stand beside him.

A tide of well-dressed Parisians swirled around them, laughing and chattering gaily. Once a grand seventeenth-century neoclassical palace, the Palais-Royal had been turned by its present owner into an elegant and very profitable series of shopping arcades and galleries that were the social center of upper-class Parisian life. By day, one could browse the most exclusive shops and dine in the finest examples of that lovely French tradition Jarvis heartily wished London would adopt: *"le restaurant."* Later, at night, when the shops closed, the city's prostitutes would come out to prowl the shuttered arcades as the focus of the Palais-Royal shifted to the theater and expensive gambling dens. But that transformation was still hours away, and Jarvis was here now looking for a gift for his young bride, Victoria, whose advancing state of pregnancy had forced her to stay behind in London rather than accompany him to Paris.

"So what have you discovered?" he asked the major.

"I'm not entirely certain yet, but I believe the information may have come from the Duchesse d'Angoulême's *huissier du cabinet.*"

"The Chevalier de Teulet? Interesting. What do we know about him?"

Kemp shrugged. "Like the Duchess herself, he believes in absolute monarchy and the need to reestablish the power of the Church. And he's utterly devoted to her."

"So why is he disturbing her with all this talk now?"

"That I haven't figured out yet."

Jarvis nodded and turned toward the shop's door. "Keep digging."

He purchased the clock for Victoria, then left it to be wrapped and delivered to his hotel while he crossed the rue Saint-Honoré and walked along the side of the Louvre to the Île de la Cité. It was a hopelessly unfashionable area, and he crinkled his nose as he crossed the ancient stone bridge over the Seine and turned into the small triangular square of narrow Renaissance-era houses.

He found Hero in her rented house's outdated salon, writing at a desk overlooking the trees below. She jumped up when he was announced and came across the room to meet him with outstretched hands and a wide smile of welcome.

"Papa," she said, kissing his cheek and drawing him down beside her on a settee covered in a tapestry that looked old enough to date to the same era as the square. "This is a nice surprise. Tell me, what do you hear from Cousin Victoria? Is she well?"

"As well as can be expected for a woman nearly six months heavy with child."

"When do you go home?"

"Soon," he said, his gaze searching her face.

No one would ever call Hero "pretty," but she was handsome. She had Jarvis's gray eyes and, unfortunately, his aquiline nose, but otherwise her features were fine, and she had good bone structure. Her marriage had never sat well with him for a variety of reasons, but he was wise enough to bide his time, for he knew his daughter. Knew how much she was, in her own way, like him.

"I've heard about Sophia Cappello."

"Ah." Hero paused, her chest lifting as she drew in a deep breath. "And do you know—" She broke off, obviously struggling to find a way to put her question into words without betraying anything if he *didn't* know.

"That her real name was Sophia Hendon? What do you think?"

She was quiet for a moment, her eyes narrowing as she studied him. "How long? How long have you known?"

"That Hendon's Countess was living in Paris? For some time. It's my business to know such things."

"And do you know who killed her?"

"No. That I don't know." He didn't care, either, but he saw no reason to add that. "This can't be pleasant for you."

"I'm all right," she said in an offhand way that didn't deceive him. "But there's no denying it's hitting Devlin hard."

"I assume he's determined to investigate the death?"

"You know he is."

"Even though such an investigation could reveal the truth about her identity to the world?"

"I don't think he cares about that."

"He should. It won't be good for either you or Simon if it becomes known that Lady Hendon has been living with one of Napoléon's marshals for the last ten or fifteen years."

"Perhaps it won't come out."

"How could it not?" He paused, his gaze drifting over her elegant long-sleeved gown of creamy muslin topped by a paisley shawl. "You're not going into mourning?"

She shook her head. "Unfortunately it would provoke exactly the sort of speculation we're most anxious to avoid."

"I suspect there'll be plenty of speculation when enough members of Parisian society get a good look at Devlin. He hasn't gone about much yet, has he?"

"No, but . . ." She shook her head, obviously not understanding him. "What do you mean?"

He saw the frown lines that formed between her brows, saw the puzzled way she tilted her head, and realized that she didn't know yet. But all he said was "I believe there is some resemblance."

"Some. But I suspect he mainly resembles his unknown father."

"Of course," said Jarvis, and left it at that. He pushed to his feet. "And now, where's my grandson?"

Chapter 12

*S*ebastian had hired a pair of sweet-going bays and a sporty phaeton for the duration of his stay in Paris. But he hadn't had the heart to leave his young groom or tiger, Tom, behind in London. And although the tiger had no use for foreigners in general and the French in particular, Tom was adjusting surprisingly well to his sojourn in the city.

"I'm 'earin' there's a lady was found dead 'ereabouts last night," said Tom when he brought the carriage and pair around from the livery stable a short time later. He was small and sharp faced, with a shrill cockney accent, a gap between his front teeth, and brown hair that had a tendency to stick out in all directions. "Did ye 'ear about it, gov'nor?"

Sebastian hopped up to the high seat to take the reins, then paused to look back at his tiger's eager young face. He'd never known exactly how old Tom was, for the boy was vague on details such as his age and even his last name. When they'd first met, he'd been an orphaned pickpocket living by his wits on the street; now he had ambitions of becoming a Bow Street Runner. There was far more to their relationship than the simple one of master and servant, and Sebastian realized the boy deserved to be told the truth.

"You'll probably figure it out eventually," said Sebastian, "so I might as well tell you now. The lady who died last night was known here in France as Sophia Cappello, but her real name was Sophia Hendon." He paused, then added, "My mother."

Tom stared at him, his mouth slightly agape.

Sebastian said, "I know I can trust you to keep that detail to yourself."

Tom closed his mouth and nodded vigorously. "Oh, aye, m'lord." He swallowed dryly, then said softly, "Was she really murdered?"

Sebastian gathered his reins again. "She was. And I don't intend to rest until I get whoever did it."

In the flat light of the cloudy day, the *hôtel particulier* on the rue du Champs du Repos looked aloof and drawn in upon itself, with a cold wind flattening the foliage of the bulbs in the formal parterres beside the entry court and banging a loose shutter somewhere out of sight. Limping badly, the dark-haired, one-legged, one-armed ex-soldier opened the heavy wrought iron gates for Sebastian, his face closed and unreadable as he swung the gates shut again with a *clang*.

"Might as well go ahead and stable them for now," Sebastian told Tom as they drew up before the portico. "We're going to be here awhile."

"Aye, gov'nor."

Hopping down, Sebastian turned toward the house to find Geneviève Dion standing at the open front door, watching him. The aubergine-colored silk gown and colorful shawl she'd worn the night before had been replaced by a ruthlessly plain black mourning gown with a black shawl and black cap. "I've warned the servants you'll be wishing to speak with them this morning, my lord," she said as he walked toward her. "And I've had a fire lit in the small salon in case you'd like to make use of that room?" Her voice rose at the end of the sentence, turning it into a question.

"Yes, thank you. I think I'd like to start with her ladyship's abigail."

"Francine?" Madame Dion cupped her hands around her bent elbows and held them close to her sides. All traces of the emotions she'd shown the previous night were now gone, ruthlessly tucked away behind that stoic, unreadable facade so many residents of France had perfected over the past twenty-six years of war and dangerous turmoil. "But she's not here, my lord. Since they'd been gone for so long, her ladyship gave the girl permission to visit her family for a few days. Francine left yesterday evening."

"Where does her family live?" he asked, thinking perhaps the girl could be sent for if they lived close by.

"Faubourg Saint-Antoine, my lord."

"Ah." It was a rough, impoverished neighborhood, the Faubourg Saint-Antoine. Lying on the eastern edge of the city, the faubourg was known for its textile workers and furniture makers, and for having been the source of the furious *sans-culottes* who'd spearheaded the Revolution's bloodiest *journées*. "In that case," he said, swinging off his greatcoat as he turned toward the small salon, "let's begin with the coachman, shall we?"

Sophie's coachman was a tough, wiry little man with thick graying hair, deep-set, narrowed eyes, and a face weathered to the texture of old boot leather by exposure to the elements. Clad in rough trousers and a dark coat, he limped into the room, bringing with him the scent of horses and hay, then stood just inside the door with his hat in his hands. He said his name was Noël Caron and that he'd been a soldier under Napoléon until he lost half his left foot to frostbite in Russia.

"You're lucky that's all you lost," said Sebastian, standing beside the fire.

The coachman nodded, his chest lifting on a quick intake of air. "Nearly seven hundred thousand of us crossed the Neman River with the Emperor that June, and less than thirty thousand of us came back."

He said it matter-of-factly, as if it were merely an interesting number, like the daily haul of the fishermen on the Seine or the amount of revenue taken by the Crown from the taxes levied on wine and other goods coming into Paris. As if the loss of human life on such an unfathomable scale and the grief of the mothers and fathers, the wives and lovers and children, left to mourn all those dead men were of no import. But Sebastian caught a glimpse of the faraway look that had crept into the old soldier's eyes, that veil of numbness that closed down thought and memory, and he understood. Sebastian himself had spent six years fighting King George's wars from Italy to the West Indies to Portugal. He understood all too well that men see things and do things in war that can never be examined too closely by those who survive. Not if they are to preserve both sanity and humanity.

They talked for a time of soldiering, about the lighter moments, the kind of moments that men can bear to remember and sometimes even laugh about. Then Sebastian said, "I understand you drove her ladyship somewhere last night in her carriage."

"*Oui, monsieur,*" said Noël.

"Where did she go?"

He ran his tongue along his lower lip. "Asked me to take her to the Place Dauphine, she did."

"And did you?"

The coachman shook his head. "*Non, monsieur.* We were crossing the Pont Neuf when we come up behind an ironmonger with a balking mule. Took him a bit to get the beast going again, and then just when I'm ready to move on, her ladyship says to me, 'No, Noël; stay a moment longer.' So I did."

"Do you know why she asked you to pause there?"

"She didn't say, my lord. But when I glance back at her, I see she's watching this family that's down in that stretch of grass and trees below the bridge—you know the place? Looked like a couple of little boys with their parents and an older man. Then some foulmouthed *fiacre* driver behind us starts hollering for us to get moving, and she tells me to go on across the bridge, that she's changed her mind about going to the Place Dauphine."

"What time was this?" asked Sebastian, sharper than he'd intended.

The coachman looked thoughtful. "Don't think I could say exactly, *monsieur*. Half past five? Maybe six? Thereabouts."

Sebastian felt a hollowness yawn deep within. The Earl had come to the Place Dauphine to see them the previous afternoon, and they'd decided to take the boys down to the end of the island to look at the river. *Is that what happened?* Sebastian thought with a sick thrum of certainty. Had Sophie seen them there? Had she recognized Hendon and perhaps Sebastian himself and decided to drive on, intending to come back later after the Earl had gone?

Sebastian felt the blood begin to pound in his temples. "So where did she go?"

"Had me take her to the inn that's right there on the quay, the Vert-Galant. And then she told me I might as well go home and stable the horses, because she was going to be a while and she figured she'd just take a *fiacre* when she was ready."

Sebastian stared out the window at the house's windblown forecourt, at the line of chestnut trees bordering the high stone wall, their dark branches lifting against the white sky. He was familiar with the Vert-Galant, which lay virtually at the foot of the Pont Neuf on the Left Bank. How long had she tarried there? he wondered. Until dark? Until she thought it likely Hendon was gone? And then what? Had she decided to walk the short distance from the inn to the Place Dauphine? Had someone seen her on the bridge and attacked her? Why? It would make sense if she'd been robbed.

But she hadn't.

He studied the coachman's deeply lined face, the watchful eyes that had seen half a million of his compatriots die hideous deaths in the snow and ice and numbing cold of Imperial Russia. "I'm told you also drove her ladyship on her recent journey."

A wary expression tightened the coachman's features. *"Oui."*

Sebastian shifted his position to lay one arm along the mantelpiece. "I can understand your reluctance to discuss a subject her ladyship may have asked you to keep quiet. But there's a possibility that her death is related to that journey, and any information you can give me about it could help explain why she was killed. Do you understand that?"

The man hesitated a moment, then swallowed hard. *"Oui."*

"Where did she go?"

Noël twisted his hat in his hands, his gaze sliding away from Sebastian's. For a moment Sebastian thought he meant to refuse to answer. Then he blew out a harsh breath and said, "Vienna. We were in Vienna, *monsieur.*"

"With Marshal McClellan?"

"Oui."

"The entire time?"

Noël shook his head. "After that we went to Italy."

Sebastian heard a strange humming in his ears that he knew had no real outside origin. "Where in Italy?"

"We tried driving south by way of Graz and Trieste, but there was danger of snow in the mountains. So we took a ship."

"To where?"

A tic started up beside the coachman's left eye. "To Piombino."

Sebastian was suddenly intensely aware of the wind buffeting the house's thick stone walls, of the fire crackling on the hearth beside him. Piombino was an ancient Tuscan seaport that lay some fifteen or sixteen miles from the island of Elba. And he knew with awful certainty where Sophie had been and why she had been there. "She went to Elba, didn't she?"

The tic beside the man's eye intensified. "I wouldn't know, *monsieur.* I stayed in Piombino."

"You know," said Sebastian.

But the man simply stared back at him, his face shuttered.

After a moment, Sebastian said, "How long were you there, in Piombino?"

"Less than a week."

"Then what?"

"We caught another ship, from Piombino to Cannes. Then we came north to Paris. It was a long journey, *monsieur*. We were gone months."

"I can imagine," said Sebastian. "And you would have me believe you have no idea what she was doing in either Vienna or Italy?"

The coachman stared woodenly back at him. "It was none of my business, *monsieur*. My job was to drive the horses and see her ladyship safely from one place to the next. And that I did."

"So you did," said Sebastian. But he found himself thinking of that disastrous retreat from Moscow; the long, hellish nightmare of exhausted, starving men freezing to death by inches as stragglers were picked off and cut down by the endlessly circling Cossacks. How had that brutal experience affected the man's attitude toward Napoléon? he wondered. Toward the restored Bourbon kings?

Did it matter?

"You say you've been with her ladyship now for more than two years?"

"*Oui*," Noël said guardedly.

"So you must know something of her friends—her friends and her enemies. Who do you think killed her?"

The coachman's gaze met his with a flare of alarm. "How would I know such a thing, *monsieur*?"

"Guess."

"I could not. I am a simple coachman, *monsieur*. I mind my own business, the way I should."

Sebastian studied the man's slack jaw and widened eyes. Part of his reluctance to talk doubtless came from loyalty to his late mistress. But Sebastian suspected the man was also frightened. And why wouldn't he be? What coachman in today's France would not be deeply afraid, knowing he'd just conveyed his mistress on a clandestine visit to Elba?

Elba, for the love of God.

"Thank you," said Sebastian, and let the man go.

He spoke to the other servants after that—to a footman named Guil-laume who'd also been on that strange journey to Vienna and Italy but claimed to know no more than the coachman. To the rest of Sophie's footmen and housemaids, to her cook and scullery maids, even to the gardeners and a young stable boy named Léon. With the exception of the stable boy, every male in Sophie's employment had been maimed in some way by the wars. Sebastian wondered if it was simply a reflection of how few unmaimed men were left in France or if she had deliberately gone out of her way to employ ex-soldiers.

All claimed to know nothing.

Chapter 13

*F*rustrated, Sebastian turned next to searching the house. He began with Sophie's bedroom, a large pleasant room that occupied the southeastern corner of the upper floor. Even on such a sullen, cloudy day, the room was flooded with light from the floor-to-ceiling windows that overlooked the gardens on two sides.

It was to the windows he went first, surprised to realize just how extensive her gardens were, stretching far to the east, north, and south. From here he could see a water garden, a knot garden, a spinney that might have been plucked from an English manor, a row of greenhouses, and bed after bed of roses just coming into leaf after the long, hard winter. He tried to remember if his mother had taken a special interest in the gardens of Hendon Hall. But if she had, he didn't recall it.

He turned away from the windows, his gaze running over the airy, high-ceilinged room with its garlanded cornices and white marble fireplace. It was more eighteenth century in style than Empire, but not particularly feminine. The Louis Quinze carved panels on the walls were washed a clean, simple white; the curtains and bed hangings were of dusky blue moiré; the scattered, well-proportioned chests and tables of delicate Italian inlaid marquetry. Tamping down an instinctive aversion to violating his own mother's privacy, Sebastian yanked open the top drawer of the nearest chest and then had to squeeze his eyes shut as a familiar scent drifted up to envelop him, hurtling him back in time with such ferocity that for one raw moment he imagined he heard his mother's distant laugh. He had to force himself to open his eyes and keep going.

He moved methodically around both the room and the dressing room he found beside it, searching first one chest, then the next. In the small drawer of a bedside table, he found a painted miniature of three boys and a young woman he recognized with a pang: Sophie's four children, frozen in time when they'd all been alive. Beside it lay an amethyst rosary that he fingered thoughtfully. But when he went to pull out the drawer of the chest on the far side of the bed, he found himself staring at a man's gold pocket watch with a fob in the shape of a rampant lion dangling from its chain.

Sophie had obviously not occupied this bedroom alone.

Slamming the drawer closed, he went to open the small door in the bedroom's northern wall to find a second dressing room, this one papered in a masculine stripe of hunter green, dark burgundy, and navy, and smelling faintly of tobacco and saddle soap. The chairs here were covered in gently worn leather, the gilt-framed paintings on the walls still lifes or hunting scenes set in what looked like the Scottish Highlands. A meerschaum pipe rested beside a riding crop atop the round rosewood table near the empty fireplace, as if the room's occupant had only recently set them there and walked off, forgetting them.

Standing in the center of the room, Sebastian felt a wave of anger wash over him—a raw, shaking rage at this man, this Napoleonic general who had drawn Sophie into a tangle of political intrigue that in all likelihood cost her her life.

He searched the marshal's dressing room with a ruthless thoroughness that had none of the reluctance he'd experienced in examining his mother's things. After some ten minutes, he knew that Alexandre Mc-Clellan had good taste; that his coats and shirts were impeccably tailored, his boots and gloves of the finest leather, his linen soft and expensive. Yet he was no closer to understanding why Sophie had made that damning journey to Elba or why she had been killed.

The search of the other rooms on the upper floor went quickly; all were intended for guests, well-appointed and comfortable but impersonal. He moved on to the ground floor. The grand salons and dining room were decorated in an elegant, understated Empire style, with friezes of simple grapevines or dentil moldings. The somber console tables were of marble-topped mahogany decorated with bronze fittings, the settees and lyre-backed chairs covered in dark green silk, the black marble mantels decorated with Grecian columns with Ionic capitals. The plain green-and-gold carpets in all the downstairs rooms looked new, as if recently purchased to replace earlier designs decorated with Napoleonic bees and eagles. He could easily imagine Sophie entertaining the marshal's colleagues here, moving gracefully through the elegant rooms with the ease of a practiced hostess. But beyond hinting at their owner's taste and the changing political winds, these public rooms told him little.

The morning room was considerably more intimate, more English, with its chintz-covered chairs and rose-strewn porcelains. It was here he found Sophie's harp, and he paused beside it, his heart suddenly so heavy that his chest ached. Reaching out, he ran his fingertips across the strings, the notes falling into the empty room like raindrops shattering the stillness of a quiet pond.

He let his gaze drift around the room, noting the cloth-lined basket with a half-finished embroidery that he recognized as her work. The book she'd obviously been reading before she left lay nearby and he went to pick it up. It was a French translation of Mary Wollstonecraft's *A Vindication of the Rights of Women*. A bookmark rested some three-quarters of the way through it, and he stared at it in wonder, realizing anew just how little he knew or understood about this woman who had been his mother.

He set the book aside and continued his search.

By the time he reached the library, he was no longer expecting to find anything. Sophie had been killed mere hours after returning from a monthslong mission he couldn't begin to understand, but which she had undoubtedly known was dangerous. She knew she was leaving behind a France in turmoil, that her home might be searched in her absence. Of course she had left nothing for anyone to discover.

The curtains at the library's long windows were still closed, and he moved first to throw them open, flooding the room with light. Like the bedroom above, the library looked out on the gardens, but the walls here were lined floor to ceiling with bookcases filled with everything from the works of Plato and Ovid to Byron and Donne. This was one thing he had known about his mother—how much she loved to read. He had simply accepted it at the time in that way children do, without wondering at the contradictions between her love of the works of Aristophanes and Shakespeare, and the brittle gaiety with which she threw herself into an endless round of balls, house parties, and indiscreet affairs with everyone from cabinet ministers to her handsome new groom.

Pushing the thought away, he turned from the windows to look back at the marble fireplace, his attention focusing for the first time on the gilt-framed portrait of a man that hung above the mantel, a French officer in a dark blue uniform with the four silver stars of a Marshal of the Empire. This, surely, was Alexandre McClellan.

He was a man somewhere in his fifties or early sixties, his nearly black hair heavily mixed with silver, his lean face darkened by years of fierce campaigning at Napoléon's side. Lines bracketed his mouth and fanned out beside his eyes, lines dug deep by all that he had seen and all that he had done. His cheekbones were high and prominent, his chin strong and square and lightly cleft, his brows dark and set straight. And for one suspended moment, Sebastian felt a cold shock of recognition sluice through him. For it was as if he were looking at himself, or rather at a portrait of himself in twenty-five or thirty years' time. He walked toward it, unable to look away from the eyes that seemed to stare back at him, taunting him.

Eyes of a hard, wolflike yellow.

Chapter 14

$\mathcal{S}$ebastian had always known he was different from the man he called Father. Different from both Hendon and from his two elder brothers.

Sebastian had grown up tall but lean and fine boned, whereas Richard and Cecil shared their father's large, solid build. Like his brothers, Sebastian had thrown himself into the "manly" pursuits of their class—horses and hunting, guns and swords. But he'd had other interests, too, enthusiasms not shared by his brothers, such as a love of music and poetry, philosophy and art. He'd always assumed he simply took after Sophie. But the origins of his yellow eyes and his uniquely acute hearing and sight remained a nagging mystery.

Because the intensely blue St. Cyr eyes were such a hallmark of the family, Sebastian eventually came to assume as a child that his strange yellow eyes were the main reason Hendon so often found fault with him, the reason the gleaming pride in the Earl's face could film over and become icy whenever Sebastian surpassed his brothers at some feat. And then one hideous July nearly three years ago now, Sebastian had discovered the truth, and it came perilously close to shattering him.

His sister, Amanda, sneeringly insisted that he was the get of Sophie's lowborn Cornish groom, and he'd believed her, for she was twelve years his senior and had always known him for her half brother. Then he'd encountered Jamie Knox, that ex-rifleman turned tavern keeper who looked nearly enough like Sebastian to be his twin. The two men shared the same lean, dark looks, the same feral yellow eyes, the same uncannily sharp hearing and sight and quick reflexes.

The son of an unmarried barmaid who had died in his infancy, Knox hailed from the small village of Ayleswick-on-Teme in Shropshire. Before her death, Knox's mother told her family that her son's father could be one of three men: an English lord, a Welsh cavalryman, or a handsome young Romani stable hand. Sebastian had assumed the handsome young stable hand must have later found work as the Countess of Hendon's groom—until he discovered the man had died over a year before Sebastian's birth. That left only two candidates: the unknown English lord and the equally unknown Welsh cavalry officer.

No one had ever said anything about a French officer of Scottish descent.

Which meant—what? That this exiled Scot had fathered both Sebastian and Knox, but that Knox's mother had for some reason omitted him from her list of lovers? That despite the resemblance there was no actual connection between Sebastian and Knox? Or had Sophie simply been attracted to Marshal McClellan because he reminded her of that unknown, long-ago English or Welsh lover?

Sebastian stared at the portrait of the French marshal, searching for the ways in which this man did not resemble him and trying to come up with another possibility.

But he could not.

He didn't know how long he stood there, his gaze on the man in the painting. Then he heard a faint rustle of cloth behind him and jerked around to find Madame Geneviève Dion in the library's doorway. And he knew from the stricken look in her eyes that his every thought, every emotion, was written on his face for her to read.

She lifted her eyes to the painting. "You've never seen him before?" Unspoken were the words *You didn't know how much you resemble him?*

"No." His voice sounded scratchy, hoarse, as if he hadn't used it in a long time. "I take it that's Marshal McClellan?"

"Yes. Her ladyship had it painted just last year." She hesitated a moment, then said, "I came to ask if you would like some tea."

"Thank you, but no."

She nodded and withdrew, leaving him alone.

Later, after he'd finished searching the library, they walked together in the gardens. The clouds were still pressing down low and gray, but the cold wind had dropped and the temperature seemed to be rising. Everywhere he looked he could see signs of the coming spring, fresh life bursting from the ground, bare limbs budding with green. By May or June the gardens would be breathtaking.

"She obviously liked roses," said Sebastian as they turned to walk down an allée bordered by climbing roses trained up tall posts to run along swagged heavy chains.

"They were her passion," said Geneviève Dion. "She was even experimenting with breeding them—growing them from seed."

He watched a magpie lift off the peak of one of the dormers in the house's steeply pitched roof. "Did McClellan give her this *hôtel?*"

"*Mais non.* The *maréchal's* estate is in Normandy. *Dama* Cappello bought this house for herself."

He glanced over at her. "Would you tell me now why she called herself that?"

A faint, sad smile touched the Frenchwoman's lips. "The name was given to her in jest by someone she once loved—a Venetian poet. Are you familiar with *Dama* Bianca Cappello?"

He shook his head.

"She was a famous Venetian noblewoman of the sixteenth century, beautiful and headstrong and very wayward. She ran off with a lowborn Florentine when she was just fifteen. It was a disastrous and foolish thing to do, yet somehow she ended up becoming first the mistress of Francesco de' Medici, then his wife and the mother of his son. Her court intrigues were the scandal of her day."

"And Sophie adopted the name?"

"As I said, at first it was simply a joke. But she told me she no longer felt that she had the right to call herself Sophia Hendon, and so she became Sophia Cappello."

He stared across a young fruit orchard to the ruins of an old prerevolutionary church just visible on the far side of the high wall. "How long was she with McClellan?"

"As long as I have known her."

He looked over at her in surprise. "But you've been with her some ten years."

"Eleven, I believe."

He was silent for a moment. "I was told several years ago that she was with General Becnel."

"Becnel?" The Frenchwoman frowned. "*Non.* Never."

"The person who told me that must have been mistaken." *Mistaken,* thought Sebastian, *or simply lying.* The information had come from one of the men he'd hired to find his mother. The man had resigned, claiming he was too afraid of Becnel to continue. Sebastian had no doubt the man had been afraid of someone, but obviously it was not of Becnel.

They turned to walk through a walled section of the gardens that reminded Sebastian of a traditional English cottage garden with flowers, herbs, fruits, and vegetables all tumbled together. "I understand McClellan is in Vienna. That he has sworn an oath of allegiance to the Bourbons."

"Yes."

"And Sophie? Did she likewise shift her allegiance from emperor to king?"

The chatelaine shrugged. "One does what one must to survive. One throws away one's white cockade and pins on the tricolor. And then when the tricolor is in turn outlawed, one throws it away and pins on the Bourbon white again."

"Is it that simple?"

"Simple?" The Frenchwoman's lips flattened into a straight, hard line. "No. It's never simple. But in the end, the differences between a king and an emperor are not so great, hmm? Not great enough to die for. Both take money from the poor to buy fine gowns and jewels for their women and to accumulate more horses, carriages, and grand châteaus than anyone has need of. And both send the sons of the poor off to fight and die in their wars."

Sebastian turned his head to study her tightly held profile, wondering if those cynical sentiments were hers alone or if Sophie had shared them. "From what her coachman tells me, after she left Vienna she went to Elba."

Madame Dion stared silently straight ahead.

He said, "Did you know?"

She shifted her gaze to where one of the gardeners was double digging a section of a nearby bed. "I suspected it. But did I know for certain? No. Not until this morning when Noël told me."

"Do you know what she was doing there?"

"No."

Sebastian wasn't convinced he should believe her, but all he said was "Can you think of someone in Paris who might know?"

The Frenchwoman blew out a harsh breath and shook her head. "There were those she would have called friend a year ago, but things are different now."

"You mean since the Restoration?"

She nodded. "The wives of the marshal's colleagues . . . they're now afraid to be seen as close to her."

"Because of Marie-Thérèse?"

Geneviève Dion nodded again. "Madame Cappello never made any secret of the nature of her relationship with the *maréchal*, and Marie-Thérèse . . . Well, let's just say she is very rigid in her thinking about such things. And she was already predisposed to despise anyone who served France under Napoléon."

He watched a lizard scuttle away ahead of them on the path. "And there is no one else?"

"Once I would have said she was close to her ward, Angélique La Hure. The girl's mother died just a few months after the father was killed in the Peninsula, and her ladyship and the *maréchal* took Angélique in and raised the girl as their own. But they have become estranged."

He glanced over at her. "Do you know why?"

"Her ladyship disapproved of the man Angélique wished to marry— Antoine de Longchamps-Montendre. But because she was of age, she married him anyway. They quarreled, and Angélique never forgave her."

"When was this?"

"That they quarreled? Last summer." She hesitated a moment, then said, "A woman did come to see *madame* yesterday, just hours after she'd returned home. But I don't know who it was; she was veiled."

"Would the gatekeeper or one of the servants know?"

"I can ask, but I doubt it. Her ladyship was in the forecourt consulting with one of the gardeners when the carriage pulled up. She obviously knew the woman because she told Jacques to open the gates and then walked forward to meet her as she descended from her carriage. They spoke for a few minutes, then the woman left." Madame Dion paused. "I could be wrong, but the exchange did not seem particularly . . . friendly."

"And you have no idea who the woman was?"

The chatelaine shook her head. "Whoever she was, she was very richly dressed, and her carriage of the finest quality, with a magnificent team of grays. But the coachman and footmen wore no livery, and there was no crest on the carriage's panel."

In other words, a woman who liked to travel incognito.

Sebastian said, "How long after that did Sophie leave for the Île de la Cité?"

"Not long. She asked Noël to bring round the town carriage, and they left." They'd reached the terrace now, and she turned to face him. "It's possible this may give you some of the answers you seek," she said, reaching into the pocket of her coat to withdraw a sealed envelope with Sebastian's name written across the front in his mother's elegant hand. "Before she left on her journey, *madame* asked me to keep it for her. She said that if something should happen to her, I was to find a way to get it to you."

She held the letter out to him, and after a brief hesitation he took it.

He drew a deep breath of clean country air scented with damp earth and growing green things and that faint, elusive scent from the past that still clung to the letter he now held in his hand. It was a moment before he found his voice.

"She knew what she was doing was dangerous," he said.

Madame Dion met his gaze, her eyes clouded with grief and worry and something else he could not identify. "Oh, yes. She knew."

Chapter 15

*S*ebastian was guiding his bays out through the *maison's* heavy iron gates when a carriage drawn by four magnificent matched chestnuts swept around the bend. He heard a man's shouted command, and the liveried coachman reined in hard, slewing the carriage across the road, blocking it.

"Who the 'ell is that?" said Tom as they watched the team of high-bred horses sidle and snort before them.

Sebastian drew up outside the gates, his eyes narrowing when he recognized the coachman's green-and-gold livery and the coat of arms on the carriage's panel. "The Duchess of Angoulême, from the looks of it. Or more likely someone from her household."

The near carriage door swung open and a courtier stepped down into the muddy road, a quiver of annoyance passing over his features when his boots landed with a splat. He was a tall, lanky man in his middle years, rawboned and austere-looking, his dark hair little touched by gray, his features pinched and hawklike. His dark blue coat was impeccably tailored and his boots of the finest leather, as one would expect of the *huissier du cabinet* and *premier valet de chambre* of the woman who was the daughter of one king, the niece of another, and the wife of a man who would someday, in turn, become king himself. But the clothes, although elegant, were masterfully restrained and understated.

According to legend, Xavier de Teulet had once planned to become a Jesuit priest, and there was still something ascetic and judgmental about him. He'd never married, choosing instead to devote his life to the royal family. They said the young de Teulet had chanced to be visiting Versailles with a group of *religieux* when the mobs broke into the palace during the October Days of 1789. Personally intervening to save the life of the Queen, he'd then chosen to accompany the royal family when they were dragged back to virtual imprisonment in the Tuileries. Even after they were moved to the Temple, he continued to serve them loyally. And when Marie-Thérèse was finally released from her cell, the only member of that small doomed family to survive, he'd helped escort her to refuge with Marie Antoinette's family in Vienna.

He'd remained faithfully at her side ever since, and had recently been ennobled by the newly restored King Louis XVIII. The Chevalier was one of several people around the Duchess who were said to stop at nothing to protect her interests. Sebastian had once tangled with his kind in England, and it had nearly cost him his life.

His and Hero's.

"Do I take it you're looking for me?" said Sebastian as two beefy *gendarmes* also hopped down from the carriage and ranged themselves one on either side of the Chevalier.

De Teulet's thin, aquiline nose quivered. "You were summoned to attend the Duchess this morning."

"Yes," said Sebastian, who wanted nothing so much as to find someplace quiet and undisturbed where he could read the letter that felt as if it were burning a hole in his pocket.

"You will come with us now. Your groom may follow with your carriage."

"I prefer to drive myself."

"Your preferences are immaterial, *monsieur*. You will come with us."

Sebastian held the man's dark, intense gaze for one long moment, then handed the reins to Tom. "Follow us."

They escorted Sebastian to the southern wing of the Louvre. At the time of Napoléon's abdication, the old sixteenth-century palace was being expanded by the addition of a new northern wing by the Emperor, who needed the space to display the hoards of artwork he'd stolen from across Europe. The Musée de Napoléon, he'd called it. The Bourbons had renamed the place, of course, but most of the looted treasures were still there. Sebastian could never understand why the Allies hadn't insisted on the return of their purloined art pieces as part of the peace settlements.

With de Teulet at his side and the *gendarmes* following close behind, Sebastian walked through endless long galleries crammed with Greek and Roman statues, grand old masters from the Low Countries and Italian states, religious works from the hundreds of French churches that had been torn down during the Revolution. He'd heard the Duchess was taking a special interest in the reorganization of the museum, and she was evidently here to confer with the man recently appointed to replace the Napoleonic director the Bourbons had dismissed.

She turned at Sebastian's approach, her head reared back in that exaggerated posture she considered regal but that most people simply found arrogant. She was dressed as usual in black, in the perpetual mourning widely seen as an expression of hatred for the French people she blamed for killing her family.

"So, *monsieur le vicomte*," she said in her cracked high-pitched voice. Her family had sent around the story that her voice had atrophied from disuse all those years she was in the Temple. But Sebastian had long suspected she'd actually broken it by screaming. "We meet again."

He bowed low. *"Madame."*

She studied him with cold, faintly protuberant blue eyes. As a child she'd had fine pale blond hair, a pointed face, and a small chin. But as a woman her hair had darkened to a dull reddish brown, her chin rounded, her nose become aquiline. It had long been believed by the public that the treatment she'd suffered in the Temple had left her unable to bear children. But the royal family strenuously denied it, and thirteen years into a childless marriage, she'd finally managed to conceive. Unfortunately she'd failed to carry the child to term, and there'd been no more pregnancies. Sebastian found it impossible not to sympathize with this tall, fiercely proud, rigid woman who'd suffered so much. But she didn't make it easy. The last man Sebastian had hired to trace his mother had been found garroted in London after complaining of being followed by "the Bourbons." Impossible to know if the man's analysis had been accurate or, if so, which of the Bourbons might have ordered his death. But Sebastian wouldn't put it past this hard, severely damaged King's daughter.

"I'm told your wife the *vicomtesse* is here in Paris, as well," she said unsmilingly. "Your wife and your son and heir."

Sebastian felt the hairs on the back of his neck rise. "They are, yes, *madame,*" he said, wondering where she was going with this.

"And what do you think of our city? Hmm? It is much changed from when I left it so many years ago."

Napoléon had introduced a vast number of important improvements to Paris, building thousands of miles of desperately needed sewer lines, setting up fountains with freshly piped clean water for the people, restoring buildings ravaged by the Revolution, improving the quays and markets, and erecting new bridges to link the Right and Left Banks of the Seine. Most of the projects that were incomplete at the time of the Emperor's abdication had been halted by the newly restored Bourbons— not because they weren't needed, but out of simple hatred for anything linked to Napoléon.

"Is it?" said Sebastian. "I was quite young when last I saw Paris."

She sniffed. "I'm told your mother has lived here for a number of years, although, of course, as *Dama* Cappello rather than under her own name."

Sebastian felt himself stiffen, then saw her lips curl in a faintly malicious smile. He had forgotten this about her, how quietly nasty she could be.

She said, "We surprise you. You thought we did not know?"

The Emperor Napoléon had been famous for his spies and secret police, who'd operated under the control of a powerful, dangerous man named Joseph Fouché. That once-feared minister of police had fallen even before the Emperor, but Sebastian had heard Fouché was trying to work his way back into the good graces of the Bourbons. Was that where this information had come from?

"And now I understand we are to extend to you our condolences," the Duchess was saying. "We hear Sophia Cappello has sadly suffered a fatal fall."

Sebastian was aware of de Teulet standing silently off to one side, his face a courtier's mask. "She is dead, yes," said Sebastian.

"And did you know, I wonder, that she'd recently made a visit to the island of Elba?"

Sebastian concentrated on keeping careful control of his features. He had no intention of letting her see she'd again caught him by surprise. "I knew she'd been on a journey, yes."

"Do you know the purpose of that journey?"

Do you? he wanted to ask. Instead he said simply, "How could I? She died before I had a chance to speak with her."

"So you would have us believe you did not know?"

"I have not seen my mother in over twenty years."

"And now she is dead. *Ç'est dommage.*" And then she repeated the expression, this time in English. "It is a pity." Except she didn't look as if she thought it a pity; she was almost smiling.

How was he supposed to respond to that? Sebastian wondered. In the end he decided to say nothing.

He saw the annoyance flicker across her features, the disappointment that her barb had not sunk as deeply as she'd obviously hoped. She said, "Marshal McClellan has sworn allegiance to our uncle the King and now negotiates on our behalf in Vienna in tandem with Prince Talleyrand. And yet his . . ." She paused as if searching for a suitable word. "Let's call her his 'particular friend,' shall we? She makes a visit to the Beast, Buonaparte?" As always she gave Napoléon's name the original Italian pronunciation, as if to disparage both the man and his non-French origins. As if she herself were not half Austrian. "Do you not find that curious?"

"I have never met Marshal McClellan."

"No?" She tipped her head to one side, her gaze traveling over his face. Again that flinty, malicious suggestion of a smile touched her lips. "He looks quite like you. Are you perhaps related?"

"Not to my knowledge, *madame*. But I have a number of Scottish relatives, so perhaps there is some distant connection."

"The resemblance is quite startling. Particularly around the eyes."

"So I understand, *madame*."

"Interesting." She shifted her gaze away from him to where de Teulet still stood in silent attendance. "Let us hope the marshal honors his vow to our uncle better than he honored his vow to his upstart Emperor. The Chevalier will see you out." And then she turned and walked away from him, the black train of her gown sweeping across the ancient wooden floor, the heels of her diamond-buckled shoes echoing loudly in the long gallery.

Sebastian was turning toward the door when the Chevalier put out a hand, stopping him. "The next time the Duchess commands your presence, you will attend immediately."

Sebastian stared into the Frenchman's dark, malevolent eyes. After a moment, de Teulet dropped his hand and stepped back.

"This isn't England, you know," said the Chevalier, raising his voice as Sebastian continued walking toward the flight of broad, shallow marble steps. "We do things differently here."

"You do indeed," said Sebastian.

And kept walking.

Chapter 16

*S*ebastian left the Louvre and went in search of his mother's husband. As Chancellor of the Exchequer, Hendon was a trusted member of the Prince Regent's cabinet and one of the two men Sebastian knew in Paris who were most likely to understand whatever was going on.

The other man, Jarvis, Sebastian generally tried to avoid.

He found the Earl at a café on the Champs-Élysées. "I've discovered something," he said, walking up to where Hendon sat reading a newspaper and drinking a coffee with brandy at a marble-topped round table beside a window overlooking the grand avenue.

Hendon glanced up, his vivid blue gaze meeting Sebastian's. Whatever he saw there caused him to fold his newspaper and thrust it aside. "Let's go for a walk."

They turned up the broad avenue toward the half-built, abandoned beginnings of what had been intended to be Napoléon Bonaparte's magnificent Arc de Triomphe. The avenue was in an exclusive new area of Paris, home to some of the most expensive tailors and modistes, milliners and jewelry stores, pastry shops and perfumers. It was also one of the few streets in the city built with pavements. Most Parisian streets forced pedestrians to walk in the roadway with all the mud, manure, and hazards posed by passing horses, carts, wagons, and carriages.

"What the bloody hell was Sophie doing?" growled Hendon when Sebastian had finished telling him of her journeys to Vienna and Elba, and of his own recent interview with Madame Royale.

"I've no idea. But whatever it was, I'd like to know how Marie-Thérèse found out about it."

Hendon huffed a hard breath. "Well, Napoléon might be under British control at Elba, but you can be damned sure the Bourbons have spies on the island watching who comes and goes and immediately reporting it all back to Paris."

"You think Sophie knew that when she went there?"

"One hopes she did." Hendon worked his jaw back and forth in that way he had when he was thoughtful or troubled. "I'm more puzzled by how they knew who Sophia Cappello really was. I'll give her credit for always keeping that quiet."

"Could they have had her killed?"

Hendon glanced over at him, his jaw sagging. "The Bourbons, you mean?" He thought about it a moment, then said, "Probably not King Louis himself. But Artois or Marie-Thérèse? I wouldn't put it past them. I suppose it depends on exactly what Sophie was doing in Vienna and Elba."

"What do you know of Marshal McClellan?" asked Sebastian. He tried to keep his voice even, but he wasn't certain he'd succeeded.

Hendon's lips pressed into a thin, tight line as he stared across the avenue at a street musician with a dancing dog. It was a moment before he answered. "I knew she was with him, if that's what you're asking. But I can't say I've ever heard anything to his discredit. He's a brilliant general—never defeated on the battlefield."

Sebastian kept his gaze on the Earl's half-averted profile. "Have you ever met him?"

"No." The offhand way in which he answered convinced Sebastian of his veracity. Hendon had never been particularly good at dissembling.

"It's difficult to believe she didn't go to Elba as McClellan's envoy," the Earl was saying. "The problem is, to what purpose?"

"You've heard the rumors that Napoléon has ambitions of returning?"

"Oh, yes. Those rumors have been flying from virtually the moment he abdicated. And the more unpopular the Bourbons make themselves, the more people whisper and dream of his return."

"Do you think he has any such actual intentions?"

Hendon frowned. "Frankly, if the Bourbons wanted to deliberately goad him into making the attempt, they couldn't be going about it in a more effective way. According to the treaty by which he abdicated, Napoléon's estates and those of his family were to be respected. But the Bourbons seized most of them within months. They were also supposed to pay him a pension of two million francs a year, but they haven't, and they've made it plain they have no intention of doing so. So there he is on Elba with a retinue of nearly a thousand and no money to pay them. I understand he's also instituted all sorts of engineering works to improve the island, expecting to have the revenue to fund them. So now he's in debt."

"You're saying he might try to stage a return simply because he needs money?"

"Not entirely. But you have to admit it's a powerful incentive. And then there's the fact it's an open secret the Prussians and the Bourbons both want him dead and have already sent several assassins against him. We're not quite that vindictive, but London and Vienna would definitely like to see him sent considerably farther away from Europe than Elba—to the Azores, perhaps, or to St. Helena. And neither government has exactly kept quiet about it. Hell, reports of the discussions have been published in the Parisian newspapers, which you know damned well are regularly sent to Napoléon."

"You think we might do it? Move him, I mean."

"I wouldn't be surprised. It's one of the things Wellington and Castlereagh are both pushing for. In fact, it's the main reason Castlereagh has gone back to London—to argue for it personally. And you've got Wellington taking his place in Vienna to promote the same thing to the Allies."

Hendon was silent for a moment, his eyes narrowed.

"What?" said Sebastian, watching him.

"The thing is, the common consensus is that if Bonaparte is going to make a move, he'll do it this summer after the Congress has broken up—the idea being that the Allies will be less likely to mount a unified offensive against him if their foreign ministers are no longer gathered together in one place."

"But?" said Sebastian.

"But there's no denying that discontent in France is growing, and the Bourbons are hardly going out of their way to make themselves popular. All they can think about is reestablishing the vanished past—that and enriching themselves and their friends, of course. And then you've got Marie-Thérèse and Artois doing their damnedest to bring back the power of the Church and the Jesuits, and forcing the shops, restaurants, and theaters to close on Sundays. I heard the other day they're even refusing to allow actors and actresses to be buried on hallowed ground. Basically they're trying to reimpose the absolute monarchy of the *Ancien Régime*, and it's stirring up a lot of resentment and resistance. There are reports there could be a push to replace the Bourbons with the Duke of Orléans. And you can be bloody well sure Napoléon is hearing those reports, too."

Sebastian looked at Hendon in surprise. The House of Orléans was a cadet branch of the French royal family that traced its descent back to Louis XIV. The current Duke of Orléans, Louis-Philippe, had actually supported the Revolution as a young man, although he broke with the

Republic after the execution of King Louis XVI and fled abroad. His father, the famous "Philippe Égalité," voted for the regicide, then lost his
own head beneath the blade of Madame Guillotine.

"You seriously think Orléans could be a threat to the Bourbons?"

"Oh, definitely. He's far more liberal in his thinking than Louis, let
alone Artois and Marie-Thérèse. Many see him as a compromise candidate between the Bourbons and a republic, and there's no denying the
House of Orléans has had ambitions of taking the throne from their
cousins for decades."

Sebastian was silent for a moment, his gaze on the jagged stones of
Napoléon's unfinished Arc de Triomphe now looming before them. The
monument had been planned as a grand triumphal arch in the style of
the Arch of Titus in Rome, but all work on the structure ceased with the
Restoration. He'd heard the King was considering restarting construction, arguing that the monument was intended to honor not Napoléon
but the patriots who had fought and died for France. But Artois and
Marie-Thérèse wanted to tear it down and put in its place a memorial to
the martyred royal family.

"In other words," said Sebastian, "if Napoléon does indeed have
dreams of taking advantage of the people's discontent, he needs to do it
soon, before Orléans beats him to it, and before the Prussians kill him or
London decides to pack him off to St. Helena."

"Basically."

"So do you think he'll do it? Try to come back, I mean."

Hendon huffed a hoarse laugh. "I suppose he can try, but he won't
get far. Good Lord, he has less than a thousand men."

"The people might rise up to greet him."

Hendon shook his head. "Only in his dreams. No, when Louis dies
there might be support to replace him with Louis-Philippe. But Napoléon? Not a chance."

There was a stray black dog nosing around the base of the monument, and Sebastian was silent for a moment, watching it. "Do you think that's what we could be dealing with here? A scheme aimed at Napoléon's return?"

"I suppose it's possible. The Allies seize and read all letters sent to Elba, so anyone wishing to communicate privately with the Emperor typically does it verbally, by sending messages through those who visit the island."

"Visitors like Sophie," said Sebastian.

Hendon turned his head, his face dark and troubled as he met Sebastian's gaze. "Like Sophie."

Chapter 17

The late-winter sun was sinking low in the sky by the time Sebastian drew up in the Place Dauphine.

"Stable 'em," he told Tom, hopping down to the worn cobblestones of the old square.

"Aye, gov'nor."

Sebastian watched the boy drive away toward the livery stables. Then, instead of entering the house, he turned to make his way down to the grassy point at the end of the island. The air was cooler closer to the Seine and damp, the dark gray water gurgling as it flowed swiftly past. He stood there for a moment, the breeze off the river buffeting his face and ruffling his hair as he watched a man in a navy coat and beret row a skiff upriver. Then he drew his mother's letter from his pocket and broke the seal.

"*Mon cher Sébastian,*" she had written. "If you are reading this, then it must mean that I am dead. If only you knew how I've ached to see you again, even if it could only be a brief glimpse from afar. But perhaps it is best this way."

He paused, his throat so thick it hurt, his gaze lifting to stare almost blindly at the barge moored on the opposite quay. The letter was written half in English, half in Italian and French, as if the use of her native tongue no longer came easily to her and she kept unconsciously slipping out of it. It was a moment before he could bring himself to continue reading.

I did see you once, some years ago. It was in Italy and you were dressed as a paysan, but I was certain it was you. Then I learned from Hendon something of what you did in the army and I knew I was right.

He wrote to me once a year, giving me news of you, Amanda, and her children. It was part of the Grand Bargain we made when I left England. And so I know you have by now discovered so many painful truths—that I did not die that wretched, long-ago summer, and that other truth, the one that would be unwise to commit to paper.

Do you judge me harshly for my actions in the past? I ache for the pain I know these discoveries must have caused you. I regret much of what I did in the course of my long, miserable marriage, but not that one fateful winter. How could I, when the result was you?

Hendon tells me you have seen your way to forgive him for the past, and I hope nothing I say here damages that. The fault for the tensions between us was as much mine as his, if not more so. I know that now, although I did not then. We were not "well suited," as they say. What a disastrous brew of misery and despair those simple words can disguise.

I hope you can somehow find it within you to forgive me for leaving you that long-ago summer and for the lies you have been told. I wish this not for my sake, but for yours, for anger and resentment corrode the soul. I would have taken you with me if I could, but Hendon said no, you were legally his heir and he was determined to claim you as such. After all, I am a St. Cyr through my grandmother, and you know how important that has always been to him. By English law all children belong to their legally recognized fathers. But even if that were not the case, how selfish it would have been of me to take you with me into my unknown future—to take you away from the wealth and titles that will someday be yours. I could not do it, any more than I could stay.

And so we made our bargain, Hendon and I. I would leave England, never to return. It would be given out that I was dead, although of course neither of us would ever truly be free to remarry. Every year he would send the letter, along with a stipend. There have been times of late when I considered telling him I've no need of his financial support, but I feared that without the stipend he would no longer send the annual letter. If you knew how much that letter has meant to me these last twenty and more years, perhaps you would understand. Plus I will admit to taking a certain satisfaction in continuing to force him to pay, although I acknowledge that as petty and unworthy of me. I have not changed entirely, it seems.

He tells me you have married, that you are happy in your marriage, and that I have a grandson named Simon. Your happiness is all I could ask for—yours and Amanda's, although she has always been a troubled soul. I've often regretted I did not make more of a push to prevent her match with Wilcox; perhaps with a different husband she would not have grown so bitter. But it's difficult to say. Hendon's mother was a hard, unpleasant woman, and I fear Amanda resembles her too much. She is my daughter and I love her, but she will do you harm if she can. Please beware.

There is so much more I would like to say, but I have been writing this letter off and on now for days, and the time has come when I must go. Please believe me when I say I love you more than life itself, and always have.

Je t'embrace,

Sophie

He didn't know how long he stood there, the letter half crushed in one hand, the sound of the rushing river loud in his ears, and the wind whistling through the branches of the untidy tangle of trees beside him. He was aware of the last of the daylight leaching from the cloudy sky, of the rattle of carriage wheels on the bridge above and the scent of woodsmoke that came with every breath. But all he could think was *She didn't tell me.*

How could she not have told him the name of his father?

How?

Rather than turning back toward the Place Dauphine, Sebastian walked across the southern arm of the Pont Neuf to the Hôtel Vert-Galant. The hotel stood on the Left Bank at the corner of the quai des Augustins and the rue de Thionville. Built of stucco and brick, with a steeply pitched mansard roof, it was a pleasant, respectable hostelry that looked as if it dated to the time of Henri IV, the first and most popular Bourbon king.

He ordered a glass of wine and sat for a time beside the fire in the public room, observing the establishment and its patrons and trying to figure out why Sophie had chosen this particular inn to come to that night. Because it was so close to the island? Or for some other reason entirely?

Some reason that might help explain her death?

The innkeeper was an older man in his sixties with wispy white hair, a round pink face, and a protuberant belly that strained against his leather waistcoat. Sebastian had little difficulty drawing him into conversation about the woman who'd been found dead on the Île de la Cité, for he was a gregarious man with what was obviously an intense lifelong interest in his fellow beings. Perhaps as a result, he seemed to find nothing either peculiar or suspicious in Sebastian's questions on the subject.

"*Ah, oui,* she was here last night," said the Frenchman, his eyes wide with the excitement of it all. "Must've been not too long before she was killed, the way I figure it. Poor woman."

"She came for a meal?" said Sebastian.

"*Non*, a glass of wine only. Took it in a *cabinet particulier*, of course. You won't find a lady of her quality drinking wine in the common room."

"She was alone?"

"When she came in? Oh, yes. Left alone, too."

"And what time was that?"

"When she left?" The innkeeper pursed his lips with thought. "Seven? Half past, perhaps?"

It had been shortly after nine o'clock when Sebastian found her. *My God*, he thought with a sickening lurch in his gut. Had she lain there in the dark, alone, afraid, and in pain for as much as two hours? Then he remembered Pelletan saying that the bruises on her arms had been made at the same time as her other injuries, within an hour or so of her death. So where had she been between the time she left the Vert-Galant and the encounter with her killer an hour or so later?

Aloud he said, "She left walking?"

"*Non*. Asked me to call a *fiacre*, she did."

Sebastian knew a glimmer of hope. All *fiacres* were licensed by the Parisian police, which meant that theoretically they ought to be able to track this one down—if the police were willing. "Did you notice the number?"

"No, sorry; can't say I recognized the driver, either."

"Did you hear her give him directions?"

"*Non*." The innkeeper obviously regretted this lack of attention to and personal knowledge of such important details in the drama, and added reluctantly, "But I suppose *he* might know where she was going."

The innkeeper's emphasis on the word "he" struck Sebastian as peculiar. "He? I thought you said she was alone."

"He didn't *come* with her. Walked in just as she was leaving. Greeted her like an old friend, he did."

"Do you know who he was?"

A strange mixture of revulsion and fear came over the innkeeper's face, and he shifted uncomfortably. "Don't think you'll find anyone in Paris who doesn't know who *he* is."

"Oh?"

The innkeeper cast a quick look around, then leaned forward, his voice dropping as if he were imparting a terrible secret. *"Le bourreau."*

It took Sebastian a moment to grasp what the innkeeper was saying. *Bourreau* meant "executioner," and in Paris it was generally used to refer to one man and one man only. "You mean Sanson? Henri Sanson?"

The innkeeper made a rude noise and jerked his head toward the inn's old-fashioned entrance hall. "Stood right there and chatted for a good five minutes, they did."

Sebastian found that baffling. The office of public executioner was both hereditary and lucrative, and a Sanson had served Paris in that capacity for generations. But despite their wealth, the family had long been considered social pariahs. During the Revolution, Henri Sanson and his late father, Charles-Henri, had beheaded thousands. Their victims ranged from unlucky commoners to nobles, princes, and royals—including King Louis XVI and Marie Antoinette. No one wanted to associate with the Sansons in any way. So why and how had Sophie come to befriend such a man? And why had she been meeting with him last night of all nights?

Sebastian took a slow sip of his wine. "Did they leave together?"

"Non. After she left, he came in and had a glass of wine."

"Did she meet or speak with anyone else?"

The innkeeper thrust out his lower lip and shook his head. *"Non.* Only Sanson."

"Did she strike you as afraid or nervous in any way?"

"Non. She was tired, though; I could see that. And perhaps a bit preoccupied with something she had in her reticule."

"What was that?"

"A small red leather case of some kind. Fancy thing, it was. Don't think she wanted me to see it—tucked it away quick enough when she realized I was coming with her wine."

Sebastian raised his own glass to his lips and drained it. There had been no red leather case, either in Sophie's reticule or on the ground near it. But its absence might explain why her reticule was open when it was thrown from the bridge.

And why she was killed.

Chapter 18

*E*lba?" said Hero when Sebastian had finished telling her most—but not quite all—of what he'd learned that day. "What in heaven's name was Sophie doing on Elba?"

"Meeting with Napoléon, one presumes," said Sebastian. "But for what purpose, I can only guess. And all the guesses are more than troubling."

They had settled after dinner in the house's old-fashioned salon overlooking the ancient square, Sebastian sipping a glass of port and Hero curled up in one of the worn chairs by the fire while she mended a hem Simon had torn that afternoon.

"And Marie-Thérèse knows of their meeting?" said Hero. "My God. Could she have had Sophie killed because of it?"

Sebastian stared out the window, his gaze on the bare limbs of the plane trees moving restlessly in the wind. "I wouldn't put it past her—either her or her uncle Artois. And interestingly enough, neither does Hendon."

"And you've no idea what this red leather case the innkeeper was talking about could be?"

"No, none. All I know at this point is that it was gone by the time I found her."

"Perhaps she gave it to Monsieur Sanson." Hero kept her gaze on her sewing. "He seems an odd acquaintance for her to have."

"Beyond odd." Sebastian pushed away from the window and went to refill his drink. "But with any luck, he may be able to tell us something that will help make sense of what happened to her." He was silent for a moment, watching Hero tie off her thread and cut it. He had given her Sophie's letter to read, but he hadn't told her about Marshal McClellan's portrait and he couldn't begin to explain why, even to himself.

She set aside her mending and looked up at him. "I can't believe Hendon knew she was in Paris all this time."

"Really? I can." He watched the firelight flicker across her beloved features, watched her brows draw together in thought in that way she had, and he set aside his port to go stand behind her chair and put his hands on her shoulders. "Thank you."

She tilted back her head to look up at him, a puzzled smile on her lips. "For what?"

For meeting with that damned doctor and officier de paix, *he thought. For organizing the funeral, which I'm not sure I could bear to deal with at the moment. For not pressing me to talk about things you know I can't bring myself to talk about.* But all he said was "Everything."

She gave a faint shake of her head. "I thought Amanda might come this afternoon. Surely Hendon has told her by now. Don't you think she'd want to see her mother?"

"I suppose it depends on how much anger and resentment she harbors toward Sophie. My guess is it's a lot. No one's better at harboring anger and resentment than Amanda."

"Perhaps. But still—" She broke off as the bell sounded below. "Expecting someone?"

"No."

A moment later a footman appeared at the salon's door with a bow.

"A Monsieur Eugène-François Vidocq to see you, my lord. He says you will know who he is."

"Send him up right away."

The footman bowed again. "Yes, my lord."

"*Do* you know who he is?" asked Hero.

Sebastian reached for his glass of port and drained it. "I do indeed. He's an ex–galley slave who somehow managed to get himself appointed head of something called the *Sûreté nationale*. From what I'm told, he's very good at catching criminals and murderers—largely because he was once one himself."

Although only average in height, Eugène-François Vidocq came into the room exuding all the energy and presence of a much larger man. His shoulders were broad and bearlike, his hands meaty, his head unusually big. Even the features of his face were exaggerated, his nose and chin pronounced, his mouth wide and mobile. He looked older than his thirty-nine years, his thick, overlong dark blond hair heavy with gray. But then, he'd lived a hard life, having killed his fencing master as a youth and run away from home at the tender age of thirteen. In the course of his varied career, he'd enlisted—several times—in the Republican Army; toured with a troop of Romani; served as a cattle drover, a privateer, and a forger; seduced and defrauded a string of women; and escaped from more prisons than anyone could remember. Sebastian had never heard exactly how he'd managed to convince the Paris police chief, Jean Henry, to allow Vidocq to set up a brigade of ex-criminals dedicated to fighting crime, but it had been an inspired move. Uncannily observant, diabolically clever, and possessed of an amazing memory for faces, Vidocq had become a legend in just a few years.

Entering the salon with a rapid gait, he brought with him the city scents of woodsmoke, tobacco, and the river. His clothes were those of a middling member of the bourgeoisie, neither extraordinarily fine nor ragged—all the better to blend in with a crowd or pass unnoticed. He swept Hero a surprisingly courtly bow, then turned to Sebastian and said, "I've heard about you."

"Oh?"

"They say you like to solve murders."

"Sometimes."

Vidocq lifted his head, breathed in deeply through his nose, then smiled and said, "Ah. You've been drinking the port of the Cima Corgo. I'll take a glass, thank you."

"Of course," said Sebastian, his gaze meeting Hero's for one brief moment before he went to pour the strange man a glass and refresh his own.

"*Merci.*" Vidocq took the glass extended to him, sniffed the hearty wine's scent with smiling appreciation, then took a drink. "*Ç'est bon.*" He fixed Sebastian with a hard stare, cocked one thick arched brow, and said, "You know why I'm here?"

"Not exactly. I was told by the *commissaire* that even you were not so foolish as to involve yourself in the death of Sophia Cappello."

Vidocq pursed his lips and made a rude noise. "Balssa is like one of those little bugs that rolls itself into a hard, tight ball at the least hint of danger." He brought up one hand, finger pointed, to draw a swirling circle in the air. "He has no sense of adventure, no curiosity, and no imagination."

"Unlike you."

A crooked grin stretched the man's wide mouth. "Unlike me." He took another noisy slurp of port. According to what Sebastian had heard, Vidocq was the son of a successful merchant from Arras. But many years had passed since those days.

The Frenchman said, "I've spoken to Dr. Pelletan."

"Yes?" said Sebastian.

"He tells me your mother was stabbed before she was thrown off the Pont Neuf."

Sebastian kept his features carefully composed. "He told you she was my mother?"

"What? Ah, no, that information comes from someone at the Tuileries— although you can rest assured that I have made no alterations to the Act of Death filled out by the sadly pedestrian-minded *officier de paix* who met with the *vicomtesse* earlier today." He turned to bow again to Hero. "Even armed with this knowledge, I saw little reason to become involved . . . until this evening."

"This evening?" said Hero.

He bowed to her again. "This evening. A young woman has been found murdered in the Faubourg Saint-Antoine. It's a rough place, Saint-Antoine. But this woman's death is unusual, as is her identity: Francine Danjou, abigail to the late *Dama* Cappello—or, I should say, to the Countess of Hendon."

Sebastian's startled gaze again met Hero's across the room.

"So," said Vidocq, one swooping eyebrow raised in inquiry as he drained his glass and set it aside, "you will come with me now to Saint-Antoine, yes?"

Chapter 19

They took a *fiacre* to the rubble-strewn site of the legendary, now-vanished fortress known as the Bastille. Before his downfall, Napoléon had been building a grand public fountain here, but King Louis had halted its construction the way he had so many of the Emperor's other municipal improvement projects. From there they plunged on foot into the maze of small, crooked passages, dark courts, and impasses that formed the infamous faubourg.

This was an area of ancient smoke-blackened houses leaning drunkenly over narrow cobblestoned lanes strewn with rubbish nosed by pigs and stray dogs and small, vacant-eyed children. The Faubourg Saint-Antoine was the home of some of Paris's poorest residents as well as its most skilled craftsmen: the master woodworkers who'd made the beautiful bedsteads, commodes, desks, and tables that once filled Versailles and so many other palaces and châteaus; the bronze turners who'd made the grand chandeliers and intricate doorknobs; the textile mill workers who toiled fourteen- and sixteen-hour days from the age of four or six; the laborers in the noxious wallpaper manufactories who seldom lived to be old.

In April of 1789, one such luxury wallpaper manufacturer, a Jean-Baptiste Revéillon, had tried to lower his workers' wages. The workers, whose families were already starving, protested. The soldiers sent by the government to quell the unrest fired into the crowd, killing dozens. Sebastian had heard there were many who saw that uprising as the real beginning of the French Revolution. Just three months later, these same angry Parisians stormed the Bastille, and France was never the same again.

"You've been here before, yes?" asked Vidocq as Sebastian followed him down a twisting, malodorous lane.

"Actually, no," he admitted.

"Wise." Vidocq turned to dart down a narrow passage lined with workshops. The air here still smelled of sewage and rot, but the pervasive stench of the faubourg now mingled with the sweet smells of freshly cut wood—of pine, walnut, cedar, and other exotic scents Sebastian couldn't identify.

"Here," said Vidocq, drawing up to knock at an ancient battered door with peeling blue paint.

The dead abigail's father was an ebonizer named Marcel Danjou, who lived with his wife and surviving children in a room behind his workshop. As the craftsman ushered them into the small, dimly lit space, Sebastian counted six children ranging from a babe in arms to a boy of perhaps sixteen.

The mother, a worn-looking woman of indeterminate age, sat on a rush-bottomed stool in the glow of a meager fire, her infant clutched to her breast, the other children huddled wide-eyed around her. The eldest boy stood protectively behind her, his hand on her shoulder.

Marcel Danjou himself was ashen faced, his eyes red rimmed and bloodshot, his shoulders slumped as if beneath a weight suddenly too great to bear. "Monsieur Vidocq," he said, bobbing his head in a way that told Sebastian the chief of the *Sûreté* had already been here once. "We haven't done anything with her yet, as you asked."

"*Merci.*"

He led Sebastian and Vidocq to where his dead daughter lay on a straw pallet in a darkened alcove. The woodworker then fetched over a smoking tallow candle, which he handed to Vidocq.

"*Merci,*" said Vidocq again.

Danjou nodded and backed away.

Vidocq waited until the father had rejoined his wife by the fire before extending his arm so that the candlelight flickered over Francine's waxen face and the ripped, blood-soaked bodice of her gown. She looked to be perhaps twenty or twenty-one, sturdily built, with medium brown hair and pleasant, even features.

"I take it she was stabbed?" said Sebastian, keeping his voice low so the family wouldn't hear.

"Multiple times. But she didn't die easily. Look at her hand."

Sebastian shifted his gaze. Four of the fingers on her right hand were a broken, swollen, mangled, discolored mess. "My God," he whispered. "Why?"

"It's a crude but effective form of torture, yes? Smash one finger; ask your question. If you don't get the answer you want, you break another, and so on. The other hand is fine, which suggests they could have decided she had nothing to tell them and simply killed her. Although it's also possible that whoever was doing it didn't have the stomach for it and just gave up and killed her. Or . . ."

"Or?" prompted Sebastian.

Vidocq met Sebastian's hard gaze. "Or she told them what they wanted to know, and then they killed her."

After that, they retreated to a dimly lit *bar à vins* near the corner, with a carafe of red wine and an earthenware bowl of nuts on the rickety

wooden table between them. The smoky bar was crowded with a malodorous mixture of craftsmen and workmen, all shouting and laughing
and almost drowning out the musician screeching out an old Provençal
love song on his fiddle.

"I suppose what happened to the girl could have been worse," said
Vidocq, cracking a nut, then digging the meat out of the shell with one
thick finger. "In the old days, before the Revolution, the Bourbons used
to break those they hated on the wheel. You know what that means, to
be broken on the wheel?" He leaned forward and continued without giving Sebastian the chance to answer. "They used to set up a wheel on the
scaffold, tie the condemned to it, naked, and literally break their bones,
one by one. The executioner would start at the shins and work his way
up. Then the broken body and the wheel to which it was tied would be
erected on a pole. If the poor bastard was lucky, the executioner would
be allowed to garrote him. If not, the condemned might be thrown into
a fire and burned alive, or left to die slowly. I've heard of men who lived
broken and tied to the wheel for up to four days."

Sebastian took a deep drink of his wine and said nothing.

"Of course, they got rid of all that with the Revolution. Everyone
was then guaranteed the right to a quick, merciful death thanks to Madame Guillotine." He slammed the edge of one hand down into the flat
palm of the other. "Chop."

"Undoubtedly an improvement," said Sebastian.

"In its way, yes." Vidocq cracked another nut. "Certainly quicker. But
it's curious, wouldn't you say? A gentlewoman is knifed and thrown off
the Pont Neuf one night, and the next day someone tortures and kills
her abigail?"

"The girl was killed today?"

"Danjou says she went out to pick up a chicken for her mother and
didn't come back. Her brother went looking for her and found her body
behind some rubbish in an alley not far from the workshop."

Sebastian took another sip of his wine. "If you're looking to me to explain it, I can't."

"No? Danjou tells me his daughter returned just yesterday from a long journey with Madame Cappello—a journey he thinks may have taken them to Italy, although he doesn't know for certain because *madame* swore Francine to secrecy and she was a very loyal girl."

When Sebastian remained silent, Vidocq leaned back in his seat, his eyes narrowing as he let his gaze rove over Sebastian's face in a way he didn't like. "Anyone ever tell you how much you resemble Marshal McClellan?"

"Yes, actually. I believe we may be distantly related."

Vidocq snorted. "Can't be too distant." He leaned forward again, his voice lowered almost to a whisper. "So tell me, *monsieur le vicomte*: Who do you think killed your mother and her abigail?"

Sebastian met the Frenchman's questioning gaze and held it. "I don't know."

"No ideas?"

"Not really," said Sebastian. Or at least, not any ideas that he intended to share.

"And do you know where her ladyship went on her recent long journey?"

"How could I?"

Vidocq's lips pulled into what might have been a smile, but his eyes remained hard. "How am I to help you discover your mother's killer if you are not honest with me, *monsieur*?"

"Where do you think she went?"

The man's smile widened into something that glittered with faint malice, yet somehow looked more genuine. "Vienna and then Elba."

Sebastian kept his own expression utterly bland. "Do you know why?"

"No."

Sebastian reached for a walnut. "Neither do I."

For a moment Vidocq stared at Sebastian with brutal intensity. Then he punched the air between them with a pointed finger. "Now, that I believe."

Sebastian cracked the nut against the table with the heel of his palm. "Who do you think killed her?"

"Me? I don't know yet. France today is a witches' brew of whispers and swirling threats of conspiracy, but not everything is political. People do still kill for other reasons."

"You think that's the case here?" said Sebastian, wondering what the man knew that he wasn't telling.

"Perhaps."

Sebastian reached for another nut. "When I first left the Place Dauphine last night, there was a young *fille publique* standing near the empty statue base in the center of the bridge. She was gone by the time I came back and found the Countess, but it's possible she saw something. Something she can tell us if we could find her."

Vidocq's features sharpened with interest. "How young?"

"Fifteen, maybe sixteen. Very thin, with a square face and a small nose. Medium brown hair, no more than five feet tall. She was wearing a light blue dress with a ragged red cloak and no hat."

"You saw her only from a distance?"

"Yes."

Vidocq frowned. "It was very dark and cloudy last night, *monsieur*. How can you be so certain what she looked like—right down to the color of her dress and cloak?"

"I see exceptionally well in the dark," said Sebastian.

"You must."

Sebastian reached for another nut, but rather than crack it, he bounced it up and down thoughtfully in his palm. "I understand your brigade is known for its close connections to bars and brothels and the people of the streets. If you could find her—"

"We can try. But there are many prostitutes in Paris. And what are the odds she actually saw anything, hmm?" The Frenchman cupped his hand to swipe it across the tabletop, sweeping his pile of shells onto the floor. "We have spoken to the Countess's coachman, of course. Do you know why she went to the Vert-Galant last night rather than to the Place Dauphine as planned?"

"No."

Vidocq's eyes narrowed. "Once again, I'm not certain I believe you."

"Believe it." Sebastian hesitated a moment, then said, "If you know the Countess went to the Vert-Galant, then you know she left there in a *fiacre*. Have you found it yet?"

The Frenchman's lips pressed into a flat line. It was obvious he did not like having his competence questioned. "We're looking."

The men at the table beside them began singing along with the fiddler's song, two tenors blending with a bullfroglike bass, and Sebastian leaned forward so that he could be heard. "I'm also told she had a small red leather case with her when she was there. But I didn't find anything like that with the scattered contents of her reticule, so it's possible someone picked up the case and pawned it—someone who might have seen something."

"And you want me to question all the pawnbrokers in the area, do you?"

"I suspect they'll answer your questions more readily—and honestly—than mine."

"Huh," grunted Vidocq. He drained his wineglass, then reached for the carafe to refill it. "Do you know, I have encountered many men in my lifetime, but I can only recall one with yellow eyes."

"Oh?"

"Mmmm. It's interesting, yes? Like yours, his eyesight was also abnormally acute—his eyesight and his hearing both."

Sebastian simply sipped his wine and said nothing, and after a moment the Frenchman continued. "He was quite famous in our regiment because of it. I served under him, you see. Of course, he was only a captain then, for it was long ago. But he's a marshal now."

Chapter 20

The night was blustery, the clouds overhead bunching and swirling in the darkness. Sebastian stood at the bedroom window watching the shadows cast by the trees dance across the facades of the old Renaissance-era brick-and-stone houses that surrounded the small triangular square. The Place Dauphine had been built early in the seventeenth century, in the reign of Henri IV, the laughing, boisterous, gallant king who'd saved France from the long and bloody religious wars of the sixteenth century. Henri had been raised a Protestant, but he'd pragmatically converted to Catholicism, famously saying, "Paris is worth a mass." Some one hundred and fifty years after that, the father of Alexandre McClellan had fled his native Scotland for Paris. Was he driven by religion? Sebastian wondered. Or was his allegiance not to the mass but to the descendants of the dispossessed Stuart King?

Did it matter?

He was aware of Hero coming up beside him, the touch of her hand light on his arm. "Can't sleep?"

"No." He hadn't told her what Vidocq had said about McClellan, just as he hadn't told her about the portrait hanging in the library of the house in the rue du Champs du Repos. It was as if by telling her his suspicions he would somehow make them more real, and he wasn't ready to face that yet.

He said, "I keep thinking, why torture and kill the abigail? *Why?*"

After he'd left Vidocq, he'd made a painful trip out to the rue du Champs du Repos to break the news of Francine's death to Madame Dion. The aged chatelaine had taken the news with silent stoicism that both awed and vaguely troubled him.

Hero gave a faint shake of her head. "Given that Marie-Thérèse already knew of Sophie's visit to Elba, what could the girl possibly have told them that they needed to hear?"

"We don't know that Marie-Thérèse is the one who had her killed." He paused, then added, "She simply seems the most likely candidate at the moment." He slipped his arms around her waist, drawing her close enough that he could rest his forehead against hers. "At least this new death suggests we can definitively dispense with the *commissaire's* theory that Sophie threw herself off the bridge in a fit of quiet despair and somehow managed to impale herself on the way down."

"I didn't know her, but from what I've heard, Sophie never struck me as the kind of woman to take that way out of her problems."

"No, she wasn't."

Hero was silent for a moment, and he had no idea what she was thinking until she said, "I've been trying to figure out where I heard the name of the young woman Madame Dion told you about this afternoon— the one who was Sophie's ward."

"You mean Angélique de Longchamps-Montendre?"

Hero nodded. "And I finally remembered. She was at that salon I attended last week."

"Madame de Staël's?"

She smiled softly at whatever she heard in his voice. Germaine de Staël was a flamboyantly eccentric but highly celebrated essayist and novelist who also happened to be the daughter of Louis XVI's notorious finance minister, Jacques Necker. She'd returned to Paris soon after the fall of Napoléon—a man with a well-earned reputation for disliking smart, sharp-tongued, critical women—and ostentatiously resumed her famous salons. Hero had attended one shortly after their arrival in Paris, but Sebastian had begged off with a look of horror that had brought Hero to tears of laughter.

"I talked to her for some time," Hero was saying. "She has a special interest in astronomy."

"She does?"

At that, Hero laughed out loud. "Don't sound so surprised. My point is, having been formally introduced, I could call on her tomorrow. She might know something."

"That would help."

She leaned back so she could see his face. "Now will you come to bed?"

He cupped her cheek with his palm, gazed into her beautiful eyes, slid the pad of his thumb across her soft lips. There was so much he wanted to say to her, to tell her, but it was as if the words were piling up in his chest, burning there, unable to get past the obstruction in his throat.

He saw her eyes narrow, saw the concern that pinched her features. She said, "What is it, Sebastian?"

He shook his head, not denying that there was something, only denying his ability to express it.

She slipped her arms around his neck, her body pressing close to his, her lips soft as she brushed his mouth with hers. "Tell me when you're ready," she whispered.

He felt his love for her wash through him, easing the pain and submerging everything else in a rush of hard-driving desire that swirled him away. . . .

For a time.

Saturday, 4 March

The next morning dawned cold but gloriously clear, with a crystal blue sky and a bright sun that bathed Paris in a rich buttery yellow light.

Sebastian began the day with a meeting with Sophie's *avocat,* an aged, scholarly-looking lawyer named Jean Cloutier. He confirmed what Sebastian had been told about her will and promised to do everything possible to expedite its settlement.

There were no surprises. Sophie had left a handsome pension to Madame Dion and generous sums for her other servants; there was also a list of small items ranging from a Turner landscape to a Murano glass bird that she wished set aside for Marshal McClellan. Everything else she left to Sebastian to share with his sister and her family "or otherwise dispose of as he sees fit."

The *avocat* cleared his throat. "I shall of course be writing the marshal to apprise him of her ladyship's death and to ask if he would perhaps wish us to forward his personal items to his château in Normandy."

Sebastian nodded. "Please assure him that they may remain at the rue du Champs du Repos until such time as he is able to deal with them."

Cloutier nodded. "And will you be interested in selling the *hôtel, monsieur?*" he asked, peering at Sebastian over the rims of his gold-framed spectacles.

"Perhaps at some point in the future," said Sebastian, "but not just yet."

He tried to imagine simply disposing of everything connected with Sophie—her home, her gardens—and was surprised to find the thought unbearable.

Cloutier nodded. "As you wish. If you prefer, I could arrange to have someone manage the place when you return to England."

"Yes, thank you," said Sebastian.

He signed the necessary preliminary papers and clarified a few details. Then he went in search of Henri Sanson, the hereditary executioner of Paris.

Henri Sanson lived with his extended family in a large stone house on the rue de Marais. Sebastian had heard that the family also owned a comfortable estate in the country to which Henri's father and predecessor, Charles-Henri Sanson, had retired in the mid-1790s. He'd killed thousands of men and women, young and old, rich and poor, powerful and powerless; but then his nerves failed. He began seeing spots of blood on his tablecloth at dinner and hearing the terrified shrieks of those he'd beheaded. And so he'd turned the family business over to his son and retired to a peaceful life of reading and gardening and playing his violin.

Sebastian wondered if he'd still seen the phantom blood splatters, still heard the screams echoing in his mind.

The current *guillotineur* was a sturdily built, neatly dressed man in his mid-forties, jowly and serious-looking, with hooded eyes and the quiet, assured demeanor one might expect from a family physician rather than a man who chopped off heads for a living.

He received Sebastian in a pleasant garden at the rear of his house. He had a pair of secateurs in one hand and a basket looped over his arm, and he was clearing the winter-killed canes out of a large rosebush just beginning to come into leaf.

"The sun is lovely today, yes?" he said, glancing over at Sebastian. "You will pardon me for continuing with my task?"

"Of course," said Sebastian, his gaze taking in the rows and rows of roses bordered by low miniature box hedges. "Thank you for agreeing to see me." He hesitated a moment, then said, "Do you know why I'm here?"

"I can guess," said the Frenchman, not bothering to look at him again. "Even here in Paris, we have heard of your reputation for solving murders, *monsieur*. I know that Sophia Cappello was killed not long after I spoke with her Thursday evening at the Vert-Galant, so it is logical to assume you have heard of that, yes?"

"Did you arrange to meet her there?"

"What? Oh, no. Our meeting was by chance only."

"How did you happen to know her?"

The *bourreau* was silent for a moment, his nostrils flaring as he drew a deep breath. "I am the fifth Sanson to serve as the executioner of Paris; did you know? The first—my great-great-grandfather—was an impoverished minor nobleman who married the daughter of the executioner serving at that time, back in the seventeenth century. He had no sons, that executioner, so when he died the office passed to the husband of his daughter. They say that particular Sanson fainted at his first execution. It is always best if the office descends within a family, father to son. The son grows up watching his father work and so becomes accustomed to it."

Sebastian found himself thinking about this man's own father, who'd grown up in the profession and still ended his days seeing imaginary blood splatters on his dinner table. But all he said was "Must be hard on those sons who might prefer a different profession."

"It is, indeed. My father dreamt of becoming a physician—he wanted to save lives rather than take them. But when his father's illness forced him to retire and there was no other heir, he had to drop out of medical school and don the red coat and blue sash of our office." A silence descended on the garden, filled only by the *snip-snip* of the secateurs and the rustle of some unseen creature in the nearby hedge. "Of course," said Sanson, "in the old days there were not so many executions."

"But they were decidedly more brutal."

Sanson lifted his shoulders in a shrug. "Most were hanged—except of course for heretics, who were burned, and counterfeiters, who were boiled alive." He paused, then added, "And murderers and highwaymen, who were broken on the wheel."

Sebastian thought of the gruesome torture so graphically described by Vidocq and now casually dismissed by this man. Henri Sanson hadn't taken over from his father until 1795, but he'd acted as one of his assistants for years before that. Sebastian tried to envision the seemingly normal man before him inflicting such hideous agonies on his fellow beings—tried to imagine Sophie befriending such a man.

He could not.

"The crowds were not happy when the guillotine was first introduced," Sanson was saying. "It was too quick, and they missed the old spectacles. There were riots. People were killed."

"I suppose the rapid increase in the number of heads being chopped off must have alleviated that concern."

Sanson sighed and nodded in agreement. "Poor Dr. Guillotin. He was against the death penalty, you know. But since he couldn't get the Assembly to abolish it, he worked to have it made more humane. And now he will forever be associated with mass executions. I hear his family has changed their name."

Who could blame them? thought Sebastian. He suspected Sanson's descendants might be inclined to do the same someday.

Sanson stood back to evaluate the rosebush, his eyes narrowing as he searched for more dead wood. "At one time Madame Guillotine was called the 'Louisette,' after the Royal Surgeon Antoine Louis, who actually designed it—with the help, of course, of Monsieur Guillotin, my father, and the musical-instrument maker who built the first one. But the name didn't stick for some reason."

"'Louisette' does have a rather diminutive sound that doesn't seem quite appropriate."

"True." Sanson moved on to the next bush. "And have you discovered anything yet about the death of Madame Cappello?"

"Not a great deal," said Sebastian. "How was she when you saw her Thursday evening at the Vert-Galant? Would you say she seemed nervous or afraid?"

Sanson pursed his lips in thought. "She was tired from her recent journey and perhaps troubled in some way. But afraid? No, I wouldn't say so."

"Troubled in what way?"

"Perhaps 'preoccupied' would be a better word."

"She spoke to you of her journey?"

"Not really. All I knew was that she had until that day been gone."

"She didn't tell you where she'd been?"

"I assumed Vienna, but we did not discuss it."

Sebastian studied the Frenchman's calm profile, looking for any suggestion of subterfuge. But the executioner had a lifetime's training in the art of disguising his emotions; he was giving nothing away. "I'm told she asked the innkeeper to call a *fiacre* for her when she left. Do you know where she was planning to go?"

"No. Sorry."

"Did you happen to see the *fiacre* driver?"

Sanson frowned as if with the effort of memory. "Briefly, through the open door when she left. Why?"

"Can you describe him?"

The executioner rolled his heavy shoulders in a shrug. "All I remember is that he struck me as quite frail—not old, you understand, but frail, as if he were unwell. I remember thinking he must be one of the returned prisoners of war one sees all over the city or perhaps a soldier still suffering from his wounds."

"You didn't notice the number?"

"If I did, I don't recall it."

Sebastian watched Sanson shift to work on the next rosebush. "You never told me how you and Madame Cappello came to know each other."

A faint smile curled the Frenchman's full lips. "You mean, why would a woman such as her befriend a man shunned by all of Paris?" He paused. "How much do you know about Madame Cappello?"

"Some."

"Then you would know that a woman with her history is not generally acknowledged by other women at Court—at least, not at a court dominated by Marie-Thérèse."

"You're saying that's what you had in common? Your status as outcasts?"

"In a sense. That, and our interest in roses."

"What can you tell me of her politics?"

"Politics? We didn't discuss politics, *monsieur*. It's the safest way to preserve friendships in France these days—as it has been the past twenty-six years."

"Do you have any idea who might have wanted to kill her?"

Sanson's heavy jowls sagged. "No. Why would anyone want her dead?"

"Do you know Marshal McClellan?"

"I have met him, but that is all." He cast a sideways look at Sebastian, then said, "You know him?"

"I've never met him."

Sanson nodded as if this answer had confirmed a previous suspicion. "And Madame Cappello, did you know her?"

"Long ago, when she lived in England."

"Ah, yes." He kept his attention focused on his task. "It must have been a shock to you, discovering her like that."

Sebastian found himself studying the executioner's half-averted profile. He thought of this man tying his terrified victims facedown on the guillotine's bascule and slipping the lunette strap around their heads to keep them steady before stepping back to release the blade and let it fall with a rattling *thwunk-thwunk*. They said that the guillotine was painted red to hide the blood that inevitably splattered it. But the arterial blood from a severed neck must surely splash over anyone standing on the scaffold when the blade descended. He'd heard that during the Terror, this man's older brother, Gabriel, had slipped in the pool of blood around the guillotine while holding aloft a severed head to show the cheering crowds. Unable to catch himself, he'd shot off the edge of the scaffold and died of a broken neck.

And again Sebastian found himself thinking, *How could Sophie have befriended this man?* Nothing he'd heard so far that morning came close to explaining it.

"A shock?" said Sebastian, becoming aware that the man was looking at him, waiting for an answer. "Yes, definitely."

"Sudden death always is," said Sanson as if he hadn't personally taken the lives of thousands.

Thousands, thought Sebastian.

Thousands.

Chapter 21

That morning, when it was still far too early for a gentlewoman to make a formal call on a young woman she barely knew, Hero took the embroidered reticule out to the rue du Champs du Repos to ask the chatelaine if she recognized it and to seek her assistance in selecting the clothes for Sophie's funeral.

Hero had visited the *maison* with Sebastian not long after they'd arrived in Paris. That day had been dark and brooding, with heavy clouds that hovered like an oppressive presence over the landscape. But today Sophie's elegant little *hôtel particulier* was bathed in glorious sunshine. The sky was a clear cornflower blue, the limestone walls glowed a tawny gold in the rich light, and the elms that framed the gray slate roof were bursting with fresh green leaves. As the carriage drew up in the graveled forecourt and the iron gates clanged shut behind them, the beauty of the place took Hero's breath.

And then she felt a heavy weight of sadness settle over her, knowing on this morning so overflowing with new life that the woman who had made this place her home would never see it again.

She found Madame Dion clad all in black and looking older than she remembered her, her face drawn and tight with grief, her flesh a worrisome gray. Seeing her, Hero felt reluctant to bring up the reticule for fear of adding to the woman's distress. But the chatelaine forestalled her by noticing it in Hero's hands and saying, "Ah, you have *madame's* reticule."

"You recognize it?" said Hero, holding it out to her.

"*Mais oui,*" said the chatelaine, taking it in her own hands. Her lips trembled as she ran her fingertips over the exquisite peacock embroidery. "It's *Dama* Cappello's work. She was carrying it that night."

"The mirror is hers, as well?"

"Yes, yes. Where did you find them?"

"Near the Pont Neuf. Is there anything missing?"

The Frenchwoman inspected the contents, her eyes narrowing as she felt the weight of the purse. "Not to my knowledge, no. I take it she was not set upon by thieves?"

"No."

"Then *why*?" The aged face contorted with a spasm of anguish and grief. "Why was she killed?"

"We don't know yet," said Hero gently. "You haven't been able to think of anything—anything at all—that might explain what happened?"

"No. It makes no sense. No sense whatsoever."

After that, with the chatelaine's help, Hero chose a high-waisted cranberry silk gown with long, close sleeves and a simple pleated bodice, which Madame Dion said had been one of Sophia's favorites, along with a pair of silk slippers embroidered with little freshwater pearls and a delicate lace cap.

"And I think she would want to be buried with these," said the Frenchwoman, laying an amethyst-and-silver rosary atop the selected gown.

Hero looked up in surprise. "She'd become a Catholic?"

A faint smile touched the older woman's lips. "Of a sort. I think she took from the religion what she could believe and what she found comforting, and simply ignored the rest. Father Paul is very accommodating in that way."

"Father Paul?"

"The priest at Notre-Dame-de-Lorette."

Hero remembered seeing the ruins in a nearby lane. "I thought the church was destroyed during the Revolution."

"Much of it was. But Father Paul still uses one of the chapels for mass." Madame Dion hesitated, then said, "There will be a funeral mass, yes? I think she would have wanted that."

Hero reached for the rosary, the faceted semiprecious stones catching the sunlight like a cascade of prisms as she turned it in her hand. "If that's what she would have wanted, then yes. Of course."

The Frenchwoman nodded, then held out a silver-framed ivory miniature. "And unless his lordship would prefer to keep it, I think she would have liked to be buried with this, as well."

Hero found herself looking at a miniature portrait of four children: Sebastian, aged perhaps six or seven; a haughty, angry-looking young woman of eighteen or nineteen who could have only been Amanda; and two unfamiliar half-grown lads, Cecil and Richard.

"Her children," said Hero softly, startled to feel the sting of threatening tears.

"Yes. She kept it always beside her bed."

Something about the way she said it made Hero look up. "You have children?"

"I had three." The woman paused, then added, "Once."

Once.

"I'm sorry," said Hero.

Madame Dion shook her head. "Don't be. They brought me much

joy while they lived, and now that I am old, the memories of them bring me a certain kind of comfort. My firstborn daughter died in childbirth, taking her infant son with her. Her little sister died of the flux when she was quite small, and my son . . ."

She paused, her throat working dryly, and it was a moment before she could go on. "My son died in Russia. At least, that's what they told me. And he was not amongst the prisoners who've found their way back to France since the peace, so I suppose it must be true."

"What was his name?" asked Hero.

"Leo. Colonel Leo Dion."

The serene expression on the Frenchwoman's face mystified Hero. If Simon had disappeared into the frozen wasteland of Russia, Hero knew she would never stop raging against God, fate, and the arrogant, ambitious Emperor who'd led him to his death.

"I'm sorry," Hero said again, because what else, really, was there to say? She wondered what had happened to this woman's husband, or if there'd been other grandchildren who, perhaps, still lived. She hoped there were other grandchildren.

But she doubted it.

Afterward, Hero found herself restlessly wandering the quiet rooms of the *maison*, her thoughts on the beautiful, enigmatic, intrepid woman who had been Sebastian's mother.

It wasn't easy to move beyond the resentment Hero had long harbored against Sophia Hendon for the deep and lasting pain she had caused the man Hero loved. And yet a part of her could understand the suffocating misery that had driven Sophie all those years ago, the desperation with which she had reached for a better life. Could Hero forgive her for abandoning her own child? No. But it was impossible not to admire the woman for shrugging her shoulders at the rules and restrictions of her world, for braving the unknown, for flouting the social conventions and moralistic censure of zealots such as Marie-Thérèse to live with the man she loved. And as she paused at the entrance to the library, Hero had to admit that a part of her also envied Sophie. Hero might defy conventions by pursuing the kind of education normally considered suitable only for a man, by writing her articles and speaking her mind. But she had always been very careful not to cross the boundaries that Sophie had simply laughed at.

Hero hadn't seen this room on her previous visit to the house, and she was struck now by how lovely it was, with its stately Empire-style mahogany desk and built-in dark oak bookcases trimmed with fluted columns and arched moldings and filled with books. So many books. And she felt her heart swell again with sadness for the meeting between mother and son that would never be, for all that Sophie and Sebastian, too, had lost.

She was turning away when she noticed the portrait over the mantel.

She stood perfectly still, staring at it. She was painfully aware of the tick of the ormolu clock on a nearby console table, of the rasp of her own breath sawing in and out. She didn't know how long she stood there before she realized that Madame Dion had come up beside her and was watching her.

"You see the resemblance, too, eh?" said the Frenchwoman, her expression giving nothing away.

"Who is he?"

"Why, Marshal Alexandre McClellan, of course."

Oh, Sebastian, thought Hero, staring at that familiar pair of uncanny yellow eyes. *So that's what you haven't been able to bring yourself to talk about.*

Chapter 22

The headquarters of Vidocq's *Sûreté nationale* lay in a back court of the labyrinth of grim, soot-stained structures that housed the judicial and law enforcement apparatus of France.

Located near the western end of the Île de la Cité, this massive, forbidding complex was once known as the Palais de la Cité, the magnificent primary residence of the medieval Capetian Kings of France. Built of golden limestone on the banks of the Seine, it had been a fairy-tale-like place of soaring, conically roofed towers, grand banqueting halls, fragrant private gardens, and dank, hidden dungeons. Much of that imposing palace was gone now, with little remaining beyond the chapel, a few grim towers, a vast, thickly columned hall, and the haunted prison cells and official chambers that had become known as the Conciergerie. It was in the dark, vermin-infested cells of the Conciergerie that Marie Antoinette and so many others had passed their last days; here that they were dragged before the Revolutionary Tribunal to hear their death sentences pronounced; here that they were loaded into the crude tumbrels that would carry them through roaring crowds to the waiting blade of

Madame Guillotine. It was a haunted and haunting place, and Sebastian found himself hesitating on the narrow cobbled street that ran between the Conciergerie and the river, his thoughts on the place's dark, ugly past.

He was still standing there, his head tipping back as he stared up at the sinister medieval towers flanking the main portal, when he heard himself hailed by someone on the Pont au Change. Turning, he scanned the press of hurrying pale-faced functionaries and ragged ex-soldiers, bonneted housewives and servants, roughly dressed artisans and laborers, who filled the quay along the riverfront. He didn't see anyone he recognized. Then a cocky grin split the dirty face of a stocky water carrier striding toward him with a rollicking gait.

"Didn't recognize me, did you?" said Eugène-François Vidocq, coming up to him.

"I did not," admitted Sebastian.

Vidocq laughed. "I've been making some discreet inquiries in another matter. I take it you're here looking for me?"

"I am," said Sebastian as the two men turned to walk together along the river. "I have a description of the *fiacre* driver from that night: thin and frail-looking, but not old. The person who saw him thinks he might be a former prisoner of war recently returned from England or Russia." It shamed Sebastian, the treatment the French prisoners of war had received at the hands of Britain and her allies—shamed and appalled him.

"Interesting," said Vidocq, jerking his chin toward a trio of emaciated, gaunt-faced men huddled over a charcoal fire beneath a nearby crumbling arch, their uniforms reduced to filthy rags. "God knows there are enough of them. But between the disbanding of the army and the Bourbons' cancellation of Napoléon's public improvement projects, a lot of people are starving. This person didn't happen to see the *fiacre*'s number, did he?"

"No."

"Pity."

Sebastian was silent for a moment, watching a ragged little flower girl sink down on a nearby set of stone steps leading up to a stout wooden door that didn't look as if it had been opened in a hundred years. Her feet were bare, her thin, wan face streaked with dirt, her golden hair hanging in tangled clumps. The tray of flowers dangling from a strap around her neck was pitted with rust, the posy clutched in her pale, bony fist beginning to wilt. She couldn't have been more than six or seven, and the look of despair in her soft blue eyes was horrible to see.

Such children were an all-too-familiar sight in London as well as in Paris. And yet for some reason he couldn't explain, this child touched his heart and filled him with a tide of hot rage that caught him by surprise. And he found himself wondering why. Because the people of this land had risen up against the grinding inequality and injustice of their age, only to lose their way in a morass of hatred, bloodshed, and terror that would surely taint any such movements for generations to come? Because the reimposition of the oppressive rule of the Bourbons made a brighter, more just future seem somehow less likely than ever? Because something about this little girl reminded Sebastian of his mother, and for one piercing moment he found her death so painful that he wasn't sure he could bear it?

"You all right there?" said Vidocq, watching him with an expression on his homely, scarred face that Sebastian couldn't read.

Sebastian blinked and turned his head to stare out over the sun-dazzled waters of the Seine. "Yes, I'm fine."

He bought all of the little girl's flowers.

Afterward he went to stand in one of the curved stone bastions of the Pont Neuf, not far from where Sophie must have been attacked. He dropped the bunches of flowers one by one into the river below him, then watched as the dark waters swirled them away downstream. From here he could see the ancient limestone walls of the Louvre and the Tuileries Palace, the long green swath of the old royal gardens, the graceful iron arches and thick stone supporting columns of Napoléon's Pont des Arts. The sun was surprisingly warm on his face, the wide sweep of the Seine reflecting the rare blue of the sky, the breeze off the water fresh and smelling faintly of fish.

Lowering the brim of his hat against the glare, he rested his arms on the old stone parapet before him and tried to make sense of a series of events that seemed to have begun with a troubling visit to the island refuge of an exiled emperor and had ended here, on this ancient bridge, on a dark, misty night that would forever be seared into Sebastian's memory.

Except that it hadn't ended here. Because the next day, Sophie's young abigail, Francine, had in turn died a painful, terrifying death. And he couldn't begin to understand why.

He became aware of an elegant carriage drawn by a fine team of white horses pulling up behind him and turned as the carriage's near window came down with a rattle to reveal the fleshy, unsmiling face of his father-in-law, Lord Jarvis.

"Climb up," snapped Jarvis. He glanced at the man in the carriage with him, a tall, fair-haired man Sebastian recognized as one of the many former army officers in Jarvis's employ, and said, "Leave us for a moment."

The major nodded, said, "Yes, my lord," and hopped down without waiting for the steps to be lowered. For one piercing moment, his gaze met Sebastian's. Then he turned to walk across the bridge toward the Louvre.

"Well?" said Jarvis when Sebastian hesitated.

The last thing he wanted at that moment was a conversation with the British King's powerful, Machiavellian cousin. But he leapt up and settled in the seat opposite his father-in-law anyway. "I take it you have something you wish to say to me?"

The carriage started forward again as Jarvis drew a pearl-studded gold snuffbox from the pocket of his finely tailored coat and flipped open the lid with his thumbnail. "You're upsetting Marie-Thérèse."

"Oh?"

Sebastian watched the older man lift a delicate pinch of snuff to one nostril and sniff. "The French King's niece is easily distressed," said Jarvis. "And it is not in Britain's interest that she be . . . disturbed."

"And precisely what am I doing that is 'disturbing' Madame Royale?"

Jarvis closed his snuffbox with a snap. "You know."

"I gather you're referring to my investigation into the death of *Dama* Cappello? I must admit I fail to understand why that would upset her." Sebastian paused. "Unless of course she's the one who ordered the killing."

"Don't be absurd."

"Is it so absurd?" Sebastian watched Jarvis tuck his snuffbox away. "What do you know of Sophia Cappello's death?"

"Absolutely nothing. Why would I?"

"You do have a decided interest in maintaining the Bourbon restoration."

The shrewd gray eyes that were so much like Hero's narrowed. "Are you suggesting *Dama* Cappello was a threat to the Restoration?"

"I honestly don't know. But Marie-Thérèse is aware of her recent visit to Elba. Were you?"

Jarvis hesitated just a fraction too long before saying, "I was not."

Sebastian found himself faintly smiling. "You lie extraordinarily well, you know. I've no doubt most people would accept that statement without question."

Jarvis's steely gray eyes narrowed. "There are things going on here about which you have no idea. Things that are of far greater importance than the death of one woman."

"Not to me." Sebastian signaled the driver to pull up, then thrust open the door and hopped down before the carriage had come to a complete stop.

Leaning forward, Jarvis put out a hand to hold open the door when Sebastian would have closed it. "I will not tolerate your interference in an already volatile situation."

"I'm not dropping this investigation. You and I both know why."

"I mean what I say."

Sebastian met his father-in-law's dangerously glittering gaze and held it. "So do I."

Chapter 23

*H*ero timed her formal call on Sophie's onetime ward, Angélique de Longchamps-Montendre, for shortly after three o'clock.

The former Mademoiselle La Hure lived on the Left Bank of the Seine in a grand house in the rue du Bac in the part of Paris known as the Faubourg Saint-Germain. This was an affluent area of embassies and *hôtels particuliers* with paved forecourts and elegant gardens, where the floors were of marble and the ceilings painted with frescoes and the carriages drawn by highbred horses driven by liveried coachmen. Here in the Faubourg Saint-Germain, it was as if the Revolution had never occurred. The names of some of the families had changed, of course. But not all of them.

Angélique herself was a slender, fine-boned, breathtakingly lovely woman of twenty-two with very fair hair and enormous violet-blue eyes fringed by thick, dark lashes. She received Hero in an elegant salon decorated in the soft, gracious style of Louis XVI rather than the more masculine, austere look of the Empire period. The young Frenchwoman was obviously trying to put on the brave front society required of mourners who considered themselves well-bred. But her eyes were bloodshot and her nose red, and there was no doubt at all that she had been crying.

"I've heard Viscount Devlin is looking into Sophie's death," she said, her hand shaking as she poured tea into a delicate Sevres cup.

"Where did you hear that?" asked Hero, taking the cup held out to her.

The girl looked up from pouring her own cup. "At Court. But I don't think anyone knows of his relationship to her, if that's what concerns you."

Hero sucked in a quick, startled breath. "Yet you know?"

"She never actually told me. But it's difficult to keep that sort of secret from people you live with."

"How long were you with her?"

"From the time I was thirteen." She settled the teapot back on the tray, then paused for a moment, her features pinched and troubled. "The papers say she died from a fall. But that's not true, is it?"

"No," said Hero baldly. "She was stabbed, then thrown off the Pont Neuf."

Angélique's chest jerked and she looked away, blinking rapidly. "*Mon Dieu.*"

Hero said, "I'm sorry, but I must ask: Can you think of anyone who might have wanted her killed?"

"Sophie? *No!*" The word came out almost like a wail, and the young Frenchwoman paused to swipe the heel of one hand across her eyes. "Oh, God. I've been so angry with her, but I never thought . . . I never thought she'd *die.*"

"I'm told the two of you quarreled over your marriage."

Angélique pressed her lips together and nodded in a way that seemed to accentuate both her youth and her vulnerability.

"Do you mind if I ask why?"

The younger woman huffed a watery laugh. "Why? Because Antoine's family fled the Revolution and his father fought against both the

Republicans and Napoléon." There was much resentment in France against the hordes of returning émigrés who'd spent the past twenty-five years living abroad—especially if they'd taken up arms against France and killed their fellow Frenchmen. "Antoine is related to the Bourbons and the House of Orléans, you know," Angélique was saying, "and Sophie despised both with equal fervor." Her face hardened. "Why do you ask? What does any of this have to do with what happened to her?"

"I don't know that it does," said Hero. "When was the last time you saw her?"

The younger woman set aside her cup and carefully wiped her wet face with her handkerchief. "I don't recall exactly. It's been some time."

"You knew she'd gone to Vienna?"

Angélique sniffed quietly and nodded. "To see the marshal."

"You know him? Marshal McClellan, I mean."

She nodded again. "Since birth. He and my father were old comrades."

"Do you know where Sophie went after she left Vienna?"

"No. I didn't know she'd been anyplace else."

The blank expression that accompanied those words looked real enough, but Hero wasn't entirely convinced. "She went to Elba."

Angélique stared at her. "Truly? You are serious? To Elba? But . . . why?"

"We don't know. We were hoping you might."

She shook her head. "No. She didn't tell me. There was a time when she might have, but . . ." Her voice trailed away.

Hero sipped her tea. "I take it Sophie was not a monarchist?"

"Sophie? Good heavens, no. She was a great admirer of the United States."

"An interesting philosophy to appeal to an English countess."

"I don't think she considered herself one anymore."

Obviously not, thought Hero. Aloud, she said, "She doesn't seem to have had many close friends."

Angélique paused as if considering this. "She did, once. But the return of the Bourbons changed things. The wives of the *maréchal's* fellow officers who were once her friends began to shun her. Marie-Thérèse is always appallingly rude to the wives of anyone who served under Napoléon, but she liked to pretend as if Sophie didn't even exist."

"Why?"

"Because of the irregularity of her relationship with McClellan, of course."

"Did it bother Sophie, do you think? That she was shunned, I mean."

"Sophie? No. I suspect she'd always known that most of the officers' wives were only friendly to her because of the *maréchal*. And if truth be told, I think the sanctimonious posturings of Marie-Thérèse and the Court amused her . . . although I know she was sad to lose her friendship with Madame de Gautier."

"Who?"

"Madame de Gautier. She's the wife of a French colonel, but she was born in England. I understand she was a novelist before coming here, although she wrote under her English name. Fanny . . . something. She was at Madame de Staël's salon the other day."

"Fanny Carpenter?" said Hero in surprise, remembering the unassuming, bespectacled older woman who had spent most of the afternoon sitting in quiet amusement, listening to the ostentatious pronouncements of their colorful hostess as if storing them away for a future book.

"Yes, that's it. You've read her work?"

"I have, yes."

The daughter of a composer and music historian, Fanny Carpenter had published a number of successful comedies of manners in the 1790s that reminded Hero of the works of Jane Austen. There'd been a time when Fanny had even served as Keeper of the Robes to Queen Charlotte, but she'd retired from the position because it interfered too much with her writing. Married relatively late in life to an émigré artillery officer, she'd returned with him to France after the Peace of Amiens in 1802, only to be caught in Paris when war broke out again just a year later.

Hero supposed it wasn't surprising that the two women had become friends. Fanny might have been of genteel rather than aristocratic birth, but there couldn't have been many Englishwomen married to French officers living in Paris.

Not that Sophie was married to McClellan, of course.

"Colonel Étienne de Gautier has sworn the oath of allegiance to Louis XVIII and now serves in the King's Guard," Angélique was saying. "I understand he has grand ambitions of rising in the King's service, so it's important for such a man that his wife has managed to be accepted at the new Court. I suppose being English helped Fanny overcome the prejudices Marie-Thérèse normally displays toward the wives of those who served Napoléon, but even with that, for her to be seen as the good friend of a notorious fallen woman would have put her beyond the pale."

"Was Sophie notorious?"

"Oh, far, far too notorious for the likes of Marie-Thérèse. Her court is so different from that of the Empress. Sophie took Joséphine's death last year quite hard, you know."

"You mean Joséphine Bonaparte?" said Hero. "Napoléon's wife?"

A faint smile curled the Frenchwoman's lips. "His *first* wife. He divorced her, remember? To marry Marie Antoinette's great-niece. He thought it would tie Europe's old monarchies to him and make him one of them. But they never stopped seeing him as an illegitimate upstart, and now they've swept him aside like so much unwanted rubbish."

"So Sophie was close to Joséphine?"

"Yes, very. They were both mad about gardening, you know. Gardening and roses."

Hero found herself remembering the lovely gardens of the rue du Champs du Repos—the extensive beds of roses, the greenhouses and cold frames and seedbeds. There was no denying that Sophie was serious about gardening, while Joséphine's own gardens at Malmaison were said to have been exquisite.

Angélique's eyes narrowed as if with a sudden thought.

"What?" asked Hero, watching her.

"You asked if I knew of anyone who might have wanted Sophie dead," said the younger woman, leaning forward. "There actually is someone, a particularly nasty Corsican count. She's been quarreling with him for years. When Joséphine died, I remember Sophie said that if she didn't know better she'd have suspected him of having killed her—he was that jealous of Joséphine's rose collection. He was jealous of them both."

"But surely she must have been jesting?"

"Perhaps," said Angélique. "Although you might not think so if you'd met him. He is . . . very intense."

"You say he's a count?"

"Well, Napoléon made him one. I can't remember his name, but Redouté would be able to tell you who I mean."

"Redouté?"

She nodded. "The artist Pierre-Joseph Redouté. You know him, yes? He's producing a book of prints of the flowers at Malmaison, especially the roses. He's been working on it for years."

"Oh, yes, of course," said Hero.

Redouté's plates of roses were so exquisitely done and instantly recognizable that he'd been dubbed "the Raphael of flowers." An official court artist under Marie Antoinette, he'd somehow managed to survive the Revolution and the Reign of Terror it spawned to emerge under the Empire as an artist patronized by both of Napoléon's wives—first the Empress Joséphine, then the Austrian Emperor's daughter, Marie-Louise.

"He would surely know, and—"

Angélique broke off as the sound of footsteps in the corridor brought the younger woman's head around, and Hero saw her face light up with delight as Antoine de Longchamps-Montendre appeared in the doorway. He was a slim, extraordinarily handsome man of about thirty, his dark hair worn fashionably disarrayed so that one errant curl fell romantically over his high forehead. His eyes were dark and deeply set, his nose long and straight, his lips full and sensual. And for one suspended moment, it was as if husband and wife were the only two people in the room; they had eyes only for each other.

Watching them, Hero thought she understood the quarrel that had flared between this girl and the woman who had cared for her and raised her since the death of her parents. If Sophie had dared to criticize the man Angélique obviously adored so intensely, the girl would never have forgiven her.

"My apologies if I interrupt," he said with a smile.

"No, no, Antoine, do come in." Angélique jumped up to go catch his hand and drag him forward to make introductions.

His bow was everything it should have been, his smile charming, his dark eyes looking intently into Hero's as if to emphasize his sincerity. "So it's true, is it?" he said, taking a seat on the silk-covered settee beside his wife. "Lord Devlin is looking into Lady Cappello's death? It's good to know that someone is doing it." Reaching out, he covered Angélique's delicate hand with his own larger one. "My wife has been most distressed."

Angélique turned her hand within his to clasp it. "Lady Devlin has been asking if we know of anyone who might have wished Sophie harm. But I can't think of anyone except that nasty rose collector she was always quarreling with."

The look that passed between them was meant to be private, but Hero caught it. It was as if Angélique was reassuring him that she hadn't divulged—what?

"And what about you, *monsieur?*" said Hero, pausing with her teacup raised halfway to her lips. "Can you think of anyone?"

He shook his head. "No. I'm sorry, but I did not know Madame Cappello well."

Hero had the niggling impression that, unlike his wife, de Longchamps-Montendre had anticipated something like this visit and already decided how to arrange his answers to any questions that might come his way. She took a slow sip of her tea, then said, "A woman came to see Sophia on Thursday evening, shortly after she arrived home—a veiled woman in a carriage drawn by a fine team of matched grays. Do you have any idea who that might have been?"

Both husband and wife stared at Hero blankly. It was de Longchamps-Montendre who finally answered. "No. How very strange." He squeezed his wife's hand, then let it go to reach forward and touch the teapot on the table before him as if intending to pour himself a cup. "Ah," he said. "It's grown cold." He looked up at Hero. "I could order fresh if you'd like, Lady Devlin?"

It was a smiling but not-so-subtle cue. Hero set aside her own cup and rose to her feet. "Thank you, but no."

Husband and wife rose with her. "Are you quite certain?" said Angélique. "It would be no trouble."

"Thank you, but I must be going."

"I'm sorry we couldn't have been of more assistance," said de Longchamps-Montendre, walking with Hero to where a footman waited by the front door. "My wife and Lady Cappello were estranged, but the affection between them was strong. This death grieves my wife very much."

"Yes, I'm sorry. I can see that," said Hero. In fact, it was so obvious, she found herself wondering why he had felt the need to emphasize it.

Chapter 24

I take it you didn't think much of Monsieur de Longchamps-Montendre?" said Devlin later as they watched the two little boys sail a wooden boat across the Grand Basin in the Tuileries Gardens. The afternoon had turned gloriously warm, with a faint breeze that stirred the fresh new leaves on the double allée of stately chestnut trees and danced shadows across the wide, sun-sparkled pond.

"Not exactly," said Hero, smiling as the boat dipped, then righted itself, and Simon squealed with delight. "But I've always been instinctively suspicious of overly smooth handsome young men."

Devlin looked over at her, his eyes crinkling with his smile. "Is he smooth and handsome?"

"Very."

They had brought the boys here, to that long stretch of public gardens that ran along the right bank of the Seine from the Tuileries Palace and the Louvre in the east to the newly renamed Place Louis XV in the west. The gardens were hundreds of years old, having been begun by Catherine de' Medici back in the mid-sixteenth century. The Revolution had declared them public property, and they still were, although Hero wondered how long it would be before the Bourbons tried to reassert their control here as they were doing with so much else.

"It seems an unusual match," said Hero as the boys lifted the boat, dripping, from the water. "For a son of the grand de Longchamps-Montendre family to marry the daughter of one of Napoléon's dead generals, I mean."

"Not when you realize that some of Napoléon's generals were very good at amassing a considerable fortune."

She looked over at him as they turned to walk up the gardens' Grand Allée, the boys running ahead of them. "Was General La Hure?"

"He was. Not only that, but he married the daughter of a Swiss banker. And Angélique was their only heir."

"Ah. It begins to make a lot more sense."

"It does indeed—especially when you think about how much the de Longchamps-Montendre family lost during the Revolution. And don't forget that Antoine is a younger son. He has a grand ancient name and a host of royal and noble connections, but no real wealth—at least, he didn't until he married Mademoiselle La Hure."

"So that's why Sophie didn't want Angélique to marry him," said Hero, watching a squirrel creep cautiously down the trunk of a nearby chestnut, ears alert and eyes scanning the area for danger. "She thought he was a fortune hunter."

"Probably. Although it's also possible she shared your prejudice against pretty young men."

Hero laughed softly. They walked along in silence for a time, enjoying the fresh breeze lifting off the river and the sweet song of the birds in the trees. The gardens were bursting with new life, the long canes of the climbing roses that had been trained over a series of wrought iron arches just beginning to come into leaf. Looking at them, she said, "Did you know your mother had such a profound interest in roses?"

"I didn't, no. But Madame Dion and Sanson also mentioned it."

The breeze was picking up. Hero could feel the mist from the fountains in the Octagonal Pond before them, hear Simon's laughter as Patrick slung his arm around the younger boy's neck and leaned in close to whisper something. She said, "I wonder if Sanson is telling the truth when he claims he met Sophie at the inn that evening simply by chance."

Devlin let out a harsh breath. "I honestly don't know. We're talking about someone who was helping his father break men on the wheel when he was little more than a child. I suspect he's very good at keeping things to himself."

They'd reached the Fer à Cheval at the end of the gardens, and Devlin drew up at the stone balustrade, his face growing solemn as he stared out over the broad sweep of the former Place de la Révolution, where so many had lost their heads. They could smell coffee and freshly baked bread from a nearby café, hear laughter from the bath barge tied up at the quay below the embankment.

After a time, he said quietly, "I remember reading somewhere that Napoléon once encountered Sanson's father here, in the Place de la Concorde. The Emperor asked Sanson if it bothered him, knowing that he'd killed so many thousands of men and women."

Hero looked over at him. "What did Sanson say?"

"He said it was kings and emperors, judges and tribunals, who imposed the death sentences; all he did as executioner was carry those sentences out."

Hero was silent for a moment, her gaze on the vast square where crowds had once gathered to cheer while so many died. She couldn't help but think of the doomed men and women who'd made the tortuous journey here by tumbrel from the Conciergerie. What must it have been like, she wondered, listening to the roar of the spectators who'd gathered for the pleasure of watching you die? She thought of the unimaginable courage and fortitude it must have taken for them to face the terror of mounting the scaffold's steps, of being thrust facedown beneath that great slanting blade. She thought about being forced to lie there, waiting to hear the swoosh of the falling blade, to feel the cold bite of its edge and then . . . what? Before she could stop herself, she shivered.

"I suppose in a sense he was right," she said. "And yet if no one had been willing to do the actual killing, no one could have been executed."

Beside her, Devlin's face was solemn, the breeze ruffling the dark hair at his neck as he stared out over the death-haunted plaza. "I think I'd have been tempted to ask Napoléon if it bothered him, knowing how many young soldiers he'd led to their deaths."

"I've no doubt Napoléon would argue that everything he did was for the greater good and glory of France," said Hero.

The light had begun to soften and the warmth fade from the day. Calling the boys away from the Octagonal Pond, they turned to walk back up the gardens along the terrace that overlooked the Seine below. She saw Devlin's eyes narrow against the sparkling flashes thrown up by the shimmer of the setting sun bouncing off the choppy surface of the river beside them, and he said, "Are you still interested in attending the Duchess of Wellington's reception tonight?"

"Oh, Lord," said Hero. "Is that tonight?" The Wellingtons had taken over one of Paris's grandest old *hôtels particuliers*, and Hero had long nourished a burning desire to see inside it—which was why they hadn't sent in their regrets. "I'd completely forgotten about it. And no, of course we don't need to go."

He shook his head. "Actually, I was thinking this English novelist that Angélique was telling you about will probably be there. What did you say her name is again?"

"Fanny Carpenter. I take it you've never read any of her books?"

"No," he admitted.

Hero smiled. "She probably will be there, although I don't know how much she'll be able to tell us. It doesn't sound as if she's seen much of Sophie since the Restoration."

They walked on in silence for a time, the light of the day fading around them. They'd almost reached the ancient stone walls of the Louvre when Hero said, "I went into the library when I was at the rue du Champs du Repos this morning."

She was aware of Devlin stiffening beside her, his gaze focused straight ahead. He was silent for a long, painful moment, then said, "I take it you saw McClellan's portrait?"

"Yes," she said simply.

He kept his face turned half away from her, his expression unreadable as he watched the boys running ahead of them. But a muscle bunched along his jawline. "Do you think he's my father?"

"It's obviously a possibility, but . . ." She paused, trying to find a way to put her thoughts into words. "I think most women are attracted to a certain type of man. Perhaps Sophie was attracted to McClellan for the same reason she was attracted to your father—or because he reminded her of him."

"Perhaps."

He didn't sound convinced, and she said, "Would it bother you if you were to discover it's true—that McClellan is indeed your father?"

He glanced over at her. "I spent six years of my life fighting Napoléon. McClellan was one of his most brilliant marshals."

"You would hold it against him that he fought for the nation that granted his family a place of refuge when they were in need?"

"When you put it that way, I suppose it does sound a tad churlish." He paused, his features intent as he watched a barge making its way down the river. "I keep thinking I could have met my own father on the field of battle and I wouldn't even have known it." He turned his head, his strange yellow eyes looking directly into hers. "Although at the same time I find myself circling around and coming back to what Jamie Knox and his sister told me: that according to their mother, their father was either a Welsh cavalry officer or an English lord. McClellan is neither."

"You don't know for certain that Knox's father and your father were the same," Hero said softly.

"Don't I?" Devlin shifted his gaze to where the two little boys were now hunkered down to study something on the ground before them, their heads close together. They looked so much alike in that moment that they might have been twins, only one was slightly larger than the other. "Vidocq told me last night that he served under McClellan. He says the marshal's eyesight and hearing are legendary." He paused, then added with a faint twist of his lips that wasn't quite a smile, "Like mine."

It was something they'd noticed about the boys—that both Simon and Patrick shared Sebastian's abnormally acute senses, as had Jamie Knox. She said, "Perhaps it has something to do with having yellow eyes."

Devlin's lips curved now into a smile. "I suppose that's one explanation." Then he turned his head as Simon shouted.

"Mama!"

Together they watched as the boy came running up to Hero, his cheeks red with the day's sun, his amber eyes gleaming with delight. "Look what I got!"

He thrust his hand out toward her, uncurling his fingers, and Hero braced herself, anticipating anything from a bug to a tree frog. But it was simply a chestnut, its shell glowing a warm reddish brown. "Ah," she said, "what a find!"

Beside her, she heard Devlin smother a laugh and knew he'd seen her tense. She looked over at him, saw the glint of amusement in the unusual eyes he'd gifted to their son, and found herself aching for him. Aching for the heartbreak that comes from the loss of a mother, which she understood only too well.

And for the endless pain and confusion swirling around the question of his father, about which she could only guess.

Chapter 25

*Y*our vulgar curiosity turned out to be fortuitous," said Sebastian later that evening as their carriage wound its way through the dark, misty streets of Paris toward the British Embassy.

Hero gave a soft laugh, the light from the swinging carriage lamps casting a golden glow across her features. She was wearing a low-necked gown of deep blue silk embroidered with tiny seed pearls on the bodice and vandyked around the hem, and a gossamer-fine silk shawl with more pearls knotted in the fringe. "*If* Fanny Carpenter is there," she said.

"If her husband is assiduously currying favor with the Bourbons in an attempt to overcome the sin and shame of having served under Napoléon, then they'll be there. What better way to play up your English wife's connections?"

The carriage lurched to a crawl as they were caught up in the crush of vehicles descending on the embassy, and he watched her turn her head to stare out the window at the crowd of ragged spectators gathered to gawk at the parade of highbred horseflesh, elegant carriages, and richly liveried servants.

"It must have been awkward for her, being trapped in France by the collapse of the Treaty of Amiens like that. Especially when you consider that her brother is a British admiral."

"Is he? Awkward, indeed."

They were close enough to the British Embassy now that its blazing torches lit up the night around them, flaring across the upturned faces of the thickening crowds. Some of those who'd gathered were the gaunt, skeletal ex–prisoners of war one saw in the streets all over Paris. But there were also a number of other ex-soldiers, many of them missing an arm or a leg. In Sebastian's opinion it was one of the worst of the many unwise things the Bourbons had done—disbanding Napoléon's army and casting hundreds of thousands of proud, loyal French soldiers out onto the streets to starve.

Hero kept her gaze on that ragged mass of wretched humanity. And he realized her thoughts must have been running along the same lines as his because she said, "Britain and France have been at war on and off for the last hundred years or more. It seems difficult to believe this new peace will last for long."

"I don't know about that. I suspect the Bourbons are going to be too busy trying to solidify their control over France to worry about challenging British colonial supremacy in the rest of the world. After all, it was their expensive wars against us in India and America that helped bring about the Revolution in the first place."

"You think they've learned their lesson? Have we?"

He huffed a strained laugh and said, "No," just as the carriage shuddered to a halt before the embassy's gates.

The Hôtel de Charost, now the British Embassy, dated from the early eighteenth century, to roughly the same period as the Élysée Palace just a few doors down, nearer the Champs-Élysées. Built in the French classical style of golden white limestone with a gray slate mansard roof, it had until recently been the home of Napoléon's beautiful, scandalous, irrepressible sister, Pauline Bonaparte Borghese. But she'd prudently sold it to the Duke of Wellington before the Bourbons had time to confiscate it. They said Pauline had demanded Wellington pay her in installments of Louis d'or, so that was what he had done.

After what seemed an interminable wait, they finally arrived at the top of the red-carpeted steps to find Kitty Wellington, the British ambassador's plump wife, greeting her guests in the *hôtel*'s soaring white-and-gray-marble-tiled entrance hall. With her husband absent at the Congress of Vienna, she was playing her part as hostess alone. She was in her forties now, with an increasing tendency to squint, thanks to her shortsightedness. But she had a reputation amongst those who knew her as being amiable, kind, faithful, and loving—everything her famous husband was not.

It was said she'd been very young when they first met, pretty and lively and clearly smitten with the newly commissioned Ensign Arthur Wellesley. But she was the daughter of a baron, while Wellesley had been nothing more than a younger son yet to make his way in the world, and so her father refused his suit. Vowing to come back and claim her, Wellington went off to make his fortune at war, succeeding far, far better than anyone had anticipated. When he returned a decade later to honor his commitment, he'd found her still devoted to him. But after ten years, he didn't think her anywhere near as pretty or desirable as he once had. Begrudgingly going through the wedding ceremony, he'd made no secret of his dissatisfaction with his new wife, and the marriage had been going downhill ever since. The more famous and feted he became, the more fault he found with his children's aging mother and the more he sought "comfort" in the arms of a succession of young, ambitious, fawning mistresses he flaunted openly with little regard for his neglected wife's feelings. Sebastian might admire Wellington's military acumen, but he had little respect for the general as a man.

"Lady Devlin," said the Duchess now, her smile widening as Hero came close enough to be seen clearly. Kitty Wellington had never been a great beauty, but she had gentle features and a pretty smile, and Sebastian could never understand Wellington's cruel dismissal of her to his friends and fellow officers as "ugly." "And my lord," she added as Sebastian came into focus. "How lovely of you both to come." She took Hero's hands in hers and gave them a friendly squeeze. "Given your interest in historic architecture, I can't wait until you see the *hôtel*, Lady Devlin! Everything is just as Pauline Bonaparte left it, and whatever one might say about her more risqué activities, one must concede her taste is stunning."

"The stories can't all be true, surely?" said Hero, returning her smile.

Kitty Wellington lowered her voice and leaned forward to whisper, "Believe me, they *are*—including the ones about her circulating *au naturel* amongst her guests! The servants have confirmed that and more." She gave Hero's hands another squeeze before letting her go. "You must come for tea one afternoon so I can show you the rest of the house."

"Do you think she meant it?" Hero asked Sebastian as they moved through the throng of chattering, elegant guests and into a magnificent long salon hung with red silk damask and massive gilt mirrors that endlessly reflected the light from the hundreds of candles blazing in the crystal chandeliers overhead.

"I'd say so. There's no artifice about her—she'd probably get on better with the Duke if there were. I wonder if she finds it a relief to have him gone again."

"I doubt it. They say she is truly devoted to him, grieves when he is away, and feels the pain of his infidelities deeply."

"Well, I've no doubt the local farmers are more than happy to see the back of him—although unfortunately for them I suspect he'll be finished in Vienna in time for the next hunting season."

Proud of his reputation as a bruising rider to hounds, Wellington had made himself hated around Paris by heedlessly leading his huge entourage at a gallop through the local peasants' fields and then refusing to pay for the crops he ruined.

Hero let her gaze rove over the noisy press of well-tailored men and silk-clad, bejeweled women. "I don't see Fanny Carpenter, but Marie-Thérèse is looking daggers at you from over by the orchestra."

"Lovely." He resisted the urge to turn and look. "So tell me, is she wearing black?"

"Of course she is."

Sebastian snagged a glass of wine from a passing waiter. "Perhaps we should split up."

"Would you recognize Fanny if you saw her?"

"No," he admitted with a smile.

Hero gave Sebastian a brief description of the small, unassuming Englishwoman, and they split up.

He was working his way through the Blue Salon when he heard a familiar female voice behind him say, "What on earth are you doing here?"

Turning, he found himself staring into his sister's angry blue eyes.

Amanda, Lady Wilcox, was a tall woman, slender and elegantly built like their mother, with Sophie's golden hair and graceful carriage. In most other respects, she resembled Hendon, with the Earl's rather blunt features and the famously intense St. Cyr blue eyes. But her temperament was all her own, bitter and self-absorbed and laced with more than a touch of cruelty. She was twelve years Sebastian's senior, the firstborn of Sophia Hendon's four children, and if she'd been a boy, Amanda would now be Viscount Devlin, heir to the earldom and all the wealth that would someday be Sebastian's. But because she was female, she'd watched that title and honor pass from one younger brother to the next until it came to Sebastian, the heir who wasn't even Hendon's own flesh and blood. Sebastian had always known she resented and disliked him, but it wasn't until she'd tried to see him hanged that he'd realized just how much she hated him.

She was a widow now and had been for four years. But she still wore a palette of grays and silvers in an ostentatious display of perpetual semimourning for the dead husband she'd loathed. Her gown this evening was of a shimmering silver satin made high at the waist in a way that showed off her still-youthful figure, with long sleeves ruched at the shoulders and a low round bodice edged with a band of the finest Brussels lace. The diamonds at her neck and ears refracted the candlelight like dazzling prisms.

"Do I take it that's a rhetorical question?" said Sebastian. "We were invited, of course."

There was a pinched look about her nostrils. "You never come to these things without an ulterior motive."

"Not usually. But the house is rather famous, and Hero was anxious to see it."

She gave a faint, dismissive shake of her head. "I know that's not why you're here. Hendon told me about her, of course."

"I expected him to. If you'd like to come by the Place Dauphine to see her before the funeral—"

"Why would I?" Amanda's upper lip curled. "She's been dead to me these twenty years and more."

Sebastian searched his half sister's hard, closed face, looking for . . . *What?* he wondered. Some trace of compassion? An echo of the love she must once, surely, have felt for their mother? "She left a letter written not long before she died. She said she wanted nothing more than your happiness."

Amanda sniffed. "She used to write to me, you know. Every year. I never answered her, but she kept writing anyway. Finally I had Hendon tell her that I was simply burning her letters unopened. But she still didn't quit."

"Did you? Burn her letters unopened, I mean."

"Of course."

He found he could only stare at her, utterly at a loss. Amanda had been married with children of her own by the time Sophie sailed away in a desperate attempt to grab a life of happiness in a difficult world. Unlike Sebastian, his sister had always known the truth. And yet her hatred burned with a bitterness that mystified him.

He said, "Do you know that when the French Revolutionaries made divorce legal and easy to get, the vast majority of the thousands of people who rushed to dissolve their miserable marriages were women? I suspect it's the main reason most states are so averse to the idea of easy divorce—because they know women are the ones most eager to obtain them."

"Yes, well, that's one thing Napoléon did right, isn't it? He might not have completely outlawed divorce, but he did make it considerably more difficult to secure."

Sebastian simply shook his head. And he found himself wondering if this might explain what Amanda held against their mother—that Sophie had had the courage to escape her wretched marriage, and Amanda never had.

"I'm told you're determined to look into her death," she said, keeping her voice low as she glanced around to make certain no one was in earshot. "Why? Why stir up trouble, making people think she was murdered, when she simply fell? Have you no sense?"

"She didn't 'simply' fall, Amanda. She was stabbed in the back and then thrown off that bridge."

"Nonsense. It's bad enough that people are already talking about her as much as they are. If you're not careful, her connection to our family is going to come out."

"And that's the most important thing, is it? That you avoid embarrassment? Not that her murderer be brought to justice?"

"She was not murdered."

He studied the tight, angry set of her lips. "Had you seen her, Amanda? Since you've been in Paris, I mean."

"Good heavens, no. As if I would have anything to do with some common soldier's whore."

"I don't think many would describe Marshal Alexandre McClellan as a 'common soldier.'"

"He's a traitorous Jacobite who fought against us, first with the Americans and then again with the Republic and Napoléon."

"You seem to have made it a point to look into him. Did you ever meet him?"

"Why would I have met him?"

"I have no idea."

He could see the pulse beating in her neck, see the raw fury tightening her features. "Will you give up this nonsense or not?"

"No."

She reared back her head, her lips parting as she sucked in a quick breath. "I should have known."

"Yes, you really should have."

A glimmer of rage leapt in her eyes, all of her loathing and animosity laid bare for him to know. Then she turned and walked away from him, the train of her elegant silk gown swishing across the polished floor behind her.

ero came upon Fanny Carpenter in the Yellow Salon. The novelist was standing with her head tipped back, her mouth slightly agape as she stared in wonder at the gloriously risqué bacchanal feast painted on the ceiling above. She was a small, energetic woman somewhere in her fifties, with a fashionable crop of curly light brown hair still only lightly threaded with gray, a pixielike face that made her look much younger than her years, and a small pair of round silver-framed spectacles. Her nose turned up like a child's, her chin was small and pointed, and her wide hazel eyes were bright with intelligence and a boundless curiosity about her fellow beings. Hero had met her briefly at Madame de Staël's, but she couldn't be certain the woman remembered her.

"Of course I remember you, Lady Devlin," the author exclaimed when Hero spoke to her. "I've been reading your articles in the *Morning Chronicle* on the poor of London for years."

"You have?" said Hero.

Fanny laughed at the surprise in Hero's voice. "My Étienne used to bring the London papers home for me when he could. There were usually several copies of the *Chronicle* smuggled across the Channel every day."

"I wouldn't have thought the newspapers revealed much of interest to the French government."

"More about popular thinking and the palace's attempts to influence it than anything else," she admitted. She paused a moment, then said, "I used to share them with Sophia Cappello."

Hero met the older woman's frank gaze and saw the understanding that blazed there. "I take it you've heard Devlin is looking into her murder?"

"Is it murder?"

"Yes."

Fanny sucked in a quick breath and turned half away for a moment, her eyes blinking rapidly as if to hold back tears. "Dear Lord, I'd hoped that was nothing more than a vicious rumor."

"How long have you known her?"

"Since I first arrived in France during the Peace of Amiens. She was always very kind to me. She knew I was homesick for England, and seeing her—talking to her—always made me feel so much better." Fanny hesitated, then colored faintly as she added, "I'm afraid I haven't seen much of her lately. With the Restoration, Étienne . . . Well, let's just say he's asked me to be careful."

"Because of Marie-Thérèse, you mean?"

The color in Fanny's cheeks deepened. "Yes."

Hero found she had to try hard not to judge this small, birdlike woman who had allowed her husband's career ambitions to destroy a yearslong friendship that had been so important to her. And yet Hero knew she wasn't being fair. Easy enough for a wealthy and powerful nobleman's daughter to scorn such behavior as weakness. But for the aging daughter of an impoverished historian who'd found herself caught up in the dynastic upheavals of a foreign land and pressured by a determined husband? How many could have resisted all the forces brought to bear upon her?

Hero said, "Would you by any chance know why Sophie quarreled with her ward, Angélique?"

Fanny let out her breath in a soft sigh, obviously relieved to have the topic shift to something less personal. "Oh, yes, that was because of Antoine."

"Antoine de Longchamps-Montendre?"

"Yes."

"I take it Sophie didn't like him?"

"No. She thought him a fortune hunter, and I suspect she was right. But she made the mistake of saying as much to Angélique, and Angélique accused her of being against him because the de Longchamps-Montendres are Orléanists."

"Are they?"

"Oh, yes, vehemently. They think the Allies should have put the Duke of Orléans on the French throne rather restoring the Bourbons, and they've never made any secret of it."

"And Antoine himself? Does he agree with his family?"

"Quite passionately. He says Artois and Marie-Thérèse are so ultra-monarchist and ultra-Catholic that they're endangering the restoration of the monarchy. He's convinced the people won't stand for it and will eventually revolt again—that the only way to preserve the monarchy and the aristocracy is to replace the Bourbons with the Duke of Orléans."

As much as Antoine de Longchamps-Montendre had rubbed Hero the wrong way, she had a sneaking suspicion that in this respect, at least, he and the Orléanists might be right.

"And Sophie? She supported the Bourbons against the Orléanists?"

Fanny's eyes crinkled with silent amusement. "Oh, no. As far as Sophie was concerned, there was little to choose between the two."

"Well, there isn't really, is there?"

"Not as much as the supporters of the Duke would like to believe."

Hero watched as a tittering cluster of silk- and satin-clad British gentlewomen paused nearby to admire one of Pauline Bonaparte's nude Roman statues. "What do you think would happen if Napoléon were to try to come back now?"

"Escape from Elba, you mean?" Fanny looked thoughtful for a moment. "Honestly? I think he'd be killed within hours of landing in the south of France. The French people want peace, and only the Bourbons can give that to them."

"Because the Allies are behind them?"

"Well, yes. Don't you think? Napoléon tried for years to get the British to sign a peace treaty, but they wouldn't do it because they saw his very existence as a challenge to the entire concept of monarchy. Now he's gone and France has peace—and the Bourbons. It's been made more than obvious we can't have one without the other."

It was not lost upon Hero that Fanny had just called the British "they" and the French "we," although she suspected the woman herself was totally unaware of it. What must it have been like, Hero wondered, to be living in a country that was at war with the land of your birth? Married to a man fighting against your own countrymen—against your own brother?

What had it been like for Sophie, loving a man who was fighting against her own son?

"Ah, there you are, my dear," said a low French voice coming up behind them.

Turning, Hero found herself facing a lean, middle-aged man wearing the elegant dress uniform of a colonel in the King's Guard. He was of above-average height, his features ruggedly attractive and weathered by years of campaigning, his dark hair still untouched by gray. This, surely, was Colonel Étienne de Gautier.

"Étienne!" said Fanny, her smile flooding her face with a joyous affection that was impossible to miss.

So, a love match, thought Hero as the novelist hastened to perform the necessary introductions.

"I have met your father," the colonel told Hero with a bow. "He's proved to be a true friend to France in her hour of need."

"Yes, he has many fond memories of his days in Paris before the Revolution."

De Gautier's eyes lightened with his sad smile "What a different world that was."

Hero knew something of the man's history. Born the younger son of a provincial noble family, he'd served proudly in the French army under Louis XVI before going into exile with his father and elder brother at the time of the Reign of Terror. He looked younger than his wife, perhaps by as much as five or ten years. But those lean years in England would have been hard, Hero figured. It must have seemed a good move for such a man to marry the only sister of a British naval captain on his way to becoming an admiral—a woman who'd once served as Keeper of the Robes to the Queen. Surely neither had anticipated being caught in Paris when war broke out again between their two countries.

And yet the colonel had not only survived and prospered, but somehow found a way to weather the transition from Empire back to monarchy. It suggested a man who valued practicality above dogmatism and love of country above partisanship. A man whose English wife would now be seen as an asset rather than a liability . . .

As long as she was careful about her friendships.

"Do you think Fanny was right?" Devlin asked as their carriage rolled through the dark streets of the city toward the Seine. "About de Longchamps-Montendre and the Orléanists, I mean."

Hero stared out the window at the glorious silver moon just beginning to rise on the eastern horizon. "I don't know. If Sophie truly saw little to choose between the two houses, then why would she care if he supported the Duke of Orléans rather than the Bourbons?"

"She'd care if she thought the Orléanists were doomed to lose. Or—" He broke off.

"Or what?" said Hero.

His troubled gaze met hers. "Or if she knew Napoléon was planning to return."

Chapter 27

Sunday, 5 March

*T*he next morning Hero walked the grand allées and winding paths of the Jardin des Plantes, looking for Pierre-Joseph Redouté. The air here was gloriously fresh and clean, and all around her was an explosion of spring, with an achingly blue sky above and only faint puffs of white clouds on the horizon.

Ancient and vast, the botanical gardens lay on the Left Bank of the Seine, slightly to the southeast of the Île Saint-Louis. The Jardin had been begun in the early seventeenth century as a medicinal garden for Louis XIII, but the Bourbons had long ago thrown it open to the public, and Redouté was known to spend his Sunday mornings here, sketching or painting. She finally came upon him seated on a folding canvas stool beside a bed of gold-laced polyanthus, a sketch pad propped on one knee and a drawing pencil in hand. So intense was his concentration that he didn't glance up until Hero was almost upon him.

"*Bonjour*, Monsieur Redouté," she said cheerfully, her smile friendly. It wasn't the "done thing" to accost a famous artist in the park without a proper introduction. But when it came to murder, Hero had no patience for such social niceties.

Redouté stared at her a moment, then let out a sigh and said, "I know why you're here."

Whatever she'd been expecting, it wasn't that. "You do?"

He was a man somewhere in his fifties, his gray hair lanky, his nose long and straight, his chin lightly cleft, his expression kindly and good-humored. As she watched, his soft brown eyes crinkled with the sugges-tion of a smile. "It is Lady Devlin, is it not?"

"It is, yes," she said, returning his smile. "Do I take it Angélique de Longchamps-Montendre warned you I might wish to speak with you?"

He shook his head as if not understanding. "What does Madame de Longchamps-Montendre have to do with anything?"

"She's the one who suggested I talk to you."

"Ah." He glanced off across the orderly garden beds to a nearby butte crowned with a magnificent cedar of Lebanon. Something she couldn't quite read flickered across his features, and he said, "Actually, it was Henri Sanson—although now that I think about it, he suggested I might expect to see your husband, Lord Devlin."

Sanson again, thought Hero. Aloud, she said, "I'm told you knew *Dama* Cappello."

He nodded, his chin falling to his chest as he gazed down at the del-icate black-and-gold flowers nestled in the litter of winter-browned leaves before them. "She was an amazing woman, Sophia Cappello, bril-liant and talented, and yet so openhearted and good. Her death grieves me a great deal."

"How did you meet her?"

"Through the Empress Joséphine. They both loved roses, you know— roses and gardens in general." He sighed again. "The gardens at Malmai-son have deteriorated dreadfully since Joséphine's death, but *Dama* Cappello has been allowing me to paint her own gardens out at the rue du Champs du Repos. She sent me a note just the other day telling me her plum trees were about to bloom and inviting me to come capture them."

"When was this?"

"That she sent the message? Thursday afternoon. Why? She said she'd just arrived back in Paris to find the orchard coming into bloom, and she wanted to make certain I didn't miss it. I'd been planning to go tomorrow, but . . ." He gave a faint shake of his head.

"So why don't you?"

"How can I, under the circumstances?"

"It's what she'd want, don't you think?" Hero was silent for a moment, watching him deftly add more shading to his sketch. Then she said as casually as she could, "So you knew Sophia Cappello had been out of town?"

"Oh, yes. I believe she was in Vienna, visiting the *maréchal.*"

"She was. But then she went to Italy. Do you know anything about that?"

"No. Sorry."

Hero wasn't convinced she believed him. "How much do you know about *Dama* Cappello's politics?"

He gave a tight-lipped smile. "I served as an official court artist to Marie Antoinette and yet still managed to survive the Reign of Terror and be honored with the patronage of both the Empress Joséphine and Marie-Louise. Do you know how? I'll tell you," he continued without giving her a chance to answer. "By keeping my nose out of politics. My friends understand that and are kind enough to leave me out of all that nonsense."

"Was Sophia Cappello your friend?" said Hero.

He paused for a moment, a faint faraway look creeping into his kindly face. "I like to think so, yes."

It occurred to Hero that Sophie had accumulated a strange collection of friends for a countess: a botanical watercolorist, a novelist, a divorced empress, and the hereditary executioner of Paris. But then, as

Angélique had said, Sophie hadn't really considered herself a countess anymore.

Hero deliberately focused her attention on the purple violets scattered amongst the feathery little cushions of moss at her feet. "I'm told she quarreled with someone recently about roses. A count, I believe."

He glanced over at her. "You mean Aravena?"

"Who?"

"Niccolò Aravena—the Count of Cargèse, to give the man his full name and title. He has an estate just outside of Paris. Or I suppose I should say one of his estates is there. He has another in Corsica."

"Why precisely did they quarrel?"

Redouté shrugged. "Some people are simply quarrelsome."

"By which I take it you mean the Count?"

"Oh, yes, of course. Not Sophie."

Sophie, Hero noticed. Not *Dama* Cappello or even Sophia, but Sophie. She suspected Redouté didn't even realize what he'd said.

"There must have been more to it than that," said Hero.

"Not much. Aravena has the Empress's and *Dama* Cappello's interest in and love of roses, but his is a selfish love. He wishes to possess, not to share. And he is—or should I say 'was'?—intensely jealous both of their collections and their knowledge. It's his ambition to be known as the premier rosarian of France, and he isn't above practicing all sorts of underhand trickery to achieve that end. He frankly hated them—hated them both."

Hero drew a quick breath scented with damp earth and green growing things and the sweet perfume of jonquils blooming somewhere just out of sight. "Do you think he hated Sophia enough to kill her?"

"Oh, surely not," he said.

But Hero saw the flare of doubt in his eyes and knew he did not discount the possibility.

Chapter 28

The Château de Marigny, the sprawling ancient estate now possessed by Niccolò Aravena, the Count of Cargèse, lay in the hills to the northwest of Paris, not far from Montmartre.

This was an area of sun-drenched rolling fields covered with the vivid green shoots of newly sprouted wheat and rye, of slopes hatched with ancient gnarled grapevines, of peach and cherry orchards just coming into bloom in sweet-smelling drifts of white and delicate pink. The air here was gloriously fresh, the sky a crystal clear blue unmarred by the smoke from the crowded city's chimneys. As Sebastian turned his phaeton in through the estate's open, rusting gates, he could hear the purling of a rain-swollen stream mingling with a chorus of birdsong and the rustling of tiny unseen creatures in the brambles lining the rutted winding drive.

Nestled in the midst of well-kept Italian-style gardens, the château looked to be several hundred years old, built of golden limestone with circular towers capped by conical gray slate roofs. As they drew nearer, Sebastian found himself wondering what had happened to the noble family who'd once owned the estate. Had they been murdered by their own brutally oppressed peasants? Fallen victim to the guillotine? Fled to Britain and fought against their own countrymen? Were they even now trying to regain what they'd lost? So far the restored Bourbon King had stood firm against the émigrés' demands that their land be returned, but Sebastian wondered how much longer Louis would be able to hold out.

"So what exactly did this cove do, that Boney made 'im a count and gave 'im all this?" asked Tom as they drew up in the château's graveled forecourt.

"That I don't know yet," said Sebastian.

"Musta been somethin' big."

"Indeed." Sebastian let his gaze drift over the sunny slopes rising beyond the roofs of the greenhouses. Rather than being covered with grapevines, these fields were filled with rows and rows of roses grown like a crop.

Hopping down, he went to bang the knocker on the château's weathered front door.

No one answered.

He was banging for the third time when a blue-smocked gardener pushing a wheelbarrow full of manure came around the side of the house.

"He's not here—if you're looking for the Count, that is," said the man, setting down the handles of his barrow so that he could scratch the side of his unshaven face. "You could try Montmartre or Clichy if you'd like. He usually spends his Sundays in one of the *guinguettes* up there."

"Any particular one?" asked Sebastian, turning to face him.

The man sniffed. "Might start with the cabaret by the Blute-fin."

"*Merci*," said Sebastian. But the man had already lifted his barrow to push it away.

Hugging the crest of the craggy heights that overlooked the city, the ancient village of Montmartre dated back to the days of the Romans, when the top of the hill had been the site of a temple dedicated to the god Mars. According to legend, it was here that St. Denis, the first bishop of Paris, had suffered martyrdom in the third century. Except that rather than immediately falling down dead, his decapitated corpse simply picked up his head and carried it to the site of what became the Benedictine abbey of Saint-Denis. The hill had been crowded with monasteries and convents since the early Middle Ages.

The Revolution destroyed them all.

The area had also suffered badly in the Battle for Paris the previous March, when eight hundred thousand Russian, Austrian, and Prussian soldiers stormed the outlying villages of Montmartre, Belleville, and Pantin. Setting up their artillery on the ruins of the old twelfth-century Benedictine monastery at the top of the hill, the Russians had threatened to level the city of Paris below unless it surrendered. While the warring nations' leaders hammered out their peace agreement, the invading soldiers amused themselves in the time-honored tradition of conquering armies, ransacking and looting houses, raping women, and bayoneting dogs and little children. It was the Russian Cossacks who'd made the old windmill known as the Blute-fin famous by nailing the miller to the wings of his windmill and then laughing as he spun round and round.

As Sebastian drew closer to the village, he found himself driving past the shattered stone walls and charred timbers of empty houses and ruined monasteries.

"Gor," whispered Tom, his head craning around. "Who did this?"

"Well, the Revolutionaries destroyed the abbeys, and then the Russians, Prussians, and Austrians did the rest."

"Gor," said Tom again in a way that reminded Sebastian this was the boy's first look at what war could do.

"Water 'em," he told the tiger, drawing up beside the fountain in the old village square. "I'm not sure how long I'll be."

Tom scrambled forward to take the reins. "Aye, gov'nor."

Sebastian could hear the sails of the old windmill flapping in the

warm breeze as he turned toward the *guinguette*. *Guinguettes* were a particular kind of drinking-and-dancing establishment popular with French
craftsmen and workers. Clustering on the outskirts of the city, they
owed their success to the existence of what was called the *Mur des*
Fermiers-généraux—the Wall of the Farmers General, a thin fifteen-mile-
long curtain wall built around Paris shortly before the Revolution. Constructed at enormous expense, it was designed not to protect Paris from
invaders but to enable the nation's notorious tax farmers to better collect the tariffs levied on all goods taken into the city. They were called
"tax farmers" because, rather than collect the nation's taxes directly, the
Crown had given the lucrative contracts to private operators who grew
enormously rich while brutally oppressing the people with impunity.
The Revolution had ended the system, but the Directory soon brought
back a modified version to help finance their wars.

And so the *guinguettes* had grown up in the villages outside the wall.
Because they didn't pay the city's taxes, their alcohol was considerably
cheaper. And because they were away from the censorious eye of the
Duchess d'Angoulême, many also still stayed open on Sundays.

The *guinguette* next to the Blute-fin windmill was a terra-cotta-roofed,
plastered building with a grapevine-covered arbor, a blue-painted door,
and wooden casement windows thrown open to the unseasonably warm
afternoon. Laughter and voices spilled out into the lane, almost drowning out the traditional folk tune played by a couple of fiddlers on the
rickety wooden platform set up in one corner. A dozen or so men and
women were already dancing, the men's heavy shoes clomping loudly on
the worn floorboards, the women's colorful skirts swirling around them.
The air was thick with the smell of cheap wine, tobacco smoke, roasting
meat, freshly baked bread, and unwashed bodies.

A few quiet questions addressed to some of the workers at the bar
led Sebastian to a man in his mid-forties who sat by himself at a table
near one of the open front windows, his fingers toying with the stem of
his wineglass, a half-empty carafe resting nearby. His dress was more

that of a gentleman farmer than that of a nobleman, his hair nearly black and a little ragged, his complexion lightly scarred by smallpox and darkened by long hours in the sun. His eyes were narrowed and faintly smiling as he watched the dancers circle the floor.

Much like Napoléon himself, Niccolò Aravena had been born in Corsica to a family from the minor nobility. Sent to study at the École Militaire in Paris, he'd graduated a year behind Napoléon, been commissioned a second lieutenant, and was serving in Auxonne at the outbreak of the Revolution. At one time he'd fought at Napoléon's side in both Italy and Egypt, then left the army to marry the plain but well-dowered daughter of a war profiteer and sire two sons, only to lose them all in an outbreak of influenza. After that, he'd poured both his fortune and his passion into collecting and breeding roses.

How or why Napoléon had made the man a count and rewarded him so handsomely remained a mystery.

"I've been looking for you," said Sebastian, pulling out the empty chair opposite the Corsican and sitting.

Cargèse shifted to stare at him, his head tilted sideways, his bloodshot eyes widening. "I know who you are." He raised an unsteady hand to point at Sebastian in a way that suggested the half-empty carafe in the center of the table was not his first.

"Good." Sebastian turned to order a glass of wine for himself, then said, "So you know why I'm here."

Cargèse shook his head. "Not exactly. Why does an English viscount care what happened to a French general's whore?"

Sebastian set his jaw against the spurt of anger the careless words sent pounding through him and somehow overcame the urge to haul the bastard up by his shirtfront, slam him back against the nearest wall, and shove the ugly phrase down his throat. "I found her when she was dying."

The Corsican studied him in silence for a moment, his eyebrows raised as if in thought. "And you care. Interesting."

The man was obviously not as foxed as he'd first appeared.

Sebastian waited while the barmaid set his wine before him, then said, "I understand you're interested in roses."

A slow smile spread across the other man's scarred face. "*Non, monsieur.* You might be *interested* in solving murders. Me? I am *passionate* about roses." His French was good, but it still carried the heavy inflections of his native Corsica.

Sebastian said, "Is that why you quarreled with *Dama* Cappello? Over roses?"

"Who told you we quarreled?"

"Several people, actually."

Cargèse shrugged. "We had a friendly rivalry. Nothing more. I was interested in purchasing some seedlings she was developing, but she refused to sell them to me. That is all."

"When was this?"

"That she refused to sell the seedlings? Late last summer. She's been gone, you know. For months."

"And you haven't seen her since her return?"

"No. I didn't even know she had returned until I heard she was dead." He leaned forward and lowered his voice. "If you want to know who killed Madame Cappello, you should look at the Bourbons or perhaps the Orléanists. Not some simple rival rosarian."

"Why the Bourbons and the Orléanists?"

Cargèse threw a quick look around, then dropped his voice even lower. "You know she went to Elba?"

Sebastian stared at him. "How do you know about that?"

A slow smile spread across the Corsican's face as he brought up a finger to hook it behind his right ear and fold it forward. "Sometimes the roses, they whisper things to me."

"Oh? What else have they whispered to you?"

He shrugged again and let his hand fall. "Nothing else so consequential. But believe me: If I, Niccolò Aravena, know she went to Elba, then others know it, as well. And some of those who know would have cause to wish her harm."

"Why?"

"Why?" He huffed a soft, disbelieving laugh. "What do you think she was doing in Elba?"

"I don't know. Do you?"

The Corsican pressed his lips together and shook his head, his eyes still dancing with amusement and wine. "No."

Sebastian took a slow sip of his own wine. "How well do you know Napoléon Bonaparte?"

"I've known him since we were boys in Corsica. Why?"

"Were you with him in Russia?"

"No, thank God. Got this eight years ago in Italy—" Twisting sideways, the Corsican thrust out a leg that ended in a peg at the knee.

"Ah."

Cargèse shifted to stare silently out the window at a donkey pulling a cart loaded with firewood up the steep, narrow street. In the distance rose the ruins of the old medieval church of Saint-Pierre and the new semaphore tower that had been built almost on top of it. They were a French innovation, semaphore towers, used to send messages over great distances.

Sebastian said, "What do you think of the rumors that Napoléon might try to return from Elba?"

The Corsican drained his wine, then reached for the carafe and poured the last of it into his glass. "What do I know of such things?"

"The roses don't whisper about the Emperor?"

Cargèse expelled his breath in a crude noise and took a deep swallow of his wine.

Sebastian said, "What do you think would happen if he tried it?"

The Corsican paused with his glass still raised to his lips. "Have you noticed how fond Paris has become of violets?"

Sebastian had noticed. Everywhere he looked he saw violets: cheap prints of the delicate spring flowers propped up in the windows of shops; bunches of violets crafted of silk and worn on hats or in buttonholes; gay patterns of violets strewn across the muslin of women's dresses.

A strange smile curled the other man's lips. "The violets are just coming into bloom."

"And?" said Sebastian, not understanding.

"They were blooming last year at this time, when Napoléon left for Elba. You know what they say about violets?"

At the table beside them, a ragged band of ex-soldiers raised their glasses in a toast. "To *Père Violette!*" they cried, their glasses clinking together.

The toast was taken up by the next table, then the next, until the words echoed around the room. "To *Père Violette!*"

Sebastian felt a chill sweep over him. *Père Violette* meant "Father Violet." "What do they say about violets?" he asked Cargèse.

The Corsican's eyes crinkled in a smile as he raised his own glass high. "They go away. But then the next year they come back again."

Chapter 29

*R*ather than turn toward the village square when he left the *guinguette*, Sebastian walked downhill, to the abandoned gypsum quarry that lay at the foot of the butte. Thousands of the Revolution's victims had been buried there in hastily dug mass graves. But the only sign of that now was a simple black cross that stood above a pile of rubble and weeds. The rest of the open mine was a sun-blasted stretch of white rock with, here and there, the burned ruins of the site's old kilns and red-tiled sheds.

Even before the mass deaths of the Revolution, the ancient Church-affiliated cemeteries of Paris had been filled to overflowing. Les Innocents, the huge graveyard beside the central marketplace known as Les Halles, was said to have been so full that the ground level rose more than six feet above the surrounding land, and the area perpetually stank of decay. By the early 1780s, Louis XVI decided something had to be done about it. His solution became known as the catacombs.

But Paris's catacombs were not originally constructed as ossuaries. The remnants of ancient limestone quarries and tunnels that honey-combed the ground beneath the Left Bank of the city, the old forgotten tunnels had begun collapsing in the late eighteenth century, occasionally taking houses and people with them. After a particularly spectacular cave-in, the King named a commission to inspect, chart, and shore up the old mines, and that project was already underway when a house next to the teeming Innocents cemetery collapsed beneath the weight of the centuries of bulging burials behind it. A macabre nightmare of bones, grinning skulls, and half-decomposed corpses spilled out of the fetid earth.

In response to the public outcry, the city's old cemeteries were closed and interments within the city itself forbidden. But the question of what to do with the millions of bodies already overflowing the old burial grounds remained. Then someone got the clever idea of combining the two problems by emptying the contents of the city's cemeteries into the old mines. Every night, caravans of black-cloth-covered wagons filled with bones converged on the catacombs. Sebastian had heard it took two years to empty the worst of the city's old cemeteries. Some of those closed burial grounds were temporarily reopened during the Revolution for the victims of the guillotine and the various bloody *journées*. But many of the decapitated corpses were simply brought here to the abandoned gypsum quarry, dumped, and covered with quicklime and earth.

Much of the old gypsum quarry had been a surface mine, and the hole gaped like a vast open wound in the midst of a blighted landscape. Like the kilns and sheds on the quarry floor, the houses and workshops that had once clustered around it had been burned by the Cossacks, the broken stone walls now quickly disappearing beneath mats of weeds and festoons of vines that draped the yawning doorways and empty windows. The place was utterly deserted except for a black-and-white goat nosing a pile of refuse at the base of a jagged cut and a gray cat that ran off, tail held high, when Sebastian's foot rolled a loose stone.

The cry of a hawk circling overhead drew his gaze to the hard blue sky, where small puffs of white clouds were forming on the western horizon. *So much death,* he thought; so much death and heartache, terror and disaster, resentment and fury, had gripped this troubled land for more than twenty-five years. And he had a sick feeling he could not shake that it wasn't over yet; that they were simply stumbling through a deceptive interval of peace that could be shattered at any moment.

Sliding down one of the rocky slopes, he went to stand beside that single forlorn black cross. He'd heard that many of the mass graves from the Reign of Terror were now being emptied, with the guillotine's victims joining their ancestors in the catacombs below the city. Just that past January, Marie-Thérèse had had the remains of her mother and father exhumed from a mass grave at the Madeleine cemetery and transferred to the royal vaults in the basilica of Saint-Denis. But looking at this mound of rubble now, Sebastian found himself wondering how the remains of the King and Queen had truly been identified from amongst those thousands of decades-old, quicklime-doused headless corpses.

The faint sound of stealthy footsteps was barely perceptible, but Sebastian's hearing was abnormally acute—his hearing and those other senses that no one had ever adequately defined. He slipped the dagger he always carried in his boot from its sheath and turned.

Three men were sliding down the steep edge of the quarry toward him. Two were dark, their hair showing the first touch of gray, their clothes the rough trousers and coats of workmen. The third man, younger and fairer, wore the sun-faded shako hat and tattered white trousers of a French infantryman, his blue coat sporting a crowned "N" for Napoléon on the turnback. A fourth man, noticeably better dressed than the others, remained standing above, just at the edge of the quarry's cut, his hat pulled low and his back to the brightness of the sun so that Sebastian could not see his face.

"Gentlemen," said Sebastian in French, his eyes narrowed against the harsh sunlight glinting off the quarry's shattered white gypsum. "I take it you have something you wish to say to me? An unusual setting to choose for a conversation."

"*Un gros malin*," said the younger, fairer man in a low voice to his companions. *A smart-ass.*

He carried a long, sturdy length of wooden tamping rod with a broken, jagged end. One of his companions held a knife half hidden in the folds of his ragged coat hem, while the third gripped a stout cudgel.

"The choice of location was yours, *monsieur.*"

"Oh? I wasn't expecting company."

The young ex-soldier shifted his grip on the long wooden rod. "Life is strange that way, yes?"

The ex-soldier charged him then, running ahead of his companions, the tamping rod held up and back like a long, narrow cricket bat.

Sebastian stood his ground, the blood coursing through his veins as he let the man run at him. The Frenchman's eyes were a soft blue, his rawboned face darkened to a nut brown by the sun, his lips curled away from his teeth in a determined, focused grimace.

"*Salaud!*" swore the man, the rod whistling through the air as he threw all his weight behind it, aiming at Sebastian's head.

At the last instant, Sebastian ducked and stepped into his rush.

The momentum of the missed swing carried the Frenchman's body around, opening his right side. Sebastian thrust his knife in deep, then quickly jerked it out and danced away.

The ex-soldier's eyes widened, his knees crumpling beneath him, his hands spasming open, dropping the rod. Sebastian heard it clatter on the rocks as he pivoted around to smash his bootheel into the man's face, sending him flying back so hard that the breath left his body in a *whoosh* when his backbone slammed against the quarry's rock floor.

Swooping down, Sebastian jammed his bloody dagger back into its sheath and snatched up the rod, gripping it in both hands. "Stop," he said to the two men still advancing on him. "Just stop."

"*Sac à merde*," hissed the one with the knife, and charged. He was a pace or two ahead of his companion, and Sebastian ran straight at him, the tamping rod held like a cavalry lance.

Gritting his teeth, he rammed the rod's jagged end straight through the man's chest. It made an obscene popping noise, the Frenchman's jaw sagging, his mouth opening to send dark blood pouring down his chin as he toppled backward.

Sebastian yanked his dagger from its sheath again, his gaze meeting the remaining man's startled, frightened eyes. "Give it up," said Sebastian, his hand clenched around the knife's grip, his breath coming hard and fast. "I don't want to kill you." *There's been too much killing in this land already.*

The Frenchman's gaze slid sideways to where the young ex-soldier was trying to lurch to his feet, one hand held to his bloody side, his face a dusty mask of pain. "And Baptiste?"

Sebastian squinted up at the rim of the quarry. The watching gentleman had disappeared. His blood still pounding in his ears, Sebastian said, "Take him with you."

Dropping his cudgel, the man sidled over to his fallen companion to loop the ex-soldier's arm over his shoulders and help him to his feet. He cast a quick, anxious glance at Sebastian, but Sebastian simply shook his head and said, "Go on. Get him out of here."

The two men staggered awkwardly away toward a path that led up the quarry's steep side.

Sebastian swiped a forearm across his hot, grimy face and let them go.

Chapter 30

*H*e arrived back at the Place Dauphine to find Eugène-François Vidocq sitting with Hero in the salon, waiting for him.

"Ah, there you are, *monsieur,*" said the stocky, broad-faced head of the *Sûreté nationale*. He took a deep swallow from a glass of Sebastian's port, smacked his lips, and said, "*Ç'est bon.*"

Sebastian exchanged one significant glance with Hero, then walked over to pour himself a brandy. "I'm glad you're enjoying it, *monsieur.*"

Vidocq smiled and took another sip. "I heard about your little scuffle in the quarry up at Montmartre. But not to worry: I told her ladyship here that you were unharmed."

Sebastian paused with the decanter in hand and swung to stare at his guest. "How did you know about that?"

"I have good informants."

"Obviously. And did your informant tell you that all traces of my attackers—living and dead—had vanished by the time I returned with the authorities to the quarry?"

"*Non.* He must have sent his report too quickly to include that detail.

Interesting but not unexpected. At any rate, that's not why I'm here. I've had some of my men talking to the residents of the rue du Champs du Repos to see if anyone in the area recognized either the carriage or the team of grays belonging to the unknown woman who visited *Dama* Cappello on Thursday. A woman can wear a veil, keep her servants out of livery, and ride in a carriage without a crest. But it's not so easy to disguise a team of prime cattle when a man knows his horseflesh."

Sebastian went to stand beside the fire, his brandy glass cradled in his hand. "I take it someone in the area knows his horseflesh?"

"One does. Swears the team belongs to Hortense. And since he used to work in her stables, I suspect he knows what he's talking about."

Sebastian's hand tightened around his glass. *"Hortense?"*

Vidocq nodded. "You heard me right: the erstwhile Queen of Holland herself."

Hortense Eugénie Cécile Bonaparte, née de Beauharnais, was the daughter of the Empress Joséphine by her first husband, who'd been one of the many thousands of victims of the Reign of Terror. Under pressure from her stepfather, Napoléon, Hortense had married his brother Louis Bonaparte, who eventually became the King of Holland. But the marriage was not a success, and she'd spent little of her time in the Netherlands. Louis himself had long ago fled the country, but despite the Restoration, Hortense still lived in Paris, protected by the Russian Tsar, who'd reportedly been more than half in love with her now-dead mother. The young former queen had a reputation as a competent amateur composer, a good watercolorist, and a mean billiards player.

Sebastian said, "Any idea what she was doing there?"

"None whatsoever." Vidocq emptied his glass and set it aside to push to his feet with a grunt. "A man like me can't exactly approach the ex–Queen of Holland and expect to get much of an answer, now, can he? You'll have much better luck, I'm sure." He turned to bow to Hero. "Thank you, my lady, for the honor of your company."

"My pleasure, *monsieur*," she said, rising with him.

He turned toward the door. "Don't bother ringing to have someone show me out; I know the way."

But at the top of the stairs, he paused, clapped his hands to the sides of his coat, and said, "Ah, I almost forgot." Fumbling, he extracted something from a pocket and held it out. "Here."

Sebastian found himself holding a small, gem-studded red leather case emblazoned with a familiar gold monogram. "Where did you find it?"

"A lemonade seller pawned it at a small shop off rue de Rivoli. Swears he came upon it lying in one of the bastions on the northern stretch of the Pont Neuf on Thursday night, and I'm inclined to believe him, given that my boys weren't exactly gentle with their questioning after we picked him up."

Sebastian lifted the box's flap to reveal the empty gold-silk-lined interior. "He says it was empty when he found it?"

"Swears it. And it was sure enough empty when he pawned it. Monsieur DuBois—that's the pawnbroker—knows better than to lie to me."

Sebastian studied the ex–galley slave's saber-scarred face. "Have you ever seen it before?"

"The case? *Non.*" Vidocq settled his tricorne hat on his head. "But maybe you can ask the Queen of Holland about it."

After the man had shown himself out, Sebastian turned to Hero and handed her the case without a word.

"Dear Lord," she whispered, running the pad of her thumb across the monogram emblazoned there: the intertwined initials "JB" surrounded by a wreath of laurel leaves surmounted by an imperial crown. "*Joséphine Bonaparte.*" She looked up. "You think that's why Hortense was at the rue du Champs du Repos that evening? To give this to Sophie?"

"Seems a logical assumption, doesn't it?" He went to stand at the window, his gaze on the short, sturdy man walking rapidly away. "I wonder what it could possibly have contained?"

That evening, as was their habit, they were gathered before dinner in the salon with the two little boys and their nurse, Claire, when a knock sounded on the door below.

Patrick had been helping Simon sort a collection of silk cards of gaily painted wood, but at the sound of murmured voices from below, his head came up, and Sebastian saw a shadow cross his features before the boy said quietly, "'Tis 'is lordship."

Simon was already jumping up, a wide grin spreading across the face that was so much like that of his adopted brother. "Grandpapa Jarvis!"

Sebastian's gaze met Hero's. "Do you know what this is about?"

She shook her head. "No."

Jarvis came in, bringing with him all the scents of the cold Parisian night. His face was set in stern lines, his gray eyes flinty with quiet anger, and he said without preamble, "I must speak with you alone." He took off his greatcoat and cast it aside. Then his gaze fell on Simon, and for a moment his expression softened as he held out his arms to his grandson. "Come give your *bon-papa* a kiss and tell him good night."

Simon ran to him, while Sebastian went to help Patrick put away the wooden pieces and softly kiss the top of the little boy's head.

"What's wrong?" asked Hero as soon as Claire had left the room with the children.

Jarvis went to stand with his back to the fire, his jaw set hard as he rocked back and forth on his heels. "Bonaparte landed near Cannes four days ago."

Sebastian felt a strange sense of inevitability sluice through him, followed swiftly by a sickening lurch of his gut as the landing's full implications struck him. *Oh, Sophie.* "Any chance it could be a hoax?"

Jarvis glanced over at him. "I doubt it. Word came by semaphore this afternoon. We'd have heard sooner, but the weather interfered with the signal transmissions."

Hero sank into a nearby upholstered armchair. "But how is this even possible?"

Jarvis's nostrils flared on a quick, angry intake of air. "There's a reason we wanted the bastard exiled far away from France—and with a proper guard set upon him. No one knows the details yet, but word is he has fewer than a thousand men with him. I don't think there's much cause for alarm. They'll stop him soon enough—and hopefully this time they'll kill him."

Sebastian went to stand behind Hero's chair and rest his hands on her shoulders. "Does Hendon know?"

"I've just come from meeting with him. I'll be leaving for the coast within the hour, and I've advised the French King not to send word to the Prince Regent just yet. Hopefully I'll reach London before the news breaks there or at least not long afterward. But we don't see any reason at this point for Hendon to leave, too. The last thing we want is to create a sense of alarm with a sudden exodus of British subjects. The palace intends to keep the news from the French public for now, but it's difficult to say for how long they'll manage to do so. If nothing else, the truth is bound to get out as soon as travelers from the south of France begin reaching Paris."

"So why keep it secret?" said Hero.

"Because they're hoping the army can capture the bastard before anyone realizes he's returned."

"Is that likely?" she said.

"I don't see why not. Pretty hard to conquer a country with a thousand men."

"But if the people rally to him—"

"They won't," snapped Jarvis.

"And the army?" said Sebastian.

"The Grand Army has been mostly disbanded, and what's left is firmly under royal control. All his former marshals have sworn allegiance to the King. No one is going to rally to him. If he tries to come up through Provence, they'll hang him the way they tried to do a year ago when he was on his way to Elba. And there's snow in the Alpine passes. He's not going to get far."

Sebastian met Hero's gaze. Provence had always been heavily royalist and staunchly Catholic. If Napoléon was planning to march on Paris, his only choice would be to take the mountain route through Grenoble. And if there was snow . . .

Hero said, "No one had any warning this was going to happen?"

Jarvis's lips flattened into a tight line. He operated a vast network of spies and informants that gave him a well-deserved reputation for omniscience. But somehow they'd missed this. "Obviously there's been talk about him returning since last September. But few thought he'd actually be foolish enough to try it."

"Is it so foolish?" said Hero.

"It's madness." He reached for his greatcoat. "I must be off. And remember: not a word of this to anyone until King Louis announces it."

Sebastian walked with him to the street door. "If Bonaparte was near Cannes four days ago, then where is he now?"

Jarvis paused to look back at him. "We don't know. But with any luck, he's already dead."

Later that night, Sebastian lay awake with Hero in his arms, his cheek resting against her hair. He could hear the wind kicking up outside, tossing the newly leafed-out lime trees in the square and sending something clattering over the old cobblestones. He kept telling himself that Jarvis must be right, that Napoléon was probably already dead and his desperate bid to regain his faded glory dead with him. But he found he couldn't believe the deposed Emperor's chances of reaching Paris were that slim, and he knew with a sick dread that it was all about to start again. The fighting. The executions. The mass graves with silent black crosses . . .

"That's why Sophie was in Elba, isn't it?" Hero said softly, one hand resting on his bare chest. "She knew this was coming and was somehow involved in helping to coordinate it."

Sebastian was conscious of a strange ache that pulled across his heart. "I don't want to believe it. And yet I can't come up with any other explanation that makes sense."

She tilted back her head so she could look up at him. "And Joséphine's red leather case? Where does it fit in?"

"I don't know yet." He tightened his arms around her, drawing her closer. "But I intend to find out."

Chapter 31

Monday, 6 March

 he erstwhile Queen of Holland, Hortense Bonaparte, née de Beauharnais, lived in a graceful *hôtel particulier* on the rue Cerutti—or the rue
d'Artois, depending on which street sign one read. The new sign at the
southern end of the street carried the name of the King's powerful brother,
Artois, while the old one at the other end still had the Revolutionary-era
name. Lying not far from the ruins of Notre-Dame-de-Lorette and Sophie's own estate, this was a genteel area of grand homes that included
the massive Hôtel Thellusson, now serving as the Russian Embassy.

Sebastian found Hortense on the rear terrace overlooking a lush
English-style garden, a paintbrush in one hand and a palette in the other.
Dressed in figured muslin with a burgundy velvet spencer unbuttoned
enough to show her cleavage, she was roughing in a watercolor sketch of
a picturesque stone bridge that arched over the garden's ornamental
brook. When the powdered, liveried footman escorted Sebastian out to
her, she looked around with a smile and said, "I trust you don't mind me
continuing, *monsieur?*"

"Thank you for agreeing to see me, *madame*," said Sebastian, sweeping her a low bow.

What was the protocol, he wondered, when addressing a deposed queen who was also the stepdaughter of a deposed Emperor? Vidocq's optimism not withstanding, Sebastian had expected to be asked simply to leave his card. Now he was wondering why she'd agreed to see him.

Her smile widened. She was an attractive woman in her early thirties, slim and of medium height, with rich dark hair, a long face, a long nose, and a small pointed chin. "I understand you're looking into the death of *Dama* Cappello," she said, her attention returning to her painting. "Is that why you're here?"

"It is, actually."

She hadn't invited him to sit, so he went to lean against the stone balustrade edging the terrace. The day was still sunny, but cooler than yesterday, with increasingly heavy clouds building on the horizon.

"How horrible that she should die so violently," said Hortense, dabbing her brush in a bit of green. "And so . . . randomly."

"You think it was random?" said Sebastian.

She glanced over at him. "How could it not be?"

He studied her wide, pretty blue eyes and full, sensuous lips. It was said she'd left her husband because she couldn't stand him and because she missed the social whirl of Paris; that she'd had a tempestuous affair with a handsome count, borne him a child out of wedlock, then reluctantly severed all ties with the man when it emerged he was simultaneously involved with an actress; that she had now embarked on another scandalous romance. Was any of it true? Probably.

Sebastian chose his words carefully. "I'm told you paid a visit to the rue du Champs du Repos on the afternoon of the day *Dama* Cappello died, and I'm wondering if she said anything to you that might explain what happened to her just a few hours later."

He saw her hesitate, as if she were tempted to tell him he was wrong, that she hadn't called on Sophie that day. But she must have decided against it because she sighed sadly and said, "Ah, if only I had known it would be the last time I'd see her."

"You knew she'd been away?"

"Yes, of course. She was gone for months."

"Do you know where she went?"

The erstwhile Queen of Holland kept her attention on her painting. "I assume Vienna."

"You didn't discuss it?"

"No. I actually spoke to her for only a few minutes."

"I'm told your interaction that afternoon was . . . tense."

She froze, then tilted back her head to give a light, practiced society laugh that displayed her even white teeth. Sebastian had heard that her mother, Joséphine, had such bad teeth that she'd trained herself to smile without showing them. "Tense?" said Hortense. "Oh, I don't think I'd go so far as to say that. But I won't deny that she was unhappy with me."

"May I ask for what reason?"

Hortense gave a faint twitch of one shoulder. "Nothing of any real importance, in retrospect. She was upset with the state of the gardens at Malmaison. They've deteriorated dreadfully, I'm afraid, since my mother's death. Unfortunately her debts were of such magnitude that my brother and I have been forced to sell her various collections, and it still isn't enough. So we've had to let most of the gardeners go."

"Why not simply sell the house?"

"But how could we? She loved it so much—as does my stepfather." Her stepfather, of course, being Napoléon Bonaparte, who until five days before had been permanently banished to the island of Elba.

Sebastian gazed out over the sun-soaked gardens, now bursting into new leaf with the promise of spring. "Do you mind if I ask why you went to see her that day?"

She gave another one of those breathy laughs. "But I thought I'd just told you, *monsieur*. I'd heard she was unhappy with the state of the château's gardens and wished to help her understand the reason."

She said it airily, as if it explained everything, when it actually made no sense at all. But one could not exactly call a queen a liar—even if she was deposed.

Sebastian said, "If she'd been gone for months, why choose the very afternoon of her return to discuss the situation with her?"

"Ah, but I didn't realize she'd only just returned. I assumed she'd been back for weeks. She was originally expected sometime in January."

"Was she? I didn't know." *So what happened while she was in Vienna*, he wondered, *that sent Sophie on an unplanned trip to Elba?*

Reaching into his pocket, he drew forth the red leather case with Joséphine's entwined initials and held it out to Joséphine's daughter. "Have you ever seen this?"

She stared at him, her full lips parting on a hastily indrawn breath that shuddered her half-exposed breasts. *"Mon Dieu."* Setting aside her brush and palette, she reached to take the case from him, her eyes widening when she saw that it was empty. "Where did you get this?"

"It was found on the Pont Neuf the night Sophia Cappello was murdered there."

"And it was empty?" she said sharply in a way that told him the case's original contents were important to her.

"It was, yes. You recognize it?"

"Of course. It was my mother's."

"Why would *Dama* Cappello have it?"

"I can't imagine. I haven't seen it since my mother died. We've wondered what happened to it—my brother and I both."

"What did it contain?"

She looked up at him, her blue eyes narrowed and thoughtful. Speculative. She was a spoiled, self-indulgent, but very shrewd woman, and one underestimated her at his peril. "You don't know?"

"No."

"Napoléon had the case made for her to hold the Charlemagne Talisman."

He shook his head. "What's that?"

"The Charlemagne Talisman? It's a ninth-century amulet that once belonged to Charlemagne. It's a lovely thing, with gold filigree and repoussé work studded with gems. I suppose technically it's a reliquary medallion, since there are two pieces of the True Cross inside."

"So why is it called the Charlemagne Talisman?"

"Because it was found on a chain around Charlemagne's neck when his tomb was opened back in the eleventh or twelfth century." She ran the pad of her thumb across the case's embossed monogram. "The Bishop of Aix-la-Chapelle gave it to Joséphine not long after she was crowned Empress. It was part of a collection of Charlemagne relics held at the cathedral, and when she admired it while on a visit there, he gave it to her."

"How large is it?"

"Perhaps three inches." She held her thumb and forefinger apart to illustrate the size. "It's still on a gold chain, although I don't know if it's the original one. There are two large sapphires in the center, one cut oval, the other square, with smaller emeralds, garnets, amethysts, and pearls set around them."

A sudden gust of wind lifted the leafy branches of a nearby maple against the sky, bringing with it the sweet scent of apple blossoms and throwing a dancing pattern of light and shadow across the terrace. Sebastian said, "Why would the Bishop give her something of such incalculable value?"

Hortense shrugged as if the question had never occurred to her, and it probably hadn't. People had been giving her family things for most of her life—ever since she'd been that fatherless child of thirteen whose mother married the then-General Bonaparte.

"I believe it was to thank Napoléon for returning the church's relics after they'd been confiscated during the Revolution."

"Do you have any idea why Sophia Cappello would have had this case with her when she was killed last Thursday night?"

Napoléon's stepdaughter looked Sebastian straight in the eyes and said, "No. No idea whatsoever."

He knew it for another lie. And he found himself wondering again why she had agreed to see him rather than simply telling her servants to deny him. To find out what he knew, perhaps?

About what?

There was an inescapable aura of exhilaration about her, of waiting, of guarding an exciting secret. And Sebastian thought, *She knows. She knows Napoléon has left Elba and landed on the southern coast of France.* But because Sebastian couldn't talk about it yet, he couldn't ask her about it directly in case he was wrong and she didn't know. So he came at it obliquely. "Is there any truth, do you think, to the rumors that the Emperor might return?"

The faint smile that touched her lips confirmed his every suspicion. "Why do you ask?"

"I've heard that many grow dissatisfied with the Restoration and yearn for the past."

"Is it any wonder? When the Bourbons raise taxes and destroy our French industries by allowing British goods into the country without duty? When our returning prisoners of war are left to starve to death in the streets and the brave officers of the Grand Army are reduced to half pay—which is never actually paid? When Marie-Thérèse pushes to bring back the Jesuits and all the oppressive powers of the Church?" Her lip curled. "You've seen the way she swans around Paris in her black gowns, indulging in an endless public display of self-pity and acting as if she's the only person who suffered as a result of the Revolution. There's not a family in all of France that hasn't lost loved ones these past twenty-six years, but she doesn't care. The only suffering she cares about is her own, and she's made that more than obvious to everyone."

There was a faint break in this formidable woman's voice that reminded Sebastian of the stories he'd heard about Hortense's own childhood. She'd been only eleven in the spring of 1794 when her father, the vicomte de Beauharnais, was thrown into prison. A month later she'd seen her mother dragged off to the Carmes prison, leaving her alone with her thirteen-year-old brother. In July, their father was marched up the steps to the guillotine, with their mother sentenced to follow him. Joséphine was only days away from being beheaded when the fall of Robespierre brought the Reign of Terror to a shuddering end.

Now Sebastian watched as Joséphine's daughter fingered the case's open flap, a frown drawing a fine line between her brows. But he couldn't begin to guess what it meant.

"You're suggesting this might be why Sophia Cappello was killed?" she said. "Because she had the talisman and someone took it from her? But who would do such a thing?"

"Do you have any idea why she would have had it with her that night?" he asked again.

She shook her head without looking up. "No."

"Is it possible she was planning to take the talisman to someone or at least show it to them?"

She did look up then, a speculative and faintly malicious gleam shining in her eyes. "Have you spoken to Monsieur Landrieu?"

"Who?"

"Émile Landrieu. He's the director of the Monuments Museum. I know he has expressed interest in the talisman in the past."

Sebastian had heard of the museum. When the churches, cathedrals, and monasteries of France were being ransacked and destroyed during the Revolution, a group of horrified historians and artists banded together in an effort to save as many of the country's priceless ancient art objects as possible. At first they'd simply warehoused them in one of the abandoned monasteries, but eventually the collection was organized into what was known as the Museum of French Monuments.

"I believe she worked with him," Hortense was saying.

"Worked with him on what?"

"On securing objects for the museum. It was one of her passions. Didn't you know?"

"No," he said.

He was beginning to realize just how much he didn't know about the brilliant, beautiful, complicated woman who'd been his mother.

Chapter 32

*W*hy would Hortense send you to the Monuments Museum?"

Hero asked the question over nuncheon at a small cloth-covered table in one of the Palais-Royal's fine eating establishments. Even at midday, the shadows beneath the arcades were deep, so candles blazed in the crystal chandeliers overhead, their light reflected in the towering mirrors that lined the room's rear wall. In London, a respectable woman who wished to dine out could only do so secluded from the public eye in a hotel's private parlor. But Paris was thick with these so-called restaurants, where both sexes of all ranks could eat and drink in public without censure or scandal.

Sebastian kept his voice low as an aproned waiter escorted two expensively dressed women past them to a nearby table. "I could be wrong, but I suspect it has more to do with her dislike of the museum's director than any real interest in helping me find Sophie's killer."

"Now, that sounds like Hortense. The explanation she gave for her visit to Sophie that day is ridiculous. Why would Hortense suddenly decide—after months of not seeing her—to drive out to the Champs du Repos and explain to her late mother's friend the reasons for the neglect of Malmaison's gardens?"

"It makes no sense at all. Which means that the real reason for that visit is something Hortense feels the need to keep quiet. And I don't think it's too much of a stretch to suspect it's somehow related to a certain someone's return to France."

"Which we can't talk about yet."

"Which we can't talk about yet . . . although I'm fairly certain Hortense knows about it." He was suddenly acutely conscious of the urbane Frenchmen and -women who filled the tables around them—laughing and talking and utterly, blithely unaware of the fact that their former Emperor was at that very moment marching toward Paris, determined to retake his throne and turn their world upside down. Again.

Hero leaned forward. "If Hortense knew—and presumably approved—of her stepfather's plan, and if Sophie had just visited him there, then why the tension between them?"

"Perhaps the discussion was simply serious—which it would have been, wouldn't it? Madame Dion could have misinterpreted what she was seeing."

"Yes, that makes sense." She waited while their waiter set soup plates before them, then said, "Perhaps the talisman doesn't have anything to do with Sophie's death. Perhaps Sophie simply happened to have the amulet with her when she was killed."

"Perhaps. Although I can't see a common thief stealing the amulet while leaving its valuable jeweled case—and everything else in her reticule."

"Yet it must be an extraordinarily delicate piece. So if it wasn't stolen that night, why wouldn't whoever has the talisman keep it in its case?"

"I don't know; that's a good point. And the thing is, while Hortense seemed genuinely surprised that I had the case and that it was empty, she was definitely lying when she claimed she had no idea why Sophie might have had it with her that evening . . . which seems oddly contradictory." He reached for his wine, then looked thoughtfully over the glass's brim at Hero. "What do you know of this Émile Landrieu?"

"Not a great deal, although I have seen his multivolume publication on the museum's collection. He worked as an artist himself once, you know, before deciding to dedicate his life to the preservation of France's artistic and historic heritage."

"A rather courageous thing to do in the midst of a revolution."

"I don't think anyone ever faulted his courage. But there's no denying he's an extraordinarily controversial figure. Some hate him with that peculiar passion that scholars reserve for those with whom they disagree professionally, while others admire him enormously. And yet . . ."

"And yet?" he prompted when she hesitated.

"Well, let's just say that even those who admire him seem to think he's a tad peculiar."

"Peculiar? In what way?"

Her lips curled up in a smile he couldn't quite read. "I suspect you'll understand when you meet him."

The former convent of the Petits-Augustins nuns lay on the quai Malaquais, on the left bank of the Seine just south of the Louvre. A graceful collection of limestone buildings dating from the Middle Ages through the seventeenth century, the museum was open two days a week to the general public and at other times by appointment for those willing to pay for a private tour.

Sebastian met the museum's director in what was once the convent's magnificent Gothic church but was now stuffed floor to ceiling with everything from a Roman altar—whose label announced it had been found beneath Notre Dame—to marble busts of some of France's most illustrious citizens.

"*Monsieur le vicomte,*" said Émile Landrieu with a bow, "we are honored by your visit."

He was a thin, gray-haired man in his early fifties, with protuberant dark eyes and narrow, high-arching eyebrows that had the effect of making him look perpetually surprised. His face was gaunt, his cheekbones sharp, his mouth small, his chin dimpled. His pride in his collection hummed through him with an intensity that was impossible to miss.

"I've heard much about your museum," said Sebastian, his gaze roving the cavernous space.

"It's organized chronologically," said the director, his hands sweeping out in a loving, expansive gesture that took in a nearby marble baptismal font and a row of intricately carved architectural fragments, "with the church serving as an introductory hall to provide an overview of our collection. From here we visit each century of France's history in a mounting progression, moving from the Darkest Ages to the High Renaissance." A quiver of indignation passed over his features. "Some of our critics object to the inclusion of the more primitive medieval monuments and sculptures, saying they lack artistic merit and thus have no place in such a collection. But this isn't simply about art; it's about *history*—the artistic history of France."

They turned to walk along the cloister, its paving stones worn by the feet of centuries of devout nuns. "Look at this," he said, ushering Sebastian into a stone-vaulted chamber filled with a collection of ancient monuments dating back a thousand years and more. "Here we have kings going all the way back to Dagobert and Pepin the Short." He spoke as if the mortal remains of the long-dead monarchs themselves were present, rather than simply their silent, empty tombs. "Pepin was descended from two of Charlemagne's sons, you know: Louis the Pious and Pepin of Italy."

"No, I didn't know," said Sebastian,

Landrieu nodded as if he had expected such ignorance. "And here we have Hugh Capet. Technically Hugh's predecessors ruled as *regis Francorum*, kings of the Franks, rather than as kings of France."

Sebastian felt a strange sensation creep over him as he stared down at the empty tomb of a ruler who had been dead for over eight hundred years. Hugh's Capetian dynasty had ended in the early fourteenth century, yet when Marie Antoinette was tried and executed by the Revolution, they'd no longer referred to her as queen but simply as "the Widow Capet." He let his gaze rove over the rows and rows of long-dead rulers.

"These all came from the royal vaults at Saint-Denis?"

"Many of them, yes. I was fortunate enough to be able to stop the complete destruction of most of the basilica's monuments and bring them here."

Sebastian had heard about the weeks-long emptying of Saint-Denis's crypt. The moldering remains of the tombs' royal inhabitants had been either burned or unceremoniously dumped in mass graves behind the old abbey church. "I wouldn't have expected the Revolutionaries to be very enthusiastic about keeping these."

An expression Sebastian couldn't quite define passed over the Frenchman's features. "Many were not. But fortunately we were able to make them see the importance of preserving France's *cultural* heritage even as we jettisoned her *political* heritage. The remains of the various kings, queens, mistresses, royal offspring, and ministers these tombs once contained are no longer preserved and revered; the sculptures' value comes entirely from their status as unique representations of the artistic output of the centuries."

Sebastian glanced around the gloomy chamber, keeping his voice casual. "Did you manage to acquire any of Charlemagne's reliquaries?"

"Alas, no." Landrieu sighed as they moved on to the next room, their footsteps echoing in the vast stone-vaulted space. "I did try. That failure is one of the greatest disappointments of my life."

"I can imagine. You're familiar with the Charlemagne Talisman, I assume?"

Landrieu looked over at him, his eyes blinking rapidly. "Yes, of course. According to legend, it was a gift to Charlemagne from the Caliph Harun al-Rashid. We don't know for certain if that's true, but the workmanship certainly looks Saracen, and the Caliph did give the Emperor many gifts."

"You've seen it?"

"Oh, yes." His expressive brows lowered with what was obviously a long-festering and deep-seated aggravation. "I was fortunate enough to be able to study it before the bishop of Aix-la-Chapelle decided to gift it to Joséphine."

"Do you know that it's missing?"

Landrieu drew up and swung to face him. "Missing? What do you mean, missing?"

"According to Hortense, it hasn't been seen since Joséphine's death. But last Thursday, when Sophia Cappello was murdered on the Île de la Cité, this was found nearby." Sebastian drew the jeweled leather case from his pocket and held it out. "Hortense tells me Napoléon had it made especially for the amulet."

"*Mon Dieu*." Landrieu took the case with hands that were noticeably shaking. He was silent for a moment, his features pinched and grave. Then he said, "You think this is why she was killed? Because of the talisman?"

"Perhaps. It's obviously extraordinarily valuable, both for its gold and precious stones and for its historic associations. But what I don't understand is, why would someone take the talisman and leave the case, which is also studded with jewels?"

Landrieu sniffed and handed the case back to Sebastian. "The case has monetary value, obviously. But it is of little historic interest."

Sebastian suspected future historians might disagree with that dismissal, but he kept the thought to himself.

"Are you familiar with the legend associated with the amulet?" said Landrieu as they continued along the stone-vaulted aisle of the ancient cloister.

"No. Why?"

"They say Charlemagne wore it as a talisman in battle. There are many who attribute his military successes to it. According to the legend, the Empire of Europe goes to the man who possesses the talisman."

An unsettling possibility presented itself to Sebastian as he gazed along the cloister's row of weathered limestone columns. "Is Bonaparte a superstitious man? Do you know?"

Landrieu's lip curled in a way that suggested the museum director was no fervent Bonapartist. "He's Corsican. They're all superstitious."

"Then I'm surprised he allowed Joséphine to keep the talisman when he divorced her."

"I've heard he regretted it. None of the military campaigns he waged after the divorce were successful."

"Do you have any idea why Sophia Cappello might have had the talisman with her when she was killed?"

Landrieu looked over at him, his strange eyebrows arching even higher than usual. "Me? No."

"But you did know her."

"Oh, yes. She believed strongly in what we are doing here. She even helped source sculptures for the museum. She had a keen sense of history and a good artistic eye."

"Did she ever mention the talisman to you?"

"No. Why would she?"

Why indeed?

They had reached the Seventeenth-Century Room, its collections dominated by the magnificent carved tomb of Cardinal Richelieu, which stood in its center. Landrieu paused beside Girardon's glorious sculptures, his head falling back, his features convulsing with an expression of awe and pride mingled with an echo of painful memories. Sebastian had heard that when Revolutionaries armed with sledgehammers broke into the Sorbonne, the museum director had thrown his own body between the vandals and the tomb's priceless sculptures. He'd suffered a bayonet wound in the fray, yet somehow still managed to save the statues.

"When the Revolutionaries broke open Richelieu's tomb," Landrieu said softly, "they decapitated his corpse, then paraded the headless body through the streets."

"Why?" said Sebastian.

Landrieu looked over at him. "Why? I suppose it was their way of showing that the kings and their minions of old had lost their power. That those who had oppressed the people were now thrown down and destroyed."

"His body must have been well preserved."

"It was, yes. Extraordinarily so." He let his gaze rove lovingly over the marble grouping. "The state of preservation of the remains in these tombs varied tremendously. Francis I, for instance, was in such a state of liquid putrefaction that he was little more than an oozing, foul-smelling black liquid that made us all ill. But Henri IV was so perfectly mummified that I could take his hand in mine."

Something about the way it was said made Sebastian think that Landrieu had, in fact, taken the long-dead king's hand. But then, of all France's monarchs, Henri IV was the one who seemed to arouse the least hostility amongst Republicans. And Sebastian found himself wondering again about the man's politics. How had he managed not only to survive but also to somehow protect this precious collection of sculptures through so many decades of political upheaval?

To have survived the early years of the Revolution, Landrieu must have at least presented himself as a fervent Republican and Jacobin. With the coming of the Directory and the Empire, he would have needed to renounce radicalism and then, in time, swear fealty to Napoléon. Now he'd declared for the Bourbons. But what did he actually believe? Or did he believe in anything beyond his lifelong mission of rescuing, preserving, and protecting his nation's artistic and architectural heritage?

"The sixteenth century was the high point of French art," said Landrieu as they turned away from the room. "After that, we see a two-hundred-year slide toward degradation. Good art requires good govern-ment." His face twisted with scorn. "Not decadent sycophants."

So, thought Sebastian; *definitely not an admirer of the Bourbons.* Aloud, he said, "Have you heard anyone express interest lately in the talisman?"

"What?" said Landrieu blankly as if his thoughts had passed on to other concerns. "Oh. Oh, no."

But his eyes slid away as he said it, and Sebastian knew it for a lie.

Chapter 33

When Sebastian walked out of the *Musée des Monuments Français* half an hour later, it was to find an elegant town carriage with a team of snorting, head-tossing blood bays drawn up outside the ancient convent's door. The servants' green-and-gold livery and the gleaming crest on the carriage's panel both identified the owner.

"The Duchess will speak with you," said the Chevalier de Teulet, stepping forward from where he stood waiting, his arms crossed at his chest. "Now."

Sebastian eyed the two *gendarmes* flanking the Chevalier. "Again?"

The Chevalier simply grunted.

Sebastian assumed he was about to be strong-armed into the carriage and whisked off to the palace. Instead, the Chevalier yanked open the carriage door, and Sebastian saw the somber, black-clad Daughter of France herself sitting rigidly within, a meek-looking, colorless maid at her side.

"*Madame*," said Sebastian, leaping up to take the seat opposite her, "how did you know I was here?"

He said it in French, but she answered him in her clipped English. "It is I who will ask the questions." Sebastian glanced at the maid, and she followed his gaze. "Elise does not understand your language."

"Convenient," said Sebastian.

Her nostrils flared. "I know what you are looking for."

"You do?"

"Let us not play games, *monsieur*. The Charlemagne Talisman: *Dama Cappello* had it, yes?"

Sebastian chose his words carefully. "She had the case. I honestly don't know if she ever had the amulet itself."

Marie-Thérèse pushed her breath out between her teeth in a hiss. "Where did she find it?"

"I have no idea."

"The amulet belongs to *us*—to the descendants and successors of Charlemagne."

Sebastian would have said it belonged to the people of France, but he kept the thought to himself.

"Where is it?" she said, her harsh, strident voice cracking.

"I suspect that's a question that might be more profitably addressed to whoever killed her." He paused, then added, "Unless of course her killers found only the empty case, in which circumstance one assumes that they, too, are now looking for the talisman."

It was a subtle way of saying that he hadn't eliminated her and her nasty ex-Jesuit henchman from his list of suspects.

But subtleties were lost on Marie-Thérèse. She said, "I will have it. It never should have been given to that *putain* Joséphine."

Sebastian studied her tight, angry, haughty face. "I wonder what makes you think Madame Cappello ever had it."

"It's obvious."

"It is? How?

Her features quivered with disdain. Rather than answer him, she simply turned her head away to stare out the carriage window at a cart of turnips trundling up the quai Malaquais. "Leave us. Now."

Protocol required him to sketch a courtly bow—or at least as courtly a bow as one could execute within the confines of a carriage—and mumble humbly, *Oui, madame.* Instead, he simply thrust open the carriage door and hopped down.

He was turning toward where Tom was waiting with the phaeton when de Teulet put out a hand, stopping him.

"She will have it," said the Chevalier.

Sebastian met the Frenchman's blazing, fanatical eyes. "How did you know I was here?"

But de Teulet simply smiled and walked away.

Chapter 34

$\mathcal{T}$he funeral mass for the woman who had called herself Sophia Cappello was held that evening in the ruins of the old church of Notre-Dame-de-Lorette.

Sebastian had approached her parish priest, a sad-eyed, white-haired old man named Father Paul, who apologized for the condition of his church, saying, "The Revolutionaries tore off the roof for its lead and then sold what was left to a contractor who tore down most of the nave for its stones. But thankfully the Lady Chapel is still usable." He hesitated, then added, "As long as it doesn't rain."

It didn't rain.

Beyond Geneviève Dion and the other members of Sophie's household staff, the number of mourners present was small. Hendon had realized his attendance was liable to provoke precisely the sort of speculation they were anxious to avoid and so stayed away, while Amanda didn't even bother to acknowledge Sebastian's note apprising her of the funeral's time and place. Sophie's former ward, Angélique, was likewise absent, although whether from guilt or anger they had no way of knowing.

But Sophie's strange collection of friends all came. Émile Landrieu and Pierre-Joseph Redouté were there, as was the hereditary executioner of Paris. In explicit acknowledgment of his status as a social pariah, Sanson stood by himself at the rear of the small half-ruined chapel and left immediately after the mass without speaking to anyone. Even Fanny Carpenter came, although she arrived without her ambitious French colonel.

Afterward she stood with them in the disused old churchyard, which like most Parisian churchyards had been closed and emptied of its burials decades ago. Only a swath of uneven grass and some of the weathered gray headstones remained, leaning together like stacks of thick, broken boards against what was left of the ruined walls.

"I still can't believe Sophie's dead," she said, her voice breaking with emotion. "I've never known anyone so joyously full of life. It just . . . doesn't seem possible." Her eyes were red and swollen, for she had been silently weeping throughout the mass. But there was a stubborn tilt to her chin that suggested the colonel had not approved of her attendance. "Have you learned anything—anything at all—that might explain what happened to her?"

"Not really, I'm afraid," said Sebastian.

The older woman sucked in a deep, shaky breath and let it out slowly. "And now we have these shocking rumors that Napoléon has escaped from Elba. No one seems to know if it's actually true but . . . God help us if it is."

Sebastian and Hero exchanged guarded glances. It was Hero who answered. "Even if it is true, surely he will be stopped soon."

It was what everyone was saying—that if Napoléon had indeed returned, his mad adventure had no chance of success, that he would be caught long before he reached Paris. But Fanny looked troubled.

"I don't know. There are so many hungry ex-soldiers and returned prisoners of war, so many officers on half pay. The commanders have all taken oaths of allegiance to the King, but if the men were to go over to him—" She broke off as if suddenly realizing that her words might be misinterpreted, and said quickly, "Of course Étienne would never dream of forsaking his oath."

She said it firmly as if anything else would be unthinkable. But Sebastian wasn't convinced. Colonel Étienne de Gautier might say that now; he might even believe it. But for how long would he and the thousands of others like him stay true to the King if Napoléon did manage to confound everyone and arrive before the gates of Paris with his ranks swelled with tens of thousands of his former soldiers?

It was a painful choice that might soon be forced upon all Frenchmen.

They buried Sophie at Père Lachaise, one of the vast new burial grounds established by Napoléon in the countryside outside of Paris. Perched serenely on a hillside, the cemetery had been landscaped like an English garden, its winding, tree-shaded cobbled lanes lined with rows of templelike white tombs that made it look like a ghostly city of the dead.

As Sebastian stood beside Hero and watched the *fossoyeurs* lower Sophie's coffin into the earth, a faint mist began to swirl with the coming of evening. He could feel the dampness against his face, feel his grief pressing down on him like a heavy weight that left him aching and exhausted. He was aware of a strange sense of unreality. How had it come to this? he thought. How could his yearslong search for his mother have ended with him standing here now beside her raw grave? For decades he had moved through the days of his life thinking her dead. And then he'd learned the truth, and through all the anger and hurt and sense of betrayal, he'd still rejoiced in the knowledge that, somewhere, she lived. Somewhere, *she* was going through the days of *her* life. He had been so bloody confident that somehow, someday, he would find her. See her. Look into her eyes, watch her smile, hear her laugh, and learn from her that painful truth he was so desperate to know. Instead, here he was, once again struggling to accept the reality of her death. Except this time

there was no denying it. The finality of it, the undeniability of this moment, stole his breath. And it struck him for the first time that she would
forever be a part of this land he'd spent so many years of his life fighting.
Should he ever wish to visit her grave in the future, he would need to
return to France to do so.

It was a simple thought that came perilously close to causing him
to lose the rigid grip on his self-control that he had somehow managed
to maintain for five long days. And he wondered what showed on his
face, for at that moment, Hero reached out to take his hand in hers and
hold him tight.

"I wish I could have met her," she said quietly as the *fossoyeurs* turned
to sink their shovels into the loose pile of dirt beside the open grave.

Sebastian nodded, his lips pressed tightly together as he swallowed
hard. "I wish . . . I wish all my memories of her weren't more than twenty
years old. I should have come to France myself last summer, rather than
simply sending agents to try to find her."

"You didn't know what was going to happen."

"No," he agreed, "I didn't know."

He knew she'd said it to comfort him, but he doubted there was anything that could ever truly ease this crushing sense of guilt and regret.

It was when they were turning away from the grave that they noticed
the waiflike young woman watching them from beneath a nearby spreading maple. Her stylish black pelisse was buttoned high at the neck
against the coming chill of evening, her hair covered by a black capote
worn *à l'anglaise*. Her face was pale, her lips swollen, and her eyes red-
rimmed from obvious weeping. Then their gazes met and she took a
step back, her hands tightening on her black reticule as if she meant to
turn and walk away.

"Madame de Longchamps-Montendre," said Hero, starting toward her.

Angélique quivered a moment, then stepped forward to take Hero's hands in both of hers and kiss her cheeks. "I didn't think she'd want me at her funeral mass," said the younger woman. "But I couldn't stay away completely."

"I can't believe she wouldn't have wanted you here," said Hero, pressing the girl's delicate hands before letting her go.

Angélique shook her head, although Sebastian couldn't tell if it was in denial of Hero's statement or for some other reason entirely. A tear spilled over to run down the girl's cheek, and she dashed it away with one black-gloved fist. "You've heard about Napoléon? That he's landed near Antibes?"

"Where did you hear that?" asked Sebastian.

"Everyone's whispering about it at Court. Most people think it's only a wild rumor, but Antoine says it's true." She gave him a look he found difficult to interpret. "He also says you've been asking questions about the Charlemagne Talisman."

"You're familiar with it?" said Sebastian.

Angélique nodded. "Joséphine showed it to me once when I was at Malmaison with Sophie. But . . . what could it possibly have to do with what happened to her?"

"It seems to have disappeared."

"Yes, right after Joséphine died. I remember because Hortense was furious. She always expected to inherit it."

"So what happened to it?"

"No one knew."

A cool breeze kicked up, lifting the leaves of the darkening trees against the sky and fluttering the curls that framed the girl's strained face.

Hero said, "Do you know if Sophie believed in the talisman's power?"

Angélique put up a hand to hold her windblown hair from her face. It was a moment before she answered. "I don't know if I'd say she believed in it herself. But something like that can be powerful if other people think it's powerful—if you understand what I mean?"

"Yes, I think I do."

"But why are you asking about it now?""

"Because the talisman's empty case was found on the Pont Neuf the night Sophie was killed there."

Her lips parted, and she gave another faint shake of her head as if it all made no sense. "Why would Sophie have had it?"

"We don't know. Do you have any idea what might explain it?"

"Me? No." Angélique's gaze strayed some distance away, to where a tall, fashionably dressed man in a caped greatcoat waited beside one of the white marble tombs, his arms crossed at his chest and his hat pulled low against the setting sun. Something flickered across her face, and she said in a rush, "I must go. Antoine is waiting for me."

And then she walked away, her lower lip held between her teeth and her focus turned inward as if a disturbing possibility had just opened up before her.

"Interesting that Antoine de Longchamps-Montendre knows for certain the rumors about Napoléon's landing are true," said Sebastian as they watched Angélique hurry away. "I wonder who told him."

"His kinsman the Duke of Orléans, perhaps?" suggested Hero.

"Probably."

They watched in silence as Angélique drew up beside her husband. For one intense moment, Antoine de Longchamps-Montendre glanced over to where they stood. But his face wore a courtier's mask, revealing nothing.

Then he drew his wife's hand through the crook of his arm and turned her away.

Chapter 35

*T*he early-morning light streaming in through the soaring stained glass windows bathed the ravaged interior of Notre Dame in a soft, colorful glow. Sebastian had lost his faith long ago on the bloody battlefields of Europe, but he still found the destruction of the venerable old cathedral wrought during the Revolution's first years painful to see.

He had come here this morning in search of peace and a place to think—a place to think about Sophie and Napoléon and a strange, twisted series of events he couldn't begin to understand. He still had no idea exactly how or why Sophie had come into possession of the amulet—or at least its jeweled case. But he was convinced that Hortense had lied to him, that she knew far more than she was trying to pretend. What he couldn't decide was exactly what that meant.

Had Hortense gone to the rue du Champs du Repos that evening to give Sophie the amulet? Why would she do that? And why would Sophie then take the amulet—or at least its case—with her on what was supposed to be a painful personal trip to the Place Dauphine to come to terms with her long-estranged son? In a desperate attempt to safeguard it? Was that it?

Safeguard it from whom? Whoever had killed her?

It was easy to make the assumption that Sophie had been killed by someone who'd then taken the famous talisman. But if so, how then to explain what happened to her abigail, Francine?

He let his head fall back, his gaze traveling over the vaulted stone ceiling soaring so high above. What if . . . what if the killer—or killers—had attacked Sophie only to find the talisman's case already empty? What if they'd yanked open Sophie's reticule looking for the amulet, found the case, and tossed the reticule off the bridge only to discover that the talisman wasn't there? He could see them throwing the case itself aside in anger, leaving it to be found by the passing lemonade seller who'd then pawned it.

It was a theory that would explain why Sophie's abigail, Francine, had been tortured: because the killer—or killers—thought the girl might know where the talisman was. But *had* she known? Sebastian found himself doubting it.

So where was the talisman now? If he was right—and that was a significant *if*—why would Sophie have been carrying the empty case with her that night in the first place? Unless . . .

Unless the case hadn't been empty when Sophie left her house. Unless she'd spent that lost hour or two between the time she left the Vert-Galant and the attack on the bridge taking the amulet to—whom? Hortense? That made no sense.

Émile Landrieu?

Perhaps.

Bloody hell, he thought, swiping his hands down over his face. He hadn't slept well in days, and it was beginning to catch up with him. *Think*, he told himself. Who would be desperate enough to kill to get their hands on the Carolingian amulet?

The obvious answer was Marie-Thérèse, but who else? What about the Duke of Orléans—or one of his supporters? Would someone like Antoine de Longchamps-Montendre kill to possess an amulet with such legendary powers? Possibly.

Who else?

Hortense? Hortense, who according to Angélique had been furious when the amulet disappeared after her mother's death. Hortense, who would be eager to pass the talisman on to her stepfather as he began his dangerous campaign to retake his throne. Hortense, who had come to see Sophie hours before her death for reasons she'd never adequately explained.

And what about the Republicans, those opposed to the Bourbons, the Orléanists, and the Bonapartists alike; those who still believed in the Revolutionary creed of *liberté, égalité, fraternité*, who still yearned to see France once again a republic? One need not believe in the amulet's power to understand the allure of superstition and the danger of allowing the piece to fall into the wrong hands.

So the Bonapartists, the Bourbons, the Orléanists, and the Republicans. *Bloody hell*, he thought again; France had far, far too many rival factions. How could anyone ever put this broken country back together again?

He bowed his head, one hand coming up to unconsciously massage the tight muscles at the base of his neck. Then he heard brusque footsteps and a brush of cloth, smelled the reek of charcoal, tobacco smoke, and cooking fat, and looked over to find a stocky coal seller sliding into the pew beside him.

"Mind if I join you?" said Eugène-François Vidocq, his face so blackened by coal dust that the whites of his eyes seemed to glow out of the gloom.

"Why are you dressed like that?" said Sebastian.

The chief of the *Sûreté nationale* lifted one corner of his rough, grimy coat and grinned. "It's a good disguise, yes? I'm trying to catch a gang of thieves who've been helping themselves to coal from the quay. But that's not why I'm here."

Sebastian leaned back in the pew. "You've found the *fiacre* driver from that night?"

A quiver of frustration passed across the Frenchman's features. "Not yet. And I must confess I don't understand why not. Normally it would be a simple matter. It makes no sense."

"What about the prostitute I saw by the statue that night?"

Vidocq sighed. "Do you have any idea how many *filles publiques* we have here in Paris? I swear, there are as many women on the streets as there are French soldiers in their graves."

"I suspect the one has much to do with the other."

The gallerian pursed his lips as if the possibility had never before occurred to him. "You may have a point."

"So why are you here?"

Vidocq leaned forward. "There's a body in the morgue I want you to see. I'm thinking he could be one of the men who attacked you in Montmartre the other day."

"What makes you think that?"

A slow grin spread across the man's dirty face. "I'd like to say 'exemplary police work.' But the truth is, they found your name and address in his pocket. Care to come and have a look at him?"

Sebastian had heard that, at one time, the unidentified dead fished from the River Seine or picked up in the streets of Paris were put on display in the prison of the Châtelet. That practice had been far from satisfactory, for the air of the prison was noxious and unhealthy for visitors, and the dead were often tossed into piles on the ground and left to putrefy.

As Napoléon had done with so much else in Paris, from the water supply and the sewers to the market facilities and wharves, the Emperor

had set about improving that situation. On his orders, a long, low building was constructed specifically to serve as the city's morgue. Conve-
niently located at the quai du Marché on the Île de la Cité between the
city's police station and the river, the morgue featured a large *Salle d'expo-
sition* where the bodies of the unidentified dead were put on display on
slanted marble slabs. Men and women alike were stripped completely
naked except for a small cloth draped across their genitals, with their
clothes hung from iron hooks over the bodies in the hopes they might
help with identification.

But the truth was that few of the hordes of people who visited the
morgue were actually there in the hopes of identifying someone. Most
came for the spectacle and the titillation. The morgue was even listed in
the city's guidebooks. Personally, Sebastian could never understand it.
He'd seen more than enough dead bodies to last him a thousand life-
times.

Making their way along the quay from the cathedral, he and Vidocq
found the morgue's simple, plain building surrounded by a boisterous,
disorganized queue of noisy, shoving men, women, and children of all
classes.

"Please tell me they're not all waiting to get into the morgue," said
Sebastian.

"*Mais oui.* The newspapers must have reported on a particularly
gruesome discovery," said Vidocq, raising his voice to be heard over the
din as they threaded their way through the crowd toward the door. "The
lines are always worse when there's something gory to see."

"*Alors!*" protested a butcher in a bloody apron. "Get in line and wait
your turn like everyone else."

"Shut up or I'll have you arrested," growled Vidocq.

He might be dressed as a coal seller, but his voice carried authority
tinged with a hint of brutality. The complainer shut up.

"Unfortunately, whoever designed the building didn't think things
through," said Vidocq as they broke through the throng into the exhibi-

tion room itself, which Sebastian was surprised to find was considerably less crowded. "There's only the one entrance, which means the gawkers and the bodies all have to come in through the same door. Imagine trying to get a corpse through that crush. Fortunately they've learned not to allow too many spectators into the *salle* at once—cuts down on the tussles and fights and the women and little ones getting trampled to death."

"Lovely," said Sebastian, trying not to breathe.

The stench in the place was eye watering, both from the decaying corpses on the other side of a series of long, tall windows and from the unwashed men, women, and children pressing up against the glass to stare.

"It's a clever idea. London could use a central morgue like this— although I can't see the British government allowing it to be turned into this kind of a spectacle."

"Ha," snorted Vidocq. "A goodly percentage of the people waiting in line out there are probably British tourists." He tapped one finger against the glass window that allowed a clear view of the dead on display. "There, the second from the left in the first row. Recognize him?"

There were two rows of inclined stone slabs supported on an iron framework. Seven of the slabs were currently occupied. Sebastian tried to ignore the other bodies at various stages of decomposition and focus on the cadaver Vidocq had indicated.

It was the fair-haired ex-soldier from the quarry. Like the other corpses, he'd been stripped naked, with his tattered uniform hanging above his body. The knife wound Sebastian had given him in his side was clearly visible and had festered horribly.

The gaping slit across his throat was new.

"So," said Vidocq, "did you kill him?"

Sebastian took an involuntary step back as a giant gray rat ran across the toes of his boots. "My knife caused that wound in his side, but I'm not the one who slit his throat."

Vidocq nodded. "Word on the street is that he was hurting so bad, he wanted to go to the Hôtel-Dieu, and he was delirious enough that his mates were afraid he'd let slip something he shouldn't. So they killed him."

Sebastian looked over at him. "I thought you didn't know who he is."

"We don't. Sometimes people can tell you why a man died even when they don't know exactly who he is."

"Where was he found?"

"Faubourg Saint-Antoine." Vidocq stared at him expectantly. "So do you know his name?"

"One of the men called him Baptiste, but that's all I heard. Just Baptiste."

Vidocq sighed. "I suspect they're going to end up having to take a wax cast before sending him off to the medical school."

"They do that? Take impressions of their faces, I mean."

"Oh, yes—in case someone comes along hoping to identify them after the bodies have been disposed of." The Frenchman nodded to the headless cadaver of a man at the far end of the row. "That's what the crowds have come to see. The more gruesome the bodies we pick up, the bigger the crowds we get. They particularly like anyone who's mutilated, although wee babes and pretty young girls who find themselves in the family way and throw themselves into the river are also popular, for obvious reasons."

Sebastian was beginning to feel vaguely ill, although he couldn't have said if it was from the sight of the cavalierly displayed naked corpses, the rowdy, malodorous crowd, the thick, oppressive stench of death, or the way a little boy of perhaps five, held up by his mother for a better view of a comely young dead woman, clapped his hands and chortled, "I can see her boobies!"

"It's like free theater, yes?" said Vidocq.

"Frankly, I find it rather appalling."

Vidocq laughed out loud and poked Sebastian with one stubby, grimy finger. "At least it's not you on that slab over there, eh?"

Sebastian watched the little boy's father light a clay pipe, then blow smoke against the glass partition. "You do have a point."

They emerged from the fetid, lantern-lit gloom of the morgue to find the crowd outside unexpectedly dispersing, with people shouting and milling about in confusion. Some were grim faced and stunned; others were laughing. Near the water's edge, a man threw his hat in the air and whooped.

"What the hell?" said Sebastian.

Vidocq called to one of the policemen stationed nearby, "What is it? What's happened?"

"Haven't you heard? Napoléon has escaped from Elba. They say he landed near Antibes a week ago." The policeman's eyes sparkled with what looked very much like hope. "*Père Violette* is back!"

Chapter 36

Sebastian returned to the Place Dauphine to find Hendon drinking a cup of tea with Hero in the salon.

"You've heard the King finally made a formal announcement about Napoléon's landing?" said Hero as Sebastian slung off his greatcoat and tossed it aside.

"Is that how the news got out? I wondered." He walked over to the tea tray to pour himself a cup. "Any idea yet as to how Boney managed to get away from Elba?"

Hendon brought up one hand to pull at his earlobe. "Well, he wasn't exactly under close guard, although of course we did have a commissioner on Elba and a small naval force patrolling the waters between the island and the mainland."

Sebastian looked up from stirring his tea. "So what happened?"

"Seems Colonel Campbell—that's the commissioner—sailed to the mainland in February to make certain his dispatches to London were sent in a timely manner." The Earl gave a strange half smile. "Dispatches warning the government that he feared Bonaparte was definitely planning to leave the island."

"Brilliant."

"Indeed. As soon as the colonel sailed out of the harbor, Napoléon ordered the *Inconstant*—that's his personal brig—fitted out for a journey, along with several other vessels he'd hired."

"He hired vessels? With what? I thought he was supposed to be broke. And no one found that suspicious?"

"Evidently not," said Hendon dryly. "They say the flotilla left the island on the twenty-sixth. They'd have landed in France sooner except they were becalmed at one point."

"And the naval vessels that were supposed to be patrolling the area?"

"Didn't see him."

Sebastian shook his head. "Do we know where he is now?"

"Estimates put him near Laffrey, but it's difficult to know for certain. The weather has been terrible, making it impossible for many of the semaphore towers to be used."

"So what finally convinced the King to make the announcement?"

"The palace has been awash in whispers, of course," said Hendon. "But I suspect the main reason for finally announcing it was the need to explain why an army of six thousand men just left for the south of France."

"That would be a tad difficult to conceal," said Sebastian. "Who's commanding them?"

"Ney himself."

"Ah," said Sebastian, his thoughts drifting back for a moment to another time and another place, when Sebastian himself had fought against French forces under Ney's command.

Born the son of a cooper, Michel Ney began his military career in 1787 as an enlisted man, for under the monarchy only those with four quarterings of nobility were allowed to enter the French officer corps. All that changed with the coming of the Revolution, and Ney was commissioned in 1792. By 1796 he was a general, and Napoléon made him a marshal just a few years later. When the *Grande Armée* invaded Russia, the ruddy-faced Ney was at Napoléon's side, and in the long, disastrous withdrawal from Moscow, it was Ney who commanded the rear guard. "The last Frenchman on Russian soil," the people called him, while the Emperor called him *le*

Brave des Braves—the Bravest of the Brave. Ney was the most prestigious and popular of Napoléon's marshals, and it had fallen to him—along with McClellan—to negotiate with the Russians last April and convince Napoléon to abdicate. As a reward, the newly restored King Louis XVIII had made Ney a peer—although Marie-Thérèse was said to despise him both for his service under Napoléon and for his common birth.

"Is the King certain Ney can be trusted?" said Hero.

"Oh, yes, no doubt of that," said Hendon, setting aside his empty teacup. "Before he left, the marshal swore to bring Bonaparte back to Paris in an iron cage."

Sebastian took a slow swallow of his own tea. "There isn't actually anything in the Fontainebleau Treaty that requires Bonaparte to stay on Elba, is there?"

"No, but it was understood that he was to remain there. His leaving will be seen as an assault on the peace of Europe."

"Or at least as an assault on the rule of kings," said Sebastian, "which I suppose amounts to the same thing."

Hendon's lips flattened into a tight line. "Napoléon can survive only by war, and everyone knows it."

"Actually, if he does succeed in retaking France, I suspect the last thing he'll want is war, given the unpopularity of the taxation and casualties it would inevitably bring. He'd be a fool not to seek peace with the Allies, and Napoléon is no fool."

"No, that he's not. And there's no denying he's playing this all quite cleverly. According to the reports, a small detachment of his troops was captured by the local guard and taken to Antibes. Not only is he insisting he wants peace, but he's ordered his men not to shoot even if they're confronted. Seems he has the conceit he can reach Paris without firing a shot." Hendon snorted in derision. "He's also issuing all sorts of proclamations—to the people of France, to the army, to his old officers—cloaking himself in the mantle of the Revolution, portraying himself as the nation's liberator, and flying the tricolor." Hendon snorted again. "As

if he didn't have himself crowned Emperor in a betrayal of everything
the Revolution supposedly stood for."

"Well, not exactly everything," said Sebastian. "Under Napoléon, a
private could rise to become a marshal, and did. You won't see that anymore. Not under the Bourbons."

Hendon stared at him. "Good God. You sound like a bloody Jacobin."

Sebastian huffed a soft laugh. "You have to admit that promotion by
merit rather than noble birthright was a significant factor in France's success in conquering Europe."

"I will admit to no such thing!"

"You say the King is still confident Napoléon can be stopped?" said
Hero, calmly intervening.

Hendon glanced over at her. "Oh, yes. Marie-Thérèse is scheduled
to leave on a monthlong tour of Bordeaux, and he's told her to go ahead.
He's not worried. In fact, I wouldn't be surprised if Napoléon has already
been defeated; we simply don't know it yet."

Hero said, "Are you still planning to leave for London?"

Hendon nodded and pushed to his feet. "This Friday evening. Amanda
has decided to come with me, but that's only because she's received word
that Stephanie is in the family way." Amanda's only daughter, Stephanie, had
recently scandalized London society by marrying "beneath her" less than a
year after the death of her first husband. "But I don't see any need for you to
leave if you're not so inclined. Even if Napoléon really is near Laffrey, that's
still a two-week march from Paris, and they're sure to stop him at the pass."
He settled his beaver hat on his head. "With fewer than a thousand men—
and those with orders not to fire even to defend themselves—he doesn't
stand a chance. It's a desperate fool's gamble, and he must know it. I suspect
he's simply decided he'd rather die on a battlefield than in his bed."

"What do you think?" said Hero after Hendon had taken himself off.

Sebastian went to stand at the window, his gaze on the small triangular square below, where an old man in a beret had struck up a sprightly tune on an accordion. A crowd of laughing men and women was gathering around him, some clapping, some dancing.

"Honestly? I think the King might be misreading the mood of his people. Look at that."

Hero came to stand beside him. "Perhaps no one has told Louis that his subjects are literally dancing in the streets at the thought of his rival's return."

"Perhaps. Or perhaps he simply thinks it's irrelevant because he trusts the army to protect him. It would be more worrisome if Napoléon had more men."

Together they watched as someone brought out a wineskin and began passing it around. Then the accordion player switched to a familiar tune that Sebastian recognized with a jolt: It was *"La Marseillaise,"* the beloved Revolutionary-era song outlawed by the Bourbons.

After a moment, Hero said, "Who do you think has the talisman now? Sophie's killers?"

"I honestly don't know. But now that word of Napoléon's escape is out, I can at least have a more frank conversation with Hortense." He paused. "It might also be interesting to talk to the family of Sophie's abigail. She was with them for the better part of a day before she was killed. Her loyalty to her mistress might have kept her from telling them much, but she could inadvertently have let something slip—something her parents might not have been eager to tell the head of the *Sûreté nationale.*"

"You think they might tell you if you went there alone?"

"Given that they know I was with Vidocq? Probably not. But . . ."

He hesitated, and after a moment she said, "Let me guess: You think they'd be more likely to talk if I went to see them."

He looped his arm around her neck and drew her to him for a kiss as she laughed.

Chapter 37

The dethroned Queen of Holland was in the Passage des Panoramas, gazing at the array of fine chocolates displayed in a shopwindow, when Sebastian walked up to her.

Paris's *passages* were the envy of the horde of aristocratic tourists visiting the city from London. Built in response to the wretched state of the city's streets, the covered arcades protected shoppers from the rain, snow, traffic, and mud. Hortense Bonaparte was dressed for her outing in a walking gown of ruby sarcenet topped by a corded spencer with a Stewart neck, a high-crowned straw hat with a ruby plume, and delicate ruby kid slippers, all of which would have been ruined if she were forced to venture out into Paris's crowded, manure-fouled streets.

Her attention was focused on the delights in the chocolatier's lantern-lit window, so Sebastian had a moment to observe her before she turned and saw him. He watched as her lips curled into a practiced sultry smile, and she said, "I thought I'd be seeing you again. I take it you've heard about Napoléon?"

"Is there anyone in Paris who hasn't at this point?"

"Probably not." She tilted her head to one side, the smile still in place as her gaze searched his face. "And now you're remembering the things I said to you and you've come to the conclusion I may have been less than honest?"

"Understandable under the circumstances, wouldn't you say?"

"Is it?"

Rather than answer, he said, "I take it you knew of Sophia Cappello's visit to Elba?"

Her eyes danced with what looked like genuine amusement. "Now, how would I have come to know that, hmm?"

"How, indeed."

She turned to walk up the passage, and he fell into step beside her. "And when you went to see her that evening, was it to give her the Charlemagne Talisman?"

"Good heavens, no," she said loudly enough to attract the attention of her two liveried footmen trailing some ten or fifteen feet behind them. "What a thought! I told you, I have no idea what happened to it—apart from which, why on earth would I give it to her if I did have it?"

"So how do you think Sophia Cappello came to have the amulet—or at least its case?"

"I've been giving that some thought, actually."

"And?"

"My mother always said she'd leave the amulet to me, and I know she still had it when she took ill. Yet when she died, it was gone. Obviously she must have given it to someone, and one of the people who came to see her often in her final days was *Dama* Cappello."

"Why would your mother give her the amulet?"

She looked him straight in the eye and said, "I've no idea."

"I think you do."

She laughed. "Are you calling me a liar, *monsieur?*"

Her voice was warm and low, seductive. This was a woman accustomed to using her sexual allure to captivate and manipulate men. After all, she'd grown up watching her mother seduce everyone from the powerful Director Paul Barras to Napoléon Bonaparte himself. After Joséphine's failure to produce an heir led Bonaparte to divorce her (and, as he so bluntly put it, "marry a womb"), Joséphine retired to Malmaison, where, after the Emperor's abdication, she struck up an intense flirtation with the Russian Tsar Alexander. She'd caught the cold that killed her while riding out with the Tsar in the rain.

Rather than answer, Sebastian said, "Did you ever ask Sophia Cappello if she had the amulet?"

"As it happens, I did. She said she did not." Hortense paused beside a stationer's shop, her gaze roving over the display of fine papers, quills, and inks. "Obviously she was being less than truthful."

"Not necessarily. The case was empty when it was found, remember?"

"So it was." She turned to walk on.

"Do you think *Dama* Cappello was planning to give the amulet to Napoléon when he returned?"

"But that would require her to know what Napoléon was planning, now, wouldn't it?"

"So did she?"

Hortense shrugged. "Anyone who knows Napoléon would know that he could never be content to remain on that island for long. But did she know exactly when he was coming? I couldn't say."

"But you knew."

She gave another of those soft laughs. "Well, the violets are blooming, aren't they?"

"So they are."

She paused again, her gaze fixed on him this time rather than on the shops beside them. "Did anyone ever tell you how much you resemble Marshal McClellan?"

"I believe we may be distantly related. My paternal grandmother was Scottish."

"Ah. Then that would explain it. You know of course that he is with Talleyrand in Vienna, taking part in the negotiations at the Congress?"

"Yes."

"How will he react, I wonder, when he hears Napoléon has returned?"

"I've never met the man. How do you think he will react?"

She gave a faint shake of her head. "It is a difficult choice that all of Napoléon's officers will now be facing, yes?" She hesitated, her lips parting as she drew a quick breath. "I assume someone has told McClellan that the woman who was his wife in all but name is now dead?"

"I believe her *avocat* has contacted him," said Sebastian in a flat, colorless voice.

He was aware of Hortense watching him closely. She said, "I wonder, has it occurred to you that Sophia Cappello may have been killed by someone who wanted to stop her from giving the amulet to Napoléon?"

"That had occurred to me."

"Ah, yes, of course it has. They do say you are very clever."

"Oh? Who says that?"

But she simply smiled and shrugged.

Sebastian was aware of the two footmen watching them from a discreet distance, their faces wooden. He said, "So tell me this: Why did you send me to Émile Landrieu?"

She opened her eyes wide as if in astonishment. "You mean to say you haven't figured that out yet? Perhaps you need to look more closely into the museum director's history, hmm? And now you must excuse me, *monsieur*; I promised an old friend I'd visit her this afternoon."

"Of course," said Sebastian, touching his hand to his hat with a bow.

He stayed where he was and watched her walk away, her two bodyguards ignoring him as they passed. He knew she was still lying to him, still hiding things from him, still toying with him. He knew it, and yet he was damned if he could untangle the morass of her entwined tales to understand where the truth lay.

There was no way, obviously, that this elegantly dressed, pampered ex-queen could have stabbed Sophie in the back and thrown her body over the edge of the bridge. This was a woman who never did anything for herself, who paid people to draw her bath, manicure her nails, and dress her hair.

She was more than capable of hiring someone to do her killing.

Chapter 38

*V*enturing into the Faubourg Saint-Antoine was like stepping back in time to medieval Paris. The crooked, fetid streets were narrow and dark, the houses mean and crumbling, the wretched, ragged figures on the streets gaunt and hollow eyed. Hero took the carriage as far as she could, then continued on foot with two stout footmen at her side. The day was cloudy and cold, and she had dressed simply in a gray pelisse and a round hat. But she was aware of hostile stares following her, and as she passed a chandler's shop, a man leaned against the rotting doorway, his thumbs hooked in the pockets of his canvas trousers as he began to sing *"Ça ira!"*

Ah! ça ira, ça ira, ça ira
les aristocrates à la lanterne!

The words of the old revolutionary song followed her up the street.

If we don't hang them
We'll break them.
If we don't break them

We'll burn them.

Ah! It'll be fine, it'll be fine, it'll be fine. . . .

Hero felt a chill run up her spine. It had been less than thirty years since revolutionary mobs had literally torn gentlewomen apart in the streets of Paris. And it occurred to her as she turned into the woodworkers' passage that it wasn't simply Napoléon and his tiny advancing army they needed to worry about.

The real threat might well come from the pent-up popular anger and lingering animosity his return could unleash.

She found Francine's father, Marcel Danjou, out making a delivery. But the towheaded little girl who answered Hero's knock whispered shyly that her *maman* and sister were washing clothes "out the back."

"Can you take me to them, sweetheart?" asked Hero, hunkering down to the little girl's level.

The child stuck her thumb in her mouth and nodded.

Francine's mother was using a big stick to stir the clothes boiling in a massive kettle set up over a charcoal fire in the tiny flagged court behind the shop. She looked up at Hero's approach, eyes narrowing against the steam. Claudine Danjou was a large woman, broad of face, with wide shoulders and heavily muscled arms. She looked to be somewhere in her late fifties or early sixties, her once-fair hair now mostly gray, her face lined and coarsened by work, deprivation, and sorrow. But judging by the age of the babe that slept in a basket by the hearth, the six-year-old assigned to watch it, and the four- or five-year-old who'd answered Hero's knock, Hero suspected the woman was probably closer to forty or forty-five.

Wiping her red work-chapped hands on her tattered apron, Claudine took the basket of fruits and cheeses Hero had brought, eyes widening at the unmistakable *chink* made by the coin purse tucked within.

"Take over here, Julia," she said to the thin, lanky-haired young girl helping her.

The girl nodded, her face an indecipherable mask as Claudine drew
Hero back inside.

They sat on wooden stools drawn up before the hearth, where a thin
stew simmered in a heavy iron pot slung over the fire, its aroma filling
the small, meanly furnished room. Hero admired the babe in her basket,
nibbled one of the biscuits she herself had brought, and slowly worked
the conversation around to the woman's dead daughter, the girl's service to *Dama* Cappello, and who Claudine thought might have killed them
both.

"If I knew, I'd say, *madame*," whispered the heartbroken mother, a
handkerchief wrapped around one fist as she stared into the fire. "Truly I
would. But I don't. I just don't."

"Did Francine tell you they'd been to Italy?" Hero was careful not to
say *to Elba*.

Claudine looked up, her lips parting as she drew a quick, startled
breath. "Is that where they went? We knew she'd been on a ship because
she talked about being so dreadfully seasick and about how kind and
gentle Madame Cappello was with her. But she never said where they'd
been. She wasn't supposed to tell, you see."

"She sounds like a good, honest, faithful girl."

"Oh, she was," said the dead girl's mother, her voice breaking. "Truly
she was. I think that's why whoever killed her hurt her like that—to
make her talk and say where they'd been."

Hero suspected it was more likely the girl's killers had been after the
missing talisman. But all she said was "Did Francine ever talk to you
about an ancient amulet called the Charlemagne Talisman?"

The Frenchwoman looked at her blankly. "*Non. Jamais.*" Never.

"Did she mention anyone *Dama* Cappello might have had reason to
fear?"

"Fear? I don't know that *Dama* Cappello was afraid of anyone. She was a strong woman, that one."

"What about someone with whom she'd quarreled?"

The baby began to fuss, and Claudine went to pick her up. She stood for a moment beside the basket, her hips swaying back and forth as she patted the infant's back. "Well, I don't know if you could say they 'quarreled,' exactly, but I do know she had issues with Marie-Thérèse. The Duchesse d'Angoulême treats the wives of Napoléon's marshals and generals like cockroaches, and she was even worse with Madame Cappello because of . . . well, you know. But it wasn't just that. *Madame* was furious because of what Marie-Thérèse was doing to France—how she was bringing back the power of the Church and trying to make it so the nobles won't have to pay taxes again. Everything the Revolution fought for, Marie-Thérèse wants to destroy."

"Did Madame Cappello have a recent confrontation with the Duchess?"

Claudine came to sit down again and put the babe to her breast. "Recent? No. How could she have? She was gone."

"True," said Hero.

She was silent for a moment, searching for a delicate way to phrase her next question. But then Claudine herself said, "I know *madame* has long been troubled by her falling-out with her former ward, Angélique." The word the Frenchwoman used was *éloignement*—estrangement. "She blamed Angélique's husband, Antoine de Longchamps-Montendre."

"I've heard he's an Orléanist," said Hero. "Is that true?"

"*Bien sûr.* It's not as if he makes a secret of it. He's quite open about it, you know."

"What about Hortense Bonaparte?"

Claudine fell silent, her gaze on the suckling babe. "You've heard they're saying he's landed near Antibes? Napoléon, I mean."

"Yes," said Hero.

Claudine looked up, her eyes surprisingly shrewd. The woman might be poor and ground down by childbearing and despair, but she was not stupid. "You think that's what this might all be about? The death of *madame* and my Francine, I mean. You think it has something to do with Napoléon's return?"

Hero met her gaze squarely. "I honestly don't know. It's possible."

Claudine nodded and turned her head to stare into the fire. "Hortense is a Bonapartist, of course. But then, how could she not be? They say her new lover is a Corsican—a relative of Napoléon's mother. But that's all I know."

"Can you think of anything—anything at all—that might help us find Francine's killer?"

Claudine's face grew pinched, as if she were holding back tears. "She was my firstborn, you know. I've birthed ten children and I'd buried three before I lost Francine. But I never thought I'd be burying her. She was always so healthy—healthy and strong. I still can't believe she's gone. I keep expecting her to walk back in that door, laughing and chattering in that way she had and bringing us presents from *Dama* Cappello."

"She did that? *Dama* Cappello, I mean. She sent you gifts?"

"Oh, yes. All the time. She was a good mistress to my Francine. Believe me, if I knew anything that could help you and the *vicomte* find who killed them, I'd tell you. But I can't think of anything."

"I'm sorry I've had to ask you to talk about something I know is so painful for you," said Hero quietly.

"No, no. In truth, I am glad to know someone is looking into what happened. Someone . . . independent," she said in a way that told Hero that Sebastian was right to suspect the family of not entirely trusting Vidocq.

It was later, when Hero was leaving, that Claudine suddenly said, "There is one other person I know *Dama* Cappello quarreled with." Her brows drew together in thought. "I don't know his name, but he's mad about roses. He was originally from Corsica, and Napoléon made him a count."

Hero turned on the stoop to look back at her. "You mean the Count of Cargèse?"

"Yes, that's it. Francine told me he was mixed up with Fouché and the spies Bonaparte had in Britain—that they used to send their reports with his shipments of roses. Plants were allowed to pass freely during the war, you know. It was all in the interest of science, they said. But it wasn't only plants going back and forth across the Channel."

Hero stared at her. She was only too familiar with Joseph Fouché, the ruthless, bloodthirsty former Jacobin who'd risen to become Napoléon's feared Minister of Police. For years he'd controlled a network of spies and informants that was said to rival Jarvis's own.

"Is that why Napoléon made Cargèse a count?" she said.

A ghost of a smile touched the woman's lips. "Why do you think, hmm? You think it was because the Emperor likes roses?"

Chapter 39

*P*ierre-Joseph Redouté was painting the plum blossoms in Sophie's garden when Hero walked up to him. The afternoon sky was growing increasingly gray, with a blustery breeze that lifted the branches of the trees against the tumbling clouds. At her approach, he looked over at her and smiled. "And so we meet again," he said. "Not so nice today, is it?"

She brought up a hand to catch the wind-buffeted brim of her straw hat. "No, indeed."

The painter sighed. "Unfortunately the blossoms are a fleeting delight. One hard rain or too much of this wind, and they will be gone."

"Until next year," she said. *Just like the violets.*

His eyes crinkled. "Until next year." He focused for a moment on his work, then said, "I take it you've sought me out for a reason?"

Hero was wearing a navy velvet spencer over her muslin walking dress, but the temperature was dropping rapidly and she hugged her arms across her chest for warmth. "I'm told that roses and other plant samples were allowed to pass freely back and forth across the Channel during the war. Is that true?"

"They were, yes. Both governments agreed it was important that the war not be allowed to interfere with science. A rare instance of cooperation in a world otherwise run mad."

"I'm also told that Napoléon's spies in England used to send their reports to Paris with the roses, and that the Count of Cargèse was somehow involved. Do you know anything about that?"

Redouté's lips parted as he drew a quick breath. He was no longer smiling. "Are you asking as your husband's wife or as your father's daughter?"

"I am asking as myself. My father has returned to London, and I can assure you that you need have no fear of my passing on anything you tell me, either to him or to anyone else connected to the British government."

Redouté added a touch of blue to his brush. "Me, I'm just a painter. But if I were a wartime spy looking for a way to get my reports back to France, I think those rose shipments would have come in very handy." He glanced over at her. "What does this have to do with Sophia Cappello's death?"

"I don't know that it has anything to do with it."

He nodded and returned to his painting. "There was a man at one of the large nurseries in London—Kellogg was his name. As soon as the war ended, he left London and came over here to work for Joséphine."

"I understand Hortense and her brother have dismissed most of their mother's gardeners."

"Yes, it's shocking the way they've let the place go to ruin in just a year. I don't understand how anyone could allow that to happen."

"Hortense says her mother left massive debts."

"Oh, yes, Joséphine was a terrible spendthrift. Napoléon was always complaining about it."

"So, is this Kellogg still at Malmaison?"

Redouté studied the row of wind-tossed plum trees with narrowed eyes. "I'm afraid not."

"Do you know where he works now?"

A shadow drifted across his face, and he gave a quick shake of his head. "He was found dead a few weeks ago."

"Dead? How was he killed?"

"Someone hit him in the back of the head—bashed in his skull."

Hero felt a shiver run up her spine, and she hugged her arms tighter across her chest. "Was the killer ever found?"

"Not to my knowledge, no."

"And was he still at Malmaison when he died?"

"No, I believe he went to work at the Château de Marigny some four or five months ago."

"De Marigny?" said Hero.

Redouté looked over at her, his face flat and carefully emptied of all trace of emotion. "The Count of Cargèse's estate near Montmartre."

Before she left Sophie's house, Hero walked through the shadowy rooms of the elegant little château. She could hear the growing wind buffeting the sturdy walls of the house, feel the energy of the storm coming in as she went to stand before the library fireplace, her head tipping back as she stared up at the portrait of the man who had been Sophie's lover.

The man who might or might not be Devlin's father.

Taking off her straw hat, she studied the features that seemed so familiar—the hard yellow eyes; the sharp, high cheekbones; the unexpectedly sensitive mouth. *Is it just a coincidence?* she silently asked that painted image. *Is it just a coincidence that you look so much like him? Or are you indeed his father?*

She became aware of footsteps crossing the entry hall behind her and turned to find Geneviève Dion standing in the doorway, watching her.

Hero nodded toward the portrait of the general. "What manner of man is he?"

"The *maréchal?*" The chatelaine came to stand beside her, her gaze, like Hero's, on the painting above the fireplace. "How does one reduce a man to a few words? He is brilliant but good-humored . . . noble but quick-tempered and hardheaded . . . cynical and yet somehow also idealistic. And deadly when he needs to be."

Like Devlin, thought Hero, although she didn't say it. "What do you know of his family?"

Madame Dion shrugged. "Little, really, beyond the fact his father came here after Culloden."

"Does he have siblings?"

"I don't believe so, no."

"What about his mother? Was she Scottish, as well?"

She shook her head. "*Non*. I believe she was Welsh."

"Welsh?" Hero felt her pulse quicken. Patrick's father, Jamie Knox, had come from a Shropshire village not far from the Welsh border.

"Mmm. But I could have that wrong."

"Do you know if McClellan was ever in Britain?"

"I don't know, *non*. But I do know that he fought in America, with Lafayette."

"Ah," said Hero softly.

She had read enough about the French involvement in the American War to know that Lafayette had returned to Paris from America in 1782—which would have been too late for anyone who'd sailed with him to have traveled to England and sired Sebastian. *So it's just a coincidence that he has those strange yellow eyes*, she thought, conscious of an odd combination of relief and disappointment.

She was aware of the chatelaine watching her and said, "So he was with Lafayette at Yorktown."

Madame Dion shook her head. "*Ah, non*, not then. He went with the Marquis on his *first* voyage to America, not the second."

"I didn't realize there were two voyages. When was the first?"

"Several years before."

"Oh," said Hero, her voice sounding hollow even to her own ears. "So if he didn't return to America with Lafayette, then where did he go?"

"That I don't know. It was long before I knew Madame Cappello." She hesitated a moment, then said, "You've heard about Napoléon?"

"Yes." Hero found her gaze returning, once again, to the *maréchal*. "What do you think McClellan will do?" she asked the chatelaine. "Stay loyal to the King? Or honor his previous oath to the Emperor?"

Geneviève Dion turned her head to stare out the window at the wind-swirled clouds, her features drawn and troubled. "It's a terrible choice to force upon an honorable man, isn't it? A terrible choice."

Chapter 40

*N*iccolò Aravena, the Count of Cargèse, was humming softly to himself as he inspected a flat of rose seedlings in one of the Château de Marigny's greenhouses. He wore rough canvas trousers and an old stained coat; his face was unshaven, and he had a black kerchief tied at the open neck of his rugged shirt. Anyone who didn't know better would have mistaken him for one of his own gardeners going about his work. He glanced up, saw Sebastian walking toward him between the rows of raised wooden flats, then went back to what he was doing.

"I take it you've heard about Napoléon?" said the Corsican without looking up again.

Sebastian paused nearby. "I have."

"And now you're thinking it must have something to do with Sophia Cappello's murder? Is that it?"

"You don't?"

Cargèse jotted down an observation in the notebook he carried. "I don't know what to think."

"But you knew that Bonaparte was planning to return."

A wry smile twisted the man's lips. "And if I said no, would you believe me?"

"No."

Cargèse huffed a soft laugh. "So here we are."

Sebastian breathed in the warm, humid air as he let his gaze wander
over the rows of raised platforms. "We've been hearing some interesting
tales about how reports from Napoléon's spies used to be smuggled out
of England with your rose shipments."

The Count shrugged. "We were at war. When it comes to war, we
all do what we must, eh? You slaughtered the sons of poor farmers and
sans-culottes on the battlefield, while I helped pass information with roses.
I've done nothing of which I'm ashamed. Can you say the same?"

Sebastian stared out the open doors of the greenhouse to where a
workman was shoveling manure from a cart onto an enormous pile. Could
he say the same?

No.

He brought his gaze back to the rosarian's pockmarked, beard-
stubbled face. "Tell me about the British gardener named Kellogg—the
one who was at Malmaison before he came to work for you."

Cargèse made another notation in his book. "You mean the one who
got his head bashed in a few weeks ago?"

"Yes, that one."

"What is there to tell? He was a good rosarian, but not so good an
Englishman, hmm? Obviously not many around here would hold that
against him, but he also had a bad habit of drinking too much *vino* and
picking fights. I assume someone must have grown weary of his belliger-
ence and put an end to it."

"And that's all there is to it?"

The Corsican shifted to the next row of seedbeds. "What do you
think? That his death is somehow linked to what happened to *Dama*
Cappello? Because if it is, I don't know about it. I know nothing about

the deaths of either Kellogg or *Dama* Cappello, and nothing about Bonaparte's return. Why would I?"

"Napoléon made you a count for your services."

Cargèse grinned. "He did, yes. But of what use would I be to him when he was in Elba? I ship roses from England, not Elba."

"In my experience, people involved in intrigue rarely completely retire."

"Yes? Well, perhaps you have more experience in such things than I. Or so I hear."

"And where did you happen to hear that?"

The Corsican shrugged again. "I hear things now and then." He paused, then added deliberately, "For instance, I heard something just yesterday you might be interested in."

Sebastian was beginning to find the man tiresome. "Oh? What's that?"

"I was talking to one of the few gardeners who are left out at Malmaison, a fellow by the name of Gaston. He's getting on in years, Gaston. I don't suppose he can do much around the place anymore, so it says something for that *putain* Hortense that she keeps him on. Anyway, he was telling me about how Sophia Cappello was just there—last Thursday, to be precise."

Sebastian stared at him. "You're saying she was at Malmaison? *On Thursday?*"

Cargèse bounced his heavy eyebrows up and down. "Mmm."

"What would she have been doing there?"

He gave a very Italian shrug and turned to run his gaze over the rows of seedlings. "I've no idea, but that's what the man said. One assumes she stopped there on her way back to Paris that day, yes?"

"Malmaison would not have been on her way back to Paris."

"No? Then she must have gone out of her way to get there." The Corsican looked up and drew back his lips in a smile that showed his tobacco-stained teeth. "Which makes it even more interesting, hmmm?"

❧

Sebastian arrived back at the Place Dauphine to find a small, slightly built gentleman in an elegant black greatcoat, an intricately tied snowy white cravat, and an expensive beaver hat standing beneath the trees in the square. He looked to be somewhere in his fifties, with a long, narrow face, an aquiline nose, and straight dark brows that contrasted sharply with the silver white of his hair. His flesh was pale, almost pasty; his thin, tightly held lips bloodless; his cheeks sunken. His piercing blue-gray eyes, as he walked toward Sebastian, held a faint smile that was utterly bone-chilling.

"*Bonsoir, monsieur le vicomte,*" said the man as Sebastian turned from his door to face him.

"Do I know you?"

"I think not." The man let his head fall back, his gaze drifting over the upper windows of the narrow old house in a way Sebastian did not like. "But I know your father—and your father-in-law, of course. Perhaps you have heard them speak of me? I am the Duke of Otranto."

Somehow, Sebastian kept his reaction off his face. The lofty title was a new one, bestowed by Napoléon. The man was better known by the name he'd been given at birth, a name generally spoken only in hushed, frightened whispers: Joseph Fouché.

Born into a middling family in Nantes, he'd risen quickly in the tumult of the Revolution to become one of the principal Jacobins. Although educated by the Jesuits, he'd taken the lead in the movement to ransack the nation's churches and strip them of their valuables. But it was as the Butcher of Lyon that he'd first become truly infamous. Sent to the city to put down resistance there, he'd engaged in such an orgy of brutal slaughter that even Robespierre was sickened.

Fouché responded by helping to overthrow him.

Landing always on his feet, Fouché somehow emerged from the fall of the Jacobins to become Minister of Police under first the Directory, then the Consulate, and finally the Empire. It was a position he'd used to create a formidable network of spies and informants, and he'd made himself so powerful that even Napoléon was said to have feared him. Now, according to some reports, Fouché was on the verge of once again being made Minister of Police, this time by King Louis XVIII. He was, thought Sebastian, a mirror image of Marie-Thérèse's *huissier du cabinet*—one was fanatically religious, the other out only for himself, but both were ruthless and cruel and very, very dangerous.

"You wished to speak to me?" said Sebastian.

"Only briefly. I am told your father leaves for London this Friday."

"And?"

A faint, frosty smile curled the man's thin lips. "Let's just say you would be wise to leave with him."

"Oh? Why is that?"

"Things are about to become . . . uncomfortable in Paris."

"How . . . generous of you to take the time to . . . warn me."

The unpleasant eyes narrowed. "You mock me?"

"No. Although I can't help but wonder why you felt the need to deliver your message in person."

"I think you know why," said Fouché, and turned to walk away to where a magnificent barouche and team awaited him on the far side of the square.

Sebastian was still standing there, watching him drive away, when Hero's carriage pulled up before the house.

"Who was that?" she asked when he went to help her down, her gaze on the departing barouche.

"Fouché."

He saw her lips part. "*Fouché?* Dear Lord. What was he doing here?"

"I could be wrong, but I think he was sizing me up."

"Why?"

"I have no idea. But it's worrisome."

That night Sebastian dreamt of his mother as she was in his memories—
young and gay and laughing in the golden English sunshine. In his dream
she walked through a rose garden surrounded by a high brick wall. The
sky above arced a clear, sparkling blue, the air was fresh and clean and
faintly scented with mint, the wind sighing through gently swaying leafy
trees, echoing with joyous birdsong. Then the sky darkened in that way
of dreams, became instantly filled with lightning-split, threatening black
clouds that tumbled and swirled with tortuous menace.

His mother was no longer laughing. She was running, her face a
white mask of fear, and he watched her throw a quick glance over her
shoulder at whoever—or whatever—was chasing her.

"No!" he screamed. He tried to run toward her, to save her, but his
limbs were heavy, paralyzed. He could not move.

"No!" he screamed again as he saw her whirl—

"Shh," Hero whispered, her breath warm against his cheek, her hand
solid and reassuringly real on his chest. "It's just a dream."

He sucked in a deep, jerking breath and opened his eyes, blinking
at the shadowy room around him, momentarily disoriented, his heart
pounding. Turning his head, he met Hero's dark gaze.

"Sorry if I woke you," he said, reaching for her.

She came into his arms, her body soft and warm and smelling sweetly
of lavender and the night and herself. He hauled her up so that she lay
upon him, her weight braced on her forearms as she arched her back to
look down at him. For a moment she gazed into his face, and he wondered what she saw there because as he watched, her brows drew together
in a frown.

She dipped her head, her lips finding his in a kiss that began as something comforting, then caught fire.

He ran his hands up her back, entwined his fingers in her dark tum-
ble of hair, holding her head steady as he deepened the kiss. He drank

her in, felt himself fill with her love and tenderness and want. With murmured urgency, she shifted to take him inside her. He held her to him,
moved with her, let her whirl him away to a place where there was only
exquisite sensation and glorious pleasure and love, so much love.

But afterward, as she lay beside him in his arms and he listened to
her breathing ease as she drifted back to sleep, memories of the dream
returned. . . .

The dream and the sense of helplessness and impending failure that
it had provoked.

Chapter 41

Wednesday, 8 *March*

$\mathscr{T}$he next morning Sebastian drove out to the rue du Champs du Re-pos. He wanted to ask Sophie's coachman if they had indeed returned to Paris via Malmaison, and if so, why the hell he hadn't seen fit to tell Sebastian about it.

The day had dawned cloudy, blustery, and cold, more like winter than the last few balmy, springlike days they had so briefly enjoyed. He found the *hôtel particulier* looking joyless in the flat white light, its court-yard littered with browning blossoms blown from the fruit trees in the orchard.

A tall, gangly young stable boy was pushing a wheelbarrow piled with fouled straw through the stable doors when Sebastian drew up and handed the curricle's reins to Tom. "You're Léon, aren't you?" said Sebas-tian, hopping down.

"*Oui, monsieur,*" said the boy, his ears red from the cold, his face tense and anxious, as if he were wondering what he'd done to be singled out like this.

"I'm looking for the coachman. Do you know where he is?"

"Noël?" Léon set down the barrow and swiped the sleeve of his coat across his runny nose. "He took off when we heard about what happened to Francine."

Sebastian felt the wind gust cold and damp against his face. "Do you know why?"

"He said he wasn't gonna wait around for somebody to do to him what they did to her."

"He was afraid?"

The boy shrugged his shoulders. "Guess he was."

"Do you know why?"

The boy stared at Sebastian wide-eyed. "*Non, monsieur.*"

Sebastian wasn't convinced the lad was as ignorant as he claimed, but nodded across the courtyard to the silent house. "What about the footman *madame* had with her on her trip—Guillaume, wasn't it? Is he around?"

"*Non, monsieur.* He took off, too."

Damn. Sebastian studied the stable boy's silent, watchful face. "You wouldn't happen to know if *Dama* Cappello stopped at Malmaison on her way back from the south of France, would you?"

To his surprise, the boy nodded. "*Oui, monsieur.* I heard Noël talking to one of the gardeners about it, telling him how changed the place is these days."

"Did he happen to mention why they were there?"

"I don't think he knew, *monsieur.* Pierre—that's the gardener—asked him that, but he said he couldn't figure it out. Said there's hardly anyone there anymore, just the housekeeper and a maid and a few groundsmen. Everything in the château has either been sold or is under holland covers, and the gardens are a ruin."

"So what did *madame* do while she was there?"

"Noël said she went into the house, but came out again just a few minutes later. And then they left. That's it."

"Was she carrying anything with her?"

"Not that he mentioned, *monsieur.*"

A hawk circled low over the nearby fields, its dark wings silhouetted sharply against the heavy white clouds. Sebastian watched it for a moment, thoughtful. "Where would Noël go if he wanted to hide?"

"I don't know, *monsieur.* Always kept pretty much to himself, Noël. He's not one to sit around the table in the servants' hall and talk."

"What about the footman?"

"Guillaume? He said he was going back to Poitou. That's where he's from, you know—Poitiers. He and another of the footmen left together. Their fathers are both tailors there."

"They must have been frightened, indeed."

The boy's worried dark eyes looked directly into Sebastian's. "Reckon they were."

Chapter 42

Shortly after Devlin left for the rue du Champs du Repos, Hero and Claire bundled up the two boys and took them to the weekly market that sprawled along the quai de l'École on the Right Bank.

Beneath the heavily overcast sky, the waters of the Seine looked gray and choppy, the wind kicking up a fine spray that filled the air with the smell of the river. This was a street market devoted to all manner of fine used goods, with everything from massive, fancifully carved Renaissance-era chests to delicate porcelains and the gilt-framed, centuries-old portraits of someone's illustrious ancestors. Many of the objects had at one time been looted from the homes of aristocrats, and Hero spotted several returned émigrés, pomanders held to their delicate nostrils, walking up and down the rows of stalls in the hopes of spotting some long-lost prized possession.

"A part of me finds it sad to see them here, knowing the pain they must feel at having lost so much that was dear to them," said Claire as they watched an elderly woman in a puce velvet pelisse with a sable collar disentangle an ormolu clock from a pile of architectural fragments. "But then I remember what France was like before the Revolution, the way they used to dash through the streets in their gilded carriages without a thought to the poor people they so often killed or maimed with impunity. The way they dressed in silks and velvets and wore diamond buckles on their shoes while tens of thousands of women and children starved to death. And I think, *They could have done something to avert it all.* They could have, except they were too selfish to share any of their massive wealth and power, and too arrogant to believe the people could ever rise up and take it from them. And because of their hubris and their greed, millions died. Millions."

Hero studied Claire's pinched, sad face. She knew some of the Frenchwoman's story—knew about the husband and children she'd buried. But there was much she didn't know, much that Claire never talked about—and probably never would. "I suppose they thought it was their due," said Hero. "And so they took it all for granted. It never occurred to them that it could end—and end so horribly."

"And they've learned nothing," said Claire, watching a middle-aged exquisite in a caped greatcoat and gleaming top boots kick at a ragged little boy who stumbled before him. "Learned nothing and forgotten nothing."

"*Top!*" said Simon, one hand reaching toward a stall selling wooden toys. "Red top!"

Hero and Claire looked at each other and smiled.

"You like that, sweetheart?" said Hero, balancing him on her hip as they turned toward the stall.

"I like tops," he said, "and horses."

It was when Hero was studying the stall's array of gaily painted wooden horses that she felt it again—that intense awareness of being watched. Of being watched by someone who did not wish her well.

She turned, her gaze sweeping the crowded stalls hung with colorful banners that flapped in the wind, the street sellers of pastries and coffee and hot chocolate, the mimes and acrobats and strolling musicians. The sandy-haired hunchbacked poodle trimmer with his box and clippers.

Hero felt her breath back up in her throat as she recognized him. She hadn't seen him at the parvis de Notre Dame the first time she'd had that sense of being watched. But he'd been there later, near the *pompes funèbres*, when she felt it again. She told herself it didn't necessarily mean anything. The quai de l'École ran from behind the Louvre to the Pont Neuf; it was logical that such a man would tend to ply his trade in the same general area. She understood that. And yet . . .

"I think we should go," she said to Claire, keeping her voice low.

The Frenchwoman had been holding Patrick up so that he could watch a dancing monkey. But at Hero's words, she turned, the laughter dying on her lips when she saw Hero's face. "Something's wrong; what is it?"

Hero shook her head. "I don't know, but I feel—"

She broke off as a huge, beefy man dressed in the rough smock of a bricklayer plowed into her hard enough to send her staggering into the stall beside them. She had a brief glimpse of beady brown eyes and a full-cheeked, ruddy face. Then he snatched Patrick from Claire's arms and ran.

"*Patrick!*" screamed Claire.

"Oh, my God," whispered Hero, her heart pounding as her breath came hard and fast. "Here, hold Simon." She thrust the little boy into the Frenchwoman's arms, grasped fistfuls of her skirts in both hands, and tore after the screaming child and the man running away with him. "*Stop him!*"

"*Mama!*" cried Patrick, his hands reaching out to her over the meaty shoulders of the bricklayer.

The little boy had never called her that before, and Hero felt as if her heart were being torn open. "*Stop that man!*" she shouted in French, dodging startled shoppers and staring stallkeepers and a braying donkey that kicked out as she ran past. "He's stealing my child!"

Careening sideways into a juggler, the bricklayer sent the man's balls flying through the scattering crowd of onlookers, then darted out into the traffic backed up on the quay at the entrance to the Pont Neuf.

"Patrick!" screamed Hero as a horse reared up between the poles of a shabby gig, its hooves flashing and nostrils flaring.

"*Salaud!*" swore the gig's driver, cracking his whip.

"Stop him!" Hero shouted again, then felt herself jerked back as someone grabbed her arm and yanked hard enough to swing her around.

The poodle clipper's sharp-featured, grimly smiling face swam before her. He stood perfectly upright, the padding he'd used to simulate his hump hanging off to the side.

"Let me go, you bloody bastard," she swore in English.

Reaching out, she snatched a rusty old iron from the jumble of metal on the stall beside her and swung it with all her strength into his face. She heard bone and cartilage smash, felt the hot spurt of his blood across her cheek. The poodle trimmer staggered back, his nose and mouth a blood-smeared mess. She threw the iron at his head and whirled around to sprint across the bridgehead.

"Stop that man!" she screamed again, dodging a ratty old *fiacre* and a fine barouche. *"He's stealing my child."*

A tall, elderly gentleman with an umbrella made a halfhearted attempt to whack the running man's legs with the tip of his umbrella, but the bricklayer swerved easily out of his way, then grabbed a potted geranium and threw it at the old man's head.

They were on the quai de la Mégisserie now, that stretch of the riverbank devoted to the sale of plants and flowers as well as birds, fish, and other animals. Holding the screaming, thrashing child to him with one hand as he ran, the bricklayer grasped first a birdcage, then a fishbowl, then a heavy spiked dog collar to send them flying behind him.

"*Madame,*" shouted an indignant nurseryman as Hero streamed past him, her skirts lifted up above her flashing knees, her breath coming in panting gasps. Her hat was gone, her hair hanging around her face in sweaty clumps, her fine paisley shawl slipping off her shoulders to trail behind her in the breeze.

There was a row of *bateaux-lavoirs*, or laundry barges, tied up along the quay here, and Hero saw the bricklayer swerve toward them. *"Stop him,"* she shouted as he dashed past a staring footman to clamber down a rickety set of wooden steps and scramble across the pontoons that lashed one of the barges to the bank.

The laundry barges, like the bath barges, were a peculiar feature of Paris, for the city had long lacked an adequate supply of water to its neighborhoods. Banished from the quay beside the Louvre, they had retreated here, a row of ancient, rickety flat-bottomed boats with tattered canvas awnings that sheltered a string of boiling vats and scrubbing ponds crowded with the washerwomen who daily lugged old wicker baskets overflowing with the vast city's soiled laundry down to the river.

Slipping and sliding on the wet, mossy wood, Hero tore after the bricklayer.

"Merde, que faites-vous?" and *"Casse-toi!"* cried the wet, aproned laundresses on the barge as the bricklayer charged through them, tripping over piles of wet shirts, snagging his rough boots in a sheet, the air filling with the sound of ripping cloth and outraged shrieks and the smell of soap and lye. Scrambling and swearing, he shoved his way to the far end of the boat, one angry arm sweeping a slow-moving laundress out of his way. Teetering, arms windmilling, she tumbled into the water, her shrieks mingling with the other women's angry shouts and cries.

Ignoring them, the bricklayer clambered up onto the barge's low railing. Patrick screamed and squirmed in his arms.

"No!" shouted Hero.

Brutally pushing her way through the milling crowd of screeching washerwomen, she lunged forward to wrench the boy from the bricklayer's grasp just as he leapt into the choppy gray river.

His head and shoulders reappeared almost immediately. Hero saw him shake his head, flinging water and streaming dark hair from his eyes as his gaze met hers for one intense moment. Then he turned and struck out toward the bank with strong, sure strokes.

"Mama!" screamed Patrick.

"Oh, Patrick."

Trembling with exhaustion and the afterwash of terror, Hero sank to her knees on the wet, filthy deck of the barge, the little boy clutched in her arms. The wind lifting off the water felt suddenly cold against her wet cheeks.

"I have you, darling," she kept saying over and over, her breath coming in painful gasps as she desperately hugged his small, shaking body to her, and he wrapped his arms around her neck to bury his tear-streaked face in her hair. "It's all right; I have you, and I'm never, ever going to let anyone hurt you."

Chapter 43

*N*ot good, this," said Eugène-François Vidocq, shaking his head. They were in the salon of the house on the Place Dauphine, Sebastian standing beside the fire while the policeman lolled in a chair near the front window and sipped a glass of Sebastian's port. "Why would someone want to steal one of your children?"

"You tell me," said Sebastian, his voice rough with a powerful combination of fear and rage. Patrick wasn't technically his own child, of course. But the boy looked enough like Sebastian that people tended to assume he was, and his affection for the child was obvious. "This is your city, not mine."

Vidocq shook his head again. "You've obviously made some dangerous enemies, *monsieur*."

"So why not come after me directly, the way they did at Montmartre? Why target my wife and children?"

"Could be revenge," mused Vidocq. "Someone nasty enough to want to take one of your children and watch you suffer rather than simply kill you outright. Or the idea could have been to seize your son in order to exchange him for something."

Sebastian looked over at him. "Something such as the Charlemagne Talisman, you mean?"

Vidocq paused with his glass halfway to his lips and stared at Sebastian with one eyebrow raised. "The what?"

"The Charlemagne Talisman. It's what was in the jeweled red leather case you recovered from the rue de Rivoli pawnshop. And now it's missing." He gave the head of the *Sûreté nationale* a brief description of the amulet and its history.

"You think that's what whoever came after your family wants?" Vidocq pursed his lips, opened his eyes wide, and rocked his head back and forth. "I suppose it's possible."

"Except that I don't have it."

"Perhaps someone thinks that with enough motivation you could find it."

"As if catching my mother's murderer weren't motivation enough?"

"Ah, but they don't know she's your mother, do they?"

Sebastian grunted and went to pour himself a brandy. "Still no luck finding the *fiacre* driver from that night?" he asked, glancing back at Vidocq.

The policeman's broad, scarred face took on a pained expression. "*Non.* And I don't understand why something that should be so simple is proving to be so difficult. I would have said it's impossible that we should not have found him by now. How does one explain it?" He took a slurping sip of his port. "I've no idea."

"And the *fille publique?*"

The ex-*gallerian* let out a heavy sigh. "Alas, she too remains elusive. You haven't by chance seen her hanging around again?"

"No." Sebastian was always looking, everywhere he went. But in a city the size of Paris, the odds of his finding her were slim.

Vidocq drained his glass and set it aside. "I hear Napoléon marches onward with not a shot being fired. They say the soldiers sent to stop him are simply tearing off their white cockades and joining him."

"Where did you hear that?"

Vidocq laughed. "Not from the palace."

"Do you think he'll reach Paris?"

Vidocq met his gaze. "You want the truth?"

"Yes."

The policeman brought up a hand to pluck thoughtfully at one earlobe with his thumb and forefinger. "I think the people of France are torn. They accepted the return of the King as the price of peace. They were tired of conscription, tired of losing their sons and brothers, husbands and fathers, to war. But the last ten or eleven months have reminded many of why they hated the Bourbons in the first place. They resent the favors being heaped upon the returned émigrés and the scornful disrespect shown by Marie-Thérèse and her women toward the wives of French heroes such as Jourdan and Ney. They miss the tricolor and the old days of French *gloire*. Nostalgia is a powerful drug—as is wounded pride. Will Napoléon prevail in the end? Who knows? But I think the Bourbons underestimate the attraction of everything he represents." He pushed to his feet with a grunt. "There. You asked for my honest opinion, and I have given it."

Sebastian met the Frenchman's hard gaze. "Thank you."

Vidocq nodded and turned toward the door. "Good day to you, *monsieur*. I'd say I wish you luck, but I think we're all going to need it now."

After Vidocq had gone, Sebastian went to the dining room, where Hero sat at the table quietly cleaning the brass-mounted muff pistol her father had once given her. Later, he knew, she would tuck it into her reticule to carry it with her, loaded. She would not be taken by surprise again.

"Vidocq's thoughts on Napoléon are interesting," she said without looking up from her task.

Sebastian let his gaze drift over the strong features of her face—the square jaw, the aquiline nose that was so much like Jarvis's, the fierce gray eyes that glowed with an uncanny intelligence. He was still shaking from what had happened today, terrified by how close they had come to losing Patrick, and furious with himself for not being there to help save him.

"I'm wondering if we're making a mistake," he said, "if perhaps you and the children should go with Hendon when he leaves this Friday."

She looked up then. "Is that what you want?"

"No. But I'm worried about you."

"And if the children and I leave, would you still stay?"

He met her gaze and held it. "You know I must."

She nodded. She knew this about him—knew that he would never rest until he found his mother's killer. She said, "I don't like the idea of running away simply because someone attacked us. And I don't think . . ." She paused as if searching for a way to put her thoughts into words. "I don't think that under the circumstances it would be good for you to stay here alone."

"What does that mean?"

She met his gaze. "You know."

He reached out to caress her cheek. "You're not afraid?"

"Of Napoléon? No."

"And the mood on the streets?"

"That might be more problematic. But I'm not going to let some humpbacked poodle clipper and overgrown bricklayer chase me away. And I'm not leaving you here to do this by yourself."

"We could send the boys with Claire."

He saw her lips part, her brows contract in a quick frown. She had never been one of those aristocratic women who relegated all care of her children to nursemaids. "I honestly don't know if I could do that. But . . ." She sucked in a deep breath, let it out slowly. "Let me think about it."

He nodded, then turned as the sound of childish laughter on the stairs heralded the arrival of Claire and the boys. And it came to him, as he watched Hero set aside the small flintlock to step forward and sweep both children up into her arms, that she might not be afraid, but he was.

He was terrified of losing all three of them.

Chapter 44

Thursday, 9 March

ᚆendon arrived at the Place Dauphine early the next morning, while they were still at breakfast. He tossed his hat onto a nearby chair and sat down heavily, his face grim.

"You'll have something to eat?" said Hero, reaching out with one hand to stop Simon from pouring more sugar into Patrick's porridge. Most families of their station left their children's breakfast to the nursery staff, but Hero and Sebastian had long ago decided such families were missing out on far too much of their children's lives.

The Earl shook his head. "Just tea, thank you."

Sebastian poured him a cup. "I take it you've heard something?"

Hendon let out his breath in a long, heavy sigh. "A message arrived this morning from the King's commander at Grenoble. The man's a loyal monarchist, and he sent the entire Fifth Regiment to stop Bonaparte at the Laffrey Defile. It should have been easily accomplished—the men were drawn up in battle order, completely blocking the pass."

"But?" said Hero when Hendon paused.

He took his cup, then simply held it a moment, his jaw working back and forth in that way he had when he was thoughtful—or troubled. "Napoléon ordered his own troops to trail their muskets. Then he dismounted and simply walked toward the King's men on foot. He was wearing that familiar greatcoat of his—you know the gray one he always wore when he was campaigning? As he neared the King's regiment, he threw open his coat to bare his breast and shouted, 'Here is your Emperor! Kill him if you wish!'"

"My God," said Sebastian. "You have to admire the man's courage."

"Courage? He's mad! All it would have taken was one shot. One shot!"

"So what happened?" said Hero.

Hendon took a sip of his tea and grimaced. "The commanders ordered their men to fire. Instead, they threw down their guns, broke ranks, and surged forward shouting, 'Vive l'Empereur!'"

"They went over to him?"

Hendon nodded. "The entire regiment."

"And when he reached Grenoble?" said Sebastian.

"We don't know yet. He hadn't arrived there by the time the message was sent. The commander says he's confident the gunners on the city walls will fire. But it's still concerning."

Hero's gaze went to meet Sebastian's. He raised one eyebrow in silent inquiry, and she pressed her lips together and nodded.

He said to Hendon, "You're still leaving tomorrow?"

"I am, yes. Kitty Wellington is coming with me now, as well as Amanda." A faint smile lightened the tension in his face. "Three carriages and three baggage wagons, plus a troop of cavalry detailed to protect the ambassador's wife. We'll be quite the little cavalcade."

Sebastian hesitated a moment, then said, "If you're willing to add a fourth carriage to your party, we'd like to send Claire and the children with you—and possibly Hero's abigail and my tiger and valet, as well, unless they choose to stay."

"Of course I'm willing," said Hendon. Then he glanced at Hero. "You won't be coming, too?"

She said, "You think I should?"

To Sebastian's surprise, the Earl looked at him and said, "I take it you're determined to stay and continue your search for Sophie's killer?"

"I am, yes. But do you think Hero should go?"

Hendon considered it a moment, then gave a faint shake of his head. "No, I don't see why she would need to. This mad adventure of Bonaparte's can't possibly last much longer. Ney's army will stop him—there's no doubt of that. Some of the rank and file might be defecting, but the marshals are all standing firm. If Napoléon was counting on them to come flocking back to his standard, he was sadly mistaken. For all we know, Ney could have defeated him already."

"I hate not knowing what is happening *right now*," said Hero. "Everything we hear is already days old."

Hendon nodded. "Just imagine how much worse it would be without the semaphores." He gave a grim smile. "I have no doubt we'll hear soon enough that it's all over, and historians will laugh at us for taking this nonsense so seriously. But I'm more than happy to take the boys with me if you'd like. If by some freak chance the unthinkable should happen and you decide later that you must leave, it will be easier to arrange without the children—not that I think it will come to that."

He pushed to his feet. "And now I must get back to the Tuilleries. I'd like to leave by noon tomorrow, if their nursemaid can have the lads ready by then."

"They'll be ready," said Sebastian, rising with him.

After the Earl had gone, Sebastian looked at Hero and said, "I'm beginning to think perhaps you should go with him, too."

"No. I'm not leaving you here to deal with this alone."

"Then perhaps we should all go."

She reached out her hand to press her fingers to his lips. "No. You heard Hendon. This mad gamble of Napoléon's will soon be over. But if we leave now, we'll never find who killed Sophie. And I don't want to live with the knowledge that I let a bad case of the nerves stop us from bringing her killer to justice."

"And if the killer is Marie-Thérèse? Or even Hortense Bonaparte? How will they ever be brought to justice?"

Her face clouded in a way that told him this fear had already occurred to her, too. "Perhaps they can't be brought before a court of law," she said, "but they can be exposed for what they've done. And *we* will know. I'm not sure why that should feel so important, but it does."

Painfully aware of Simon and Patrick's looming departure, they devoted the day to the children: walking along the Seine in a fine mist; eating warm chocolate crepes purchased from a vendor who'd set up his stall in the shadow of Notre Dame; exploring the ancient winding streets of the Latin Quarter.

"I know it will only be for a few weeks," said Hero as they wandered the paths of the Luxembourg Gardens. "So why does even thinking about it hurt so much?"

Sebastian was silent for a moment as they watched the boys scramble over a ruined wall that had once been part of a vanished Carthusian monastery. "We can always change our minds. Keep them here."

"No," she said with a faint shake of her head. "I can't begin to explain it, and it almost embarrasses me to say this when everyone is so convinced Napoléon will be stopped, but . . . I have a bad feeling about this."

He reached out to take her hand in his and hold it tight. Then his gaze met hers, and what she saw there mirrored all her own unspoken thoughts and fears. "I know. So do I."

It was late in the afternoon, when Sebastian was off making final arrangements with Hendon, that Fanny Carpenter stopped by the Place

Dauphine. She perched on the edge of the tapestry-covered settee in the salon, her reticule gripped so tightly in her lap that her fingers turned white. "I'm hearing rumors that Kitty Wellington is leaving Paris tomorrow, along with the Earl of Hendon and Lady Wilcox. Please tell me it's all a hum."

"No, it's true," said Hero, settling into the armchair opposite her. "But Hendon's return to London has long been planned, and Amanda is going because she's recently learned her daughter is in the family way."

Fanny studied her quietly for a moment, her hazel eyes narrowed and shrewd. "Perhaps. But that doesn't explain Kitty Wellington. It's rather ominous when the British Ambassador's wife turns tail and runs, wouldn't you say?"

Hero paused while a maid brought in the tea tray, then said, "Has Colonel de Gautier heard something new?"

Fanny shook her head. "No. But then, Étienne is busy with the artillery; he doesn't hear much of the palace chatter." She hesitated, then added, "You knew Marie-Thérèse has left for Bordeaux?"

"I knew that was her intent, but I didn't know she'd actually gone, no. Surely her decision to go ahead with her tour can only mean the palace is not overly concerned about Napoléon."

"They say she is going to rally the troops."

"Ah." Privately, Hero suspected Marie-Thérèse's presence might not have the effect the palace was hoping for. But she kept that to herself. "I hadn't thought of that."

Fanny took the cup Hero handed her, then simply sat holding it in her lap. "There are even rumors that the King has asked Kitty Wellington to take the crown jewels with her."

Hero poured her own cup. "Oh, surely not. How can that be when the King is convinced Napoléon will be stopped before he gets much farther?" She set the teapot aside. "You've lived in Paris under Napoléon before. I would think his approach wouldn't worry you as much as it might some."

The Englishwoman met her gaze. "Étienne has now pledged his loyalty to the King."

"As has everyone from Marshal Ney to Jourdan," Hero said gently.

"Yes, I suppose," said Fanny. She hesitated a moment, then said, "Do you know, when I first heard Napoléon had landed near Antibes, I laughed. I actually *laughed*. It seemed such madness for him to think he could conquer France with fewer than a thousand men. They say he slept on the beach that night and started marching toward Paris in the morning. It sounds like something from a play at the Comédie-Française, does it not? And yet here we are a week later, and the British Ambassador's wife is fleeing Paris in terror."

"I suspect she'll feel very foolish in a month's time," said Hero.

Fanny gave her a trembling smile. "Perhaps you are right. For some reason I can't quite explain, Marie-Thérèse's departure threw me into something like a panic."

Hero took a slow sip of her tea and kept her voice casual. "Have you ever heard Marie-Thérèse mention the Charlemagne Talisman?"

"The Charlemagne Talisman?" Fanny was silent for a moment, her brows drawn together as if in thought. "I know she's been furious with the Bishop for giving it to Joséphine—she thinks it should by rights be hers. At one point she demanded Hortense return it, but Hortense claimed she didn't know what had happened to it. Why do you ask?"

"The talisman's empty case was found on the Pont Neuf the night Sophie was killed."

Fanny's eyes widened. "Good heavens. But . . . why?"

"We don't know."

Fanny set her cup in its saucer with a clatter. "You can't think *Marie-Thérèse* had something to do with what happened to Sophie?"

"No, not at all," Hero lied. "Devlin was simply wondering if anyone associated with the palace had recently expressed interest in the talisman."

"You're thinking Sophie's murder is somehow connected to Napoléon's return? Oh, surely not."

"Can you think of any other reason someone might have had to kill her?"

"No, but . . . why would Sophie have had the talisman in the first place? I always assumed Hortense was lying when she claimed she didn't have it."

"It is curious," said Hero, taking another sip of her tea. "You can't explain it?"

"No. I wish I could." Fanny fiddled with the handle of her own cup. "It's so bizarre, these endless changes in government the French have endured these last twenty-six years. Whatever else one might say about the British monarchy, at least it's stable."

"Well, except for the Civil War and the Glorious Revolution. And the sticky bits in 1715 and 1745."

Fanny's eyes crinkled with amusement. "Yes, I suppose that with the exception of the Civil War, the events of those years must have seemed far more dire to those who lived through them than they do to us now in retrospect. Who was it said that the periods of greatest happiness are the missing pages in our history books?"

"I don't know. But whoever it was, they knew what they were talking about."

Fanny set aside her cup and reached out to clasp one of Hero's hands in both of hers. "Thank you. You've made me feel better."

"Have I? Yet if you are truly concerned, perhaps you could go on a visit to your family in England. Just for a while."

A pinched look crept over the novelist's face, making her look both older and frailer than she was. "But Étienne couldn't come with me. And how could I leave without him? What if the worst were to happen so that I wouldn't be allowed back in again as an Englishwoman?"

"It would be a risk," said Hero. And she thought, *All over France, people are facing these same torn loyalties, these same painful and heartbreaking decisions. And for what?*

For what?

Devlin returned from seeing Hendon not long after the novelist's departure. He poured himself a glass of brandy, then went to stand at the arched window, looking out at the square as the light faded from the day. "So many innocent lives being disrupted," he said after a moment, echoing Hero's own thoughts. "All over France. Again."

Hero rattled the cups in their saucers as she stacked them back on the tray. "All because the Bourbons believe they have a divine right to rule France and because Napoléon was bored on his little island."

He looked over at her. "Why do you think Fanny came?"

"She's afraid, and she was hoping that thanks to Hendon we might know more than she does. It's the inevitable result of the King's decision to hide the truth about Napoléon's landing for those two days, isn't it? Now no one believes anything coming out of the palace. And who can blame them?"

"Not I."

"No."

She came up beside him, and they watched in silence as the lamplighter worked his way around the square. Unlike in London, where lamplighters had to use a ladder to reach the streetlamps, Parisian lamps were suspended by a cord that allowed them to be lowered and raised.

After a moment, she said, "Once Hendon leaves, how will *we* know what's actually happening?"

"Vidocq?"

She looked over at him. "You trust him, a former brigand and galley slave?"

"About everything? No. But in this?" He reached out to draw her to him and hold her close. "Perhaps," he said, pressing his cheek against her hair.

Then he added, "At least for now."

Chapter 45

*H*endon's plans to leave Paris by noon proved optimistic. Both Kitty Wellington and Amanda were still packing hours after the scheduled departure time, so it was closer to six before the long line of carriages, carts, baggage wagons, and armed escort was ready to roll.

Hero's abigail, Molly, had opted to return to London and was anxious to get away. But Tom and Jules Calhoun, Sebastian's valet, were both vaguely insulted by the suggestion that they might wish to abandon their employer in the wilds of a foreign land.

"Ye ain't gonna make us go, is ye, gov'nor?" the tiger had demanded when Sebastian offered them the opportunity.

"No. But I don't want either of you to feel as if you are obligated in any way to stay."

The boy sucked in a quick, high breath. "I ain't afeared of Boney!"

Jules Calhoun's eyes crinkled with his slow smile. "I'll be staying as well, my lord . . . unless you'd prefer I go to help Claire with the two little lads."

"I think Molly and Claire between them should be more than capable of handling the children," said Sebastian.

"Good," said Calhoun. "Because I must admit it would go sorely against the grain with me to leave."

And so there were only the women and two children to load into the fourth waiting carriage. The sun was already low in the sky, and Hendon sighed as he pulled out his pocket watch and squinted down at the time.

"You'll be lucky to get twenty miles before you have to stop for the night," said Sebastian, watching him. "Are you sure you don't want to wait and leave in the morning?"

Hendon closed his watch with a snap and tucked it away. "Quite certain."

"Grandpapa is taking you for another ride on the big ship," Hero told Simon, lifting him up in her arms.

The little boy's eyes shone with excitement. "I like da ship!"

"Thank God neither of them suffers from seasickness," said Hendon under his breath.

Sebastian gave a soft laugh. Then his gaze fell on Patrick, his small hand fisted tight in Claire's skirts, his face solemn. He seemed to have come through his recent ordeal little the worse for wear, but he hadn't taken the news of this impending separation well.

"We'll catch up with you soon," Sebastian told Knox's son, hunkering down beside him. "I promise."

Patrick blinked and looked away, his lips pressing tightly together. "Me mum promised me, too. Only she ain't never come back, has she?"

Sebastian felt his throat thicken as he reached out to ruffle the little boy's hair. "Except this time you're not going alone, lad. You've got Simon, Claire, and Hendon with you. And you're going home to Brook Street, remember?"

The boy's chin trembled, but he managed to drudge up a game smile.

As Sebastian straightened, Hendon said gruffly, "If you haven't sorted this out in another ten days—and if against all odds Bonaparte is still on the march—you should leave anyway. You can always come back later when things are more settled."

There was a defensive tone to his voice, as if he expected his words to put up Sebastian's back. But Sebastian wasn't inclined to argue. Molly was already in the carriage, and he was watching Hero lift Simon up to the abigail's waiting arms. Hero was putting on a cheerful face for the boys' sake, but he knew by the stiff set of her shoulders and the brittle glitter in her eyes just how much this brief separation was going to cost her.

"I've already decided I'm giving it one more week," Sebastian said quietly as the bells of Notre Dame began to chime the hour, the low *bong*s echoing solemnly across the slate rooftops of the ancient island. It cut him to the quick to say it, but he knew it was right. "We can't stay here forever."

That night they went for a walk around the island, the lights of Paris glimmering on the dark waters of the Seine beside them, the air cold and clear and scented with the smell of wet stone and burning charcoal and the river. They could hear the water lapping at the base of the stone embankment, the faint strains of a violin, the sound of distant voices and children's laughter. Their own children's departure was like an ache that lay heavily on both their hearts, lending a new sense of urgency to a search that had already loomed as the most important endeavor of Sebastian's life.

After a time, Hero said, "I keep thinking that if we could understand the part Sophie played in Napoléon's escape from Elba, we might be able to understand why she was killed."

It was something that had been haunting Sebastian for days, and he felt the weight of all its implications as he gazed across the choppy black waters of the Seine to the Place de Grève, the vast open square in front of the ancient building known as the Hôtel de Ville that housed Paris's city government. Before the Revolution this had been Paris's traditional site for executions, and when the guillotine was removed from the Place de la Révolution, it was eventually erected there. It was still there, standing silent and ominous in the darkness, and it occurred to Sebastian, looking at it now, that it was difficult to walk anywhere in this city without being reminded of the turmoil, bloodshed, and terror of France's last twenty-six years. It tore at his gut to think that Sophie might have played a part in the desperate, dangerous scheme that could easily cause it all to start up again.

He had to force himself to say, "Given that the Allies open and read all of Napoléon's correspondence, I think we can safely assume she was carrying a message."

"From McClellan to Napoléon, you mean?"

"It seems likely, doesn't it?" Madame Dion had confirmed Hortense's contention that Sophie was originally expected to return to Paris much earlier.

"So what was the message?"

"Well, if I were Napoléon and I were plotting my return, I think I'd contact my most faithful generals and ask for their support."

Hero looked over at him. "You're saying McClellan and the others must have known Napoléon was planning to escape from Elba?"

"The ones Napoléon thought he could trust, yes."

"You think that's why Sophie went to see him? To deliver McClellan's reply and pledge his support?"

"I think she went to deliver McClellan's reply. But I'm not convinced we can assume that means McClellan intends to support Napoléon. Just because McClellan and the others didn't betray the Emperor's plans doesn't mean they agreed to join his cause."

He knew he was doing it again, grasping at possible excuses, trying to convince himself that his mother hadn't done what he was so terribly afraid she had. And he knew from the set of Hero's profile that she understood exactly the emotions that were driving his thinking.

She was silent for a moment, glancing up at a weathered plaque fixed high on the wall beside them, which still read "quai Napoléon." The Bourbon functionaries who were so busy chiseling bees off buildings, tearing down statues of the Emperor, and changing every offending place-name had obviously missed this one.

"Even if that's true," said Hero, "I think she might also have carried a message from Napoléon to Hortense, perhaps giving her the exact date he planned to leave Elba. Why else would Hortense have shown up at the rue du Champs du Repos within hours of Sophie's arrival back in Paris?"

Why indeed? thought Sebastian with a heavy heart.

"What I can't figure out," Hero was saying, "is why Sophie stopped at Malmaison on her way back to Paris. At first I was thinking she must have gone there to get the talisman, but that makes no sense. It wouldn't still have been there."

"No, it wouldn't," he said.

They had reached the narrow stretch of water that separated the Île de la Cité from the Île Saint-Louis, the other, smaller island that lay just upstream. There had been a bridge here once, but a recent storm carried it away and the Bourbons hadn't bothered to replace it.

"My guess is that Joséphine sent the talisman to Napoléon when she realized she was dying. She knew he'd never won a campaign after he divorced her and lost the talisman, and she thought having it might help him, should he ever decide to attempt to regain his throne."

"That makes sense," said Hero as they turned to walk along the nave of the cathedral. Even at this hour the square before it was crowded, the air ringing with voices and laughter and the joyous trill of an accordion. "Except why would Sophie have brought the talisman's case back to Paris with her?"

"Perhaps it was intended as a signal to whomever she was meant to give it. Only she never managed to deliver it."

"That doesn't explain her stop at Malmaison."

"No, it doesn't."

Hero linked her hand through the crook of his arm. "What if her meeting with Sanson wasn't as innocent as he would have you believe? What if, once she changed her mind about going to the Place Dauphine, she sent Sanson a message asking him to meet her at the Vert-Galant? Did you ever ask him about the talisman case?"

Sebastian shook his head. "It hadn't been found yet when I spoke to him." He was silent for a time, his thoughts on the past as they wound their way through the narrow old streets that lay beyond the square. "What I'd like to know is where she went between the time she left the inn and when she was attacked on the Pont Neuf. I'd also like to know what the bloody hell she was doing out on that bridge. If she was coming to see us, why didn't she have the *fiacre* driver take her into the Place Dauphine, to the door of the house?"

"Is it possible she was stabbed someplace else and brought to the bridge by her killer? If he thought she was dead, he could have meant to dispose of her body by throwing it into the Seine."

"And simply missed the river, you mean?" He thought about it, then said, "I doubt it. There are much less public places from which to quietly slip a body into the river. I think she was attacked on the bridge, although I'll be damned if I can figure out what she was doing there."

Their walk had now brought them full circle, back around to the Pont Neuf, and they crossed the bridge's roadway to step up on the platform that had once supported the statue of Henri IV.

Eight days, thought Sebastian as he stared out over the shadowy tangle of overgrown shrubs and trees that thrust like the prow of a ship into the silently flowing black waters of the river. It had been eight days since he'd found her here, and he felt no closer to unmasking her killer now than he had been then.

"It's an odd place for a woman to be walking alone," said Hero, turning to gaze across the bridge.

The breeze coming up off the water was growing colder, and Sebastian put his arm around her shoulders to draw her in closer to the warmth of his body. "It is."

He was aware of the lamplit carriages and carts rumbling across the bridge beside them, of the laughter and voices spilling from the café on the corner of the quai de l'Horloge, and the tall, familiar figure of a man who stood by himself near the darkened entrance to the Place Dauphine.

"*Bloody hell,*" whispered Sebastian as the man started across the road toward them.

"Why? Who is it?" said Hero, following his gaze.

"Someone who must sincerely regret having missed the joys of the Spanish Inquisition." Raising his voice, Sebastian said, "*Bonsoir,* Monsieur de Teulet."

Marie-Thérèse's gaunt, austere *huissier du cabinet* stepped up onto the platform, the golden light from the oil lamp that dangled from the post beside them limning his pale face and somber clothes. "*Bonsoir, monsieur le vicomte.*" He bowed to Hero. "And *madame.* A chilly evening for a walk."

"Not too chilly," she said.

A tight smile twitched the Chevalier's face as he turned back to Sebastian. "I understand your father, the Earl of Hendon, left Paris today, along with your sister and the wife of the British Ambassador."

"Yes," said Sebastian.

"And your children went with them."

"Yes."

"And yet here you are."

Sebastian glanced up as the breeze swayed the lantern above them, casting a macabre pattern of light and shadow across the platform. "Why should we leave, when the King assures us that Napoléon will never reach Paris?"

"Oh, Napoléon will be stopped long before he reaches Paris. Never fear that. And then the time of retribution will begin."

"Retribution against whom?"

"All those who should have been dealt with a year ago. The anti-monarchists. The atheists and secularists. Their accomplices and sympathizers."

"A new Terror, in other words."

"Except a just and godly one this time."

"Yes, of course."

"The final result will be glorious, but some might find things a bit"—de Teulet paused as if searching for the right word—"uncomfortable for a time. You would be wise to follow your father and children to London. Soon."

"Is that a threat?"

"A threat? Now, why would I threaten you?" The Chevalier touched his hand to his hat and bowed again to Hero. *"Madame,"* he said, and turned to walk away.

"It was a threat, wasn't it?" she said quietly as the Frenchman continued on across the bridge.

Sebastian watched de Teulet climb into a carriage waiting on the far side of the bridge, in the Place des Trois-Maries. As the green-and-gold-liveried driver turned his horses toward the Tuileries Palace, the crest of the Duchesse d'Angoulême was plainly visible on the coach's panel. Marie-Thérèse might have left Paris, but for some reason, her faithful minion had remained.

"It was a threat," said Sebastian.

Chapter 46

$\mathcal{T}$he next morning dawned clear but cold, with a brilliant aqua sky that slowly turned into a smudged blue-brown as the smoke from Paris's tens of thousands of chimneys rose to hang over the city.

Painfully aware of the clock ticking away the hours of their last days in Paris, Sebastian arrived early at Henri Sanson's sprawling complex in the rue de Marais. A flustered, nervous young housemaid left him for a time cooling his heels in a withdrawing room, but returned to escort him through the house and across the gardens to a large stone outbuilding the girl referred to as "the family museum."

"Thought you'd be back," said the High Executioner of Paris, looking up from where he sat at a workbench beneath one of the room's windows, wiping oil on the honed blade of what Sebastian realized must be a headsman's ax.

More axes and swords hung from the walls and filled the cabinets that crowded the room, along with a macabre collection of torture implements: fire-blackened pincers, an iron maiden, branding irons, ancient

doloires, huge wagon wheels stained dark with old blood, and a towering wooden frame with a worn, bloodstained bench and massive slanted
blade: Madame Guillotine.

"Why is that?" said Sebastian, drawing up beside a glass-fronted display cabinet crowded with a collection of small toy guillotines, brooches
made in the shape of guillotines, pipe bowls decorated with guillotines,
even necklaces and earrings dangling tiny guillotines.

Sanson grunted. "You think I can't put one and one together to get
two? Napoléon's landing in the south of France casts Sophia Cappello's
death in a slightly different light, yes?"

"You knew she had returned to Paris via Elba?"

Sanson's normally expressionless features contorted with a hint of
surprise, quickly smoothed away—although whether it was because
he'd been ignorant of the details of Sophie's journey or was merely startled to discover that Sebastian knew of it was difficult to say. "She went
to Elba?"

"She did. You would have me believe you didn't know?"

Sanson pursed his full lips. "No, I didn't know. I told you: We discussed roses, not politics."

"And yet you suspect that Napoléon's return might have had something to do with her death?"

"Just because we didn't discuss politics doesn't mean I'm incapable of
deduction."

"Oh? So tell me this: Do you think she would have supported Napoléon's return?"

Sanson set aside the newly oiled ax and reached for a heavy, nasty-
looking sword, his eyes narrowed as if in thought. "Well, she didn't have
much use for the Bourbons, that's for sure. But she told me once she'd
seen far too much killing in her life. And whatever the end result of Napoléon's current mad adventure, there will be more killing. Make no mistake about that."

Sebastian watched the executioner test the edge of the sword's blade with his thumb. A new possibility was beginning to occur to Sebastian, unformed but chilling in its implications. He said, "Are you familiar with the Charlemagne Talisman?"

"I know of it," said Sanson. "Why do you ask?"

Sebastian drew the jeweled red leather case from his pocket and held it out. "Have you ever seen this?"

Sanson glanced at it, then returned his attention to his task, his oiled cloth moving reverently over the deadly blade. "No. Why?"

"Madame Cappello didn't show it to you the evening you met her at the inn?"

"No. Why would she?"

"It's the case Napoléon had made for the talisman. Sophie had it with her at the Vert-Galant, and it was found later that night on the Pont Neuf—empty—after she was attacked there."

"She had the Charlemagne Talisman?" The executioner sounded puzzled.

But that didn't mean that he actually was.

Sebastian studied the man's impassive, unreadable profile. "We don't know that she had the amulet itself; all we know is that she had the case. Did she ever speak to you of the talisman?"

"No. Never."

"And you have no idea where she went after she left the inn that night?"

The headsman stared back at Sebastian as if defying disbelief. "No."

"Are you familiar with her former ward, Angélique de Longchamps-Montendre?"

"I know of her, although I don't believe I've met her. Why?"

"What about her husband, Antoine de Longchamps-Montendre?"

The executioner's lip curled in open contempt. "Him I have met. Briefly."

"I take it you don't think much of him."

Sanson pushed out a rough breath in a faint, derisive huff of amusement. "He is a spoiled, arrogant young man who was brought up to believe he is better than others and that the world owes him far more than it has given him. That kind can be dangerous."

Dangerous. It was an interesting word for the executioner to choose. "Do you think he was a threat to *Dama* Cappello?"

"Why would he be?"

"What about Hortense Bonaparte?"

Sanson was thoughtful for a moment. "Her kind is different. She's a woman who has been feted as the stepdaughter of an emperor and a queen in her own right, so she has the arrogance of Antoine de Longchamps-Montendre. But she has also known adversity and hardship, want and fear. And she is a woman, of course—a beautiful, seductive woman with her mother's cunning." He paused, then added, "Although not, perhaps, her mother's shrewdness."

"What was her relationship with Sophie?"

"I have no idea. *Dama* Cappello was close to Joséphine, but I don't believe Hortense ever had much interest in roses."

"Did you know Sophia stopped by Malmaison on her way back to Paris?"

Sanson frowned. "No. Why would she do that?"

"I was hoping you might be able to tell me."

Sanson shook his head. "No."

"She didn't mention it when you saw her at the Vert-Galant?"

"No." He hesitated. "You're quite certain she'd just been there?"

"Yes. That surprises you. Why?"

"Because we discussed the condition of the gardens that very evening. Why wouldn't she have mentioned it?"

Why indeed? thought Sebastian as he watched as the High Executioner of Paris set aside his oiled sword. "Do you know the Count of Cargèse?"

Sanson swiveled on his stool to look directly at him. "Niccolò Aravena? Oh, I know him, all right. The man takes his interest in roses to a degree one might well describe as fanatical. Why do you ask?"

"Fanatical enough to kill, do you think?"

"To kill *Dama* Cappello, you mean?" He opened his eyes wide, pulled down the corners of his mouth, and rocked his head back and forth as if in thought. "I honestly don't know."

"Did you know he used his rose shipments to smuggle reports from Napoléon's spies out of Britain?"

"I've heard some such talk, yes."

"How well-known was it?"

"It was known amongst those of us with an interest in roses. Beyond that?" He shrugged. "I could not say."

Sebastian let his gaze drift around the grisly collection, his attention coming to rest, inevitably, on the guillotine. "You don't use that anymore?"

Sanson rose to go rest his hand on the worn wood of the guillotine's bascule. It was a tender, almost loving gesture. "Not this one, no. This one is old. After a while, the blade and wood wear; the joints are no longer true. If the uprights stand even a fraction off vertical, the blade won't descend properly. And then what should be quick and relatively painless becomes something else entirely."

Sebastian stared up at the towering crossbar and *mouton* with its deadly angled blade. "And yet you keep it."

"It's a part of history, this guillotine. Thousands met their end upon its bascule: Marie Antoinette, Louis XVI, his young sister, Princess Élisabeth . . . so, so many."

Sebastian suddenly found it hard to draw breath. "And Robespierre?"

"Of course." Sanson's lips twitched with what might have been a smile. "Did you know that the brain remains aware for thirty or more seconds after the head is cut off from the body? Thirty seconds is a long time, yes? Think about all that can happen in thirty seconds. When a man's or a woman's head is cut off and lifted up by its hair to be shown to the roaring crowds, those people's brains are still alive. They are *aware*. They hear the cheers, see those jeering, laughing faces. Feel the wind on their flesh."

Sebastian stared at him. "How can you know that?"

Sanson tilted back his head, his gaze, like Sebastian's, on the blade towering above them. "I know. I see their eyes track movement, see their expressions alter."

"What is their expression?"

"At first? Fear. Afterward?" He paused. "Astonishment. And then the head is dropped into the basket with all the others; the person sees the equally bewildered faces of those who have gone before and then . . . knows no more."

The horrors concentrated in this death-haunted private museum were suddenly too much for Sebastian to bear. "Thank you for your assistance," he said, turning toward the door.

"I wouldn't have said I told you much." Sanson went to settle back on his stool and reach for a long, curving knife whose purpose Sebastian had no desire to speculate upon. "It's interesting you do not ask about Marie-Thérèse—if I thought she might have been a threat to *Dama* Cappello."

Sebastian paused with one hand on the door to look back at him. Sanson kept his focus on the ghastly blade in his hands, but the conversation had shifted into delicate territory, and the tension in the low, macabre building was suddenly so thick as to be palpable.

Sebastian said, "Are you familiar with the Duchess's *huissier du cabinet*?"

"Xavier de Teulet? Oh, yes."

"What do you know of him?"

Sanson ran his oiled cloth up and down the knife blade, his expression once more completely unreadable. "I know he is a man with the zeal and righteous moral certitude of a religious fanatic. And like all such persons, he can justify anything in the name of heaven."

"You think that's what this is about? Heaven?"

Sanson looked over at him then. "To those such as Marie-Thérèse and the Chevalier de Teulet, everything is about heaven, if they wish it to be. In their minds, they are on the side of the angels, which means that anyone who stands against them is standing against God."

"And Sophia Cappello was standing against God?"

"Well, she was standing against Marie-Thérèse. And as far as de Teulet is concerned, that might actually have been worse."

Chapter 47

*S*o Sanson claims he and Sophie discussed Malmaison's gardens, and yet she didn't mention she'd just been there a few hours before?" said Hero when Sebastian returned to the Place Dauphine.

"That's what he says. And while I could be wrong, I suspect that in this, at least, he's telling the truth. After all, he didn't need to tell me the topic had come up."

"Yes, but . . . what could she possibly have been doing out there that she felt the need to hide?"

"I can't imagine," said Sebastian. "But I think it's time we try to find out, don't you?"

They drove out to the Empress Joséphine's famous seventeenth-century château in Sebastian's sporty little phaeton. Normally such a journey would be made by carriage, except that the carriage, team, and coachman Sebastian had hired for the duration of their stay in France had all disappeared.

"I wonder who's responsible," said Hero, adjusting the angle of her parasol against the shifting direction of the sun as they wound through the gently rolling vivid green hills to the west of Paris. She was dressed for the excursion in a heavy dark blue carriage dress made high at the neck with a satin collar, and had a jaunty broad-brimmed hat with a short veil to help keep out the dust. "The coachman or the stable owner?"

"If I had to guess, I'd say both working together," said Sebastian, keeping his pair at a brisk trot. There was still a bite to the air, but the sun was now higher in the sky, bathing the fresh new growth of the fields with golden light and giving warmth to the day that hadn't been there before. "From what I'm hearing, it's becoming virtually impossible to buy, hire, or steal a decent carriage within a hundred miles of Paris."

An ancient wagon piled high with trunks and bits of furniture and drawn by a blown team wallowed in the road ahead, and Sebastian dropped his hands, urging his horses out and around it. They'd already passed a dozen or more such overloaded wagons and carts, carriages and buggies and gigs.

"The rats are fleeing the Bourbon ship of state in a panic," said Hero, tipping her parasol just so as they rounded another bend in the road. "And it hasn't even hit the rocks yet."

Sebastian reined his horses in to a more sedate pace as they left the overloaded wagon far behind. "I'm glad we sent the boys with Hendon."

She turned her head, her gaze meeting his. "So am I."

The Château de Malmaison lay some nine miles to the west of Paris, just beyond the small, prosperous village of Rueil. Built in the classic French Renaissance style of pale limestone with a gray slate roof and neat rows of long, symmetrical windows, it stood in the midst of some five hundred acres of English-style gardens that had once been the toast of Europe. Known for their extensive collection of exotic plants and animals from as far away as New South Wales and Joséphine's native Martinique, the château's gardens were now sadly neglected, with overgrown and half-dead borders stretching out on either side of the rutted drive.

"I wouldn't have expected gardens to deteriorate so badly in less than a year," said Sebastian as he stared across the abandoned park to where an elegant black swan was coming in to land on a weed-choked ornamental lake.

"Last summer was hot, even in England. And if there was no one to water the more delicate exotic plantings . . ." Hero's voice trailed away as they swept around a bend in the drive and the golden-stoned château rose up before them, looking forlorn and deserted. She gave a faint, disbelieving shake of her head. "I can't understand Joséphine's children. How could they allow this to happen? They surely know how much the house and gardens meant to their mother."

"They obviously don't care," said Sebastian, reining in before the château. To Tom, he said, "Baby them. We'll need to rest them well before we head back to Paris."

"Aye, gov'nor," said the tiger, taking the reins.

"It's too bad Tom's French isn't better," said Hero as they turned toward the château's tentlike glass-and-metal entry. "It would be interesting to hear what the servants are saying amongst themselves."

Sebastian reached for the bell. "It would, indeed."

They rang the bell five times before they finally heard approaching footsteps and the sounds of various bolts and bars being drawn back. The door creaked inward, revealing a bony, imposing-looking woman dressed in the severest black. In age she could have been anywhere between fifty-five and seventy-five; her back was ramrod straight, her once-dark chignon heavily threaded with silver, her long, narrow face hook nosed and lined with a fine crisscross of wrinkles. She looked at them through unblinking dark eyes and said, "No family here anymore."

"We know, *madame*. I am—"

The housekeeper made as if to shut the door in their faces, then looked beyond them to the empty sweep before the house. A puzzled frown scrunched her aged face, and she hesitated. "How did you get here? Never say you walked."

Sebastian handed her his card. "Lady Devlin and I have taken the liberty of sending our carriage around to the stables. It's a long drive back to Paris, and I've given instructions to have the horses fed and watered."

"Ah." She squinted down at the card. "Well, I hope your men can manage for themselves, *monsieur le vicomte*, because they won't find anyone there to help them. Not anymore."

"The stable hands and grooms have all been dismissed?" said Sebastian. He saw no reason to disabuse her of the assumption that they had arrived in a proper carriage with a coachman and footmen in attendance.

"*Mais oui.* And all but a couple of the groundsmen, as well."

"And in the house?"

"It's just me and CeCe."

"CeCe?"

"The housemaid. All the others have gone, you know. Trying to get wages out of Hortense and Eugène is almost more trouble than it's worth."

Sebastian exchanged a quick glance with Hero, who gave the woman a friendly smile and said, "You must be Madame . . . ?" She left the question dangling.

"Sorel. Anaïs Sorel."

"Of course. Madame Sorel, we understand the Empress's friend *Dama* Cappello was here recently. Is that true?"

The question seemed to puzzle her. "*Oui, madame.* Must've been last . . . hmmm, a week ago last Thursday."

Sebastian felt a strange sensation crawl over his skin. It was what they'd been told, and yet he realized that he hadn't quite believed it until now.

Hero said, "She came to look at the gardens?"

"*Non, madame.* Didn't stay long enough for that. Came into the house, disappeared up the stairs for a few minutes, then came back down, thanked me, and drove off. If the Empress hadn't warned me on her deathbed that *madame* might be coming, I'd have thought it strange. But I was expecting her, you see."

"The Empress Joséphine told you to expect Sophia Cappello's visit?"

"*Oui.* Said her ladyship might come one day, and if she did, I was to let her in and leave her alone. So that's what I did."

Sebastian said, "Do you know why *Dama* Cappello came?"

Madame Sorel tucked her chin back against her neck and looked vaguely affronted. "*Non, monsieur.* She didn't say, and it's not my place to question such things."

Hero gave the woman another of those warm, coaxing smiles. "No, of course not; I understand completely. But why do you think she came?"

The housekeeper raised her eyebrows and shrugged. "Well, stands to reason she must have come to get something, now, doesn't it?"

Again, Sebastian and Hero exchanged glances. He said, "And when *Dama* Cappello went upstairs, do you have any idea which room she went to?"

"Well, I could be wrong, but it sounded to me like she went into the Empress's bedchamber. Not the tented, red formal room in which she used to receive the Emperor when he was here, you understand, but her own private chamber."

Sebastian said, "May we see it?" The housekeeper stiffened, and he added quickly, "We will of course recompense you for your trouble."

He thought for a moment she still meant to refuse them. But the lure of remuneration was too tempting for a servant whose wages had become erratic since the death of her mistress.

She led the way across the black-and-white marble-tiled entrance hall to a flowing, surprisingly simple staircase that swept up to the first floor. Many of the house's rooms and galleries were virtually empty, with the remaining furniture buried beneath holland covers. Yet even without

the priceless artifacts and art treasures that had been either sold or transferred to the Louvre, the rooms were magnificent, with gleaming mahogany paneling and Classical frescoes inspired by the recent discoveries
at Pompeii.

But in contrast to the opulence of the rest of the house, the Empress's private bedroom was a comparatively modest chamber, with a
small bed simply draped in plain pale gold satin and tall windows that
looked out over Joséphine's beloved gardens.

"She died here, of course," Madame Sorel was saying as their footsteps echoed on the room's dusty floorboards. "In that bed right there."

Hero tipped back her head, her gaze taking in the exquisitely decorated ceiling. "We've heard that *Dama* Cappello came to visit the Empress
frequently when she was ill."

"*Oui, madame,* that she did."

Sebastian went to stand beside one of the windows overlooking the
gardens. The room's focus on the garden views reminded him of Sophie's bedchamber, and he found himself thinking of the vastly different
backgrounds of the two women: Joséphine, who'd been raised on a
French colonial island in the Caribbean and suffered through all the
horrors of Revolutionary Paris, and Sophie, who'd grown up in the safe,
bucolic world of an English nobleman's country estate. In that sense they
seemed unlikely friends. And yet were they really so different? Both had
experienced miserable first marriages and lived lives of luxury mingled
with hardship and heartache. Both loved gardens and roses, and both
had joined their fates to that of military men of non-French origin who
prospered fighting for France. . . .

"Do you have any idea what *Dama* Cappello might have come here
last week to get?" he heard Hero ask the housekeeper.

Madame Sorel shook her head. "No. Don't see how she could have
found anything, either. Hortense and her brother went through the
house quite thoroughly after the Empress died." She paused, then said
again with emphasis, "*Quite* thoroughly."

Sebastian turned from the window. "Have you ever heard of the Charlemagne Talisman?"

The housekeeper thought about it a moment, then shook her head. "*Non, monsieur.*" She could have been lying, but Sebastian found it impossible to tell. She cocked her head to one side. "If you're so interested in what her ladyship did here that day, why not simply ask her? *Hmm?*"

"You haven't heard that *Dama* Cappello was killed not long after she left here?"

He watched as the Frenchwoman's features went slack and the color drained from her face. "*Non.* Where? How?"

"She was stabbed. In Paris, on the Pont Neuf. Do you have any idea why someone would want to kill her?"

Her hand crept up to press against her lips. "*Non.* How could I?"

"Did anyone ask you to let them know if *Dama* Cappello should ever come here?"

She stared back at him, her features now carefully wiped of all betraying emotions. "*Non.* Why would anyone do that?"

It was a lie—a lie so obvious that it strengthened his belief that up until then she had been telling the truth. He said, "The housemaid who still lives here with you—you said her name is CeCe?"

"*Oui.*" She glanced from him to Hero, then back again. "Why?"

"Just wondering," said Sebastian. He found his gaze drifting again to the gardens beyond the windows. From here he could see an aged man hacking back the arching canes of a massive climbing rose that was threatening to swallow a nearby greenhouse. A husky, dark-haired lad of perhaps fifteen worked nearby, gathering up the cuttings. "Can you think of anything—anything at all—that might help explain why *Dama* Cappello came here last week, or why someone would have wanted to kill her?"

"*Mais non.*"

Sebastian studied the older woman's tensely held face. He could press her, of course. But he doubted it would accomplish anything and it might even do more harm than good. He was a foreigner here, an Englishman, and this woman's country had been fighting his for most of her life. France and Britain might now be at peace, but old attitudes died hard, and he suspected that in many ways she still saw him as her enemy.

"It's such a lovely room," said Hero in that friendly, chatty voice that hid a steely purpose and iron will. "It must have been even lovelier when the Empress was still alive. I'm wondering, where would we find the woman who served as her abigail?"

"You mean Bernadette?"

"That's right, Bernadette . . . ?"

"Agasse is her name. Bernadette Agasse. But I don't know where she's found a new position, and I don't see how she could tell you anything. She's been gone from here ten months and more." The housekeeper's eyes narrowed as if a thought had only just occurred to her, and she fixed Sebastian with a challenging stare. "What is all this to you anyway?"

"Sophia Cappello was a friend of my mother," he said. "I'd like to find out who killed her and why."

The Frenchwoman's features relaxed as she nodded sympathetically. "Ah. She was a lovely gentlewoman, *Dama* Cappello. So many deaths."

Her gaze drifted back to the silk-hung bed where Napoléon's Joséphine had breathed her last, and she sighed again. "So many."

Chapter 48

*H*er abigail?" said Eugène-François Vidocq when Sebastian stopped by the headquarters of the *Sûreté nationale* that evening. "You want me to find Empress Joséphine's abigail? Whatever for?"

"I have a theory," said Sebastian, his gaze drifting around the policeman's unusual office.

It was a small, messy room, crowded with bureaus and tables piled high with note cards and folders and a strange variety of objects—wigs and broken-down hats, crutches and canes, tattered old coats and jars of theatrical makeup, which Sebastian realized the ex–galley slave must use for his famous disguises. From the office's dirty windows he could see a cramped courtyard and, beyond that, the delicate flying buttresses of Sainte-Chapelle, the magnificent thirteenth-century chapel that dated to the time when the Palais de la Cité had been the residence of the Capetian Kings of France.

"A theory," said Vidocq, his voice flat. "A theory about what?"

"Malmaison is not on the way back to Paris for anyone traveling up from the south of France. And yet for some unknown reason Sophia

Cappello stopped there briefly just a few hours before she was killed. I think she went there to get something, and I'm hoping Joséphine's abigail can help us understand what that was."

Vidocq frowned. "You think she went there for the talisman, do you?"

"It's seeming more and more likely. And yet according to the housekeeper, the Queen of Holland and her brother effectively ransacked the château after their mother's death, looking for anything and everything they could sell. So why would it still have been there?"

"And that's what you're hoping the Empress's abigail can tell you?"

There were several things Sebastian was hoping the woman might know, but all he said was "Perhaps."

The head of the *Sûreté nationale* studied him intently for a moment, then shrugged. "I can try." He fished in one of his pockets and came up with a tobacco-stained clay pipe. "And no, we haven't managed to track down either the *fiacre* driver or your *fille publique*," he added when Sebastian opened his mouth to ask just that.

"You don't find that odd?"

"Yes, I find that odd," snapped Vidocq, reaching for a pouch of tobacco.

"They could be dead. Or in hiding."

"That had occurred to me."

Sebastian watched the Frenchman tamp down the tobacco in the pipe's bowl, then reach for a taper. "There is one other thing."

Vidocq didn't even bother to look up from lighting his pipe. "Oh?"

"It's possible one of the servants out at Malmaison—most likely the housekeeper, but perhaps a housemaid named CeCe or even one of the gardeners—notified someone of Sophia Cappello's visit. It might be worth your sending someone out there to question them."

At that, Vidocq did turn. "That would imply someone was anticipating her visit to Malmaison."

"Yes," said Sebastian.

The policeman's eyes narrowed. "You're hiding something from me."

"Nothing I know for certain."

But Vidocq did not appear convinced.

Sunday, 12 March

They awoke the next morning to the peal of dozens of church bells calling the faithful to Sunday mass. Sebastian was forced to wait until late in the afternoon before trying to approach Hortense Bonaparte.

She was in the entry hall of her imposing *hôtel particulier,* arranging an assortment of lilies and ferns in a mammoth bloodred vase that stood on the large, round marble-topped table in the center of the space. When the footman opened the door to him, she looked up and smiled. *"Bonjour, monsieur le vicomte.* Do come in."

"Madame," he said with a low bow.

She was wearing a high-waisted gown of delicate white muslin sprigged with embroidered bouquets of pastel pink, blue, and yellow flowers, and her smile widened as she picked up one of the large white calla lilies lying on the table before her and added it to the arrangement. "I hear you paid a visit to my mother's château."

"And how did you hear that?"

She reached for another lily. "Did you think I would not?"

"It's a lovely place," he said noncommittally.

She glanced over at him. "And now the rooms are empty and the gardens are an atrocious mess. I know. Everyone who sees it reproaches me for it. But if you knew how much money my mother poured into that château, you would not judge me so harshly."

"I do try not to judge."

She flashed him a saucy smile. "Even if you don't always succeed?"

"Perhaps." He watched her fingers work quickly to make subtle, sure alterations to her arrangement. "You didn't tell me Sophia Cappello stopped by Malmaison on her way back to Paris, but I take it you knew. Did Madame Sorel send the gardener's boy to tell you? Or was it CeCe?"

"Does it matter?"

"I suppose not. And yet even though you knew, you kept that knowledge to yourself."

"Did I? How . . . remiss of me."

Sebastian studied her beautiful, composed lying face. "I assume *Dama* Cappello was there looking for the talisman. So tell me, did she find it?"

"How would I know?"

"You know."

She was no longer smiling. She picked up a fern frond and added it to the vase before taking a step back to study the effect.

Sebastian said, "Is that why you went to see her the day she arrived back in Paris, to demand she give you the talisman? I thought at first that she had brought you a message telling you that Napoléon was leaving Elba. But you already knew that, didn't you? Were you afraid she meant to keep the amulet from him?"

She gave one of her airy little laughs. "What a ridiculous notion. I told you: I'd heard *Dama* Cappello was unhappy with the state of the gardens. That is all." Hortense placed the last lily in the vase with studied care, then turned to face him, the flounces of her embroidered gown twirling girlishly around her ankles. "Why exactly are you here this afternoon, my lord?"

"Actually, I'm wondering if you could provide me with the direction of Bernadette Agasse."

A frown marred her pretty forehead. "Who?"

"Bernadette Agasse. She was your mother's abigail."

The frown cleared. "Ah, yes, of course. Bernadette. I've heard she found a new position, but I'm afraid I couldn't tell you with whom. *Je suis désolée.*"

He didn't believe her, and she confirmed his doubt by not inquiring into the reason for his interest in the woman. Instead, her eyes narrowed with what looked like genuine amusement.

She said, "I understand Kitty Wellington has left Paris, escorted by your father, the Earl."

"Yes," said Sebastian, wondering where she was going with this.

The smile spread to her lips. "The British Embassy—the Hôtel de Charost—used to belong to my sister-in-law, Pauline Bonaparte. Did you know?"

"So I had heard."

"And did you know she insisted that your Duke of Wellington pay her for it in louis d'or?"

"Yes, I've heard that, as well."

"Do you know why?"

He shook his head. "No."

"Pauline wanted the gold to send to Napoléon so he could hire the ships he needed to carry his men to France. In other words, your grand Duke of Wellington obligingly—and, I must say, rather foolishly—provided the gold that funded Napoléon's return. Ironic, is it not?" She tipped her head to one side, her eyes widening. "You don't believe me?"

"Oh, I believe you," he said.

After all, it was London's bankers who'd loaned the infant United States the money to make the Louisiana Purchase, which literally sent British gold pouring into Napoléon's war chest.

He kept his gaze on her face. "Tell me this: If Sophia had the Charlemagne Talisman, do you think she would have given it to Napoléon?"

Hortense shrugged. "Her lover was one of the Emperor's most trusted marshals; why would she not give Napoléon the talisman?"

"Perhaps because she was tired of people dying?"

The deposed Queen of Holland gave a faint shake of her head. "You think that if Napoléon returns to his throne, he will immediately embark on a quest to reconquer all of Europe? He won't, you know. All he wants is to govern France in peace . . . if the Allies will let him."

They won't, thought Sebastian.

But he didn't say it.

Chapter 49

*H*ero was in her dressing room, vigorously brushing her carriage dress in an attempt to rid it of yesterday's dust—and ruefully mourning the loss of her abigail—when she heard the knocker bang at the distant front door. Turning her head, she caught the vaguely familiar timbre of a Frenchman's voice drifting up from the entry hall below. A moment later came the sound of a housemaid running up the stairs.

"A Monsieur Antoine de Longchamps-Montendre to see you, my lady," said the girl, dropping a curtsy. "Jacques told him that *monsieur le vicomte* is out and that he didn't think you were receiving, but . . ." She sucked in a quick breath, obviously winded by her rapid climb.

Hero set aside the brush. "I'll be right down."

She found Angélique's aristocratic husband standing beside the fire laid on the parlor's old-fashioned hearth. He was dressed in an elegantly cut long-tailed double-breasted coat with a wide-collared red waistcoat and loose-fitting buff-colored Cossack trousers inspired by the uniforms of the Russians who'd so recently occupied Paris. He'd been staring down at the fire with one hand resting on the mantel, but at her entrance he dropped his hand and turned with a smile.

"Lady Devlin," he said, sweeping her a courtly bow, "my apologies for intruding upon your Sunday."

"That's quite all right." Hero stretched out a hand to indicate the tapestry-covered settee. "Please, won't you have a seat?"

"Merci." He adjusted the tails of his coat as he sat, a quickly disguised expression of contempt flitting across his handsome, fine-boned features as he took in the worn upholstery.

"May I offer you some refreshment? Your wife tells me you acquired a taste for tea while you were living in England. Or would you prefer a glass of wine?"

"Thank you, but I am fine." He hesitated a moment, then said, "To be frank, I wasn't certain I'd find you still in Paris. So many of the English are leaving."

"True," she said, faintly smiling as she settled in the chair beside the fire. "But we see no reason to do so."

He raised his eyebrows. "Do I take it Lord Devlin remains intent on uncovering the identity of *Dama* Cappello's killer?"

"He is, yes. Why do you ask?"

"I gather he thinks her death may have something to do with the Charlemagne Talisman." Something of Hero's surprise at his words must have shown on her face, because he added, "Lord Devlin's inquiries into the amulet have been rather extensive."

"We don't actually know yet," said Hero, folding her hands together in her lap. "But I wonder, do you have any idea why Sophia Cappello stopped at Malmaison on her way back from the south of France?"

"Did she do so? How . . . odd." His features showed mild surprise, which may or may not have been genuine. He was very, very good at playing these kinds of games. But then, so was Hero.

"Odd, indeed." She leaned forward slightly as if inviting a confidence. "Tell me, *monsieur*, do you believe in the power of the amulet?"

He appeared to find the question faintly ridiculous. "It contains fragments of the True Cross. Of course it is powerful."

"Yes, of course." Privately, Hero suspected there were enough fragments of the True Cross scattered across Christendom to build a small
chapel, but she kept that thought to herself.

"And his lordship has yet to find any trace of it?" said the Frenchman.

"No. None." Hero settled back in her chair. "And how is your wife,
monsieur? I know she has been sadly grieved by Sophia Cappello's death."

"She mourns her, of course; the woman was like a second mother to
her. But Angélique is resilient."

"I am relieved to hear it." Was it the young woman's grief, Hero wondered, that kept Angélique from accompanying her husband on this
rather transparent fishing expedition, or something else entirely?

The Frenchman's eyes narrowed ever so slightly. "I understand that
Eugène-François Vidocq is assisting Lord Devlin in his search for the
killer."

"He is, yes."

De Longchamps-Montendre gave a faint shake of his head. "Quite a
change of fortune for a onetime *cheval de retour.*"

"A what?"

"That's what they call a man who has been recaptured after escaping
from the galleys—a *cheval de retour.* They're double ironed, you know.
They say Vidocq still has the scars from the fetters on his wrists and
ankles—and around his neck from the iron collar."

"The gallerians wear iron collars?"

"They do, yes. I see you think such punishments harsh, but I fear it's
all terribly necessary. These men are invariably brutes, and Vidocq is no
exception. He was a *chauffeur,* you know." The Frenchman cocked his head
in inquiry. "You've heard of the *chauffeurs?*"

"I have not, no."

De Longchamps-Montendre breathed a troubled sigh. "Fortunately,
they're now little more than an ugly memory—just one of many from

the days of the Revolution. But when it comes to Vidocq, Lord Devlin would do well to remember always with whom he is dealing."

"You think Vidocq might do Devlin harm?"

"Let us say simply that he is not a man to be trusted."

The Frenchman stayed talking a few minutes more, then rose to take his leave. "Again, my apologies for interrupting your Sunday, my lady," he said with another of his magnificent courtly bows. "And please believe me when I say that if you or Lord Devlin requires any assistance in your quest to uncover *Dama* Cappello's killer, you must not hesitate to ask."

"Thank you," said Hero, rising with him. "I'll be certain to pass your message along."

"So why did he come?" asked Devlin when he returned to the Place Dauphine a few minutes later.

Hero walked over to the silver tray that rested on a table near the door and poured two glasses of wine. "Ostensibly? To inquire into your investigation and offer any assistance we may require. In reality? I suspect because he knew of our visit to Malmaison and was hoping to learn something of the talisman's whereabouts." She frowned, then said, "Or perhaps that's simply what he wanted me to think. He's very clever, that man. His real intent might have been to sow seeds of distrust about Vidocq. Have you ever heard of the *chauffeurs*?"

Devlin reached to take the glass she held out to him. "I have, yes. Why?"

"Who were they?"

"A band of particularly nasty brigands who operated in northern France during the darkest days of the Revolution. They acquired the name from their habit of attacking isolated farmhouses and slowly roasting the unfortunate inhabitants over an open fire until they gave up their hidden valuables."

"Good Lord," whispered Hero.

"Why do you ask?" he said again.

She took a long, slow swallow of her wine. "De Longchamps-Montendre claims Eugène-François Vidocq was one."

"I wouldn't be surprised."

"You wouldn't? And now he's head of a division of the French secret police?"

"'Every valley shall be raised up, and every mountain and hill shall be made low, and the crooked shall be made straight,'" Devlin quoted, his lips twisting into a wry smile.

"I don't think that's what that particular verse is referring to."

"Isn't it?"

Hero recklessly drained her wine and went to pour a second glass. "And did you learn anything from the erstwhile Queen of Holland?"

"Only that she also knew of our visit to Malmaison."

"Which means she knew of Sophie's visit there, as well."

"It is rather suggestive." He took a slow sip of his wine. "Oh, and I also discovered how Napoléon managed to hire the ships he used to sail away from Elba."

She looked over at him. "How?"

"The Duke of Wellington paid for them."

Chapter 50

*E*arly the next morning, Sebastian went to stand outside the Conciergerie on the quai de l'Horloge, his head tipping back as he stared up at the massive medieval towers that remained from the old royal castle, his thoughts on the past. It was when the kings of France moved across the river, first to the Louvre, then to the Tuileries, and finally out to Versailles, that the Palais de la Cité was left to the French treasury and the judiciary. The Conciergerie tended to loom large in people's minds as the epicenter of some of the worst of the Revolution's bloody excesses, yet even as early as the fourteenth century, the place had been used as a prison, its feared torture chambers discussed in furtive whispers—if at all. The oldest remaining tower, the Tour Bonbec, still carried a name that meant "good beak," an appellation derived from the way its tortured prisoners used to "sing."

The Revolution might have lopped off its *citoyens'* heads at an alarming rate, but it had done away with the breaking wheel, the rack, the head crusher, the saw, the screw press, the iron tongue shredder, and all the other hideous devices that had been used with such painful effect to convince the enemies of King and Church to confess—whether they were actually guilty of anything or not. Many of the torture implements in the Sanson family's museum had doubtless come from here, and they weren't particularly old. During the reign of Louis XVI, the Countess de la Motte had been stripped, whipped, and branded here for her part in an incident that embarrassed Marie Antoinette. For most Englishmen, the hideous death toll of the Revolution had washed away all memory of those centuries of royal cruelty and capriciousness. But that wasn't necessarily true of the French people themselves.

She didn't have much use for the Bourbons, that's for sure, Henri Sanson had said. *But she told me once she'd seen far too much killing in her life. And whatever the end result of Napoléon's current mad adventure, there will be more killing. Make no mistake about that.*

Sebastian watched a short, rotund clerk in a black greatcoat come bustling out the Conciergerie's doors, a sheaf of papers tucked under one arm. Sanson could have been wrong, of course. How well had the executioner actually known Sophie, particularly if—as he claimed— they never discussed politics? But if he was right—and Sebastian had a gut feeling the man probably was—then would such a woman risk the resumption of war by working to help Napoléon regain his throne? Her trip to Elba suggested she had been doing just that when she was killed. But what if . . .

What if that assumption was wrong?

Émile Landrieu was in the gardens of the old convent, brushing the dead leaves off the recumbent stone figures of a medieval man and woman lying side by side atop an elaborately carved sarcophagus, their folded hands forever held pressed against their chests in prayer. This was the part of the sculpture museum that Landrieu had dubbed the Elysian Garden, with the tombs of some of France's most famous artists, philosophers, and writers scattered amongst verdant plantings of rhododendrons and hollies and cherry trees just coming into bloom in a froth of pink sweetness.

"Good morning," said Sebastian, walking up to him. "It's lovely out here."

A slow smile of delight spread across the man's lined face. "It is peaceful, yes? This part of the museum is intended not to illustrate our history but to celebrate it." He lifted both hands up in the air in the manner of a priest saying mass. "One leaves the museum after having contemplated the dark centuries of domination by monarchy and the Church, then walks into the light and beauty of the garden to find here a place of inspiration and hope."

Sebastian studied the medieval monument beside them. "Whose empty tomb is this?"

"Oh, but it's not empty! Most of the tombs in the Elysian Garden are not. The idea is to assemble together in one place the greatest luminaries of French culture: Molière and Descartes, La Fontaine and Turenne— they're all here."

"You mean their actual bodies are here?"

"Yes, yes." The Frenchman looked shocked. "You can't think I would commit the sacrilege of casting such great men and women from their tombs simply to collect their empty monuments here?"

"Of course not," said Sebastian, somehow managing to keep all trace of irony from his voice. Landrieu evidently didn't consider casting the mortal remains of France's kings and queens from their coffins to be a similar act of sacrilege—which only reinforced what Sebastian had already suspected about the museum curator's political opinions.

"Unfortunately," Landrieu was saying, "the remains of some came to us without the monuments their greatness deserved. But we have sought to remedy that."

Sebastian nodded to the sarcophagus before them. "So who is this?" he said again.

A strange smile spread across the Frenchman's face. "This is the tomb of Héloïse and Abélard. They were buried near to each other in the twelfth century, but here their bones are actually mingled together, as they should be, for all time."

"But the monument itself is original?"

"Not exactly. We have created it for them from various medieval fragments saved from the destructive excesses of the Revolution."

Sebastian searched for something to say, but all he could come up with was "Oh."

"It draws many, many visitors to our museum every week," said Landrieu as they turned to walk along a path that wound through the shrubbery. "There is something about the poignancy of a doomed but eternal love that transcends the ages to both move and inspire us."

"Yes, I can understand that."

Landrieu cast him a sideways glance, the faint smile fading from his features. "You wished to see me about something in particular, *monsieur*?"

"I did, yes. I was wondering when was the last time you saw *Dama* Cappello."

"*Dama* Cappello?" The museum curator clicked his tongue against the roof of his mouth as if in thought. "I suppose it must have been late last summer sometime. Why do you ask?"

"So it was before she went to Vienna but after the return of the Bourbons?"

"It was, yes. Why?"

"Would you say she was enthusiastic about the Bourbon restoration?"

Landrieu was silent for a moment as if considering his response. "I don't think I would say that, no."

"So would you describe her as a Republican?"

Again, Landrieu took his time in answering. "A Republican? Let's just say I don't know that she would have described herself as such. One can simultaneously admire the potential of a political system and abhor the excesses of a particular example."

"Nicely put."

Landrieu pressed his lips together and said nothing.

Sebastian watched a white-backed woodpecker flit through the branches of the newly leafed-out plane trees overhead. "If she were alive today, what do you think would be her reaction to Bonaparte's return? Hypothetically, of course."

"I think . . . I think she would be worried."

"That it would lead to more bloodshed, you mean?"

The museum curator glanced over at him. "It's inevitable, is it not?"

"Is it? They say the Emperor advances on Paris without a shot being fired."

"So far."

"And if he succeeds in regaining his throne, will he be content to simply rule France in peace, do you think? Or does he still nourish dreams of reconquering all of Europe?"

Landrieu drew up and swung to face him, his features pinched with what looked like profound disquiet. "One might hope the defeats of his last years combined with all these months of exile have sobered him. But . . ."

"But?" prompted Sebastian when the Frenchman hesitated.

"There was a time when Napoléon saw himself as the successor of Charlemagne—or perhaps it would be more accurate to say he saw himself as the new Charlemagne. It was one of the reasons he took the title 'emperor' rather than simply 'king,' and why it was so important that the Pope anoint him at his coronation. His dream was to unite all of Europe beneath one law and one ruler. Has that dream died? Perhaps. But perhaps not."

"So tell me this," said Sebastian, his gaze drifting back over the celebrated tombs scattered about the gardens. "If Sophia Cappello had the Charlemagne Talisman, do you think she would give it to Napoléon?"

"I suppose that would depend on if she thought it would bring a swift peace and thus less death. Or . . ."

"Or?"

For one intense moment, Landrieu's gaze met Sebastian's. Then the Frenchman bit his lip and glanced away. "Or the opposite."

Chapter 51

$\mathcal{J}$ ebastian spent the rest of the afternoon and evening roaming the narrow, noisome streets of Paris, looking for the *fille publique* he'd seen standing on the Pont Neuf the night of Sophie's murder. It was a long shot and he knew it; the girl could easily have seen nothing. And yet he couldn't shake the feeling that finding her was vital, even though he knew that was most likely an illusion born of desperation.

And so he walked in ever-widening circles around the Pont Neuf, combing the vast central Parisian market known as Les Halles, where even that late in the day the air still rang with the guttural shouts of the sellers and every breath reeked of fish and raw meat and the tang of earth-covered vegetables. Beside the market lay what was now called the Marché des Innocents, a vast open square that had replaced the infamous, oozing Innocents cemetery that once stood there. It was to the square's towering public fountain that the poor women and children of the neighborhood came to draw water. And so he stood for a time with his hands buried deep in the pockets of his greatcoat, his hat pulled low, his breath showing misty in the frigid air as he scanned the ragged crowds, studying the dirt-streaked, gaunt faces and hollow eyes of the younger women. But the longer he stood there, the more he found himself wondering if he'd even recognize the girl if he saw her again. Poverty and despair had a tendency to grind out individual differences until every face started to look the same.

He moved on, roaming from one wretched public fountain to the next, searching raucous squares and back alleys, until night began to fall and he moved on to the Palais-Royal. By now the wealthy, privileged women who patronized the arcades and expensive shops during the day had disappeared, their places taken by a different class of women, women with exposed breasts, bold stares, and suggestive pouts. Some, he knew, would lead their customers upstairs to small private chambers. But most retreated only as far as the nearest dark corner for a quick, furtive coupling. And as he pushed his way through the laughing, shrieking crowds of drunken men and willing women, Sebastian found himself remembering that it was here, beneath the shadowy arcades of the Palais-Royal, that an eighteen-year-old Napoléon Bonaparte was said to have lost his virginity one night long ago to a comely *fille publique;* here that Camille Desmoulins delivered the fiery speech that led to the fall of the Bastille; here that Charlotte Corday came in the darkest days of the Revolution to buy the knife she would use to kill Marat in his bathtub. . . .

They were everywhere, he realized, these endless reminders of the city's dark and deadly past. Was that why he kept thinking that the past must have played a part in Sophie's death? Was it all simply an illusion, a mistake?

Troubled by the thought, he turned south, toward the Seine and the old Latin Quarter, which lay beyond it. But though he searched until the church bells of the city tolled midnight, he never found her.

"The days are slipping away," he said later that night as he lay with Hero in his arms. "And I don't even know where to look next."

"We can stay longer," she said, her soft hair sliding across his naked shoulder as she shifted to hold him closer. "We don't need to leave on Friday."

He shook his head. "I heard people saying tonight that Napoléon has taken Grenoble and is probably at Lyon by now."

"How is that even possible?"

"I don't know." He speared his fingers through her hair to draw it back so he could see her face in the golden light from the fire. "They say he still hasn't fired a shot."

She was silent for a moment, her features tense with her thoughts. "The Bourbons aren't going to be able to stop him, are they?"

"No. I don't think they can."

Tuesday, 14 March

Sebastian lost most of the next day to a seemingly interminable round of meetings with Sophie's bankers and her *avocat*, and to sorting out the myriad details involved in arranging for the care of the house on the rue du Champs du Repos after his departure. Madame Dion had offered to stay on with a reduced staff, and they had gratefully accepted.

"I take it you are still planning to leave this Friday?" said the *avocat* Monsieur Cloutier at one point.

"Yes," said Sebastian.

Cloutier nodded and started to say something, then stopped.

"What?"

The Frenchman peeled off his spectacles and rubbed his eyes with a spread thumb and forefinger. "It's probably not my place to say, but . . . well, I think you're wise to leave."

Sebastian studied the old man's heavily lined face and sad, weary eyes. He knew by now that Jean Cloutier's clients included not only Sophie, but the Marshals McClellan and Ney, as well. "You think Napoléon will reach Paris?"

"Truthfully? I'd say it's virtually inevitable at this point."

"You don't expect Ney to stop him?"

"I suppose it's possible. But . . ."

"But?"

"Ney has always served France before all else. Make of that what you will." The old man cleared his throat, settled the spectacles back on his nose, and reached for another stack of official-looking documents. "Now, let's see what's left, shall we?"

Wednesday, 15 March

Later, just after midnight, a storm rolled in from the north with a howling wind that drove the rain hard against the stone walls of the old house and lifted slates from the city's ancient rooftops to send them crashing down to the cobbles below. When the rain finally died shortly before daybreak, Sebastian gave up trying to sleep and rose from his bed. Moving quietly so as not to disturb Hero, he dressed, then crept downstairs to let himself out into the cold predawn.

A wet hush lay over the city, with the heavy, angry clouds still pressing low on the rooftops. The rows of rain-sodden trees in the square were somber things, wrapped in mist and dripping in the darkness. He cut through the narrow passage that led to the bridge, conscious of the vast, waiting city still sleeping around him.

At the top of the steps leading down to the tip of the island, Sebastian paused. From here he could see both channels of the river, twin ribbons of pale quicksilver that swept swiftly back together at the island's point. To the north stood the Louvre and the Tuileries Palace, with the leafy mass of the old royal gardens stretching away into the darkness beyond that; on the southern bank, opposite the Louvre, stood the ancient convent of the Petits-Augustins, which now housed the Monuments Museum. He could hear the rush of the river, feel the dampness of the air against his face, smell the pungent scent of wet pavement and sodden vegetation. It was a moment before he could bring himself to look down at that shadowy spot near the bridge abutment where he had found his dying mother.

Only this day and tomorrow, Thursday, remained, and then they would be leaving. Whether Napoléon's escape from Elba had anything to do with Sophie's death, Sebastian still did not know. But the Emperor's relentless, seemingly unstoppable advance on Paris could no longer be ignored. In a little over forty-eight hours he and Hero would be returning to London, and he was aware of a sense of frustration mingled with rage and a crushing awareness of having failed at the most important thing he had ever tried to do. He knew he was missing something, something that should be obvious. But what?

What?

He descended the worn stone stairs, his footsteps sounding abnormally loud in the stillness. At the riverbank he paused, the water lapping at the fine silt at his feet and filling his nostrils with the cold scent of wet mud and fish. All around him, the city dripped and slumbered, as if reluctant to awaken to the coming dreary morn. He could hear the clip-clop of a lone horse's hooves and the rattle of cart wheels on the roadway of the bridge above. A dog barked somewhere in the distance and, from nearer, came the quick, furtive scuff of shoe leather on wet paving stones.

He turned, knowing that he'd left it too late, that he'd been so lost in his own thoughts that sounds that should have alarmed him hadn't even registered. Two men came off the old stone steps in a rush, one dark and big and meaty, as much as four to six inches taller than Sebastian and a good four stone heavier. His companion was fairer and smaller, with a swollen, newly broken nose and two blackened eyes and a knife gripped purposefully in one hand.

The smaller man was lithe and agile, running ahead of his lumbering companion to come at Sebastian with the knife raised to strike. Sebastian plowed into him, catching the man's wrist with both hands and twisting it, using his weight and height to wrench the man's hand behind his back and shove it up in a brutal maneuver that ripped the arm out of its socket with an audible, tearing crack.

The man screamed, his knife falling into the mud at their feet with a dull thump. Shifting his weight, Sebastian pivoted to send the man flying into the river with a splash. But the other man was upon Sebastian before he could turn, looming up behind him to drop a garrote over Sebastian's head.

Sebastian flung up his left hand, but only managed to snag the leather thong as it tightened around his neck. He could smell the big man's rank body odor, feel the cord cutting into his hand and throat, slicing into flesh, closing off blood and air. The man's foul breath was hot against the nape of his neck, and Sebastian ducked his head forward and then slammed it back hard into the man's face. He heard the crunch of cartilage, heard the man's pained grunt. But the Frenchman simply shifted so that his cheek was pressed against the side of Sebastian's head, preventing him from repeating the maneuver.

The brutal pressure on the garrote never slackened.

His sight dimming, Sebastian eased his weight onto his left leg so that he could draw his right knee up close to his chest. He was losing consciousness, his fingers clumsy as he fumbled for the knife in his boot.

Found it.

Closing his fist around the handle, he yanked it free and drove the point up and back into the face of the man holding him. He felt the blade slice through flesh and slide across bone to plunge deep. The man let out a high-pitched shriek, and the killing pressure cutting into Sebastian's neck eased.

Wrenching the knife free, he whirled around, tearing the garrote from his throat, bringing his knee up again to send the heel of his boot slamming into the big man's chest. But the man was already dying, his face a bloody mess, one eye an oozing horror, the other glazing as he fell.

A splash drew Sebastian back around. The first man was struggling to his feet at the water's edge, his left hand cradling his dangling, useless arm against his side. He had his head down, looking for his dropped knife. Sebastian was lunging toward him when a flicker of movement jerked his attention to the bridge above.

A shadowy figure stood within the curve of one of the bridge's bastions, a gentleman with a scarf wrapped around the lower part of his face and his hat tipped forward over his eyes. As Sebastian watched, the man calmly lifted the flintlock pistol he held in his hand, thumbed back the hammer, and took aim.

Swearing loudly, Sebastian grabbed fistfuls of the sandy-haired man's wet coat and swung him around just as the figure on the bridge fired.

A burst of flame exploded into the gloom above. Sebastian felt the man in his arms jerk, then slump as the *crack* of the shot echoed across the abandoned wasteland and a hot wetness poured over Sebastian's hands.

"Bloody hell."

Shoving the dying man's body aside, Sebastian tore across the sodden grass to race up the slippery steps toward the bridge above. He heard the clatter of wheels and the rattle of trace chains, and burst up onto the platform to see a dark carriage pulling up just beyond the abutment. The gentleman at the balustrade turned, the spent pistol still in his hand. For one frozen moment, his hard gaze met Sebastian's. Held it. Then the carriage's near door flew open and the unknown man darted toward it, the grace of his stride ruined by a limp as he dove into the shadowy interior.

With a guttural oath, the driver whipped up his horses, and the carriage disappeared into the mists of the gathering dawn.

Chapter 52

*D*o you know who they are?" asked Eugène-François Vidocq, staring down at the two dead men at their feet. The morning had dawned by now, cold and wet and gray, with a faint mist that hugged the river and drifted through the half-dead trees at the island's tip.

"Not exactly." Sebastian crossed his arms at his chest, his gaze on the ex-gallerian. "But Lady Devlin identified them as the two men who attacked her on the quay. The smaller man had disguised himself as a hunchbacked poodle clipper."

Eyes widening, the Frenchman looked up at him. "You showed them to her? She has seen them? *Looking like this?*"

"Yes."

"*Sacré bleu,*" he muttered.

Sebastian said, "Do you recognize them?"

The head of the *Sûreté nationale* scratched absently at the side of his neck as he nudged the smaller of the two men with the toe of his boot. "This one looks vaguely familiar. It may come to me."

Sebastian studied the Frenchman's closed, secretive expression. Vidocq was famous for never forgetting a face, however briefly glimpsed.

So why was he pretending to have forgotten this one? Sebastian could think of several explanations, and all of them were troubling.

"What about the man on the bridge?" said Vidocq. "Did you recognize him?"

"Only his limp."

"Ah, yes." Vidocq's knees popped loudly as he hunkered down beside the larger of the silent, blood-splattered figures, tilting his head first one way, then the other, as if to study the dead man's mutilated features from different angles. "You stuck your knife in his eye?"

"I did, yes."

"*Sacré bleu,*" he whispered again, then cleared his throat and looked thoughtful. "How do you think they knew you were down here?"

"I could be wrong, but I suspect it was sheer luck. They were probably intending to break into the house and kill me there. But then they saw me leave the Place Dauphine and made the mistake of thinking I'd just made it easier for them."

Vidocq sniffed. "You are a hard man to kill, *monsieur le vicomte.*"

"I do try."

The ex-*gallerian* huffed a deep, rumbling laugh and pushed to his feet again. "You've heard Lyon has fallen?"

"No, I hadn't heard. Still not a shot fired?"

"Not a one. Artois was there, you know—with his army."

"And?"

"He ran away."

"With his army?"

"Hardly. The army went over to the Emperor. Last night, the King sent the crown jewels out of the country."

"A few days ago everyone was saying the crown jewels left Paris in Kitty Wellington's baggage wagon."

"Perhaps. Except this time, it's true. Baron Hüe was put in charge of the task. He's on his way to Calais, and from there to England."

Sebastian knew a profound sense of uneasiness. François Hüe had served as *officier de la chambre du roi* for both Louis XVIII and his ill-fated elder brother, Louis XVI, before him. This was a tale that carried with it an ominous ring of truth. "The King must be getting worried."

Vidocq shrugged. "They say he's still confident Napoléon will be stopped."

"Yet not so confident as to risk losing the crown jewels for the second time in a quarter century. I suppose he learned from his brother's mistake."

"In some ways, certainly, if not in all," said Vidocq with a wink. "And when the time comes—if the time comes—I suspect *this* Louis will run away while he still can." He cast one last, thoughtful glance at the dead men at their feet, then turned to walk back toward the steps that led up to the bridge. "I'll send someone to haul the bodies to the morgue; they shouldn't be too long."

"The sandy-haired man worked for Fouché, didn't he?" said Sebastian as they began to mount the old stone stairs.

Vidocq drew up sharply, his eyes widening as he turned to face Sebastian. "How did you know?"

"A guess. A talent for disguises isn't that common. I figured he worked either for Fouché or for you."

Vidocq grunted and continued up the stairs. "You remember how you asked us to talk to the housekeeper out at Malmaison?"

"Madame Sorel? Yes. Why?"

"She's dead."

Vidocq's men had a reputation for being heavy-handed in their questioning, and Sebastian felt a surge of anger tinged with a healthy dose of guilt for having set them after the older woman in the first place. "Your men got carried away, did they?"

"What? *Ah, non.*" Vidocq looked affronted. "They never had a chance to talk to her. Found her strangled in her own bed. The housemaid, gardener, and his grandson have all disappeared. Wise of them, I suppose—unless they're lying dead someplace, too. That remains a possibility obviously, so we are looking. But you'll be pleased to know we've located Joséphine's abigail."

"Also dead?"

"As it happens, no, she's still very much alive. But if you intend to speak to her, you'd best be quick. She's taken a position with one of your more easily spooked countrywomen, and her ladyship is intent on fleeing Paris as soon as she can get her trunks packed."

Bernadette Agasse was a petite, fine-boned woman somewhere in her thirties, with fashionably cropped auburn curls, small even features, and the air of quiet confidence that comes from having served an empress. She met with Sebastian and Hero in a withdrawing room off the entrance hall of the grand Marais district house hired by her employer, an aging baroness from Kent named Lady Bliss. The interview had been approved by her ladyship, but the abigail was obviously still feeling uncomfortable and vaguely puzzled.

She declined to take a seat and chose instead to stand just inside the room's doorway, her fingers laced tightly together, her hands pressed against the midriff of her neat gray wool gown. "I don't understand how you think I can help you," she said, looking from Sebastian to Hero and back again.

"What can you tell us about the Charlemagne Talisman?" said Sebastian.

"The talisman?" she repeated, her face carefully composed into a blank expression.

"You do know it, don't you?"

"Yes, of course. But . . . why?"

"We understand Joséphine promised to give the amulet to Hortense. Is that true?"

The abigail nodded, her lips pressed tightly together, her eyes dilated with what looked very much like a sudden upsurge of fear.

"So did she?" said Sebastian. "Give it to Hortense, I mean."

"*Non, monsieur.*"

So that much evidently was true. He said, "Do you know what happened to it when Joséphine died?"

Bernadette's gaze met his, then jerked away. "I think perhaps I should not say, my lord. It's not right, is it, for a servant to be telling tales about her previous employers? Even if they are dead."

"Your sense of loyalty does you credit," said Sebastian, his voice rough with impatience. "But I don't think you understand the implications of what you're involved in here." He drew the jeweled red leather case from his pocket and held it out to her. "On the evening of March second, Sophia Cappello was stabbed to death on the Pont Neuf; this was found lying near where she was killed. Empty. And Joséphine's housekeeper has now been found murdered in her bed. For your own sake, you need to tell us what happened to the talisman when Joséphine died."

Bernadette stared at the case's familiar gold monogram, her thin chest juddering with her rapid breaths. "*Mon Dieu.*"

"Tell us," he said again when the woman still hesitated.

The abigail brought up one cupped hand to cover her nose and mouth. For a moment she squeezed her eyes shut. Then she nodded and drew a deep breath. "It was when she realized she was dying that *madame*—the Empress—she asked *Dama* Cappello to take the amulet."

Sebastian and Hero exchanged quick glances. "Do you know why?"

"*Madame* thought . . . She knew the Emperor would soon grow restless on Elba, and she worried that if he had the talisman, then he would be more likely to try to regain his throne." She paused. "And then the Allies would kill him."

"So she was trying to protect him from the probable consequences of his own ambitions?" said Sebastian. "Is that what you're saying? That Joséphine didn't leave the talisman to her daughter because she was afraid Hortense would give it to Napoléon?"

The woman swallowed hard and nodded again.

Hero said quietly, "You say Joséphine asked *Dama* Cappello to take it. Did she?"

The abigail gave a quick shake of her head. "No, *madame*. *Dama* Cappello said she wasn't comfortable having it."

"So what happened to it?"

The abigail looked from Hero to Sebastian, then back again, her face strained.

"Tell us," said Sebastian in the voice that had once commanded soldiers into battle.

Bernadette dropped her gaze to her clenched hands. For a moment he didn't think she would answer. Then she whispered, "We hid it."

"'We'?"

"*Dama* Cappello and I. There is a secret compartment the Empress had built into the paneling in her chamber, and we put it there. *Dama* Cappello promised Joséphine that if Napoléon died, or if Hortense and Eugène ever sold the château, she would retrieve the amulet and give it to Hortense. The Empress did want her daughter to have it eventually, just . . . not yet. She hoped that if she could keep the talisman from Napoléon, then he would be less likely to attempt a return."

"And if he should decide to return even without the amulet?" said Sebastian. "What then?"

The abigail looked at him blankly. "I don't know."

Hero said, "You say Joséphine wanted it hidden. Do you know whom she was hiding it from?"

The abigail lifted her shoulders in a vague shrug. "Hortense. The Bourbons and Orléanists. Men such as the comte de Cargèse . . ."

"Cargèse?" said Sebastian so sharply that the abigail took a frightened step back. "What makes you mention him?"

The abigail's small, sharp nose twitched with scorn. "Last summer, before I left Malmaison, I found him in the Empress's chamber, tapping on the walls. I suppose Anaïs Sorel must have let him in. She does that sort of thing, you know—for money. When I asked what he was doing, he tried to frighten me into telling him where the amulet was hidden." A contemptuous smile twisted her lips. "I told him I had no idea."

"He knew Joséphine had a secret compartment in her chamber?"

She looked surprised by the question, as if it hadn't occurred to her before. "I suppose he must have, but . . . how could he?"

"Who did know of it?"

"Only the Empress and I, and—after I showed it to her—*Dama* Cappello. The old carpenter who'd built it died long ago."

"You're certain no one else knew?"

"Yes," she said, meeting his gaze unflinchingly. "Quite certain."

Chapter 53

*S*ebastian made the drive out to the Count of Cargèse's château through a cold, wind-swirled mist. The afternoon was dark, the clouds still hanging low, the road a wet ribbon that wound through sodden fields.

No matter which way he looked at it, Sebastian decided, it seemed unlikely that any of the three people who had known the talisman's location in the summer of 1814 would have shared that secret with Cargèse. Two—Joséphine and Sophie—had disliked the man intensely, and Sebastian likewise found it difficult to believe that the abigail Bernadette could have been the source of Cargèse's knowledge. So how had the Count known where to try looking?

Sebastian considered the housekeeper Madame Sorel. He supposed she might have come upon the information in some way, but he doubted it. Anyone as shrewd and calculating as Joséphine would never have trusted the woman with such a secret.

So what about Napoléon?

The more Sebastian thought about it, the more that struck him as a real possibility. The Emperor could easily have known of the existence of Joséphine's secret compartment without knowing its exact location. And whom else would he send to search for it besides his loyal comrade and childhood friend? One of his sisters or brothers, perhaps; but they were a half-mad and untrustworthy lot. Hortense? That seemed more likely, except had she even been in Paris last summer? He didn't think so, although she had surely searched the house without success many times since.

Joséphine's secret compartment must have been very well disguised indeed.

By the time Sebastian arrived at the Château de Marigny, the cloud-shrouded sun was slipping low on the darkening horizon, leaving a cold wind that burned Sebastian's cheeks and cut to the bone.

"Think 'e's 'ere?" said Tom, staring up at the dirty, darkened windows as Sebastian drew up before the neglected château.

Sebastian handed the boy the reins and hopped down to the gravel sweep. "Hopefully. It's a bit chilly to spend the evening combing the *guinguettes* of Montmartre and Belleville."

He turned at the sound of the front door creaking open behind him. A scruffy-looking retainer in a rusty black coat and yellowing linen stood in the partially opened doorway, peering out at them. In age he could have been anywhere between sixty-five and eighty, his cheeks pale and gaunt, his pate bald except for a few wisps of white hair. He held a candle in one hand and had the other palm cupped around the flame to protect it from the wind.

"Who are you?" he demanded.

Sebastian walked toward him, the gravel crunching beneath his boots. "The name is Devlin. I'm here to see the Count."

The elderly maître d'hôtel gave a slow, ponderous nod. "Ah, yes. He said I was to let you in if you were to come." He nudged the door open wider with his foot. "This way."

Sebastian stepped into a soaring, cobweb-draped entrance hall tiled in dirty white marble littered with scattered clumps of dried mud such as might have fallen from a gardener's boots. A graceful staircase with several missing spindles curled away into darkness, its carved banister dull from a lack of polish. The air inside the house was dank and musty and felt even colder than the outside; what rooms Sebastian could see opening off the hall lay in shadow and appeared virtually empty except for a disparate collection of overflowing bookcases.

Dozens of bookcases.

Here was a side of Niccolò Aravena that Sebastian would never have guessed. And as he crossed the filthy, cracked floor in the butler's wake, he found himself having to slightly readjust every assumption, every theory, he'd formed about the Corsican.

Clothed in a splendid silk dressing gown thrown casually over shiny leather breeches and a worn open-necked shirt, the Count sat in a tapestry-covered chair drawn up before a log fire roaring on the massive hearth of what had once been an elegant drawing room. Now the space contained only the tattered old chair, a gilded octagonal marble-topped table that stood at the Count's elbow, and an untidy sea of stacked books. A liver-colored hound lay at the man's feet, and he had a ginger cat in his lap; a second cat—this one white—sprawled on the back of his chair. The only light in the room came from the fire and a branch of candles perched precariously atop the pile of books on the table at his side; the rest of the room lay in shadow.

"You'll pardon me for not rising," said the Count, the fingers of one hand rhythmically stroking the cat in his lap. "But I can't disturb Rouille here. If you care for refreshment, do feel free to ring for it yourself. The bell does work, although to be honest, Jean might not answer it."

"Thank you, but that won't be necessary," said Sebastian, going to hold his cold hands out to the fire.

Cargèse watched him through narrowed eyes. "Do I take it you've discovered something you think redounds to my discredit?"

Sebastian turned to face him. "You didn't tell me you'd been caught ransacking Malmaison in search of the Charlemagne Talisman."

"I don't think I'd use the word 'ransacking,' exactly."

"Oh? What would you prefer? Thoroughly searching?"

Cargèse snorted. "Not thoroughly enough, unfortunately. I never did find the thing."

"What made you think it was still there?"

"Well, I knew Hortense didn't have it."

"How could you be so certain of that?"

"Because I knew how desperately she was still searching for it."

"Interesting that the housekeeper neglected to tell me of your visit."

"One assumes she . . . forgot."

"One might also assume that you paid her to . . . forget."

A faint smile tightened the skin beside the Corsican's dark eyes. "One could assume all sorts of things, I suppose." He shifted his hand to scratch behind the ginger cat's ears. "And now you think Madame Sorel notified me of Sophia Cappello's visit to Malmaison, do you?"

"It does seem a likely scenario."

"Does it? What a murderous fellow you must think me. So you're assuming . . . what? That having failed in my search of dear Joséphine's chambers, I then paid her decidedly greedy old housekeeper to notify me if Sophia Cappello should ever show up to retrieve the talisman? Has it occurred to you that if Madame Sorel was supplementing her income by keeping me apprised of interesting visits to the château, then she very likely had a similar arrangement with others?"

"Such as?"

"Hortense, for one. But"—the Count waved his unoccupied hand through the air in a vague gesture—"perhaps you should ask the house-keeper herself. Or get that nasty little ex-gallerian to do it for you. I understand his methods are most effective. When he wants them to be."

Sebastian thought about the housekeeper lying strangled in her bed and said simply, "Meaning?"

Cargèse tilted his head back against his chair. "Meaning that we are a divided nation of constantly shifting loyalties. A man—or a woman—considered a hero and patriot one day can easily find themselves dubbed a traitor the next . . . and be punished accordingly."

Sebastian let his gaze drift around the shadowy, once-beautiful room, with its seventeenth-century carved paneling and peeling frescoed ceiling. The contrast between the château's meticulously maintained gardens and the ruin of a house was stark.

As if following Sebastian's thoughts, Cargèse said, "My wife fell in love with this château; it was because of her that I acquired it. But while the fields and greenhouses are of use to me, the house itself . . ." The features of his face twitched, and he shrugged. "It is full of ghosts."

"And books," said Sebastian.

"And books," agreed the Corsican. "They keep me company in ways the ghosts cannot." He dropped his gaze to the purring cat in his lap. "You know, Napoléon always loved Joséphine. But she drove him mad with her spendthrift ways, and after she was unfaithful to him while he was in Egypt, he never again respected her."

"I wasn't aware that he ever had much respect for women in general."

Again that faint tightening of the eyes that suggested amusement. "Not overly much, no, although he is genuinely fond of his second wife, Marie-Louise. Not only did she quickly present him with a legitimate son whom he adores, but as a woman she was young, pretty, and quite taken with him as a man. And of course as the daughter of the Emperor of Austria, she promised to cement the acceptance of his line into the ranks of the royal houses of Europe."

"An unfulfilled promise," said Sebastian.

The Corsican sighed. "As it turned out, yes. She and her son were supposed to join him in Elba, you know, but her father stopped her. Just think: If the Austrians had allowed her to go to Napoléon—and if the Bourbons had paid the two million livres' pension as promised—he might still be on Elba, filling his days with the supervision of a never-ending program of ambitious public works and teaching his young son to ride and shoot."

"He might," said Sebastian. The last he'd heard, Marie-Louise was indulging in a torrid love affair with a handsome equerry sent by her father specifically to seduce her and wean her away from Napoléon. It had worked extraordinarily well; the Austrian emperor obviously knew his daughter. "How old is the boy now?"

"The King of Rome? Nearly four. They say Marie-Louise has no use for him anymore and has abandoned him to her Austrian servants, who use him abominably. Ironic, is it not, that his fate should so closely parallel that of the boy king, Louis XVII?"

"Last I heard, no one has locked Napoléon's son in a dark tower, sodomized and beaten him senseless, and left his wounds to fester."

"Not yet," said Cargèse. "I suppose his fate will rest upon the success of his father's last, desperate gamble."

"As will the fates of so many others."

The Corsican inclined his head. "How true."

"And for what?" said Sebastian. "To satisfy one man's exaggerated amour propre?"

"Amour propre? Or sense of destiny?"

"Is there a difference?"

"Perhaps not." Cargèse watched the ginger cat stand up, arch its back in a stretch, then hop down to trot across the dusty floor toward the door. "Telling, is it not, that no one ever attributed Louis XVIII's decades-long quest to regain his family's throne to amour propre, or blamed Marie-Thérèse's even greater dynastic drive on her own overweening pride and lust for revenge?"

"If you're looking for an argument from me," said Sebastian, "you won't get one on that score."

Cargèse opened his eyes wide. "No? Interesting." He pushed to his feet. "You've heard the King will be addressing the *Chambre Législatif* tomorrow? They say he intends to swear to maintain the Constitutional

Charter and warn of the dangers of civil war. It will be interesting to see how he is received by the crowds in the streets. He's been hiding lately."

"I hear his gout has been acting up."

"So it has."

Sebastian was aware of the Corsican studying him with an intensity he found oddly disconcerting.

"Why are you doing this?" said Cargèse. "I can understand how you might have felt compelled at first to look into Sophia Cappello's murder when you practically stumbled over her body. But it's been nearly two weeks. Seems a bit above and beyond and all that."

"Not for me."

"And not in this case, hmm?" He paused, then said, "I have met Marshal McClellan, you know."

Sebastian kept his features composed in an expression of polite boredom. "Indeed?"

A slow smile spread across the Corsican's beard-stubbled face. "Oh, yes." The smile lingered, but shifted subtly. "I did tell you once that the roses whisper to me, did I not?"

"Yes," said Sebastian, wondering where the man was going with this.

"As you are no doubt aware, there were during the war various individuals in Paris who used to pass information to Whitehall. Some were genuinely secret loyal royalists, but . . ."

"But not all?" said Sebastian.

"Thus it is always, yes? Predictably, one or two were actually working with Fouché, deliberately feeding false information to the British."

Sebastian didn't need to ask how Cargèse had come to know this. After all, the Count himself had once worked with Napoléon's extensive and highly effective intelligence service, helping smuggle French spies' reports out of England with his rose shipments.

"It seems," Cargèse was saying, "that one of these individuals was mentioned in conversation between Napoléon and *Dama* Cappello when she was in Elba." The Corsican paused, then added, "A conversation overheard by one of the spies the Bourbons have on the island. Interestingly, however, the spy was unable to catch the individual's name."

Sebastian studied the Corsican's dark, still faintly smiling face. "You're suggesting this individual would thus have had reason to kill Sophia Cappello? To prevent the true nature of his activities during the war from becoming known to the Bourbons?"

"It strikes you as a possibility as well, does it?"

"And do you know the name of this individual?"

"Unfortunately, no." The smile had faded from the Frenchman's eyes. "You do believe me, don't you?"

"Is there a reason I should?"

He shrugged. "Perhaps not. But you should, nevertheless. Fouché knows the individual's name, obviously, but Fouché is playing both sides now. They say the King is about to offer him the Ministry of Police."

"Will he accept?"

"If the King triumphs, then yes. Otherwise, I've no doubt Napoléon will offer him the same position."

Sebastian was silent for a moment, watching the fire crackle on the hearth and listening to the cold wind buffet the walls of the old château. He was remembering the sinister, pale former Minister of Police, who'd approached him in the Place Dauphine for reasons he'd never quite understood; the sandy-haired man lying dead on the blood-drenched banks of the Seine; and the bland smile of an ambitious artillery officer whose English wife had somehow managed, against all odds, to be accepted at Marie-Thérèse's court despite the Duchess's avowed hatred of anyone who'd ever served under Napoléon.

"Tell me this," said Sebastian. "How common in Paris were copies of the London newspapers during the war?"

"Common? Not common at all."

"Even amongst officers in the military?"

"Hardly. Amongst Fouché's men, perhaps. But the military? No. Why do you ask?"

Chapter 54

You can't think Cargèse was talking about Fanny's husband," said Hero later that evening as they strolled the lamplit streets of old Paris, past quiet ancient churches scented by centuries of incense and cafés boisterous with music and laughter. The wind had died but the air was still cold, and Hero kept her hands buried deep in her small fur muff. "Oh, surely not."

"He was in a position under Napoléon to acquire the kind of information that would have seemed useful to Whitehall," said Devlin as they turned up the rue Saint-Honoré. "And now his wife is close enough to the Bourbon Court to have heard whispers of the spy's report about Sophie. It's her position at Court that makes me suspect him—well, that plus what she told you about the *Morning Chronicle*. It explains why she's been accepted at Court even though Marie-Thérèse treats the wives of all the other men who served under Napoléon like—how was it someone put it?—cockroaches. I know people say it's because Fanny is English, but I'm not convinced that would be enough. It's much more believable that Marie-Thérèse made an exception for Fanny because she thinks Fanny's husband was a secret royalist who spent the Napoleonic years faithfully sending genuine reports to Whitehall."

"And now he's killed Sophie for fear she would expose him? But that doesn't make sense. By the second of March, Napoléon had already landed in the south of France. Why would a man who'd once served the Emperor so faithfully choose that moment to kill in an attempt to keep what he'd done a secret?"

"He would if he had no idea the Emperor was coming. And even if he did know, how many people thought Napoléon would actually succeed?"

"He still hasn't succeeded."

"Not yet."

They had reached the Place Vendôme, and Hero fell silent for a moment as they stared across the vast octagonal square at the towering bronze column erected there by Napoléon in honor of the victory at Austerlitz. From the monument's top, where the statue of the Emperor had once stood, fluttered the white flag of the Bourbons. But, looking at it now, she found herself wondering, *For how much longer?*

"And Fanny?" she said as they crossed the square toward the monument. "Do you think she knows?"

"I think she knows the game her husband was playing during the war. Does she know he killed her good friend? Surely she must at least suspect it."

Hero shook her head. "I can't believe it."

"Why? Because she's a small, engaging Englishwoman who wears spectacles and writes like Jane Austen?"

She gave a muffled laugh, her head falling back as she gazed up at the column's spiraling bas-reliefs. "Partially, I suppose. But also because I can't believe anyone who knew Sophie would think she could betray them—or anyone else—to the Bourbons."

"I'm not so sure about that," said Devlin. "In my experience, liars tend to suspect others of lying, and cheaters always fear they're being cheated. I can see a man who would do anything to ingratiate himself with the newly restored monarchy assuming that others would do the same."

"But Colonel de Gautier doesn't limp."

"No, he doesn't. Our friend with the limp is probably someone from Fouché's old intelligence network—the same as your poodle-clipper friend."

She gave a faint shake of her head. "None of this explains why Sophie had the talisman's case with her that night or why someone tortured and killed her abigail."

"It doesn't explain why she had the talisman case," he admitted, turning his back on the column. "But think about this: If an ambitious and ruthless traitor killed Sophie to keep his treason secret and then recognized the empty talisman case in her reticule, what do you think he'd do?"

Hero looked at him for a long, silent moment. "Try to find the talisman so he could use it to his advantage."

He nodded. "Exactly."

Thursday, 16 March

The next morning, Sebastian and Hero joined the crowds of sullen on-lookers gathered to watch King Louis XVIII's grand procession from the Tuileries to the Palais Bourbon, where he was scheduled to address the nation's combined legislative assemblies. The sky was a dreary gray and spitting rain, the crowds unnaturally quiet, the King's new state coach so absurdly heavy with ornate gilded carvings that it required eight snowy white horses to pull it at a slow crawl.

"So what precisely is the purpose of this grand spectacle?" said Hero as an advance contingent of the *Garde royale* trotted past in their splendid uniforms, their horses' hooves clattering on the wet paving stones, their grand plumes limp with the damp.

Sebastian studied the stony faces of the guardsmen beneath their tall headgear, their jaws set, their eyes fixed straight ahead. They gave every appearance of being loyal to their king. And yet one after another, every army sent south to stop Napoléon had gone over to him. The ranks of his followers were growing every day, not with callow, untested recruits but with battle-hardened men seasoned by the blood and mud of Austerlitz and Leipzig, Badajoz and Talavera, and in the long, agonizing retreat from Moscow. . . .

"I suspect," he said quietly, "the idea is to reassure the King's subjects that he intends to respect what's left of the liberties they fought so hard to win with the Revolution."

She looked over at him. "Does anyone in the palace actually think people will believe that?"

Sebastian gave a soft laugh. "Louis himself might believe it. I'm not so sure about anyone else."

The King was abreast of them now, one hand raised in a languid regal wave. Dressed in a dark blue coat with gold epaulettes, he wore an old-fashioned powdered wig that had the effect of making him look like a relic of the eighteenth century. Without the wig he was white haired and balding, and between his monumental girth and frequent attacks of gout, he typically used a wheeled chair to get around. Now fifty-nine, he'd spent more than a third of his life in exile, living in Prussia, Russia, and England, and had been restored to his hereditary dignities only by the might of the Allied armies. As monarchs went, he was fairly benevolent. But he was also childless, which meant that when he died the crown would pass to his younger brother, Artois. And Artois was anything but benevolent.

"No one's cheering," whispered Hero.

"No."

Sebastian let his gaze drift over the silent crowd. There were no huzzahs, no shouts of *Vive le roi!* By far the vast majority of those assembled to stare quietly at their King were women, old men, and the very young. And it occurred to Sebastian, as another troop of plumed, superbly mounted young guards clattered past, that most of these soldiers and more than half the ragged throng assembled to watch the King's passage today had been born since he'd fled his country a quarter century ago. Louis was essentially a stranger to them—a stranger associated in most people's minds with the past centuries of excess and oppression and the kind of nasty abuses that led to a grim stone tower being named Tour Bonbec.

"Where do you think he is now?" said Hero as another troop of cavalry clattered past. "Napoléon, I mean."

"With any luck, he's in Marshal Ney's iron cage."

Hero turned her head to look at him. "But you don't think so?"

Sebastian shook his head. "I think—"

He broke off as his gaze fell on a young woman in a tawdry pale blue gown standing beside a nearby lamppost. She was small and slightly built, surely no more than fifteen or sixteen, with a ragged red cloak and honey-colored hair she wore shoved up under a tattered straw hat with a torn brim.

"What is it?" said Hero, watching him.

He brought his lips closer to her ear. "The girl just there—the fair-haired one in the red cloak by the lantern. She's the *fille publique* who was on the bridge the night my mother was killed."

Hero was careful not to stare at her. "What do we do?"

He frowned. "I'm working on that."

Chapter 55

They waited until the last of the royal procession had passed and the somber throng that had gathered to watch it began to drift away.

Without looking at Hero, Sebastian crossed the street toward the girl. She appeared to be alone and moved away aimlessly, as if simply filling in time until the coming of evening. He didn't think she'd recognized him.

The air on the rue de Rivoli was thick with the smell of unwashed bodies and rotting teeth and the horse droppings left by the departed procession. The girl cut across to the rue Saint-Honoré, and Sebastian followed her up past a dilapidated old church. He was careful not to glance toward Hero, who was keeping abreast of the girl on the far side of the street.

It was Hero the girl noticed first. Sebastian was aware of her casting quick, anxious glances at the extraordinarily tall gentlewoman in the rich burgundy pelisse and ostrich-plumed hat who inexplicably stayed with her as she turned up the rue des Petits Champs toward the Place des Victoires. Grandly dressed ladies did not walk the streets of Paris, for without pedestrian pavements to lift them up and away from the muck and manure, their fine slippers would quickly be ruined, the hems of their grand silk and muslin gowns hopelessly soiled. And so, even though she might not understand why, the girl sensed that this unknown gentlewoman was in some way a threat to her.

Hastening her step, the girl turned down one of that warren of old streets that stretched away to the north of the Palais-Royal, then darted sideways into a narrow, noisome passage that cut between two decrepit old houses. It was there that she heard Sebastian's footsteps. She whirled with a startled gasp to see him coming up behind her, then turned to try to run.

He pushed past her, blocking her way forward. She spun back toward the street, only to find Hero already there, at the passage's entrance, trapping her between them.

"We don't mean you any harm," said Sebastian, holding his hands spread wide, palms up. "We simply want to talk to you."

"*Talk?*" The girl swung toward him again, her face pale and trembly, her chest jerking with her frightened breaths.

"Just talk. Two weeks ago I saw you standing beside the statue base on the Pont Neuf. It was perhaps half past eight; the night was cold and misty and—"

He saw her eyes go wide, her lips parting in terror, and knew she had seen something that night. She cast a frantic glance around the dark, rubbish-strewn passage as if desperate to escape, and Sebastian said quietly, "You don't need to be frightened. We only want to know what happened on the bridge that night. The woman who was killed was . . . very dear to me."

The girl bit her lower lip, her gaze falling to the wretched muck at her feet.

He said, "Tell us what you saw. I swear to you, no one need ever know where it came from."

"Why should I believe you?"

"Because I'm asking you here, now, rather than hauling you off to the *Sûreté nationale.*"

She let out a mewl of fear and scuttled sideways to flatten her back against one of the passage's old stone walls.

"We don't want you hurt," said Hero. "We only want to know what happened that night."

The girl looked from him to Hero and back again. "I don't know anything!"

"Yes, you do. You saw her, didn't you? A tall older woman in a dark blue pelisse with a velvet collar?"

The girl hesitated a moment, then gave a faint, reluctant nod.

Sebastian said, "Did she arrive by carriage or in a *fiacre*?"

"*Fiacre*," whispered the girl. "The driver drew up at the entrance to the Place Dauphine, and she got out."

Why? he thought. *Why hadn't Sophie told the fiacre driver to take her into the square itself?*

"Then what?" said Hero.

"She just stood there a moment, looking into the square. I think she was nervous."

"What makes you say that?"

The girl shrugged. "I could tell."

Sebastian believed her. This was a girl whose very survival must all too often depend on her ability to read the emotions and intents of others. He said, "How long did she stand there?"

Another shrug. "Not long. Then she turned and walked out onto the bridge. Not fast, like she was going someplace. More like she was trying to screw up her courage to do something."

To do something. Something such as enter the Place Dauphine, ring a bell, and face the son she had abandoned more than twenty years before?

Aloud, he said, "Then what?"

"Then . . ." A pinched look appeared around the girl's nostrils. "Then they came."

"'They'?"

"The man and the woman."

Sebastian's heart was pounding so hard it was roaring in his ears. He barely heard Hero say, "What did this man and woman look like?"

The girl gave a shrug that was more like a shiver. "He was tall. Lean. The woman . . . Well, I *think* maybe she was smaller, but I don't really know. I didn't pay much attention to her."

Sebastian said, "They were walking?"

The girl shook her head. "They came from the carriage."

"What carriage?"

"The one that was waiting near the entrance to the square."

"What sort of carriage was it?"

"Just . . . a carriage."

"Not a *fiacre*?"

"No."

"You say the carriage was waiting? Not following the *fiacre*?"

"No. It was there before."

Waiting for Sophie? thought Sebastian. *Except . . . how could anyone have known to expect her there?* And then he understood: They had known the same way Hortense had learned of Sophie's visit to Malmaison. They had paid one of Sophie's servants to alert them of her return to Paris, and that same informant had no doubt told them exactly where she was going that night.

Aloud he said, "What did the man and the woman do?"

"They followed her."

"You mean they followed the first woman when she walked out over the river?"

The girl nodded. "She walked almost to the Right Bank, then turned to start back. That's when she saw them—the man and the woman following her, I mean."

"Did she know them, do you think?"

"I suppose. They spoke, but I don't know what they said. I couldn't hear."

"And then?"

"Then the tall woman pushed past them and kept walking toward the island. That's when the man—" The girl sucked in a quick, frightened breath. "That's when—" She broke off again, her voice falling to a barely audible whisper. "I think he stabbed her. I don't know what happened after that. I ran."

"Was there anyone else around?"

"No, no one. Well, no one except their coachman."

"Was he in livery? The coachman, I mean."

"I don't know. It was dark."

Hero said, "Tell us more about the man—the one who stabbed the woman. You say he was tall. How tall?"

The girl twitched one shoulder. "Tall." She jerked her chin toward Sebastian. "Not as tall as him, though."

So probably not de Teulet, Sebastian thought, trying to remember the height of Colonel de Gautier. "How old?"

"Your age, maybe. More or less."

"Dark or fair?"

"I don't know." Her breathing had stilled. She was beginning to sound less afraid, more aggrieved and impatient with their questioning. "It was night. And he wore a hat."

"What about the woman? Was she fair? Dark? How was she dressed?"

Again the negligent roll of a shoulder. "She was dressed well enough, I suppose. I told you, I didn't pay much attention to her. She was just . . . a woman."

And thus not a potential customer, thought Sebastian.

Hero said, "Is there anything at all distinctive you can remember about either of them?"

The girl thought a moment, then shook her head. "They were just . . . ordinary-looking. Except . . ."

"Except?" prompted Sebastian.

"Well, the man did limp. But that's ordinary enough these days, isn't it?"

Sebastian and Hero exchanged a quick glance. He said, "When the first woman came in the *fiacre*, where was she coming from? The Left Bank or the Right?"

"The Left."

"You're certain?"

She nodded. "The mist had lifted a bit at that point, so I could see it coming along the quay."

"Along the quai des Augustins, you mean?"

The girl shook her head. "From the other direction. The quai Malaquais."

And then suddenly what had been muddled and hopelessly twisted became straight and clear.

Sebastian knew exactly where Sophie had been that night and why.

Chapter 56

ero and Sebastian found Émile Landrieu in a small stone-vaulted chamber with an ancient groined ceiling supported by a cluster of four weathered limestone columns topped with crude capitals. This was one of the oldest parts of the former convent, where the windows were high and narrow and the plaster covering the old stone walls crumbling. It was dark enough here that the museum director had set a tin lantern on a nearby ledge, and the light from the lantern cast his shadow across the worn flagged floor and the far wall as he stooped to sort through a pile of what looked like the broken pieces of a medieval architrave. At their approach he looked up, a nervous spasm flitting across his features before he straightened and turned toward them with a bland smile.

"*Monsieur le vicomte.*" He glanced at Hero. "And Lady Devlin, yes?" He yanked a handkerchief from his pocket to quickly wipe the dust from his hands. "Forgive me for my dishevelment. Have you come to view our collections?"

"Not today," said Sebastian, advancing on him. "We're here for some honest answers, and this time I intend to get them."

"*Monsieur!*" said the Frenchman, falling back one step, then another.

Sebastian kept coming. "You lied to me."

Landrieu gave a high-pitched, panicky little laugh as his heels bumped into the pile of broken carvings behind him, forcing him to stop. "There must be some mistake—"

"Oh, definitely a mistake. I asked when was the last time you saw Sophia Cappello, and you said late summer. But that was a lie. She was here at the museum the night she died."

"*Mais non*—"

"Don't." Sebastian grabbed the museum director by the front of his coat and swung him around to pin him against the nearest worn column. "Seven people are already dead because of what happened that night, so don't even think about lying to me anymore. Sophie was here, and unless you want me to think you're the one who killed her, you'd better start talking."

"But I had no reason to kill her!"

Sebastian picked him up and slammed him back again, hard enough this time that the breath left his chest in a little *whoosh*. "So why lie to me?"

"Because I was afraid! Of course I was afraid. As far as I know, I was the last person to see her alive. What if people thought *I'd* killed her?"

"Convince me you didn't."

The man's eyes bulged. "But how can I?"

"Tell me why she came here that night."

Landrieu's gaze darted away, his tongue creeping out to wet his dry lips.

"She brought you the talisman, didn't she? *Didn't she?*" said Sebastian again when the man remained silent.

"All right, yes! Yes, she did."

"Why bring it to you?"

"Why do you think? Because she knew I understood both its historical and artistic importance, and because—" He broke off.

"Because what?

He swallowed. "She said Hortense had discovered she had it, and *madame* was afraid that if she kept it herself it would fall into Napoléon's hands."

"Did she mention anyone besides Hortense?"

He shook his head. "No. But she said that if Hortense knew, then others might, as well."

Sebastian took a step back and let the man go. "She told you Bonaparte had left Elba?"

Landrieu brought up a shaky hand to straighten his cravat. "Not exactly. All she said was that it was becoming increasingly likely that he would do so."

"Why didn't she give you the talisman in its case?" said Hero.

The museum director glanced over at her. "I didn't want the case—it's too recognizable. Not many are familiar enough with the amulet to identify it on sight, but everyone knows Joséphine's monogram. I thought the talisman would be safer without it."

"So what did you do with it?"

Landrieu gave his disheveled coat a tug. "I hid it, of course."

"Where?" said Sebastian.

He didn't expect the little Frenchman to answer him, but he did. "In the museum, at first. Where better to hide a museum piece than in a museum, yes? But then my assistant—Paul Chastain is his name; have you met him? He's a fanatical Bonapartist, and he's been behaving suspiciously lately. I was afraid he might be searching for the amulet, so I moved it."

Hero said, "How could this Chastain know you had it?"

A faint tic started up beside the Frenchman's right eye. "Perhaps the knowledge of my secret simply weighed heavily upon my mind, making me nervous and suspicious of everyone. But I worried that Hortense had somehow concluded that *Dama* Cappello might have brought me the amulet and set Chastain to looking for it."

Sebastian remembered the smug little smile that had curled Hortense's lips when she told him about the museum, and it occurred to him that Landrieu's suspicions might well have been right. "You say you hid the amulet here 'at first.' So where is it now?"

The man's homely features took on a triumphant smile. "In the catacombs."

"*The catacombs?*"

Landrieu nodded. "The tunnels are miles long and labyrinthine; no one will ever find it there."

"Unless they torture you to make you talk," said Sebastian. "The people who killed Sophia Cappello also tortured and killed her abigail, you know. They broke her fingers, one by one."

The museum director's mouth sagged as he sucked in a frightened little hiccuping breath. He might have devoted the last twenty-five years of his life to saving France's artistic heritage, but at heart he was still an artist, personally illustrating each of the fat volumes of his collection's catalogue. And for an artist to lose the use of his hands . . .

He swallowed hard, his chest jerking as he sucked in a quick breath of air. "How did you know I had the amulet?"

"Once we'd learned Sophie was coming from the quai Malaquais the night she was killed, it was the only explanation that made sense."

It occurred to Sebastian that Sophie's killers must not have seen the direction from which her *fiacre* had approached that night. But he wouldn't be surprised if they eventually managed to put it all together.

"*Mon Dieu,*" Landrieu whispered, one hand coming up to swipe down over his eyes as he turned half away. "If you've figured it out, then—" He broke off and swung to face them again, his hand falling to his side, his jaw hardening. "If I gave you the amulet now, what would you do with it?"

Sebastian met Hero's gaze. Sophie might not have died because of the amulet, but keeping it from falling into Bonaparte's hands again had been important to her, and it seemed only right that they finish what she had started.

Hero said, "What would you suggest, *monsieur?*"

"Get it out of France quickly. Keep it someplace safe until Napoléon is no longer a threat to the security of Europe. Then return it to the French people." He paused, looking anxiously from one to the other. "Would you do that?"

"You would trust us?" said Sebastian.

"To keep it safe from Napoléon? Yes, of course. To return it, in time, to France?" Landrieu hesitated. "If you give me your word of honor as a gentleman, then yes, I think so."

"We leave for England tomorrow."

"Then there is no time to lose; we must get it now, quickly." He stooped to pick up his lantern, then said, "It would be best if we had a second lantern. The catacombs can be . . . dangerous."

Sebastian felt an unpleasant chill run up his spine. "A second lantern, definitely."

The official entrance to the catacombs lay far to the south. But there were other points of access scattered across the Left Bank, in the cellars of taverns and ancient houses, and in the crypts of the city's abandoned churches and monasteries.

Émile Landrieu led them through a small arched door set into the convent's back garden wall, then along a twisting string of streets to the crumbling ruins of a twelfth-century chapel. There, in the chapel's ancient crypt, they paused to light their lanterns. Then he pulled aside a tangle of ivy to expose a seemingly endless set of stone-cut steps that led straight down into the dark bowels of the earth. The air wafting up from below was dank and cold and pungent with the scent of damp stone.

"You go first," said Sebastian, holding one of the lanterns.

The museum director took the second lantern and nodded.

The stairs were narrow and steep, the low ceiling that closed over

their heads blackened by smoke from the candles and torches of centuries past. At the base of the flight of steps, they found themselves in a
vast open space hewn out of the rock by long-dead miners, with a scattering of columnlike formations supporting the low stone ceiling. Some
of the columns were simply sections of the raw sandstone that had been
left in place when the tunnels were cut; others were artificial, newer
stacks of masonry brought in to help shore up the old mines and keep
them from collapsing and bringing down the city above. As the light
from their lanterns danced over the surrounding walls, Sebastian could
see the yawning mouths of five tunnels that opened up in all directions.
He had expected utter silence this deep below the earth; instead, a
steady *drip, drip* of moisture joined with a chorus of faint moans and
groans that echoed ominously from all directions.

"What is that noise?" said Hero, her voice hushed.

"Sometimes the mines . . . settle," said Landrieu, lighting a torch that
stood in a bracket fastened to the wall near the base of the steps. The
flame flared up, casting its golden glow over the surrounding rocks.

"Lovely," she said under her breath.

"Best stay close behind me so you don't get lost," he said, and picked
up his lantern again. "It happens."

They followed him down one of the high, gaping tunnels that
opened up to the right of the stairs. "Some people don't like it down
here," he said, his voice echoing back to them.

"Imagine that," said Sebastian, and he heard Hero's soft, shaky laugh.

The shaft they followed was twisting but empty, its stone walls bare.
But after some minutes, they reached a place where the tunnel opened
up into another cavernous space, and Sebastian heard Hero give a faint
gasp. Everywhere they looked were bones—countless thousands and
thousands of bones: skulls and tibiae stacked in alternating rows to form
fat columns; ribs curving into decorative hearts; femurs stacked up and
splayed out as if to form an arch.

"My God," he whispered, playing the light from his lantern over an entire wall some thirty feet long and fifteen feet high and lined with long bones topped by rows and rows of skulls.

"These are all from an old churchyard on the Île Saint-Louis," said Landrieu. "At first the bones were simply brought here and dumped in vast haphazard piles. It was Napoléon who sent in crews to tidy things up. It's beautiful, yes?"

It was beautiful, Sebastian thought—in a profoundly horrible and unsettling way. There was no individuality here, nothing to distinguish one skull or long bone from the next. Whatever wealth, talent, power, beauty, or virtue these tens of thousands of the dead had once possessed was lost. All were reduced to anonymity, to the commonality of the one thing they'd all shared: their inescapable mortality.

And their bones.

"This is only one small section of the catacombs, of course," Landrieu was saying. "The remains of something like six million people are down here."

"How do you keep from getting lost?" said Hero, her reticule dangling half forgotten from one hand as she stared in fascination at a macabre mosaic formed entirely of vertebrae and clavicles.

The museum director nodded to a narrow black line painted up close to the near wall. "See it? There?"

"Ah," said Hero.

At one end of the cavern lay a stone slab set up on four low pillars to form a crude altar, and it was to this that Landrieu went. "Every year, on All Souls' Day," he said, hunkering down beside it, "the priests from the church come here to say mass and clean the altar." He reached out to dig behind one of the pillars and came up with a small parcel tied with twine. "I wrapped the amulet in silk and oilcloth to protect it as best I could, and included a written history of how it came to be here. I figured that if something were to happen to me, the priests would find it. I couldn't bear to think of such an ancient, beautiful piece being lost forever."

Straightening, he laid the small package atop the stone altar and carefully removed its wrappings with hands that were not quite steady. "Have you ever seen anything like it?" he said reverently, lifting the reliquary into the golden light of the lantern. "Incredible to think that it's over a thousand years old."

Sebastian sucked in a deep breath scented with damp stone, old incense, and moldering bones. The talisman was smaller than he'd expected but exquisitely made, the gold fretwork and repoussé decorations delicate, the polished gemstones shimmering in the light.

"It's lovely," said Hero.

Landrieu gazed at it a moment, his face pinched. Then he closed his fist around the reliquary and held it out. "Here. Take it."

Sebastian hesitated, then reached for it. He didn't know what he'd been expecting—a jolt of energy, perhaps, or at least some physical sense of the enormous power the piece had been believed for so many centuries to possess. But he felt only the cold of the metal and the smooth stones and the fragility of the ancient goldwork.

"Do you come down here often?" he asked, carefully tucking the talisman into an inner pocket of his greatcoat.

"Sometimes," said Landrieu, picking up his lantern. "It's a thought-provoking place, yes? Although of course there is always the danger of a collapse. Or one's lantern going out."

Sebastian was suddenly acutely conscious of the fragility of the single flame he carried, while Hero cleared her throat and said, "Shall we go?"

They followed the museum director back the way they had come. Sebastian could hear the strange murmurings of the earth settling around them in a series of groans and sighs that combined eerily with the drip of moisture and the furtive rustlings of scurrying rats. He found himself remembering the various stories he'd heard of how, in years past when the old mines had been used by smugglers and thieves, men had been known to become so lost and disoriented down here that they'd never been found. And about how the bodies of the Revolution's victims were often dumped in the mines without waiting for them to be reduced to bone; the grisly chambers were simply bricked up and sealed off. He found that the longer he was down here, the more each breath he took began to taste of the tomb. Of death.

"Thank God," he heard Hero whisper as they rounded a twist in the tunnel to see the glow of the distant torch.

They had almost reached the steep stone-cut steps when Sebastian heard the soft but unmistakable whisper of a footstep on stone, followed by the rasp of a pistol's hammer being pulled back and a woman's crisp voice saying in English, "Stop there, please."

Chapter 57

"*Mon Dieu*," whispered Landrieu, drawing up abruptly.

Wearing a delicate muslin gown with kid half boots, a soft blue velvet pelisse frogged with silver, and a jaunty plumed hat, Fanny Carpenter stepped out of the shadows of one of the tunnels behind the stairs. The identity of the man who ranged himself beside her was unknown to Sebastian, but his lean form and the set of his head and shoulders were as unmistakable as his hitching stride.

"*S'il vous plaît,*" the man added with a mocking half smile as he leveled the muzzle of his gun on Sebastian's chest.

"So, did you follow us or figure it all out yourselves?" said Sebastian, moving up to stand beside Hero and Landrieu.

Fanny simply shook her head. "All we want is the amulet. Give it to us, and you'll come to no harm."

"Sounds fair enough," said Sebastian, even though he knew it for a lie. They would shoot him first, he figured, thinking that they could then deal easily with Hero and Landrieu.

But then, they didn't know Hero.

"Give it to me," said Fanny, holding out one finely gloved hand.

"It's in my pocket," said Sebastian. "I'll need to set down the lantern
to get it."

"Move very carefully, *monsieur*," said the man with the gun.

Slowly setting the lantern at his feet, Sebastian caught Hero's gaze,
held it for one significant moment, and saw her give a barely perceptible
nod as her fingers began to work at the ties of her reticule.

"And here I thought your sole interest in all this was simply to hide
the truth about your husband's activities during the war," said Sebastian,
reaching into his greatcoat as he straightened.

An expression he couldn't quite decipher flitted across Fanny's small,
even features. "It was," she said, "until we saw the talisman case."

And he understood then how it all fit together and felt a tide of cold
rage sweep through him. "So whom will you give the talisman to? Marie-
Thérèse? Or Napoléon?"

She gave a faint shrug. "Whoever wins, of course. They will no doubt
be most appreciative."

"And thus reward you handsomely." He drew the amulet from his
pocket and held it up by its chain so that the reliquary swung back and
forth, the old mellow gold and finely polished gemstones glimmering in
the flickering torchlight.

At the sight of it, a smile of satisfaction parted Fanny's lips. "I'll never
understand why you've expended so much time and energy interfering
in the death of a woman you never even met."

"Don't you know? She was my mother," said Sebastian, and threw
the talisman at her companion's face.

Caught off guard, the Frenchman was still scrambling to catch the
piece of delicate gold when Sebastian charged.

Grabbing the flintlock's long barrel, he shoved the muzzle to one
side and twisted it hard enough to jerk the man's finger off the trigger.
He heard the man's breath expel in a startled grunt of pain, heard the
clatter of metal against stone as the flintlock fell to their feet and went
skittering away.

"*Bâtard,*" swore the Frenchman, his hands coming up to clamp around Sebastian's neck, squeezing hard as he jammed his thumbs painfully up under Sebastian's jaw.

His lips peeling away from his teeth in a grimace, Sebastian slammed his fist into the side of the Frenchman's head. The man grunted, then lost his footing as he tried to jerk away from a second blow.

He went down hard, dragging Sebastian over with him. Sebastian saw an outcropping of rock rushing toward them and twisted as they fell, driving the side of the man's head into the stone wall of the tunnel with a sickening *thwunk.*

"*Look out!*" shouted Hero.

Then a deafening roar echoed around the enclosed space and the air filled with smoke and the stench of cordite and burned powder. Sebastian felt an explosion of pain tear through his right leg, spinning him around to slam him back against the wall beside him.

He was dimly aware of Fanny crouched at the mouth of the tunnel, the Frenchman's flintlock clutched in both hands. But his sight was beginning to blur, his legs buckling beneath him.

The last thing he saw was Fanny's look of triumph. Then everything disappeared in a spray of blood and shattered bone when Hero pointed her muff pistol at the woman's chest and squeezed the trigger.

Chapter 58

*S*ebastian's dreams were disjointed, a hellish mix of searing pain and strange, disconnected images: endless mounds of hideously grinning skulls; an ominous slanting blade that hung glittering in the sun before slowly beginning to drip blood; the portrait of a man, his uniform that of the enemy, his eyes a familiar haunting yellow.

At one point Dr. Pelletan was there, bending over him, features tight with concern. Then his mother came to him, a gentle smile curving her lips as she bent to press her cool hand to his hot forehead. But when Sebastian reached for her, she disappeared in a red mist, and he felt his chest heave with a piercing sorrow and soul-wrenching sense of loss and sobs that went on and on until he thought they would never stop.

The next time he opened his eyes, it was to find Hero sitting in a straight-backed wooden chair beside him. He was in the guest bedroom of the house on the Place Dauphine, and she leaned forward in a way that told him she must have noticed him stirring. *"Bonsoir,"* she said with a trembling smile. "Feeling better?"

It seemed an exhausting effort simply to speak, but he made himself do it. His voice came out cracked and hoarse. "What day is it?"

"Saturday." She reached out to press her fingertips to his lips. "But hush. Don't try to talk. You must rest."

He shook his head. "Saturday the what?"

"The eighteenth."

"And Napoléon?"

"Don't worry about Napoléon."

"Where is he?"

"No one is sure. He was at Auxerre a few days ago."

"Auxerre? And Marshal Ney?"

He read the truth in her eyes even before she said it. "Napoléon's triumphant advance and the enthusiasm of the people and the army convinced Ney that the Bourbons' cause is lost forever. He's joined the Emperor—and his army with him."

"Bloody hell," swore Sebastian.

He fumbled with the bedcovers, meaning to cast them aside, get up, and get dressed. Instead he gasped and almost passed out as a white-hot flare of agony shot up his right leg. He lay panting, aware of the sense of something oddly heavy and immobile where his leg should be.

He knew too many men who'd awakened from amputations racked with pain from a limb that was no longer there. He had to force himself to put his worst fears into words. "My leg . . . Do I still have it?"

She put a hand on his arm as if to calm him. "You do, yes. But Dr. Pelletan doesn't want you to move for another week, at least. Please lie still."

Sebastian knew a wash of relief tempered by bitter, raging frustration. "You must go," he said, his breath still coming in painful pants. "Now. Leave Paris while you still can."

He was surprised to see her smile. "I'm not leaving you. I'll be all right. Truly. The King is still in Paris, you know. He insists he's not going anywhere."

"Do you believe him?"

Her gaze met his, and after a moment, she gave a faint shake of her head. "No."

The next time he awoke, it was to find Dr. Pelletan standing beside his bed.

"Ah, good, you're awake," said the Frenchman cheerfully. "Mind if I change your bandages and take a look?"

Sebastian nodded, then had to clench his jaw against the pain as Pelletan went to work. "So tell me truthfully: Will I keep it?"

"If you don't do anything foolish," said the Frenchman, looking up at him. "But I'd wait two or three months before trying to pull myself up on a horse if I were you."

"Has Napoléon been stopped?"

Pelletan started to say something, then seemed to change his mind and simply shook his head.

Monday, 20 March

Two days later, on a dreary gray morning, the head of the *Sûreté nationale* appeared in the doorway of Sebastian's bedchamber.

"They tell me you'll live," said Vidocq, settling with a sigh on the wooden chair beside the bed. He fixed Sebastian with a hard frown, then said, "You could have come to me, you know. We would have dealt with your lethal little countrywoman and her friend."

When Sebastian remained silent, the Frenchman grunted. "Didn't trust me, did you?"

"No."

Vidocq grunted again. "Fair enough." He leaned back in his chair. "I assume you know they're both dead? One with a broken head, the other with a bullet through the heart. Monsieur Landrieu insists he fired the fatal shot, but then he's always been a chivalrous fool, while Lady Devlin . . ." He paused as if searching for the right words. "She is a formidable woman."

"Tell me this," said Sebastian. "The man with the limp—who was he?"

"Raphael Berger was his name. He worked for Fouché—had for years."

"Along with Fanny Carpenter's husband?"

"Actually, no, with Fanny Carpenter herself."

"Really?"

Vidocq nodded. "I didn't believe the colonel at first, but he insists he knew nothing of his wife's activities. And it appears he may be telling the truth."

"It was all Fanny and Berger from the beginning?"

"So it would seem. She's the one who was working with Fouché, playing both sides of the fence and trading information both real and fake. She didn't expect Napoléon's bid to retake France to succeed, so she and her lethal friend killed *Dama* Cappello to keep her dangerous little secret from coming out. But then they found the talisman's case in her ladyship's reticule and realized something else was afoot—something they might turn to their advantage. So they tortured the abigail to try to discover the whereabouts of the talisman, but must have realized quickly that the girl knew nothing. So they killed her."

"Charming woman."

"Indeed. The women of your nation are truly frightening."

Sebastian gave a soft laugh. "So why did they leave the talisman's case on the bridge?"

"That I can't answer. One assumes perhaps they dropped it and were unwilling to take the time to search for it in the dark—not with their murder victim lying there and her blood still literally on their hands. Most do not see as well in the dark as you do, you know."

Sebastian was silent for a moment. "She would never have told on Fanny," he said. "Sophie, I mean. She would never have betrayed her friend. Not to Marie-Thérèse or anyone else."

"I know."

Sebastian nodded toward the window that overlooked the ancient square and the city beyond. "Tell me what's happening out there."

"As we speak, Paris is awakening to the realization that Louis and his entire court have abandoned them."

"They've fled? When?"

"Last night, at midnight. They've left the army with orders to defend the city, although God knows what makes them think anyone's going to fight for a king when that king himself has run away. The Bourbons are done. Finished. Surely even the Allies aren't so foolish as to try to put them back again."

Sebastian wasn't as confident, but he kept the thought to himself. "When is Napoléon expected to reach the city?"

Vidocq's eyes gleamed with expectation and what looked very much like delight. "Tonight."

That night, as the church bells of the city rang out in an endless joyous peal, Hero put on her pelisse and a modest hat and walked across the Pont Neuf to the Right Bank. A light drizzle was falling, but nothing could dampen the joy of the men, women, and children dancing and singing in the streets around her. The cold air echoed with their laughter and jubilant shouts, and every breath carried with it the heady scent of freely flowing wine. Long before she reached the Tuileries Palace, Hero could hear the excited noise of the crowd gathered before it in the Place du Carrousel. The massive iron gates stood open wide. Looking up, she saw that the white flag of the Bourbons with its golden fleur-de-lis no longer flew over the palace. There came a sudden hush; then a new standard rose slowly into view, the blue, white, and red stripes of the tricolor unfurling as the wind caught the cloth and billowed it out.

The crowd roared.

She was close enough now that she could see the men and women gathered on the steps of the palace, the officers from Napoléon's glory days once more in full dress uniform, their wives in court dress beside them. Hero caught a glimpse of Hortense, her face shining with triumph as she stood awaiting her stepfather's arrival, then lost her in the press of figures.

Burrowing her cold hands deep into the pockets of her pelisse, Hero felt her fingers brush something and realized with a start what it was: the Charlemagne Talisman. At some point after Devlin was shot, she had picked it up from the floor of the catacombs, thrust it into her pocket, and simply left it there, forgotten until now.

Someone, somewhere, began to play *"La Marseillaise"* on a pipe. A thousand voices joined in, then more and more, until it seemed as if the words of the old Revolutionary song rose up from the city itself.

The day of glory has arrived.
Against us, tyranny's
Bloody standard is raised.
Do you hear, in the countryside,
The roar—

Listening to it, Hero found her hands shifting to settle low on her belly, where a new life was beginning to grow. She hadn't told Devlin yet and would not until they were safely back in England. But standing here now, she found herself wondering what kind of world they would be bringing this child into. A world still at peace? Or one plunged once more into an endless, useless, wasteful war?

She was aware of a new wave of excitement sweeping over the crowd. Again a hush fell; then a sea of voices rose together in a deafening cheer. *"Vive l'empereur! Vive l'empereur!"*

Hero could see him now, a dark-haired middle-aged man hoisted up on the shoulders of the crowd. He looked older than the image Hero had of him, and plumper. But he still wore his familiar gray greatcoat, and his people still loved him with a passion that was palpable. Surging forward, they bore him up the stairs and into the palace he'd been forced to abandon just a year ago.

"*Vive l'empereur!*" roared the crowd. "*Vive l'empereur!*"

Hero turned away. But the rousing cheer followed her as she walked along the rain-pocked gray waters of the Seine. She could still hear it as she crossed the old stone bridge to the ancient island where she knew Devlin lay awake, listening to the same endless ominous shout.

"*Vive l'empereur!*"

Long live the Emperor.

Historical Note

I have tried to be true to the timeline of Napoléon's escape from Elba, his landing in the south of France on the first of March, and his triumphant trek north to Paris. Word of the landing did reach King Louis XVIII on the fifth, but the Palace kept it quiet for two days. Napoléon really did order his troops to trail their muskets at the Laffrey Defile; he then dismounted and walked toward the King's men to throw open his famous gray greatcoat and shout, "Here is your Emperor! Kill him if you wish!" (Different observers recorded his words with slight variations.)

He really did take Paris without firing a shot.

Kitty Wellington left Paris at six o'clock on the tenth of March, the Friday I have her leave with Hendon. There were indeed rumors that the King sent the crown jewels out of the country with her, although he did not; they left later with Baron Hüe. The Duke of Wellington was an awful husband and all-around cad; he really did inadvertently supply the gold that Napoléon used to hire his ships and escape Elba.

King Louis XVIII fled Paris at midnight on the nineteenth; Napoléon arrived less than twenty hours later, and would have been there sooner but was slowed by the people clogging the roads to greet him. He was carried by the crowd up the stairs of the Tuileries Palace, and Hortense was there to meet him.

The Charlemagne Talisman is real, although on her deathbed Joséphine simply gave it to her daughter, Hortense. At some point in the nineteenth century, the sapphires were replaced with glass. It now rests in the Abbey of Saint-Remi. The jeweled red leather case is my own invention.

The Paris we see today is a very different city from the Paris that Sebastian would have known. Many of its most famous boulevards were plowed through the old city late in the nineteenth century by Baron Haussmann under Napoléon III. Many old buildings have been burned or torn down over the years, but much also remains. The Pont Neuf, with its circular bastions and fanciful *mascarons*, is still there, joining the Île de la Cité to the Right and Left Banks. Despite its name, it is the oldest bridge in the city. The Renaissance-era triangular square known as the Place Dauphine also still exists, although its eastern range burned during the Paris Commune of 1871. I myself once lived on the Place Dauphine, so of course I had to put Sebastian and Hero there.

Before the Revolution, some wealthy aristocrats actually did amuse themselves by making gardens in open stretches of land around the city, so it is conceivable that something similar was done to the area of wasteland that existed at the time at the tip of the Île de la Cité. But if so, I have never found any evidence of it, so I have taken some liberties in putting one there. The park that exists on the point today, the Square du Vert-Galant, was laid out in the 1880s.

The Tuileries Palace stood just to the west of the Louvre. It was destroyed in the Paris Commune.

The Museum of French Monuments, located in a former convent of Petits-Augustins nuns, existed from 1793 to 1816. It is thanks to the brave people associated with it that so many precious tombs, sculptures, and other objects were not lost forever in the Revolution (the word "vandalism" was coined at that time for a reason). Émile Landrieu is based on the museum's real-life director, Alexandre Lenoir (who was himself quite a

character). After the Restoration, the museum was dissolved and the tombs and other sculptures sent back to their various churches of origin or to the Louvre; the director, Lenoir, went with the royal tombs to Saint-Denis and was put in charge of restoring them. The tombs of the various luminaries Lenoir gathered in the gardens, including the lovers Abélard and Héloïse, were moved to the Père Lachaise cemetery. A smaller, modern version of the museum has been re-created using plaster casts in the Palais de Chaillot, at Place du Trocadéro on the Right Bank opposite the Tour Eiffel; while somewhat off the tourist circuit, it is well worth a visit for anyone interested in medieval art. Much of the Convent of the Petits-Augustins still exists and now houses the École Nationale Supérieure des Beaux-Arts; it also retains some of Lenoir's historic fragments.

Napoléon did indeed build a central morgue for Paris. Compared to the crude deadhouses of London, it was a brilliant innovation, and was essentially as Sebastian describes it. In 1864 the morgue moved to a new building behind the cathedral; throughout the nineteenth century, it was a huge tourist attraction as well as being popular with Parisians themselves. When a particularly gruesome or poignant corpse was on display, up to forty thousand people a day were known to visit the morgue and gawk at the naked bodies. By the early twentieth century, changing sensibilities and concerns about the place's effects on "moral hygiene" forced its closure to the public.

What is now the famous Montmartre cemetery was at the time of the Restoration simply an open, abandoned gypsum quarry. Many of the victims of the guillotine were at one time buried there in a mass grave.

The history of the Paris catacombs is essentially as described here. Parts of them have been open to the public since Napoleonic times.

Notre-Dame-de-Lorette was just one of well over a hundred Parisian churches, monasteries, and convents destroyed during the Revolution; it was later rebuilt.

Many of Paris's streets and squares have been renamed multiple times over the years, but I have tried to use the names that would have been in place in March 1815. For example, the rue Cerutti was the rue d'Artois both before the Revolution and after the Restoration; it is now rue Lafitte.

As for people: Henri Sanson was the hereditary executioner of Paris. His father did see blood splatters on his tablecloth and hear the screams of the people he'd killed. The family did keep a museum at the rear of their house, and one of the objects there was the original guillotine used during the Terror. Henri's son, Henri-Clément Sanson, who in time inherited the position, was a drunken gambler and eventually sold the guillotine to Madame Tussaud; it was lost when the waxworks burned. The Sansons and some of their friends actually did experiments to see how long a human head remained conscious and responsive after it was cut off. They concluded thirty to forty seconds.

Hortense Bonaparte was the daughter of Napoléon's first wife, Joséphine de Beauharnais, and married his brother Louis. Their son eventually became Napoléon III.

Eugène-François Vidocq was a real historical figure. He was the inspiration for both Valjean and police inspector Javert in Victor Hugo's *Les Misérables*, for Jackal in Alexandre Dumas's *The Mohicans of Paris*, for Arthur Conan Doyle's Sherlock Holmes, for Dupin in Poe's "The Murders in the Rue Morgue," and for countless literary detectives since.

Fanny Carpenter was vaguely inspired by the real-life English novelist Fanny Burney, Madame d'Arblay. Her accounts of her life with her French husband make interesting reading. Her novels, published in the 1790s, did profoundly influence Jane Austen.

Marie-Thérèse did treat the generals who'd served under Napoléon and their wives "like cockroaches." Her treatment of Ney's wife is often cited as one of the reasons the marshal went over to Napoléon. Xavier de Teulet is modeled on the Chevalier de Turgy, Marie-Thérèse's longtime *huissier du cabinet* and *premier valet de chambre*, although de Turgy never studied to be a Jesuit.

Joseph Fouché was Minister of Police under Napoléon. A seriously nasty and sinister character, he created a formidable network of spies and informants. As Napoléon neared Paris, Louis XVIII did offer Fouché the Ministry of Police; he refused, then accepted the same position from Napoléon several days later. He is one of the historical figures who inspired my character Lord Jarvis.

Napoléon did have a marshal who was descended from Jacobites who had fled Scotland, but his name was Étienne Jacques Macdonald (and he didn't have yellow eyes). Unlike Ney, Macdonald did not go over to Napoléon during the Hundred Days. After Waterloo, Marshal Ney was executed by the Bourbons, and several other prominent generals were quietly murdered.

A few other bits and pieces: Malmaison still stands and can be visited, although the gardens were a ruin within a year of Joséphine's death and what has been re-created today is much reduced. Reproductions of the famous works of the botanical artist Pierre-Joseph Redouté are still selling. Roses and other botanic specimens did pass back and forth across the Channel during the war, and yes, Napoléon's spies in London did smuggle reports out with the roses. One of the men who worked in the London nursery they used did cross the Channel after the war and go to work for Joséphine, but to my knowledge he was not murdered. The term "rosarian" only came into general usage later in the nineteenth century, but I have employed it here for convenience. The buff-colored, loose-fitting Cossack trousers Antoine de Longchamps-Montendre wears were a style inspired by the uniforms of the Russians who'd so recently occupied Paris. Although they didn't become the rage in London until some years later, they first appeared in 1814.

And, finally, it was Talleyrand who is credited with saying the Bourbons had learned nothing and forgotten nothing.